RESCUING ARIA

Guardian Hostage Rescue Specialists: DELTA Team

ELLIE MASTERS

MASTER OF ROMANTIC SUSPENSE

JEM Publishing

Dedication

This book is dedicated to my one and only—my amazing and wonderful husband.

Without your care and support, my writing would not have made it this far.

You pushed me when I needed to be pushed.

You supported me when I felt discouraged.

You believed in me when I didn't believe in myself.

If it weren't for you, this book never would have come to life.

Also by Ellie Masters

The LIGHTER SIDE

Ellie Masters is the lighter side of the Jet & Ellie Masters writing duo! You will find Contemporary Romance, Military Romance, Romantic Suspense, Billionaire Romance, and Rock Star Romance in Ellie's Works.

YOU CAN FIND ELLIE'S BOOKS HERE:

ELLIEMASTERS.COM/BOOKS

Shop Ellie Masters Romantic Suspense and Steamy Contemporary Romance by series.

Angel Fire Rock Romance

Guardian HRS: Alpha Team

Guardian HRS: Bravo Team

Guardian HRS: Charlie Team

Guardian HRS: Delta Team

Cerberus Personal Security

The LaRouge Triplets

The One I Want Series

Angel's Peak Series

Billionaire Boy's Club

The Lovers

Changing Roles

SUGGESTED READING ORDER

START HERE

Rockstar Romance

The Angel Fire Rock Romance Series

EACH BOOK IN THIS SERIES CAN BE READ AS A STANDALONE AND IS ABOUT A DIFFERENT COUPLE WITH AN HEA.

IT IS RECOMMENDED THEY ARE READ IN ORDER.

Heart's Insanity

Ashes to New

Heart's Desire

Heart's Collide

Hearts Divided

Hearts Entwined

Forest's FALL

Hearts The Last Beat

CONTINUE HERE...

Military Romance

Guardian Hostage Rescue Specialists

Rescuing Melissa

(Get a FREE copy of Rescuing Melissa

when you join Ellie's Newsletter)

Alpha Team

Rescuing Zoe

Rescuing Moira

Rescuing Eve

Rescuing Lily

Rescuing Jinx

Rescuing Maria

Bravo Team

Rescuing Angie

Rescuing Isabelle

Rescuing Carmen

Rescuing Rosalie

Rescuing Kaye

Cara's Protector

Rescuing Barbi

Charlie Team

Rescuing Rebel

Rescuing Stitch

Rescuing Mia

Jenna's Protector

Rescuing Sophia

Rescuing Malia

Rescuing Ally (Part 1)

Rescuing Ally (Part 2)

Delta Team

Rescuing Ember

Rescuing Aria

STANDALONES IN THE GUARDIAN HOSTAGE RESCUE

By Jet & Ellie Masters

EACH BOOK IN THIS SERIES CAN BE READ AS A STANDALONE AND IS ABOUT A DIFFERENT COUPLE WITH AN HEA.

Saving Abby

Saving Ariel

Saving Brie

Saving Cate

Saving Dani

Saving Jen

The LaRouge Triplets

Asher

Brody

Cage

Billionaire Romance

Billionaire Boys Club

Hawke

Richard

Contemporary Romance

Cocky Captain

Romantic Suspense

EACH BOOK IS A STANDALONE NOVEL.

The Starling

The Swan

~AND~

Science Fiction

Ellie Masters writing as L.A. Warren

Vendel Rising: a Science Fiction Serialized Novel

If you enjoyed this book by Ellie Masters, the LIGHTER SIDE of the Jet & Ellie writing duo, and aren't afraid of edgier writing, you might enjoy reading BDSM themed books written by Jet, the DARKER SIDE of the Masters' Writing Team.

The DARKER SIDE

Jet Masters is the darker side of the Jet & Ellie writing duo!

Romantic Suspense

Changing Roles Series:

THIS SERIES MUST BE READ IN ORDER.

Command Me

Control Me

Collar Me

Embracing FATE

Seizing FATE

Accepting FATE

HOT READS

A STANDALONE NOVEL.

Down the Rabbit Hole

Light BDSM Romance

The Ties that Bind

HOT READS

Becoming His Series

Dark Captive Romance

Grab the First Book in The Guardian
Hostage Rescue Specialists Series
for Free

https://elliemasters.com/RescuingMelissa

ONE

Aria

———

I USED TO BELIEVE THE WORST THING THAT COULD HAPPEN WAS being taken. It turns out, surviving it is harder. Surviving means carrying the silence. The nightmares. The lies you tell yourself just to keep breathing.

Except you don't forget. You just get better at hiding it. You smile prettier. Wear designer jeans. Rebrand the trauma as strength. Wrap the scars in gold and call it kintsugi.

Now I sell hope in glass jars. Dreams that smell like cinnamon and safety. I tell myself this candle shop is healing. That I belong here, where it smells like light, not the cellar where they broke us. And maybe if I burn enough wicks, I'll believe it. They broke us in the dark, but now we're building light.

And I'm pretending I'm not still shattered.

Ember's on her third pass reorganizing a display of crystal vessels, fingers trembling like they remember too. The last time she touched fire, it nearly killed her. Now she bottles it in glass and calls it hope.

"If you reorganize that display again, I'm calling Blaze." I'm unable to keep the amusement out of my voice as she adjusts the same arrangement of crystal vessels for what has to be the twentieth time this morning.

Despite the ungodly hour, I've made an effort with my appearance—designer jeans and our company shirt, which I've modified to look more runway-worthy than retail. The familiar ritual of putting myself together helps calm my nerves.

"Aria, I'm fine," Ember insists, though her hands shake as the crystal vessels clink together. "Just—making sure everything's perfect."

"Everything's already perfect." I cross the space, my heels clicking against the reclaimed hardwood floors. "Including the west wall display, which you've obsessed over for three days straight."

I catch her restless hands in mine, feeling the tremor of anxiety beneath her skin. Her fingers find the small burn scar on her collarbone—an old tell I've learned to recognize.

"What if—" she starts.

"No what-ifs," I interrupt gently. "We've planned for everything. Now breathe before you work yourself into a panic attack."

The workshop door creaks open, and Ryn slips through. Six months of regular meals have softened the sharp angles of her face, but her eyes still hold shadows. She stands taller now— another survivor refusing to break.

"The first batch is ready for inspection." Her voice carries that careful deliberation of someone who went too long without speaking. "The new rose quartz vessels worked perfectly."

I follow as she leads us into the workshop, watching Ember's face light up with pride. The space is incredible—three professional pouring stations gleaming under specialty lighting, walls lined with ingredients that would make any artisan weep with envy.

"Look." Ryn lifts one of her creations, and I gasp. Rose quartz vessels hold swirls of pale pink and gold wax, tiny crystals suspended like constellations. "I tried that new technique with the suspended minerals."

"These are extraordinary," Ember breathes, and I nod in agreement. "There's real artistry here." She hugs Ryn, who immediately flinches, but then relaxes, leaning into Ember's touch.

We've all been traumatized. Ryn, perhaps more than Ember or myself.

The front bell chimes, and my hands fly to my hair, smoothing strands that are already perfectly in place.

"Three guesses who that is," Ryn mutters, a rare smile tugging at her lips.

"Anyone alive in here? Brought coffee and those almond croissants Aria likes." Jon's voice carries from the retail floor, deep and warm like coffee and promises. My heart does something ridiculous in my chest. He remembered. Of course, he remembered—Jon notices everything.

"I should, um—go help. With the coffee. Because… Reasons," I stammer, already moving toward the front.

"Subtle," Ryn calls after me, her smile widening.

I practically float to the retail floor, then try to compose myself when I see him. Jon stands near the entrance, still carrying himself with the same military bearing, despite being in civilian clothes. He sets out breakfast with careful attention to detail—pastries arranged just so, coffee cups positioned just right.

His gaze finds mine immediately, and something electric passes between us. I catch him looking when he thinks I'm not paying attention, his gaze lingering on my face, my hair, and the way I move through the space. When our eyes meet, my stomach does backflips.

"You didn't have to bring breakfast." Though I'm already gravitating toward the coffee like it's calling my name.

"I wanted to." Simple words, but the way he says them makes heat pool in my belly.

The front door chimes again. This time, it's Charlie and Brett, carrying more breakfast and looking relaxed together. Jon's shoulders tense slightly—the only visible sign of discomfort. The dissolution of their three-way relationship still echoes in moments like this, wounds that are healing but not completely healed.

I reach for the mug, fingers brushing ceramic, but they won't steady. Tremors betray me—tiny at first, then stronger, a pulse of tension radiating out from my core. The silence presses in, heavy and sharp-edged, scraping nerves already frayed raw.

The cup tips.

Time slows.

Coffee arcs in midair, splashing across the wood floor as the porcelain shatters. A sharp gasp—not mine—breaks the moment. I stare at the mess, heat rising in my throat, unable to breathe past the sudden sting behind my eyes.

Before I can even react, Jon is there. His hands catch mine, steadying me, checking my fingers for any sign of burns or cuts. His touch is gentle but thorough, professional yet intimate.

"Are you hurt?" His voice is soft, concerned, meant only for me.

"I'm fine," I whisper, though I don't pull my hands away. "Just clumsy."

He doesn't let go immediately, his thumbs brushing over my knuckles like he's memorizing the shape of them. Charlie and Brett exchange knowing looks, and my cheeks flame with embarrassment.

And then the moment passes—slips between us like breath—and the rhythm of the morning presses in to swallow it.

Brett crouches to mop up coffee with a wad of paper towels while Charlie mutters something about needing stronger mugs.

Jon finally releases my hands, his touch leaving behind a phantom heat that lingers far longer than it should.

The front door chimes again.

Controlled chaos descends like a well-rehearsed play.

Jenny strides in with Mac on her heels, both scanning the space like they're prepping a battlefield instead of a candle shop. Mitzy's right behind them, already scrolling through her tablet and muttering something about wireless dead zones.

"Don't start," Ember warns from across the counter, without looking up. "No robots, no drones, no laser grid."

I watch the familiar banter, but my attention keeps drifting to Jon.

The way he moves—deliberate, coiled, predator-smooth—makes it impossible not to stare. Six-foot-something of silent intensity, all broad shoulders and cut muscle stacked like he was carved, not born. His shirt stretches just enough across his chest to make my thoughts indecent, and when he pivots, that narrow waist and thick arms pull heat straight into my bloodstream.

He doesn't just look like danger. He wears it like a second skin. Eyes sweeping the space, cataloging exits, reading threats I can't even see. But then his gaze snags on mine—and holds.

Too long. Too deep. Like he sees everything I'm not saying.

And God help me, I don't look away.

The front door jingles, and Blaze fills the space with his effortless swagger. Ember turns like she's gravity-bound to him, her whole face lighting up. That look between them? It's a slow-burning fire. A promise. Something so real it makes my heart twist in my chest.

"Morning, beautiful." His voice is a low caress, and their kiss draws out a collective groan.

"Gross," Ryn calls from the workshop. "Some of us are trying to work here."

The laughter that follows is familiar, grounding, and I use the distraction to step toward the front shelving. One of the signs is crooked—barely, but it bothers me. I reach up, stretching onto my toes, fingertips grazing the bracket.

A shadow moves in.

"Here—let me." Jon's voice slides down my spine, all quiet power.

Before I can react, he steps in close, reaching above me, his body a wall of heat and muscle. We're not touching—barely—but my whole body buzzes like we are. I lower my arm slowly as his takes its place, and now he's towering above me, breath warm against my temple.

I turn my head. He looks down.

The moment sharpens—tense, electric.

His face is inches from mine. Sharp jawline, dark eyes with flecks of amber catching the light. One hand still raised above me, the other dropping slowly to his side. We're frozen, suspended in something fragile and dangerous.

I forget the sign. Forget the shop. Forget how to breathe.

"Are you two gonna kiss, or should I give you a minute?" Jenny's voice pierces the silence, bone-dry and perfectly timed.

We spring apart like teenagers caught sneaking out.

"I was just fixing the sign," I mutter, ducking my head.

"I was just helping her." Jon clears his throat, stepping back.

Charlie snorts into her coffee. Brett lifts a candle to his nose with exaggerated concentration.

And me? I can still feel the heat of his body like it's been branded into my skin.

"Two hours to opening," Mitzy announces, saving us from further embarrassment.

"Your Instagram announcement reached fifty thousand views overnight." I check my phone, smiling. It's a phenomenal number.

"Fifty thousand?" Ember's knees nearly buckle.

"Turns out 'Former Foster Kid Opens Luxury Candle Shop With Kidnapping Survivor Bestie' makes compelling social media," I manage to say, trying to regain my composure. "Who knew?"

The rest of the morning passes in a blur of preparation. I organize the same display as Jon, our hands brushing against each other *"accidentally"* every few seconds. Each touch sends electricity shooting through me, and I'm hyperaware of every movement he makes.

Ryn places her kintsugi candles in the front window—dark glass with golden cracks running through her creations like lightning strikes. The symbolism isn't lost on any of us. Broken, but made more beautiful by the breaking.

"One hour," Mitzy calls out. "And there's already a line forming."

I peek outside, and my heart races. The line stretches around the block—a sea of expectant faces pressed against our windows.

"Did you see? There are actual influencers out there. And is that…? Oh my God, that's the editor of Vogue," I babble, my socialite background recognizing the faces even as my nerves threaten to overwhelm me.

"Breathe." Jon appears at my elbow, steady as always. "You've got this."

Our eyes meet, holding for a heartbeat too long. A blush creeps up my neck as his hand brushes my lower back—a touch that could be accidental but isn't.

For the next fifty minutes, Ember, Ryn, and I flutter around the shop making last-minute adjustments, while Blaze, Jon, and the rest of the Delta team look on with genuine smiles.

"Five minutes," I announce, fidgeting with the register for what feels like the hundredth time.

Blaze positions himself by the door. The team spreads throughout the store, everyone in their assigned positions. I take one last look around at this makeshift family we've built, at the dreams we've turned into reality.

"Ready?" Blaze's hand finds the lock.

"Ready," Ember's voice rings clear and strong.

The door opens.

"Welcome to The Little Matchstick Girl," she says. "Where every light tells a story."

The first wave of customers floods in, their excitement as thick as cinnamon in the air. I move through the crowd, guiding people toward the candle stations, answering questions, laughing like I haven't lived through hell. My background has trained me for this kind of finesse—charming investors and navigating boardrooms.

Today, it's just wax, wicks, and wide-eyed wonder. Still, my focus drifts.

To him.

Jon lingers near the back, pretending to restock shelves he's already triple-checked. His gaze keeps returning to me, and every time our eyes almost meet, he looks away too fast, like I burn.

I duck into the supply nook behind the checkout to grab more gift bags. The curtain barely swings shut when I hear voices —low, casual. They don't know I'm here.

"Just kiss her already," Mac mutters as he passes Jon. "Before we all die of old age."

My hand stills on the bag handles.

Jon's reply is soft. Embarrassed. "I don't… She wouldn't…"

"Dude." Mac's grin is audible. "She knocked over an entire display just to get your attention."

"That was an accident," Jon protests, scandalized.

"Sure it was," Mac drawls.

I stand frozen, heart thudding in my throat. Heat crawls up my neck as I replay every clumsy moment—every stolen glance. I squeeze the paper handles tighter, cheeks flushed, lips curved into a secret smile as I step back out into the fray.

The morning passes in a whirlwind of sales and stories, the shop pulsing with warmth and movement. Customers drift from table to table, inhaling the air thick with the scents of cinnamon, lavender, and melted wax. But it's not just the scents that pull them in—it's the women behind the counter.

Ryn starts off tentative, her voice barely rising above the music. But with every sale, every compliment, she straightens a little taller. She answers questions with growing confidence, her posture relaxing, her eyes lighting up when a woman tells her the "Midnight Ember" scent reminds her of dancing barefoot in the rain.

By the time a teenager insists on buying three of Ryn's kintsugi candles "for aesthetic vibes," her smile is a mile wide. She's cracking jokes and wrapping products like she was born for retail therapy.

At the front of the store, Ember is in her element.

She doesn't just sell candles—she sells stories.

"This one's lavender," she says to an older couple, her fingers grazing the soft purple label. "It's my bestseller. I like to say it soothes your soul more than your senses."

The woman clutches the jar to her chest like it's precious.

"And this one…" Ember lifts another, her voice taking on a soft reverence. "Vanilla. I blended it to smell like my grandmother's kitchen. It reminds me of home."

A teenage boy quietly places it in his basket, cheeks flushed.

When a man in a suit picks up a pine-scented candle, Ember grins. "That one's for new beginnings. You planning one?"

He hesitates. Nods. "Just moved. Divorce was—rough."

"Then this is your fresh start." She doesn't pry. Just presses the candle gently into his palm.

I stand near the center display, folding bags, pretending to organize ribbon, but really, I'm just watching Ember shine.

This girl, who once sold candles off a milk crate on a street corner, now commands a shop filled with laughter, light, and purpose. Customers lean closer when she speaks, drawn not just to the scents but to the strength threaded through her words.

My throat tightens. Pride swells in my chest until it's almost too much. She built this. From ashes. From trauma. From nothing.

And it smells like hope.

By lunch, I'm back on my tiptoes, reaching for something on the top shelf—this time, genuinely needing it. My fingers graze the edge of the box, but it wobbles, teasing, just out of reach. I don't hear Jon approach.

I feel him.

The heat of his body brushes against my back as he steps in behind me, calm and unhurried. His arm lifts beside mine, steady as he grabs the box like it weighs nothing. Our bodies align with startling ease—his presence fitting into mine like some long-missing piece.

He lowers the box, but doesn't move away. I turn—and he's already watching me.

Close.

Too close.

Not close enough.

"Thanks," I murmur, but it comes out breathless.

My fingers twitch at my sides, aching to hold on to something. To him.

Jon's hand lifts to my cheek, his touch reverent, his gaze tracing every line of my face like he's memorizing it.

"I've waited far too long for this," he says, voice rough with meaning.

My heart stutters. My breath tangles.

He doesn't ask. Doesn't hesitate.

He just leans in—and I let him.

The kiss starts softly. A brush. A promise.

His lips barely ghost over mine at first, like he's asking permission without words. Like he's giving me the chance to change my mind.

I don't.

I tilt my chin, lean in, answer with my mouth, and the ragged inhale I can't hold back.

Then he deepens it—slow and sure. No rush. No force. Just heat blooming between us like a match struck in the dark. His hand slides to my waist, grounding me, anchoring me in place. When he pulls me closer, our bodies slot together like we were always meant to find each other.

My fingers fist in the front of his shirt. I need the feel of him —solid, warm, real—to believe this is actually happening.

His mouth moves over mine, every tilt of his head, every flick of his tongue purposeful, like he's memorized the kiss before he ever dared steal it. There's restraint in him, in the tight line of his shoulders, in how he's holding back from devouring me. But underneath? Tension hums like a wire stretched to its limit.

I taste cinnamon on his tongue, feel the low rumble in his chest when I kiss him back harder, deeper.

And then—stillness.

He pulls back just enough to look at me, our foreheads brushing, breath mingling.

"You okay?" he asks, voice like gravel and velvet all at once.

My lips are tingling, swollen, stunned. I nod, breathless.

"Yeah," I whisper. "I'm more than okay." A beat of silence. My heart hammers in my throat, but I push past it, voice smaller now. "Can we—do that again?"

"Yeah, we can." The corner of his mouth lifts in a crooked smile. He chuckles, low and warm, like I've just handed him the one thing he's wanted most. "Should've done this a hell of a lot sooner."

Then he leans in, this time with no hesitation. One arm slides around my waist, pulling me tight to his chest. My hands loop over his shoulders instinctively, fingers threading into the hair at the nape of his neck. His body is all heat and hard lines, anchoring me to something I didn't know I needed until this moment.

His mouth finds mine again—deeper this time. Hungrier. Like now that he's tasted me, he's done pretending he can stay away. The rest of the world falls away. All that exists is this—his breath, his warmth, the delicious ache blooming low in my belly as his kiss claims me completely.

"Oh, thank God," Charlie mutters from somewhere behind us. "Finally."

A cheer goes up from the team, and we spring apart, both blushing furiously.

"About time," Jenny calls from across the store. "Now, maybe we can all focus on actual work?"

But she's smiling too, and even Charlie and Brett look genuinely happy for us.

The rest of the day passes in a blur of happiness and nonstop sales. By closing time, the shelves are nearly bare, and Ryn's entire collection has sold out.

"We did it," I breathe, collapsing onto the counter as I kick off my shoes. Jon's arm slides naturally around my waist, like it was always meant to be there.

Ember leans against the door, hair slipping loose from her braid, cheeks flushed with triumph. "I think I'm actually high on lavender and adrenaline."

"Same," I laugh, rubbing at the tight knot between my shoulders.

We sweep the last of the receipts into the drawer, turn off the display lights, and do one final walkthrough—checking locks, counting cash, restocking the back room with what little remains. Ember flips the CLOSED sign with a flourish.

"Ready?" I grab the keys, glancing around the space that now smells like memories and magic.

"I've got a few last-minute things. I'll meet you there." Ember tucks a box under her arm, her eyes still bright from the rush.

"You sure? Want me to wait for you?"

"No, you go ahead. I won't be long."

"I'll see you there." I head out with the others.

Jon finds my hand without a word, his fingers lacing through mine like he's been doing it forever. It feels natural. I don't even question it.

We're all heading to Blaze and Ember's place—one last toast to mark the end of something hard-fought and the beginning of whatever comes next.

TWO

Jon
——————

Later that evening, I stand on Blaze's deck overlooking the Pacific, mesmerized by how the setting sun transforms the rolling waves into a canvas of amber and gold. The salty breeze carries the scent of grilling burgers and hot dogs, mingling with the rhythmic percussion of waves breaking against the shore below.

String lights twinkle overhead, dancing with the glow of countless candles—Ryn's creations—their golden cracks illuminating the gathering like earthbound stars.

"Your turn to flip, Blaze," Mac calls out, brandishing a spatula like a weapon. "I've done my duty as grill sergeant."

"Last time I left you unsupervised with beer, you taught CJ that ridiculous drinking game." Blaze groans dramatically.

"Which is now standard training procedure," CJ interjects, raising his bottle with a grin. "Best way to teach rookies patience during stakeouts."

"God help us all if Delta team's methods ever become standard." Jenny rolls her eyes, but her smile is fond.

The easy banter washes over me, familiar and comforting.

Charlie and Brett stand near the railing, heads bent in quiet conversation, occasionally glancing my way. There's something in their expressions that makes my chest tighten—not the sharp pain of recent months, but something softer, an anticipation.

Brett catches my eye and tilts his head slightly. A gesture I know well from years of wordless communication in the field. *We need to talk.*

I nod, and Aria shifts beside me. She knows better than most about the complicated history between Charlie, Brett, and me— the years we spent as more than just teammates. The dissolution of our relationship left wounds that are still healing, though tonight they ache less than usual.

"Go ahead," she says softly, squeezing my hand. "I'll help Ryn set out the desserts."

I follow Charlie and Brett to the far corner of the deck, where the crash of waves provides privacy from the rest of the group. The sunset casts long shadows across their faces, and for a moment, I'm struck by how familiar they still are to me—the curve of Charlie's smile, the way Brett stands with his weight shifted slightly to his right side.

"We wanted to talk to you first," Charlie begins, her voice softer than usual. The vulnerability there reminds me of late nights when the three of us would lie awake, sharing fears we never voiced to anyone else.

Brett leans against the railing, his posture deliberately casual, but I recognize the tension in his shoulders. We've been through too much together for me not to see it.

"Something's changed." It's not a question. The sea breeze carries the scent of Charlie's perfume—the same one she's worn for years, the one that still sometimes haunts my dreams.

"Jon, you've been…" Charlie takes a deep breath. "God, how do I even say this?" She looks to Brett, a silent plea for help.

"We were good together," Brett says quietly. "The three of us. For a long time."

"We were," I agree, my throat tight with unexpected emotion. Memories flash through my mind—Charlie's laughter in bed on Sunday mornings, Brett's arm slung over my shoulder during movie nights, the three of us moving together like one.

"When things ended, it wasn't because we stopped caring." Charlie steps closer, close enough that the flecks of gold in her eyes shimmer.

"I know." The admission still stings.

Our relationship dissolved not from lack of love, but from the slow, painful realization that we were growing in different directions. The arguments grew more frequent, the silences longer. Even the passion that once was our foundation began to feel like a desperate attempt to hold onto something already slipping away.

"I've missed you." Brett's voice roughens with emotion. "Not just… But you know. The way you always knew what to say when a mission goes sideways. Your terrible jokes. How you hog all the blankets."

"I do not hog the blankets." I can't help but smile at that.

"You absolutely did." Charlie laughs softly, the sound achingly familiar. "Remember that cabin in Colorado? Brett and I nearly froze to death."

The memory warms me—a rare weekend off, snow falling outside, the three of us tangled together for warmth. For a moment, I let myself remember how it felt to be part of something so complete, so consuming.

"I've missed you too," I admit. "Both of you, but we've all moved on. I'm okay with that."

"I'm happy to hear that." Charlie reaches for my hand, her fingers twining with mine the way they have countless times before. "We wanted you to know first because—because despite everything, you're still part of us."

"Charlie's pregnant." Brett moves closer, completing our small circle.

The words don't register at first, too enormous to process. I look from Charlie's face to Brett's, seeing the mix of joy and apprehension there.

"You're…" My voice trails off.

"Twelve weeks." Her free hand moves instinctively to her stomach. "We found out last month."

"We wanted to be sure," Brett adds. "Before we told anyone. Even you."

I try to imagine it—Charlie with a rounded belly, Brett hovering protectively, a child with his eyes or her smile. A life they're building together, one that doesn't include me in the way we once imagined.

What rises in me isn't the jealousy or loss. Instead, a surge of joy wells up inside of me for these two people I've loved so deeply.

"That's… Wow!" I swallow hard, emotion making my voice rough. "Charlie, Brett, that's incredible."

"Yeah?" Charlie studies my face, looking for the truth behind my words. "You're okay with it?"

"Okay?" I squeeze her hand. "I'm thrilled for you, both of you. You're going to be amazing parents."

"There's more." Brett's eyes shine bright.

"More?"

"Yeah. We're stepping down from Guardian HRS. Opening our own place, a gym focused on teaching self-defense to foster kids and trafficking survivors."

The pieces click into place—their whispered conversations, the research I glimpsed on Brett's laptop, Charlie's sudden aversion to coffee. The subtle changes I noticed but never fully registered.

"When?" I ask.

"End of the month," Brett says. "We wanted you to hear it from us, not through Guardian gossip."

I nod, processing. My relationship with them was intense. Complicated and beautiful in its own way. For years, we moved as a unit, in the field and in life. The end was messy and painful—not because anyone did anything wrong, but because we grew in different directions.

"I'm happy for you," I say finally. "Both of you. It's a perfect fit."

"We want you in our lives." Charlie studies my face, looking for the truth behind my words. "This doesn't change that you're family."

"We want you in the baby's life, as well." Brett's shoulder brushes mine, familiar and solid.

"Me? How?" I glance between them, suddenly not following. How would that work?

"As an uncle," Brett says, "and Godfather, if we could ask that of you."

"Godfather?" The request catches me off guard. After everything—the dissolution of our relationship, the careful dance of rebuilding friendship—this feels like a sacred trust. "Wow, that's… I'd be honored."

Brett pulls me into a tight embrace, his arms strong around my shoulders. The familiar pressure of his body against mine sends a bittersweet ache through my chest. The solidity of him, the scent of his skin—things I once knew as intimately as my own heartbeat. No more nights exploring every inch of him, no more lazy mornings with his body curved around mine. Something precious slips away in this moment, even as something new begins.

"We still want you in our lives." We separate, and Brett's hands linger on my shoulders, his eyes searching mine. "Different than before, but no less important."

"This wasn't how any of us planned things would go." Charlie steps closer, her hand finding mine. "But just because we're not sharing a bed doesn't mean we're not still connected." Her gaze drifts past me to where Aria stands with the others. A small smile plays at her lips. "She seems nice. And you seem— lighter around her."

"Took you long enough to make a move, though." Brett follows her gaze. "We had a betting pool going, you know."

"You did not." Despite everything, a laugh escapes me.

"We absolutely did," Charlie grins. "No one won, though. You waited way longer than any of us predicted."

"Even Mac bet you'd kiss her after the debrief from the Santa Barbara extraction," Brett adds. "That was two months ago."

"You were betting on my love life?" Heat rises to my face.

"Someone had to take an interest." Charlie squeezes my hand. "You weren't exactly rushing things along."

Something about Aria feels right in a way I can't fully articulate. A possibility I'm not yet ready to name, but I also can't ignore it.

"Are you happy?" Brett asks, his voice dropping to that register that always made me tell him the truth, even when I didn't want to.

"Getting there," I admit. "And you two? I can't believe you're starting a family."

"Yes." Charlie's hand drifts to her stomach again. "We want this, but we also want our child to know their Uncle Jon, to have you in their life. As family."

"Always," I promise, and mean it with everything in me.

When we rejoin the group, Aria's eyes find mine immediately.

Questions, but no jealousy, no insecurity. Just patience and understanding. She makes my heart swell. I slide beside her, my arm finding its place around her waist. Her body leans into mine, a silent acknowledgment of connection.

"Everything okay?" Her warm breath against my ear sends shivers down my spine.

"Better than okay." I press my lips to her temple.

The night deepens around us, and the deck is alive with laughter and conversation. Jenny and Mac trade stories from missions past, embellishing details to make Ember and Aria laugh.

"Food's ready," Blaze announces, piling juicy burgers onto a platter. "Come and get it before I feed it all to Jon. Man's been eyeing these burgers like they're intel packets."

"Occupational hazard," I call back. "Always hungry."

"For more than just food," Charlie quips with a meaningful glance toward Aria, who blushes beautifully.

The teasing, the way everyone has accepted Aria and Ember into our circle, fills me with warmth that has nothing to do with the lingering heat of the day. Delta team has always been family, but seeing how seamlessly they've embraced the newcomers makes me realize how much I want this to work. How much I want Aria to feel she belongs here, with us.

With me.

I hope I'm not moving too fast, but she feels like an inevitability, as if she's already a part of me.

"To 'The Little Matchstick Girl,'" Jenny raises her glass, her smile radiant in the golden light. "Ember and Aria, may you enjoy unlimited success."

"And to Ryn's fire-born art," Blaze adds, nodding toward the candles that illuminate our gathering. "Turning broken things into treasure."

Our glasses clink together, and the sound carries out over the ocean. I watch Aria's face in the flickering light, memorizing the way joy transforms her features. Just hours ago, in the shop, I finally found the courage to kiss her—a moment I've imagined countless times but never thought would ever happen.

I'm glad I took the chance.

The evening flows around us in waves of conversation and laughter.

CJ leans back in his chair, the fading light catching the silver threading through his dark hair at the temples. Our former Delta team commander still carries that unmistakable air of command. His promotion to head Guardian operations left a hole in our team dynamic that Jenny filled seamlessly, but having him here tonight makes our circle feel complete.

"Like old times." CJ's gaze sweeps over all of us. "The whole team is back together."

"Not quite like old times." Jenny nudges him with her elbow. "I give the orders now, remember?"

"As if I could forget." CJ laughs. "You remind me every chance you get."

"Someone has to keep your ego in check." Mac reaches for another beer. "Remember Bogotá? When you decided we should infiltrate that compound without backup?"

CJ winces. "That was—"

"The worst call you ever made," Jenny finishes. "We were pinned down for six hours."

"And yet," CJ raises his bottle, "we all made it out. With the intel. And the hostage."

"Because I had a backup plan," Jenny says smugly.

"You always do." CJ's voice carries genuine respect. "Why do you think I recommended you for Delta-One?"

Brett leans forward. "You never told us that part."

"Some things are meant to stay between team leads," CJ says, his eyes meeting Jenny's in silent communication that speaks to years of partnership. "But tonight's a night for truths, isn't it?"

"Remember the extraction in Caracas?" Mac leans forward, elbows on his knees. "When CJ had to pose as a flamenco dancer?"

CJ groans. "I thought we agreed never to speak of that again."

"Some things are too good to stay buried." Jenny's eyes dance with mischief. "Especially the part where an arms dealer tried to seduce you."

"Someone failed to mention in the intel briefing," CJ says drily.

"Not my department." Mac raises his hands in mock surrender. "Besides, you improvised beautifully."

"That was the night I knew you'd be taking my job someday," CJ tells Jenny, something like pride in his voice. "The way you stepped in when everything went sideways."

"Only because you'd taught me how to think on my feet." Jenny's tone softens. "Delta team has always been more than just a tactical unit."

"Family," Blaze says simply, his arm draped around Ember's shoulders.

"Speaking of family," CJ turns to Aria, his expression warming. "It's good to see you fitting in so well with this bunch of misfits. Not everyone can handle the Delta dynamic."

"It's—different," Aria admits. "But in the best way."

"We grow on you," Mac says. "Like a fungus."

"A highly trained, lethal fungus," Brett adds.

Blaze keeps glancing at Ember with an intensity that makes my neck prickle with awareness. Something's coming. During a lull in conversation, Blaze clears his throat, rising from his seat beside Ember. The sudden quiet draws everyone's attention.

"I, uh—" Blaze rubs the back of his neck, uncharacteristically nervous. "Had something planned. A speech. But I'm just going to—"

He drops to one knee in front of Ember, whose eyes widen. Her hand flies to her mouth.

"Ember," Blaze says, his voice steady despite the emotion plain on his face. "You walked into my life, and somehow became the best part of it."

From his pocket, he draws a small velvet box. The deck falls silent except for the crash of waves below and the soft catch of Ember's breath.

"I had this made," he continues, opening the box to reveal a ring that catches the candlelight. Golden veins run through the metal like Ryn's kintsugi work—beauty created from broken pieces. "Because that's what you did for me. Found the broken pieces and made them something beautiful."

"Blaze—" Ember's eyes shimmer with tears.

"I want to spend my life making you as happy as you make me. Will you marry me?"

"Yes," Ember whispers, then louder, "Yes!"

Blaze slides the ring onto her finger, then rises to gather her into his arms. Their kiss, tender and fierce at once, sends a cheer through our gathered family. Champagne appears, toasts are made, and the celebration takes on a new energy.

As the congratulations and toasts continue around us, my fingers twitch with the need to touch Aria. To claim her in some small way. The impulse surprises me—I'm not usually possessive. But something about tonight, about seeing Charlie and Brett together, about watching Blaze and Ember seal their future with a kiss, makes me acutely aware of what I want.

Who I want.

I catch Aria's wrist, the delicate bones beneath my fingers making my throat tighten.

"Come with me."

Her eyes meet mine, curious but trusting. She follows me to the far edge of the deck, where the crash of waves drowns out the celebration behind us. Stars reflect on the dark water, endless possibilities mirrored in the depths.

"Are you all right?" She studies my face in the dim light, her hand brushing lightly along my forearm. The warmth of her touch grounds me, but my pulse refuses to slow. She studies my face in the dim light, her brows pulling together in concern.

I nod, but it's not enough. I need to say it.

"I've been thinking about that kiss. In the shop."

"Me too." Color rises to her cheeks, soft pink even in the moonlight, and it damn near knocks the air out of my lungs. "I've wanted to kiss you for so long."

"I've wanted to for months," I admit, my thumb tracing a slow line across the back of her hand. "Just never thought…"

"That I'd be interested?" Her laughter is soft, surprised, and tinged with a hint of shyness, like she's testing the water before diving in. "I've been hoping you would for months. I just didn't think you saw me that way. Not with—"

"Charlie and Brett," I finish for her, jaw tightening. "That's been over for a while now."

Her mouth parts, but she doesn't speak. Her fingers twist nervously in the hem of her dress, and the gesture nearly undoes me.

"I just wasn't sure if you were ready…" She bites her lip, and it nearly unravels me. That uncertainty, that doubt—like she doesn't know how much I see her, want her. "For something else."

That hits deeper than it should. This fierce, brilliant woman doesn't realize how completely she's undone me. How often I've found myself watching the way her eyes light up when she's focused. How the curve of her smile ruins my concentration. How the memory of her laugh gets me through the hardest parts of the day.

"I need to ask you something." I reach out, brushing her hair behind her ear.

"Anything."

"Are you seeing anyone?" My hand stays at her cheek, my thumb tracing the curve of her jaw. "I should have asked before I kissed you. Before I assumed—"

"No." The answer is immediate. Her lips tilt into a small, teasing smile. "I'm not seeing anyone."

"Good." The relief that hits me is hot and visceral, coiled low in my spine.

"Good?" she echoes, like she's testing the word on her tongue.

I step into her space, one hand slipping to her hip, tugging her in until our bodies nearly touch. Her breath hitches. I feel it in the way her fingers grip my forearm.

"Yes." I step in closer, my hand sliding to her waist. She doesn't flinch. Doesn't move away. She lets me touch her like I have the right. "Because I don't want to share you."

"Do I dare ask—what that means?" Her tone is playful, but there's a thread of hope running through it.

"I want you. Just you. Us," I continue, voice dropping. "If that's what you want too… Say it now." I lock my gaze on hers.

"I'd like that." She sways into me, hands sliding up my chest, looping behind my neck like it's instinct.

I nod once, then let my thumb stroke the edge of her rib, just under the curve of her breast.

"Just to be clear," I murmur, my fingers tracing a slow line along her waist, "if you're not seeing anyone… I want to be the one who is. The *only* one who is. I'm done with the threesome thing, and I'm not interested in casual. Not with you."

My thumb presses gently at her waist, drawing her just a little closer.

Her lashes lower as that sinks in, a flicker of emotion crossing her face—remembering what things looked like between me, Brett, and Charlie.

"I don't want anyone else in it. Just you. Me. No additions."

Her breath hitches. I lean in, my voice dropping to a rumble.

"This is you and me. No one else. If we do this, it's exclusive. You're mine."

"Then, I'm yours," she whispers. "Just like you're mine." She leans into me, hands sliding up my chest, locking behind my neck.

That's all I need to hear.

She stares up at me, lips parted, breath shallow, eyes storm-lit with want and something deeper. Need, maybe. Or maybe it's just mine, reflected back at me.

I don't ask permission—I don't need to. Not when everything in her body is already leaning toward me, drawn like a tide to shore.

I slide a hand around the back of her neck, fingers threading through her hair, tugging gently until her mouth tilts just enough. My other hand curves around her hip, anchoring her in place.

Our mouths meet in a clash of heat and hunger—no brush, no tease. Just need. Pure and potent.

She gasps against my lips, and I take advantage, sweeping in, claiming her in a kiss that's all tongue and teeth and pent-up ache. Nothing slow about it. Nothing careful. This isn't a question. It's a fucking declaration.

Her fingers grip my biceps, nails biting through cotton, dragging me closer like she wants to climb inside my skin. Her body molds to mine, soft curves pressed tight to every inch of me. I groan, the sound guttural, ripped from my chest.

Her tongue meets mine, bold and unfiltered, a rhythm that

sets my blood on fire. She tastes like wine and sin and the first damn breath after nearly drowning.

I press her back until her spine finds the wall behind her, my thigh slipping between hers. She arches instinctively, and the friction shoots sparks straight through me.

She moans into my mouth, breath hitching when my hand slides up her side, thumb brushing the underside of her breast through fabric.

I pull back just enough to breathe, our foreheads bumping, noses brushing.

"That answer your question?" I rasp.

Her eyes flutter open, pupils blown wide. "What question?"

I grin, breathless and wild. "Exactly."

She surges up and kisses me again, deeper this time. Needier. Like she finally understands just how far I'm willing to go for her.

And hell if I'm not already gone.

I reclaim her mouth, my kiss harder now, more demanding. Possessive in a way I've never allowed myself to be. Her response is immediate, matching my intensity with her own. Her hands aren't idle, sliding beneath my shirt to trace the muscles of my back, nails lightly scoring my skin in a way that makes me groan against her lips.

When we finally break apart, we're both breathing hard. Her lips are swollen from my kisses, her eyes dark with desire. I rest my forehead against hers, struggling to regain control.

"That wasn't like the first one," she whispers, a smile in her voice.

"No." My thumb traces the curve of her lower lip. "But I've been thinking about it all day."

"Just today?"

"Longer." I laugh softly, caught. "Much longer."

I'm not a man for casual flings—never have been. Even with

Charlie and Brett, it was always more than physical. They were family, safety, and home. With Aria—I want even more.

Behind us, Delta team's laughter carries on the night breeze. My family, her family now too. Tomorrow will bring its own challenges. But tonight, with Aria in my arms and the endless horizon stretching before us, I allow myself to believe in possibilities I'd given up on finding again.

THREE

Aria

——————

Several days have passed since opening day, Ember's engagement, and the start of something wonderful with Jon. The memory of that kiss still burns beneath my skin. The shop is back in order, Ember and Blaze are tangled up in their own bliss, and somehow—against all odds—Jon asked me out on a real date.

"You never said we'd be coming here."

The gondola creaks as it glides along the narrow track carved into the cliffside, the sea glittering far below. I press my fingertips to the cool glass, breath catching with each sway. The coastline stretches out like a painting—jagged rocks, wind-tossed waves, a promise of something wild and unforgettable.

Jon stands beside me, one hand braced casually on the rail, the other stuffed in his pocket.

"Wanted it to be a surprise."

That rare smile tugs at the corner of his mouth, eyes crinkling at the edges in a way that makes something in my chest turn over. He holds a softness that I'm only beginning to see. A quiet joy he saves just for me.

The metal carriage slows, settling with a gentle bump against the landing platform on the beach. Jon pushes the door open and extends his hand. His palm burns against mine, calluses from years of fieldwork creating delicious friction that sends electricity racing up my arm.

Salt and freedom saturate the air, mingling with the scent of Jon's subtle cologne—sandalwood and something uniquely him. Waves crash against dark stones, spray catching rainbows in the fading light. A narrow boardwalk leads down to the rocky shoreline.

Jon's grip tightens as we navigate the weathered planks. "Watch your step." His body angles protectively toward mine, shoulder blocking the wind as it whips strands of hair across my face. The way he shelters me stirs something deep in my chest, a dangerous hope I'm afraid to fully embrace.

A wicker picnic basket swings in his free hand.

This beach radiates a wildness—a rugged landscape of smooth, black and gray stones with tidal pools sparkling between them, like hidden treasures. Nothing like the tourist-packed stretches of sand in Malibu, where people pose for Instagram rather than actually experiencing the ocean. Above us looms Insanity—a modernist fortress of glass and steel perched atop the cliff like a crown.

"So Angel Fire really lives up there? All of them together?" The question bubbles up through my awe.

Jon nods, never releasing my hand. "They've always been more family than bandmates. Forest's place sits just beyond that northern ridge—he shares it with Sara and Paul."

We pick our way across the stones toward a sheltered alcove where the cliff curves inward. My curiosity about Jon's past—particularly the parts he rarely mentions—surfaces despite my efforts to contain it.

"How often do you come here?"

"Not as much as I'd like." Jon sets down the basket and

unfurls a thick blanket with a swift flick of his wrists. "Forest has an open invitation, but I try not to intrude. This place means something to them."

The blanket settles on the relatively flat stone surface. Jon weighs down the corners with smooth rocks before gesturing for me to sit. As I settle onto the soft fabric, the reality hits me— alone with Jon at this magical place, the most beautiful sunset I've ever seen painting the sky in watercolor strokes of gold and crimson.

Jon kneels beside the basket, unveiling containers one by one. His hands—capable of such precise violence when necessary— move with meticulous care, arranging strawberries beside rich artisanal cheeses and crusty sourdough bread.

"You didn't have to go to all this trouble." Emotion rises unexpectedly in my throat, tightening it around the words.

"I wanted to." Jon looks up, the dying sunlight turning his eyes to liquid amber, warm and rich with something that makes my heart stutter.

The heat of his gaze sparks a fluttering low in my stomach. I turn toward the darkening ocean, needing a moment to collect myself. In the distance, a seabird wheels against the purple-orange sky, free and unfettered.

"Tell me about the tidepools." My voice emerges huskier than intended, betraying the effect he has on me.

Jon smiles and offers his hand. "Come on." His fingers inter-twine with mine, thumb brushing across my knuckles in a casual caress that feels anything but casual. "I'll show you."

We leave our shoes on the blanket and make our way bare-foot across the stones. Each rock presses cool smoothness against my soles, worn by centuries of tides. Jon leads me to a collection of shallow pools near the water's edge, each one a miniature universe glimmering in the fading light.

Jon crouches beside one pool, his finger hovering just above the surface. "Look." The word holds reverence. "There's an entire ecosystem in each pool."

I kneel beside him, our shoulders touching, sending a cascade of awareness through my body. The pool before us shimmers like polished glass, a miniature cosmos teeming with life. Bright green anemones wave their tentacles in invisible currents. A tiny hermit crab scuttles across miniature mountains. Purple sea stars cling to rocky walls, their forms perfect and alien.

"It's beautiful." The whisper escapes me, the words inadequate for the wonder I feel.

"These little worlds survive against impossible odds. Twice a day, the tide leaves them exposed and vulnerable. Yet they adapt, persist, thrive." Jon's fingers skim the surface, creating ripples that dance across the pool. The movement mesmerizes me—not just the water, but the strength in his hands, the careful control.

His words carry weight beyond their literal meaning. My gaze shifts to his profile, strong and defined against the darkening sky.

"Did you come here with them?"

The question slips out before I can stop it. My voice barely carries above the crash of waves and the distant cry of gulls.

Jon's hand stills in the water. Tension hums off him—not angry, just tightly wound. Then he nods, eyes still fixed on the tidepool.

"Yeah. Many times."

Silence stretches between us, delicate and alive. A sea anemone ripples beneath the surface, curling in on itself, then slowly opening again, vulnerable but unafraid.

"I'm sorry," I murmur. "I shouldn't have asked."

"Don't be." He turns to me then, crouched low but suddenly towering in presence, gaze steady and unflinching. "Charlie and Brett were a big part of my life. They always will be. They're family. But I'm not romantically involved with them anymore. That chapter's closed."

My heart knocks hard in my chest.

"What I want now…" His voice drops, rough-edged and reverent. "Is to explore what this could be. With you. Just you."

I reach for him before I can second-guess it, fingers sliding over his, our palms brushing. His hand tightens around mine, grounding me.

"I want to build something with you. If you're in." Then he lifts our joined hands and gently drags his knuckles across my cheek, slow and warm.

I nod, too full to speak. But my fingers curl tighter around his, and he knows.

The sun dips lower, painting the water in deepening shades of gold and crimson. Jon rises, extending his hand. His touch lingers as he helps me up, thumb tracing small circles on my palm. "Come on. Let's eat before everything gets cold."

Back at our picnic spot, Jon uncorks a bottle of white wine, pouring it into proper glasses before handing one to me. His fingers brush mine, lingering longer than necessary.

"To new beginnings." He raises his glass, eyes never leaving mine.

I clink mine against his. "New beginnings."

The wine's flavor explodes across my tongue—crisp apple notes with hints of plum and something mineral, like the ocean itself distilled into liquid. We eat as the last light fades from the sky, stars appearing one by one like shy performers taking the stage.

The food disappears, replaced by comfortable silence. Jon packs away the remnants while I wrap a blanket around my shoulders against the growing chill. When he's done, he pulls something from beneath a nearby pile of driftwood—more pieces he must have stashed here earlier, knowing exactly what this evening would need.

"Fire?" Jon gestures toward a small depression among the stones lined with blackened marks from previous flames.

"Yes, please." I watch him arrange the driftwood, the practiced movements revealing a lifetime of outdoor skills I'm only beginning to discover.

The fire catches quickly, flames licking upward, casting his face in warm light and dancing shadows that emphasize the sharp lines of his jaw. His presence fills the space around us—not just physically, but something deeper, an energy that draws me toward him like gravity.

"You've done this before." The observation slips out, my eyes tracing the confident movements of his hands.

"Spent half my childhood outdoors." Jon settles beside me, close enough that our thighs touch through layers of clothing. "My dad believed camping built character."

"Did it?"

"Maybe." His smile flashes in the firelight, a quick glimpse of white teeth against tanned skin. "Or maybe it just gave me a useful skill set for when I need to impress pretty women on beach dates."

The casual compliment heats my cheeks more than the fire. Jon's arm slips around my shoulders, and I lean into him, our bodies fitting together with surprising ease. His scent envelops me—clean sweat, salt air, and that underlying note that's purely Jon.

"I've been having the nightmares again." The confession emerges quietly as I stare into the flames. "About the van. The needle. Waking up in that warehouse."

"How bad?" Jon's arm tightens, his body tensing slightly before relaxing with deliberate control.

"Three nights this week." I trace patterns in the sand beside the blanket, focusing on the small movements of my finger rather than the memories. "Not as intense as before, but—they're still there."

"Have you talked to Dr. Reynolds about it?"

I nod, watching embers spiral upward from the fire. "She says it's normal. That trauma doesn't follow a straight line to healing. There are setbacks, loops, spirals."

"She's right." His voice softens, vibrating through his chest against my ear. "What happened to you—what Wolfe did—it leaves marks. Some visible, some not."

The thin scar on my collarbone tingles at the mention, a souvenir from my time in captivity. Jon doesn't treat it like something ugly or broken. When we kiss, his lips sometimes brush against it with deliberate tenderness, transforming it from a mark of pain to something almost sacred.

"Do you ever wonder about him?" The question barely rises above the crackle of flames. "About Wolfe? If he survived?"

Jon shifts, his body angling toward mine. "According to the reports, the upper floors of the warehouse were compromised during the extraction. Wolfe was last seen on the roof before the helicopter took off without him. Ember stabbed him with a letter opener."

"But no body was recovered," I press, needing to hear the truth.

"No." Jon's jaw tightens. "The building was structurally unsound after the operation. Too dangerous for a thorough search."

"Do you believe he's dead?"

"I believe in being prepared for all possibilities." The careful phrasing tells me everything.

A shiver runs through me despite the fire's warmth. Wolfe was obsessed with his revenge against my father, using me as a means to an end. When Ember tried to save me, she'd been taken too, not trafficked like the other children Wolfe targeted, but held as leverage over me. The thought that he might still be out there, watching, waiting…

"Hey." Jon's hand cups my face, turning it toward him. His eyes burn with intensity in the firelight. "If he's alive, if he ever comes back, we'll be ready. All of us. You're not alone, Aria. We're here and we'll protect you."

The conviction in his voice steadies me. I lean into his touch, the warmth of his palm anchoring me to the present. "Thank you for bringing me here. It's perfect."

"You're welcome." His thumb traces my cheekbone, a featherlight caress that leaves a trail of heat in its wake.

We sit in silence, watching the flames dance and listening to the ocean's eternal conversation with the shore. The vast darkness stretches before us, broken only by our small fire and the distant lights of passing ships. Under the blanket, Jon's fingers find mine, intertwining them in a casual intimacy that still takes me by surprise.

"Can I ask you something?" Courage finally gathers in my chest for the question that's been circling my mind for weeks.

"Anything." His focus shifts entirely to me, making me the center of his universe in that moment.

I take a deep breath. "You, Brett, and Charlie… Was it always the three of you? Or did you join them later?" The question remains incomplete, but Jon understands what I'm asking.

"Does it matter?" His voice holds no judgment, only genuine curiosity.

"I—I don't know." Heat floods my cheeks, which has nothing to do with the fire. "I guess I'm trying to understand how it worked. How you all fit together."

"Charlie and Brett were together first." Jon shifts to face me more directly, his knee pressing against my thigh. "I met them on an operation in Budapest six years ago. We became friends, then more. It evolved naturally."

"And you all were—together?" I bite my lip, dancing around what I really want to know.

"We were together, yes." A smile plays at the corner of Jon's mouth, amusement dancing in his eyes. "We did a lot of things together. A lot of—exploring."

The deliberate vagueness in his tone makes my cheeks burn hotter. He knows exactly what I'm trying to ask, but he's not going to make it easy for me.

"That's not exactly what I meant," I mutter, fiddling with the edge of the blanket.

"If you want specific details," Jon's laugh is low and rich, "you're going to have to ask *specific* questions."

The challenge in his eyes both embarrasses and thrills me. I'm not quite brave enough to ask outright—not yet—but the knowledge that this conversation isn't over, that stories are waiting to be told when I find the courage to ask for them, sends a strange thrill through me.

"Fine. For now, let's just say… Was it complicated? Logistically?" I hedge, still circling what I really want to know.

"The same way any relationship works." Jon's shoulder lifts in a half-shrug, though his eyes still hold that knowing glint. "Communication. Respect. Love. Just with one more person in the equation."

"Weren't you jealous? Or afraid of being left out?" The question reveals more of my insecurities than I'd intended.

"Sometimes." The honesty in his admission touches me. "We're all human. But we talked through it when those feelings came up." His eyes search mine. "What are you really asking?"

"I guess… Do you miss it?" The flames capture my attention as I gather my courage. "Does being with me feel—incomplete somehow?"

Jon's hand finds mine again, his fingers intertwining with my own.

"No." The single word carries such conviction that it steals my breath. "What I had with them was beautiful and real. What

I have with you is also beautiful and real. Different, but no less whole."

"But you were together for years." The insecurity I've been fighting bubbles to the surface. "And now they're having a baby, starting a family… They moved on so quickly."

Jon's expression softens. "We were together for nearly five years. But people change. What they need changes."

"They chose each other in the end." The words emerge smaller than I intended.

Jon exhales slowly, thumb tracing patterns on my palm.

"It wasn't about choosing one over the other. Charlie wanted children. Brett was ready for that step. I wasn't—not then. They made the choice that was right for them."

"And now?" My heart pounds against my ribs. "What do you want now?"

"Now, I want to be here, with you." His eyes meet mine, firelight dancing in their depths. "Getting to know you. Building something new."

Tears prickle behind my eyes. "I worry sometimes that you're not ready. That you're still healing from losing them."

"I am still healing." The admission comes without hesitation, his voice low and intimate. "But that doesn't mean I'm not ready for this—for us." His hand cups my cheek, thumb brushing away moisture I hadn't realized had escaped. "Healing doesn't happen in isolation. Sometimes it happens in connection with someone new."

The honesty in his voice touches something deep inside me. I lean forward, resting my forehead against his. His breath warms my skin, mingling with mine in the small space between us.

"I've been wondering," my voice drops to a whisper, "why you haven't tried to… You know. Go further than kissing. I thought maybe you weren't attracted to me that way, or…"

Jon pulls back slightly, eyes darkening.

"Aria." My name becomes something sacred in his mouth. "I am very attracted to you, but after everything you went through with the kidnapping, I didn't want to pressure you." His gaze drops to my lips, then back to my eyes. "I know trauma can complicate physical intimacy. I wanted to give you space to heal, to feel safe."

A laugh bubbles up from my chest, unexpected and genuine.

"You've been holding back because you thought I needed time, and I've been worrying you weren't interested in being with just me?"

"Seems we could both use some work on our communication skills." His smile breaks through, slow and warm.

"Maybe we should start now." Boldness surges through me, heat pooling low in my belly. "I'm not made of glass. The kidnapping was traumatic, yes, but I'm stronger than you think."

"I know exactly how strong you are." His voice drops lower, something primal threading through it. "I've seen it firsthand."

"Then stop treating me like I might break."

The fire crackles between us, sending sparks spiraling into the night sky. Jon's eyes darken, pupils dilating until only a thin ring of amber remains. A muscle ticks in his jaw—the only outward sign of his tightly held control.

"Aria." My name becomes a warning, a promise.

"Yes?" I challenge, leaning closer.

With deliberate slowness, Jon cups the back of my neck, fingers threading into my hair. The gentle possessiveness of the gesture sends shivers racing down my spine. His other hand settles at my waist, drawing me closer until I'm almost in his lap.

"I'm definitely interested in you." His voice rumbles, deeper than I've ever heard it, laced with hunger held too long in check.

In answer, I close the distance between us.

His lips claim mine with a hunger that steals my breath. This isn't like our previous kisses—polite, careful, restrained. This is

Jon unleashed, taking what he wants with a ferocity that makes my head spin. His hand tightens in my hair, angling my face to deepen the kiss, tongue sweeping into my mouth with possessive intent.

I gasp against his lips, fingers clutching at his shoulders. He tastes of wine and desire, of salt air and need too long denied. My body ignites, every nerve ending coming alive under his touch. His arm around my waist tightens, drawing me fully into his lap until I'm straddling him, the position intimate and thrilling.

Jon breaks the kiss only to trail his lips along my jaw, down the sensitive column of my throat. His teeth graze my pulse point, drawing a whimper from deep in my chest. My hands slide into his hair, holding him against me as heat pools between my thighs.

"God, you taste amazing," he growls against my skin, the vibration sending new shivers through me. "Been wanting to do this for so long."

His hands roam my back, my sides, skimming just beneath the hem of my sweater to touch my bare skin. The contact burns, his calloused fingers leaving trails of fire wherever they touch. I arch against him, seeking more contact, more friction, more everything.

Jon recaptures my mouth, the kiss deeper, hungrier. One hand splays across my lower back, pressing me tighter against him, letting me feel exactly how much he wants me. The evidence of his desire sends a bolt of feminine pride through me —I did this to him, broke his legendary control.

When we finally break apart, we're both breathing hard. Jon rests his forehead against mine, eyes closed as if gathering the last fragments of his restraint.

"If we don't stop now," he warns, voice ragged, "I'm not sure I'll be able to."

"Who said anything about stopping?" I roll my hips experimentally, drawing a hiss from between his clenched teeth.

Jon's eyes snap open, dark with desire.

"Aria." My name emerges as half-groan, half-warning. "I didn't bring protection. Didn't think we'd get this far tonight."

The admission—that he wanted to be prepared but didn't want to pressure me—touches something deep inside, but the fire he's ignited in me refuses to be extinguished so easily.

"There are other ways to touch," I whisper against his mouth, taking his hand and guiding it to the hem of my sweater.

"You sure?" A growl rumbles through his chest as his fingers slip beneath the fabric, palm hot against my bare stomach.

In answer, I arch against him, silently asking for more.

His touch grows bolder, calloused fingers sliding upward with torturous slowness until they graze the underside of my breast. My breath catches, head falling back as his thumb brushes across my nipple through the thin lace of my bra.

"God, you're beautiful," Jon murmurs, eyes locked on my face as he watches my reaction. His other hand tangles in my hair, angling my head for another searing kiss as he cups my breast fully, thumb circling the hardened peak.

A soft moan escapes me, swallowed by his hungry mouth. Heat pools between my thighs as his fingers deftly slip beneath the lace, skin against skin at last. The calluses on his fingertips create exquisite friction against my sensitive flesh.

"Jon," I gasp, arching into his touch.

He shifts us, laying me back against the blanket, his body half covering mine as his mouth travels down my neck. His hand never leaves my breast, alternating between gentle caresses and firmer touches that send lightning through my veins.

"Tell me if you want me to stop," he breathes against my collarbone, even as his free hand pushes my sweater higher, exposing more skin to the cool night air.

"Don't you dare," I manage, threading my fingers through his hair.

His lips replace his fingers, hot mouth closing over my nipple through the lace. The dual sensation of wet heat and rough fabric draws a cry from my throat. My hips buck instinctively, seeking pressure, friction, release.

Jon's hand slides to my hip, thumb tracing circles against the exposed skin between my jeans and sweater.

"Easy," he soothes, though the strain in his voice betrays his own struggle for control. "We have all night."

The promise in those words sends another wave of heat through me. His mouth returns to mine, the kiss deep and possessive as his hands continue their exploration, learning what makes me gasp, what makes me moan, what makes me whisper his name like a prayer.

Time loses meaning as we touch and taste, discovering each other beneath the vast canopy of stars. Jon's restraint amazes me —every move calculated to bring me pleasure while maintaining the boundaries he's set for tonight.

Eventually, reluctantly, we slow our exploration. My body thrums with satisfied desire, but a deeper ache lingers—unspent, smoldering.

"Rain check on the rest," I whisper against his mouth, brushing a final kiss to his swollen lips.

"Definitely." His voice is still gravel-edged, need wrapped in restraint.

He helps me adjust my clothes, his hands reverent, then pulls me against his chest, his jacket tucked around us both, sealing me in his warmth. His arms lock around my waist from behind like he doesn't want to let go.

"I'll be prepared next time," he murmurs at my temple.

Next time. The promise makes my breath hitch.

God, I can't wait to have sex with this man.

We settle back by the fire, my head resting on his shoulder, his arm secure around me. The stars shine overhead, countless and bright. The ocean continues its eternal conversation with the shore. Yet despite the serene setting, awareness hums between us —a current of desire temporarily banked but far from extinguished.

"Tell me something," I say, watching the flames dance. "Something you've never told anyone else."

Jon is quiet for a long moment, fingers tracing idle patterns on my shoulder. "When I was eight, I found a bird with a broken wing. I tried to save it, kept it in a shoebox, fed it with an eyedropper. It died three days later." He pauses, and I can feel his throat work as he swallows. "I buried it under my window and planted a wildflower over the spot. Every spring when the flowers bloomed, I'd think about that bird and wonder if I could have done something different to save it."

The simplicity of the story, along with its unexpected vulnerability, touches me deeply. I turn my face into his chest, pressing a kiss over his heart.

"Thank you for telling me."

"Your turn," he says, fingers now combing gently through my hair.

I consider what to share, what part of myself to offer in exchange for his trust. "I used to dream about running away. Even before the kidnapping, before Wolfe. I'd sit in my father's mansion with everything a girl could want, and I'd fantasize about just—disappearing. Becoming someone else, someone without all the expectations and obligations."

"And now?"

"I know what it feels like to be taken from your life. To be terrified." I stare into the flames. "I don't dream about running anymore. I dream about building something worth staying for."

Jon's arm tightens around me. "And what would that look like? This *thing* worth staying for?"

The question opens doors in my mind that I've only glimpsed before.

"Freedom to choose my own path. Work that matters. People who see me, not just my father's name or my trust fund." I pause, gathering courage. "Someone who loves me for who I am, not what I represent."

"And does your father approve of these dreams?" Jon's lips press against my temple.

"Hardly." A hollow laugh escapes me. "Marcus Holbrook has my entire life mapped out. Executive position at Holbrook Pharmaceuticals. Marriage to someone with the right connections, preferably in biotech or healthcare. Two perfect children who'll continue the dynasty."

He presses a soft kiss to my forehead. "Do you think he'd really object that strongly?"

"I know he would." Sadness threads through me. "My father measures people's worth by their bank accounts and business connections. He's never understood that some things can't be quantified on a balance sheet."

"And where do you stand on that philosophy?" Jon's fingers lift my chin, turning my face to his.

"I used to buy into it." The admission comes with a flush of shame. "Before the kidnapping, I was exactly what he raised me to be—shallow, privileged, and obsessed with status."

"And now?"

"Now I know better." My voice strengthens with conviction. "I've seen real courage in Ember, who had nothing but risked everything to help a stranger. I've seen real strength in all of you at Guardian HRS, fighting not for money but because it's right."

I shift to look directly into Jon's eyes. "I've seen what really matters. And it isn't my father's empire or his connections or his legacy."

Jon studies me, his hand warm against my cheek, thumb brushing gently beneath my eye.

I draw in a breath. "You know the first time I saw Ember? I was rushing to a board meeting downtown. Wearing Louis Vuittons. Designer coat. Wind in my face, phone in hand, already pissed about some press leak." I give a short, brittle laugh. "And there she was—standing on a frozen street corner, hawking candles from a folding table."

Jon stays quiet, listening, letting me find my words.

"I barely looked at her. She tried to sell me a five-dollar candle. I dismissed her like she didn't matter." Shame curls in my stomach, sharp and sickening. "And then it happened. That van screeched up. Two men in ski masks grabbed me. No one moved. Not a single person helped."

My voice drops, throat tightening. "Except Ember."

His brows pull together, his fingers tightening slightly at my jaw, but he doesn't interrupt.

"She didn't hesitate. She screamed and ran toward them. She fought them. With nothing but bare hands and zero regard for her own safety. The girl I ignored two seconds earlier risked her life to save mine."

I blink hard against the burn behind my eyes. "Everything changed after that. I wasn't the person I thought I was. And Ember—she's not just my friend. She's the reason I saw myself clearly for the first time. I owe her everything. So I gave her what I could—my money and my belief in her dream. But the truth is, she gave me something so much bigger."

Jon's hand slides into my hair, cupping the back of my head, his forehead pressing gently to mine.

"She gave me a chance to become someone worth saving."

"Never think you aren't worth saving." He exhales slowly, like the air's been punched out of him. His voice, when it comes, is rough. "I'd go to hell and back to save you."

He studies my face in the firelight, something profound shifting in his expression. Then he kisses me again—gentler this time, but no less intense, a kiss that speaks of understanding and something deeper I'm not ready to name.

When we break apart, the fire has burned lower, the embers glowing ruby-red in the darkness. Jon adds another piece of driftwood, stirring the flames back to life.

"So where does that leave us?" he asks quietly. "Hiding from your father indefinitely?"

The question pierces me. "No. Not indefinitely. Just until I figure out how to make him understand that my life is my own." I pause, doubt creeping in. "Unless that's not what you want? If this is just casual for you…"

"There's nothing casual about how I feel about you." Jon's laugh holds no humor.

The simple declaration steals my breath. We haven't used those words yet—the big ones that change everything—but they hover in the air between us, unspoken but increasingly undeniable.

"So we'll figure it out," I whisper, hope unfurling in my chest. "Together."

"Together." Jon seals the promise with another kiss.

We stay by the fire for hours, talking, kissing, learning each other in new ways. Jon tells me about his childhood in Montana, the grandfather who taught him to track and hunt, the mother who insisted he learn to cook and clean because "no partner of yours should have to do everything."

I share stories about my boarding school adventures, including the time I got suspended for starting an underground newspaper that exposed the headmaster's embezzlement, and the summer I spent volunteering at a clinic in Guatemala against my father's wishes.

The stars wheel overhead, the moon rises and sets, and still we talk. It's as if the beach exists in its own pocket of time, separate from the world with all its complications and expectations.

"We should head back up soon." Jon's words come reluctantly as the sky begins to lighten with the first hints of dawn. "The tide's coming in."

"Five more minutes." I curl tighter against him, not ready to leave this perfect space we've created, this magical place where it feels like we've carved out something that belongs just to us.

Jon kisses the top of my head. "Five more minutes."

The ocean continues its eternal conversation with the shore. The stars fade as night surrenders to morning. And here, in this small circle of dying light, we hold onto our moment, stretching it out like a thread of gold—fragile, precious, and surprisingly strong.

"I need to tell my father about us soon," I murmur against Jon's chest, the thought both terrifying and liberating. "About what I want for my future. All of it."

"Are you ready for that battle?" Jon's question holds no judgment, only concern.

"No." I gaze out toward the endless expanse of ocean before us. "But some things are worth fighting for, even when the odds seem impossible."

The first ray of sunlight breaks over the horizon, casting long shadows across the beach and illuminating the tidepools with golden light. New day, new beginnings. New courage for the challenges ahead.

"Whatever happens with your father," Jon says quietly, "I'm not going anywhere."

And in that moment, watching dawn break over the Pacific

with Jon's arms around me, I almost believe that love might be enough to withstand even Marcus Holbrook's disapproval.

Almost.

FOUR

Aria

———

THE SOFT CHIME OF THE DOOR ANNOUNCES ANOTHER MORNING rush customer, followed by the gentle murmur of voices discovering something beautiful. Satisfied sighs drift through The Little Matchstick Girl as customers breathe in their chosen scents. Three months ago, when I proposed this partnership to Ember, even I couldn't have predicted this level of success. Watching Ryn confidently guide a customer through our newest collection sends a swell of pride through my chest, entirely different from anything I've experienced at my father's charity galas.

"The rose quartz vessels work particularly well with our lavender blend." Ryn's voice carries steady confidence as she lifts one of the candles to catch the morning light. Gone is the traumatized girl we rescued from Damien Wolfe's basement six months ago, who barely spoke above a whisper. "The crystal amplifies the calming properties."

The customer—a woman wearing what I recognize as last season's Burberry coat—nods thoughtfully. Her manicured fingers trace the vessel's smooth surface.

"I'll take three. And could you put me on the waiting list for the custom kintsugi pieces?"

"Of course." Ryn's smile could power the entire shop. She pulls out our leather-bound appointment book, pages thick with orders. "We're booking about six weeks out for custom work."

Six weeks. The waitlist makes my business school brain practically sing. When Ember and I started this venture with her hand-poured candles and my investment capital, we never dared dream people would wait that long for our work.

"Aria!" Ember's voice carries from the back office, tinged with excitement. "You need to see these numbers."

I weave through the morning customers, past the display of bath bombs that've become surprisingly popular, toward the converted storage room that serves as our office. Ember sits surrounded by papers, her laptop open, a grin spreading across her face that transforms her entire being.

"Look at this." She turns the screen toward me, fingers dancing across the trackpad to highlight specific figures. "We're up forty percent from last month. The Instagram feature in Architectural Digest drove serious traffic, and the waiting list for custom pieces is—"

"Overwhelming." I settle into the chair across from her, the worn leather creaking beneath me. "Ryn just told someone six weeks for kintsugi work."

"That's good overwhelming though." Ember's eyes sparkle with an enthusiasm I've come to cherish, the kind that lights her from within when she talks about her work. "We're getting inquiries about wholesale accounts. High-end boutiques in Napa, that place in Carmel I told you about, even a few shops in New York."

My Stanford business degree kicks in automatically, calculations and projections dancing through my mind like familiar dance partners.

"That's—significant expansion potential."

"It's a lot." Ember's fingers worry at the edge of a spreadsheet, a familiar note of caution creeping into her voice. Unlike me, she wasn't raised to think in terms of market share and growth trajectories. Everything about business is new to her, but she's wicked smart. Incredible even. She has a true gift for her art as well as a mind for business. Nothing scares Ember. She's willing to tackle the whole damn world if she needs to.

"It's amazing." I lean forward, reaching across the small space between our desks to touch her hand. "This is what success looks like, Em. Your vision, your artistry—people are recognizing it. They want to be part of what you've built."

"What we've built." Ember is quick to correct me. The phrase sits comfortably between us now, a partnership that's grown into something deeper than business. Friendship forged in crisis and tempered by trust—something my elite social circle never provided.

"I know. It's just…" She gestures vaguely toward the shop beyond the office door, where the soft jazz mingles with quiet conversation. "I can barely keep up with the custom orders we have. Ryn's training two new girls, but they're still learning. And if we start wholesaling—"

"We maintain our quality." My voice carries the firmness that comes from absolute conviction. "That's non-negotiable. But there are ways to grow smart, Em. Scale without losing what makes us special."

The bell chimes again, and through the doorway, familiar figures enter. Jenny and Jon.

Jon's strong arms circle my waist from behind, pulling me against a solid chest that feels like home. His lips find the sensitive spot just below my ear, his breath warm against my skin as he presses a soft kiss to my throat. Electric current shoots straight through me, pooling heat between my thighs and making my knees weak.

"Missed you." His voice rumbles against my neck, low and intimate.

I melt back against him, tilting my head to give him better access. My arms cover his, fingers interlacing as he holds me tighter. When I turn my head, he captures my lips in a kiss that tastes like promise and possibility. Jon's body anchors me—solid, hard, intoxicating in ways that still surprise me.

From across the office, Ember's knowing smile tells me she's witnessed every second of my complete dissolution. Heat climbs my neck, but I can't bring myself to care. Not when Jon's thumb traces circles on my wrist, not when his presence fills every empty space inside me.

It's been a month since Charlie and Brett stepped away from Guardian HRS. A month of watching Delta team adapt and find their new rhythm.

"Jenny's becoming quite the regular." I lean back into Jon's embrace, my voice casual despite the way his thumb stroking my wrist makes concentration difficult. "I think she's buying candles for half the Guardian HRS facility."

"She says the lavender ones help the new recruits sleep better after night training." Ember watches as Jenny examines our newest display.

The office phone rings, sharp and demanding. The caller ID makes my entire demeanor shift automatically. My shoulders straighten, my smile becomes more polished, and the professional mask I've worn for twenty-plus years slides into place like armor. Jon's arms tighten around me briefly before he releases me, stepping back to give me space.

"Hi, Dad." My voice takes on the tone I use exclusively for Marcus Holbrook—dutiful daughter, successful businesswoman, everything perfectly controlled. The words taste different in my mouth when I speak to him, measured and careful. "Yes, the shop is doing wonderfully. I'm here right now going over the quarterly numbers…"

I deliberately emphasize quarterly numbers, translating our three-month success into the corporate language Dad understands. Behind me, Ember suppresses a knowing smile, her lips twitching as she pretends to focus on her laptop. Jon moves to lean against the doorframe, his presence steady and reassuring even as I navigate the familiar minefield of family expectations.

"Of course I'd love to show you around." Something tightens in my stomach, a familiar knot of anticipation and dread. "When were you thinking? This afternoon? That's perfect. I'll see you then."

I hang up and turn to face Jon, whose expression has already shifted to understanding.

"Dad's coming by at two to see the shop." Frustration rises in my chest like steam from one of our candles. "You shouldn't be here when he arrives."

"No worries." Jon's response carries easy acceptance, no wounded pride or demand for explanation. "I've got drills with the team anyway. Jenny's putting us through our paces, trying to incorporate the newbies into our flow."

Relief floods through me, followed immediately by guilt. The fact that he makes it so easy—that he understands without making me explain the complications—only makes me feel worse about the necessity.

I've managed to keep my relationship with Jon carefully separate from my father's scrutiny. Not because I'm ashamed—quite the opposite—but because I know precisely how Marcus Holbrook would view my involvement with a security specialist. Not quite the merger with the Holbrook Pharmaceuticals heir he's been hoping for.

"It'll be fine." Ember's voice carries forced optimism, though uncertainty flickers across her face. "He's seen the numbers. He knows we're successful."

"He knows I've backed a successful venture," I correct her with a grimace, my stomach twisting tighter. "In his mind, I'm the business half and you're the talent. Like I'm managing your career instead of us being actual partners."

The conversation we've had before hangs between us, heavy with unspoken frustrations. Dad's worldview operates like a finely tuned machine: people have roles, hierarchies exist for a reason, and his daughter couldn't possibly be equal partners with someone from Ember's background. Not through any malice—he's not deliberately cruel—but through an inability to conceive of any other reality.

"Maybe this time will be different." Ember offers the words like a prayer, but she doesn't believe them.

My expression suggests that it is about as likely as snow in July.

FIVE

Jon

———

The field's quiet, the kind of quiet that hums with anticipation. Cool air clings to my skin, damp with the scent of churned dirt and cut grass. I check my rifle again—third time: Bolt, sight, chamber. Everything's clean, everything's tight. Still, I go over it once more. Not superstition. Just habit carved into muscle and bone.

The others have their rituals. Mac cracks his knuckles in sequence, and Jenny recites the same three words under her breath like a prayer.

Me? I check. Then check again.

"Planning to take that rifle to dinner, or you gonna shoot it sometime today?" Mac's voice cuts through the stillness, dry as sandpaper and twice as abrasive.

Heavy footfalls thud closer, gear rattling with each step. He's already suited up, vest snug across his barrel chest, sleeves pushed to his elbows like he's daring the morning to piss him off.

"Just making sure she's still prettier than you." I don't look up.

Mac snorts. "That's not hard. But she still won't cuddle you after."

"She doesn't talk back. I'll take the trade."

"You ready?" He crouches beside me, eyes scanning the line where the targets will pop.

"Always."

My grip tightens because this isn't just a drill. Not today.

"Just making sure I don't embarrass myself in front of the new guys." I run my thumb along the edge of the magazine before slotting it into place with a satisfying click.

"Too late for that. Your face already does the job." He grins, the expression transforming his weathered features into something almost boyish despite the gray at his temples.

Jenny materializes beside us, her dark hair pulled back in a severe bun that means business. No one wears authority quite like her—it fits better than her tactical gear.

"Our new team members are getting the tour from Sam. They'll meet us at the range in ten." Her eyes scan the horizon, where the training course sprawls across five acres of Guardian HRS property. "Everyone needs to play nice. I've seen their files. They're good."

"Good enough to replace Charlie and Brett?" Blaze drops his gear bag next to mine, the thud punctuating Jenny's statement.

The question hangs in the air. Charlie and Brett left holes bigger than their tactical positions. They were family. Eight years of missions, near-misses, and triumphs don't disappear overnight because someone decided to open a gym and have a baby.

"Different skill sets," Jenny answers diplomatically. "Matias Kane—goes by Razor—former Navy SEAL, sniper qualification that makes our previous records look like amateur hour. And David Rodriguez—Storm—ex-Ranger, demolition specialist. Both decorated. Both highly recommended."

"Recommended by who?" Mac adjusts his tactical belt, skepticism etched into every line of his face.

"Forest himself." Jenny lets that sink in.

Blaze whistles low. Forest doesn't personally recruit often, but when he does, it means something. Like when he found me in that bar in Tijuana, half-dead and fully drunk, somehow seeing potential where I saw only wreckage.

"Speaking of…" Blaze sidles closer, lowering his voice to a stage whisper that's anything but private. "How's Aria? Still pretending you two aren't completely gone for each other?"

"We're taking it slow." Heat creeps up the back of my neck, traitorous and sharp beneath my collar. Years of training, and still, she gets under my skin like no one else.

"That's not what I heard." Mac doesn't even look up as he slides extra mags into his pack. "Word is you've been sneaking off to the beach… K-noodling."

"Word gets around fast," I grunt, eyes on my vest straps as I rethread the shoulder harness.

"We wouldn't say word's getting around," Blaze cuts in, grin audible in his voice. "But Aria and Ember are tight. They talk. And then Ember talks to me. And I'm telling you—you're not moving as fast as you should be, brother." He claps a hand on my shoulder, solid and loud enough to make the vest dig into my ribs. "Life's short. Especially for guys like us."

A knot tightens low in my gut. I keep my voice neutral, eyes locked on the edge of my gear. "That's what she's saying to Ember?"

Blaze doesn't catch it—too busy grabbing his hydration pack. "Nah. She says you're different. Careful. That you actually give a damn."

He moves on, but I stay still, pulse thudding behind my ears. Different.

Careful.

She notices.

I double-check the Velcro across my chest plate, buying time, letting my face settle back into unreadable lines. I don't need them catching the way her words land like a gut punch wrapped in velvet.

"She seems good for you." Blaze's teasing smile softens into something more genuine. "After everything that went down with Charlie and Brett leaving… You good?"

"I'm good. Really." I look up, meeting his eyes.

"Well, Aria seems good for you."

"Thanks, bro."

"Incoming. Best behavior, children." Jenny clears her throat, but I catch the hint of a smile before she schools her features.

Two figures approach from the main compound, flanking Sam's stocky silhouette. Even from a distance, I can read their movement patterns—the way the taller one scans his surroundings in precise arcs, the way the other moves with barely contained energy.

Military. Experienced. Dangerous.

Sam makes the introductions before disappearing back toward headquarters, leaving our potential new teammates standing before us like fresh meat at inspection.

"This is Razor," Sam says as he stops in front of us, gesturing to the taller of the two men flanking him.

The guy nods once, his dark eyes sweeping over each of us like he's cataloging weak spots. Controlled. Quiet. SEAL sniper, and it shows in every inch of him.

"And this is Storm," Sam adds, jerking his thumb toward the broader one with the twitchy energy.

Storm flashes a crooked grin, practically bouncing on the balls of his feet.

"Marine Raider," Sam continues. "Breacher, demo, CQB.

Moves fast, thinks faster, talks the fastest. You'll see. They're joining today's exercise. Trial run." Sam's tone is matter-of-fact. "Whether it turns permanent is up to all of you. And them."

Without waiting for a response, he turns and heads back toward HQ, leaving the new guys in our territory.

"So you're Delta team." Storm steps forward, voice smooth with a clipped East Coast edge. "Heard you guys were the best. That true, or just good PR?"

"Why don't you tell us after today?" Blaze snorts, his laugh sharp and unbothered.

"Jenny. Delta-One." Jenny steps up, shoulders squared, chin tipped up. She doesn't offer a handshake. "Before we start, let's establish the hierarchy. Guardian HRS doesn't promote based on gender or size. We promote based on capability."

"Wouldn't have assumed otherwise." Storm lifts a brow, expression unreadable.

"Good." Jenny's smile is a knife's edge. "Then you won't mind a quick demonstration."

"On the mat or here?" Razor doesn't hesitate, voice cool, assessing.

"Here is fine." Jenny shrugs off her jacket, flexes her fingers, and rolls her shoulders with unhurried calm. "You first."

Mac and Blaze don't say a word. Just step back in sync, boots grinding into the dirt as they form a loose perimeter. I join them, familiar with what's coming. Jenny doesn't posture. She doesn't raise her voice. She demonstrates.

Razor circles, cautious. A quick testing jab.

Jenny slips under it, her movement liquid and economical, then pivots, taking his balance with her. A breath later, she's behind him, one arm looping his neck, the other sweeping his legs. They hit the ground hard, Razor flat on his back, her forearm pressing across his windpipe, elbow locked.

He doesn't fight it. Smart.

"Good technique," Jenny says, and just like that, she's up again, offering him a hand like nothing happened. He takes it, breath steady but eyes sharper now.

"Storm?" She turns, already resetting.

"Sure," he says, cracking his knuckles. "Why not?"

He doesn't dance. Just comes straight in—fast, aggressive, low center of gravity. Jenny absorbs the first blow, redirects the second. Storm adjusts mid-strike, trying to power through with brute force.

Doesn't matter.

She catches his momentum, pivots hard, and drops her weight. He goes airborne, lands with a thud and a grunt, face first in the dirt. She's on him before he can blink, his arm twisted back in a lock that has Blaze wincing in sympathy.

"Would've popped your shoulder if I'd committed," she says mildly, releasing him.

Storm groans but grins as he rolls onto his back, shaking it off. "Fuck. Okay, yeah. Message received."

Jenny doesn't smile. "CJ—our boss, the one who oversees every Guardian HRS team—used to be Delta-One. I took over when he stepped up."

She lets that settle.

"I earned this position. And I earn it every damn day."

Razor coughs, rubbing his throat. "Where'd you train?"

"Streets of São Paulo," she says. No embellishment. No pride, just fact. "Forest and Skye found me there when I was seventeen."

That silences them both.

"Now," she adds, voice clipped, "let's see if you follow orders half as well as you fall down."

Mac grunts something that might be an expression of approval or indigestion. Hard to tell with him.

"Two-person teams," Jenny barks. "Mac and I will run

tactical opposition. Jon, you take Razor. Blaze, you've got Storm. Hostage retrieval scenario. Three potential hostiles, one civilian asset. Asset extraction is primary objective. Clean shots only—we don't want any friendly fire incidents like last month." She cuts a glance at Blaze, deadpan.

"Rules of engagement?" Razor falls into step beside me, already adjusting his gear with quiet efficiency.

"Sim-ammunition only. Blue rounds for us," Jenny says without missing a beat. "Red for you. One hit to center mass or two extremities counts as a casualty. Asset wears a yellow vest—hit them, you fail automatically."

We break off from the group, boots crunching across the gravel path that winds through the training compound. A gust of dry mountain air carries the scent of dust and cordite, familiar and grounding. Razor moves with the kind of quiet confidence that speaks louder than bravado. No wasted motion. No flash. Just precise, practiced economy.

"SEAL Team Six?" I glance sideways, watching how his shoulders tighten, just for a second. Bingo.

"Among other things." His voice is cool, unreadable. But that half-beat pause tells me I nailed it.

Not much rattles the guy. Which makes me wonder what did.

"Tell me about the team," he says, not quite a deflection—more like a measuring stick.

"Delta team specializes in boutique rescues," I offer as we cut across a scrubby clearing. "Mostly high-value targets. We get called when shit goes sideways and the FBI needs surgical precision. Most of our ops are off-book, partnered with their Black Book division."

"And the Damien Wolfe op?" Razor checks the tension on his chest rig without breaking stride.

"That one started small. Aria Holbrook kidnapping.

Supposed to be an easy extraction. Turned out Damien Wolfe's network ran deeper than anyone thought."

I pause at the concrete barrier that marks our staging position. It's cool under my palm, solid. Sightlines are clear to the mock structure ahead—a two-story building with boarded windows and entry points at the north and west.

"We adapt fast," I add. "It's what sets Delta apart."

Razor nods, eyes scanning the structure, taking mental notes. His movements are disciplined, methodical—but a beat of something else hides under the surface. Tension, maybe. Or history.

"Delta's not just a tactical unit," I say, then stop.

He turns slightly, one brow raised.

"We're family," I finish.

"Yeah." He pulls back the charging handle on his sim rifle, the faint clack crisp in the quiet. "That's why I'm here." His voice softens, just enough to reveal something unspoken.

Loss? Maybe. Or exile.

I file it away for later. Everyone's got a reason. The good ones never say it out loud.

There's weight behind his calm, something older than pride or pain. The kind of thing that doesn't fade with time. It buries itself in your spine, lives behind your ribs.

"Your file said your last unit was disbanded after Kabul."

"Storm and I were the only ones who made it out." His tone doesn't flinch. "Six months of investigations, then honorable discharges with commendations nobody wanted."

Our eyes lock. No mask this time. Just a flash of raw, unfiltered memory before he buries it again.

They're not just looking for jobs.

They're looking for what we all came to Guardian HRS to find.

Purpose. Belonging. Redemption.

"How'd Forest find you?" I scan the windows of the target

building, senses sharpening. The stillness is loaded. Jenny and Mac are in place, traps laid, waiting.

"He didn't." Razor's mouth curves, just slightly. "We found him."

His tone holds a quiet reverence, like saying Forest's name is a kind of prayer.

"After our discharge, we kept hearing about Guardian HRS. Ghost stories. Black ops without a country. Impossible missions pulled off by ghosts with call signs. Sounded like bullshit until we tracked a safe house in Morocco."

I glance at him, impressed. "You tracked Guardian HRS?"

"Watched Alpha team extract a diplomat's daughter without firing a single shot."

"Classic Alpha." I nod. "They're surgical. Quietest team we've got."

"We followed them back to their extraction point. Figured we'd get lit up. Instead, Forest offered us coffee. Told us we were wasting our talents playing shadow games."

Sounds exactly like him. Nearly seven feet of steel, and yet still the gentlest man I've ever met.

"And here you are."

"Here we are." Razor crouches behind the concrete slab, rifle steady. No tension in his shoulders. Just calm. Focus.

A beat of silence.

"So you pulled out the Holbrook heiress?"

"You've done your homework." It's meant to sound casual, but the words land heavier than I intend.

"Always do. Before joining any team." Razor's tone doesn't shift, but everything else does. Muscles coiled. Breath shallow and slow. Rifle locked against his shoulder like it's part of him. "High-profile rescue. The kind that travels fast through our circles."

He exhales once. Low. Measured. Controlled.

Then he's gone.

Not literally—but the man beside me changes in real time, right in front of my eyes. That easygoing, quiet new guy? The one who asked about the team, who told me about Morocco and sipping coffee with Forest? He evaporates.

Vanishes into thin air.

What's left is something harder.

Sharper.

Like steel being drawn from a sheath.

His spine straightens, no wasted motion. Shoulders square. The slight slouch in his posture disappears. His left hand slides to stabilize the barrel while his right adjusts the scope without a sound, no hesitation, no fumble. Just precise, practiced movements. The kind you don't learn in training—you earn it through fire.

Through blood.

His entire presence condenses—energy folding in, tightly coiled, silent, waiting to strike. There's no tension in him. None. Just readiness. Stillness with purpose.

Even his breathing shifts—barely there now. Shallow and slow, tuned to keep his pulse down, his hands steady.

"Contact." His voice is flat, razor-clean. All business. "Northwest corner, second floor. Moving east to west."

It's not just the words. It's how he says them—like reading coordinates from muscle memory. Like he's already calculated wind speed, distance, trajectory, and kill zone.

I know that tone. I've used that tone. It's the voice of a man who's been in kill-houses and deserts and rain-slicked rooftops. The voice of someone who doesn't ask questions until the job's done. Someone who's lost enough that he doesn't flinch anymore.

Razor's not just watching that window.

He's already in the room. Already five steps ahead.

And for the first time since Sam introduced him, I realize exactly what kind of operator I've just been paired with.

Not new.

Not junior.

Lethal.

I don't hesitate.

"Blaze, you copy?" My voice drops, colder now. Efficient. "Visual on second-floor movement. Target heading west. Possible hostile."

SIX

Jon

———

Razor doesn't blink. Doesn't breathe loud enough to hear. Just murmurs—

"On your call, Delta-Three."

He's not a man anymore. He's a weapon. Silent, still, and waiting for the signal to detonate.

"Reading you five-by-five," Blaze crackles in over comms. "Storm's already mapped the building. Three possible entries, two weak load-bearing walls. Kid's got a gift for structural analysis."

"Don't call me kid," Storm cuts in. "I've blown up more buildings than you've digested brain cells."

I catch the grin tugging at Razor's mouth—but only for a heartbeat. Then it's gone, and all that's left is the steady arc of his scope sweeping the window line.

"We're in position at the south entrance," Blaze says. "On your go, Jon."

I inhale once. Sharp. Grounding.

"Delta moving in three—two—one… Execute."

My finger taps the comm switch, and we flow.

Razor moves like water over stone—quiet, smooth, lethal. There's no tension, no wasted energy. Just precision. The kind that isn't learned through training. It comes from surviving shit no one should've lived through.

He ghosts through the breach point ahead of me, rifle up, eyes cutting through shadow. No hesitation. No fear.

Only purpose.

What follows is twenty minutes of flawless rhythm. Razor's not just good—he's scary good. We don't speak. Don't need to. His pace matches mine without lag, without anticipation—just pure, instinctive sync. When I pivot right, he's already watching my six. When I drop to one knee behind cover, he shifts elevation, angling for a better shot window. It's like running point with a guy I've trained with for years.

Hand signals, head tilts, sharp nods—everything lands without a hiccup. We sweep and clear methodically, converging on the interior of the warehouse structure where Blaze and Storm already hold position. The space smells like old oil and dust—fake smoke from the sim-rounds clings to the air.

"Two tangos down," Blaze reports, jerking his chin at the splattered training dummies, center mass tagged in tight blue groupings.

"No visual on the asset," Storm adds, crouched by a stack of crates, eyes scanning. His rifle is angled low, but his posture says ready.

"Third hostile's probably guarding them." I flatten against the doorway, motioning Razor to cover the opposite angle. My pulse ticks higher. Something's off. "Feels like a setup."

Razor slides into position, rifle steady, eyes sweeping the corridor ahead. "It is. Your team leader set this up to fail. She thinks like me."

Right on cue, Mac's hulking silhouette appears at the far end of the hallway, shield raised like a battering ram. Jenny's behind him, flanking left, already laying down suppressive fire. Sim-rounds crack through the corridor, blue paint spattering against the cinderblock walls and floor.

"Back exit!" I bark, diving behind a steel support column as a round kisses past my cheek and explodes against the concrete.

"This way!" Storm doesn't hesitate.

He barrels into a maintenance room, his shoulder slamming into the push bar. The metal door groans open, revealing a narrow, dimly lit service tunnel lined with exposed pipes and utility conduits.

"Service corridor leads to the basement," Storm calls back, breath controlled but urgent. "Saw it on the floor plan earlier. Could be a secondary hold."

Razor signals me forward—go—and drops back into rear cover with Blaze. I pass the word with a clipped gesture, and we file in, single line, fast and tight. Sim-rounds pepper the frame as Blaze steps through last, snapping the door shut behind him.

"Nice pull," Blaze mutters, clapping Storm on the shoulder. "Mac hates the basement routes. Gets twitchy."

"I heard that," Mac's voice grumbles through comms. "And it's called tactical awareness, not claustrophobia."

The corridor narrows, light flickering from a busted overhead bulb. Our boots crunch on gravel and debris as we press forward. The smell of damp concrete and machine oil thickens. Sound echoes weirdly down here—everything sharper, like the air's listening.

Then I see it. Far wall, behind a scaffold of rusted pipes and stacked crates—a yellow vest, unmistakable against the gray.

"Our hostage," I murmur.

Razor doesn't ease his stance. If anything, he coils tighter, scanning every shadow like it's about to strike.

"This is wrong," he says, voice low and flat. "Too exposed. Too easy."

"Jenny doesn't make mistakes like this," I agree, raising my rifle. "She's waiting for us to blink."

And I don't plan on giving her the chance.

As if summoned by Razor's unease, a soft metallic clink cuts through the quiet. Something rolls across the cracked concrete between us, slow and deliberate.

My brain processes it a second too late.

"Flash-bang!" Blaze shouts—

—but Storm's already airborne.

He dives without hesitation, covering the sim-grenade with his vest, curling around it like a human shield. The pop is muffled, more of a puff of compressed air and a cloud of chalk dust than a real detonation—but the instinct?

Flawless. No pause. No calculation. Just action.

I blink through the haze, adrenaline spiking in my bloodstream like a jolt of electricity.

That could've blinded all of us.

Storm stands, white dust clinging to his front like frost. His expression doesn't shift, doesn't falter—just that same dry deadpan.

"Hate being blinded," he mutters, brushing chalk off his gear. "Makes it hard to see the people I'm about to shoot."

Blaze lets out a low whistle. "Remind me never to startle you."

From there, the op wraps with surgical precision. Razor and I secure the asset dummy—vest intact, no paint hits—while Storm clears the last room and Blaze covers our six. The only hit comes when Blaze gets cocky, slicing the pie wide and catching a red round to the shoulder.

"Still pretty," he mutters, wincing as we haul ass to the extraction point.

We regroup at the edge of the training field, sweat slick beneath my vest, lungs still working to settle after the final sprint.

Jenny's already waiting near the debrief tent, arms crossed, hair pulled back tight, expression unreadable—except for the spark of satisfaction in her eyes.

She watches us silently for a beat. Letting the weight of the moment land.

"Solid work," she says finally. "Times were sharp. Communications tighter than I expected for a first run. Combat skills? Excellent. You followed the mission parameters. You adapted when the scenario flipped."

She takes a step forward, gaze flicking between Razor and Storm.

"But Delta team isn't just about tactical proficiency. We're more than a team. We're a family. Dysfunctional, sometimes. Messy as hell. But blood-deep."

Mac snorts. "The question isn't whether you can shoot straight. It's whether you're looking for a job…" He looks between them. "Or something more."

Storm shifts beside Razor. There's a flicker—something vulnerable beneath the iron. He doesn't say anything right away. Just meets Razor's eyes.

Then he speaks. Quiet. Measured.

"After Kabul… After everything we lost…" His voice rasps, unpolished. "We're not here for a paycheck."

Razor nods once. "We're here for purpose. For connection. For a reason to fight that doesn't get erased by a politician's pen."

Jenny studies them both, reading between the lines like she always does. Then she turns to Mac.

"In?"

Mac grunts. "They think. They shoot. They listen. Works for me."

"Blaze?" Jenny turns to Blaze.

He shrugs, smirking. "They'll do."

High praise, from him.

And then her eyes land on me.

"Jon?"

I don't hesitate. Not for a second.

"They're in."

Jenny nods once. "Razor, Delta-Five. Storm, Delta-Six."

Blaze steps forward, extending a hand to each of them in turn.

"Welcome to Delta." A beat, then that irreverent grin. "Try not to die. The paperwork's a bitch."

After debriefing and processing, we head to the mess hall. Guardian HRS's food puts military bases to shame—Forest believes in feeding his people well. Our table in the corner has been Delta's unofficial territory for years, and the new guys follow without needing direction.

"So," Storm loads his plate with an impressive mountain of pasta, "what's the deal with Guardian HRS anyway? Private company running paramilitary rescue operations doesn't exactly scream 'normal business model.' Forest Summers started it?"

"More like created it. He and Doc Summers." I dive into my chili mac, best on the planet. "Forest and Doc Summers are foster siblings," I explain, noting their surprised expressions. "Started Guardian HRS initially to rescue kids from abusive foster situations like they experienced. Expanded into human trafficking operations, then broadened further into all types of extractions."

"Forest is…" Blaze pauses, searching for words. "Different. Brilliant doesn't cover it. Self-made billionaire before eighteen, but operates on another level than the rest of us mere mortals. Savant-level smart, but his interpersonal skills are a bit off."

"You'll meet Mitzy soon," Jenny adds. "Head of tech division. You can't miss her. She's a bundle of chaos and changes her hair color weekly. Right now it's neon purple with green tips.

Genius with drones and surveillance tech. She's behind the RUFI units and the bumblebee drones."

"She's wicked smart. Not as smart as Forest," Blaze clarifies, "but nobody is."

"How's that?" Razor asks, his plate modestly filled.

"Let's just say there's nothing normal about Forest or Doc Summers," Mac answers around a mouthful of garlic bread. "But they pay well, and they don't ask us to do anything we wouldn't be proud of. Better than government work."

Storm looks intrigued. "What about the actual operations? How do you decide who to help?"

"No politicians deciding which lives matter based on polling numbers." Blaze's voice holds an edge that speaks of past experience. "If someone needs help and they can reach us, we go. Simple as that."

"Not always simple," Jenny corrects. "But that's the idea. Some missions are client-funded, others Forest takes on pro bono. Either way, we don't leave people behind."

Storm grins. "Sounds like my kind of operation."

My phone buzzes against my hip. Aria's face lights up my screen, and I can't help the smile that follows.

"There it is," Mac points his fork at me accusingly. "That dopey look. Man's in love."

"Shut up," I mutter, but there's no heat behind it.

"The Holbrook heiress, right?" Storm whistles low. "Aim high, brother."

"It's not like that." I silence my phone, promising myself I'll call her back after dinner. "She's not what people think."

"Never are," Razor says quietly, pushing food around his plate. "The good ones, anyway."

The conversation shifts to past missions, Blaze regaling the new guys with increasingly embellished versions of our greatest hits. I watch them integrate, noting how Storm naturally falls into banter while Razor observes, offering precise comments at perfect intervals.

They'll fit well, in time.

As we're finishing, the mess hall doors open to admit Ember and Ryn.

Blaze straightens immediately, his attention magnetized to Ember like she's true north. He still looks at her like she might vanish if he blinks too long.

"Ladies, what brings you to HQ?" he calls, waving them over. "Meet the new guys."

Ember approaches with confident steps, her once-haunted eyes now bright with purpose. Ryn follows more cautiously, her posture still holding echoes of her trauma despite six months of freedom from Damien Wolfe's captivity.

"Did they survive Jenny's welcome party?" Ember slides onto the bench beside Blaze, accepting his arm around her waist as naturally as breathing.

"With flying colors," Jenny confirms. "Matias Kane, David Rodriguez, meet Ember and Ryn."

"The candle makers," Storm says with recognition. "My quarters smelled like a locker room until Jenny gave me one of your eucalyptus things. Life-changing."

"Glad to help." Ember laughs, the sound still new enough to draw attention. "We're actually expanding our men's line. Forest thinks tactical teams might appreciate scents that don't make them smell like a flower shop."

"Sandalwood, leather, gunmetal," Ryn offers quietly, her eyes briefly scanning the table before dropping to the table—her way of participating without making direct contact. "For focus and grounding."

Razor's attention shifts, his careful assessment of Ryn more thorough than mere curiosity. Something in her tentative presence has caught his interest.

"I'd try that." His voice gentler than I've heard it all day. "Hard to find candles that don't smell like Valentine's Day threw up."

A ghost of a smile touches Ryn's lips before disappearing.

Progress.

"You should come by the shop," Ember offers. "Friends and family discount for Delta team."

"It's doing well then?" Jenny asks. "The business?"

"Better than I expected. We're connecting with clients who appreciate artisanal work." Ember beams with the success of her candle-making business. It's a good look on her.

"She's being modest," Blaze interjects proudly. "They're creating custom lines."

"We just make candles," Ember says, but the pride in her voice is unmistakable.

"The crystal designs in the reception area," Razor says, addressing Ryn directly. "Those are yours? The way you suspend the minerals in the wax… Not many people could do that."

Ryn looks up, startled at being directly addressed, a flush creeping across her pale cheeks. "Thank you," she murmurs, the words barely audible.

The mood at the table shifts—just a flicker, barely perceptible, but enough to prick the back of my neck.

Ryn's talking. Not to us, not to Ember. To Razor.

And she's not shutting down. No walls. No glassy-eyed retreat.

Just—talking.

"I should get back," she says softly, already halfway to her feet. "The new crystal wax needs temperature monitoring."

Ember glances at her watch, catching the cue. "We've left Aria alone all morning."

She leans in, kisses Blaze's cheek, casual as always. But her eyes linger on Ryn a little longer. Watchful.

Then both girls stand.

"Hey," Blaze calls after them, brows lifting. "You never said why you're at HQ."

"You're right." Ember flashes that sly grin of hers. "I didn't."

She tosses a wink over her shoulder. "See you later. Nice to meet you, Storm. Razor."

"Well met," Razor says—and I don't miss how his gaze never leaves Ryn.

Not even for a second.

Ryn pauses at the door. Just a heartbeat. Then her gaze flicks back to him.

Color rises up her throat, blooming fast across her cheeks like she wasn't expecting whatever that was—whatever just passed between them.

She drops her gaze, pushes through the door, and Razor finally blinks.

He watches her go like he's marking her silhouette into memory.

"She seems young," he says after a beat, voice low. Calm. But something sharp threads beneath it.

"She looks younger than she is." Jenny crosses her arms over her chest, eyes still on the mess hall door long after it swings shut. But something shifts. "She's eighteen." Her spine straightens, chin lifting slightly like she's bracing for impact.

The edge in her voice tightens—barely—but I catch it.

"What's her story?" Razor asks.

"Foster system. Then Damien Wolfe's Night Pack." Her mouth hardens around the words. "She's survived more than most people twice her age."

A beat of silence.

Then her shoulders lower, arms falling to her sides, fists unclenching. "She's been through hell," she murmurs, quieter now. "And came out standing."

Jenny's gaze flicks sideways. Sharp. Calculating.

She clocked the way Razor watched Ryn walk out—curious, quiet, focused in that way only operators get when something matters. Jenny doesn't bristle. Doesn't issue a warning. She doesn't have to. Instead, she straightens, turning to face him fully, the tilt of her chin pure Guardian.

"She's a part of the Delta team family." Her voice is steady and low. "Every single one of us would take a bullet before letting her get hurt again."

"Understood." Razor doesn't flinch. Just meets her gaze, expression unreadable.

Jenny studies him for a long second. Then something shifts— barely visible—but I feel it all the same. A loosening at the corners of her mouth. A subtle nod, almost imperceptible.

"She's got a long road ahead of her," she adds, quieter now. "Tread carefully." She turns without another word, moving toward the armory with that same fluid, coiled stride that always makes people get the hell out of her way.

I glance at Razor.

He's still watching the door, but now, there's something else on his face.

Respect. Maybe a little awe.

And the faintest flicker of something I recognize all too well. His jaw ticks once, like he's locking something down behind his teeth.

"I've got to make a call before our next briefing." I check my watch and stand.

"Tell Aria we said hi," the entire table choruses, followed by laughter.

I flip them off good-naturedly as I exit, already pulling out my phone. Their teasing is relentless, but underneath it lies the only truth that matters: we're family. Dysfunctional, dangerous, and fiercely loyal.

And now, we're two members stronger.

Outside, the evening air carries the scent of pine and possibility. I find a quiet spot near the training field and dial Aria's number.

"Hi, Jon." I smile as Aria's voice fills my ear, bright with stories about her day and questions about mine.

New beginnings all around.

SEVEN

Aria

———

THE MORNING CONTINUES ITS FAMILIAR RHYTHM. CUSTOMERS drift in and out, drawn by word of mouth and the kind of organic buzz that money can't buy. Ryn handles the newcomers with growing confidence while Ember works on custom orders in the workshop; her hands move with grace as she layers scents and pours wax.

Ryn draws my attention more closely today, the transformation striking in its completeness. Six months ago, we found her in that basement—a small, fierce girl with haunted eyes and a defiant spirit that refused to break. Damien Wolfe had kept her there, along with others, intending to shatter her. Instead, she became part of our makeshift family, discovering an artistic talent that rivals Ember's own.

The kintsugi technique has become her signature, taking broken vessels and filling the cracks with gold, making them more beautiful for having been damaged. The symbolism strikes everyone who enters our shop; the message is impossible to miss.

Broken things made beautiful.

Scars turned to art.

Stories of survival written in gold.

I'm rearranging a display of our newest scent collection when voices carry from the front of the shop. Dad's arrival, fifteen minutes early, announced by his commanding presence that seems to fill any space he enters.

"Dad. You made good time." I move toward him, automatically adjusting my posture to match his professional bearing, feeling my spine straighten and my expression shift.

"Traffic was lighter than expected." Marcus Holbrook's voice carries the kind of authority that expects attention. Not loud, but commanding in a way that draws every eye in the room. "I wanted to see this phenomenon my daughter created."

My daughter created. Not my daughter and her partner. The distinction lands like a small stone in still water, creating ripples I try to ignore but can't quite manage.

Dad stands in the center of our retail space, taking in the displays with the eye of someone accustomed to evaluating investments. He's impeccably dressed as always: a tailored Tom Ford suit, Italian leather shoes polished to mirror brightness, every detail perfect. The kind of man who's never questioned his place in the world because the world has always accommodated him.

"The foot traffic is impressive." His gaze sweeps the space methodically, cataloging everything from customer behavior to product placement. "And the price points… Well above what I expected for candles."

"They're not just candles, Dad." I step closer, gesturing toward our displays with practiced pride. "They're artisanal pieces. Each one is hand-poured, custom-scented. People are buying the story as much as the product."

"Smart positioning." He nods approvingly, the motion carrying decades of business experience. "Taking a commodity item and creating perceived value through narrative marketing. Very clever."

Narrative marketing. As if our stories of survival and healing are merely clever copy, rather than lived experiences. I resist the urge to correct him, to explain that there's nothing "perceived" about the value we've created. The words stick in my throat, held back by years of conditioning.

Dad's gaze sweeps the shop again, lingering on details—the customer flow patterns, the inventory levels, the way Ryn interacts with browsers. His assessment operates like a scanner, thorough and completely clinical.

"The staff seems well-trained." He watches Ryn complete another sale with growing confidence. "Though I imagine it's challenging to maintain quality control with artisanal production. Have you considered standardizing the process? Creating reproducible formulas?"

"That would defeat the purpose." I choose my words carefully, feeling Ember's presence as she emerges from the workshop, her hands still dusted with gold leaf. "The custom nature is what makes them special."

"Special doesn't scale." Dad's response carries the matter-of-fact tone of someone stating an immutable law of physics. "At some point, you'll need to choose between boutique charm and real growth. The question is whether you want this to remain a hobby business or become something significant."

Hobby business. Ember flinches slightly at the words, a micro-expression that ignites something protective in my chest. Three months of twelve-hour days, of building something from nothing, of creating beauty that brings people joy, reduced to a hobby.

"Ember. Good to see you again." Dad's tone warms with genuine politeness as he notices her approach.

"Mr. Holbrook." She manages a smile that looks only slightly forced, her fingers unconsciously wiping at the gold dust on her apron. "I was just showing Aria our latest numbers. We're pretty excited about the growth."

"As you should be. It's impressive what you've accomplished here." His tone carries warmth and genuine appreciation, but something underneath it makes my jaw tighten—a pat on the head for the talented child who has done well within her limitations. "Your artistic vision is resonating with customers."

Artistic vision. As if that's her entire contribution, while the real business happens elsewhere. I can't let that stand.

"Ember handles all the creative development." My voice carries a firmness that surprises even me. "The scent combinations, the aesthetic choices, the custom techniques. It's her vision that drives everything we do here."

"Of course." Dad's smile doesn't waver, but something in his eyes suggests he's humoring me. "Talent recognizes talent. You've done well to harness that creativity into something profitable."

Harness.

As if she's a resource to be managed rather than a partner with an equal investment in our success. The conversation continues, but Ember steps back, shifting from participant to observer in her own business.

Dad examines our newest display—a collaboration between Ryn's crystal work and Ember's scent blending. The pieces catch the afternoon light streaming through our windows, each one unique and stunning, selling for prices that validate our business model completely.

"These are quite sophisticated." He lifts one of the vessels, turning it to examine the goldwork. "The craftsmanship is excellent. But I have to ask—how much of your time goes into each piece? What's your actual hourly rate once you factor in labor costs?"

Classic Dad—reducing art to spreadsheet calculations.

"It's not about efficiency." Ember's voice carries quiet conviction, her hands stilling on the display she's been adjusting. "It's about creating something meaningful. Something that tells a story."

"Stories don't show up on quarterly reports." Dad's response carries gentle chiding, the tone of someone explaining simple math to a child. "I'm not diminishing the artistic value, but at some point, you need to consider whether this is sustainable long-term."

I shift beside him, caught between supporting Ember and not contradicting my father—a position I've found myself in with increasing frequency lately.

"Actually…" Dad's tone brightens as if he's just thought of something wonderful. His eyes light up with the kind of enthusiasm that usually signals he's about to solve a problem we didn't know we had. "This might be perfect timing. I've been discussing emerging brands in the luxury lifestyle space with some colleagues. There's real interest in artisanal products that can scale appropriately."

"Scale how?" Wariness creeps into my voice despite my efforts to sound neutral.

"Strategic partnerships. Distribution agreements with high-end retailers. Maybe even licensing deals for the more unique techniques." He gestures toward the kintsugi display with appreciation. "This broken-and-mended concept—that's brandable. Marketable. With the right backing, it could be in Nordstrom by Christmas."

Horror flickers across Ember's features as Dad speaks before she can conceal it. Mass production. Her careful, personal work reduced to a marketing concept to be replicated by factory workers who've never experienced the kind of breaking that makes the mending meaningful.

"That's…" Ember starts, then stops, clearly at a loss for words that won't offend.

"Generous." I finish for her, though enthusiasm remains notably absent from my voice. "Dad, that's incredibly generous, but we'd need to think about whether that fits our vision."

"Vision evolves," Dad speaks with the confidence of someone who's never had his vision questioned, never had to defend something precious against well-meaning improvement. "What matters is maximizing the opportunity while it exists. These lifestyle trends have limited windows. Strike while the market's receptive."

He pulls out his phone, scrolling through contacts with an efficiency that speaks to decades of deal-making. "Let me make a few calls. I know people who specialize in scaling artisanal brands. They could do a consultation, show you what's possible."

"Dad, we don't need—"

"Nonsense. It's just a consultation. Information gathering. No commitments." He's already dialing, moving toward the front window for better reception. "You'll thank me when you see the potential."

Ember and I stand in the sudden quiet, watching Dad pace near our carefully arranged displays while he speaks in low, urgent tones to whoever answered his call. Around us, the shop continues its afternoon rhythm—customers browsing thoughtfully, Ryn helping a teenager choose her first high-end candle, the soft jazz that provides our soundtrack weaving through conversations like silk.

"I'm sorry." The words emerge quietly, barely audible above the ambient noise. "He means well, but—"

"But he doesn't see what we've built here," Ember finishes the thought, her voice carrying resignation rather than anger. "He sees a business opportunity that happens to involve candles."

I nod, frustration building in my chest like pressure in a steam kettle. "In his world, success means going national, maximizing profits, and building an empire. He can't understand that sometimes small and meaningful is better than big and profitable."

Dad ends his call and returns with a satisfied expression, as if he's just solved a problem. "Good news. I spoke with Miranda Anderson—she's phenomenal at brand scaling. She's free Thursday afternoon for a preliminary assessment. No cost, just an expert eye on what you've built and where it could go."

"Thursday?" I keep my voice carefully neutral, though my stomach performs an uncomfortable flip. "That's very quick."

"No point in waiting. Market timing matters in this business." He slides his phone back into his jacket pocket. "Miranda will take a look at your operations, review your financials, and suggest strategic directions. Think of it as a free graduate-level business course."

I want to protest that we didn't ask for a graduate-level business course; we're happy with what we've built. Not everything needs to be optimized, scaled, and turned into something unrecognizable. But the words stick in my throat, held back by decades of conditioning and the genuine desire not to hurt him.

"That's very thoughtful." Ember manages the response with grace I couldn't have mustered, though tension radiates from her shoulders.

"It's an investment in Aria's future." Dad's smile widens, genuine warmth radiating from his expression. "And yours, of course. Rising tides lift all boats."

He spends another twenty minutes touring the shop, asking questions about inventory management and customer demographics, taking pictures of our displays "for Miranda's reference." His interest radiates genuine enthusiasm, his suggestions carry obvious good intentions, but underneath it all sits the assumption that we're playing at business until real business arrives to show us how it's done.

When he finally leaves—after scheduling Thursday's consultation and promising to "make some additional calls"—the shop feels different. Smaller, somehow. As if his vision of what we could become has diminished what we are.

"That went better than expected." Ember's words carry forced optimism, her voice suggesting she doesn't believe them any more than I do.

"Did it?" I move toward the kintsugi display, touching one of the pieces Ryn completed this morning. The gold catches the afternoon light, beautiful and meaningful in ways that spreadsheets can't quantify. "Because I feel like we just agreed to let someone explain why everything we've built is wrong."

"Not wrong. Just—limited." Ember joins me beside the display, her fingers tracing patterns in the dust motes dancing through sunbeams. "From his perspective, anyway."

"What about from your perspective?"

She remains quiet for a long moment, long enough for doubt to creep in like fog through an open window. When she speaks, her voice carries careful consideration.

"I love what we've built. I love the intimacy of it, the personal connection with every customer. But…"

"But?"

"But, what if he's right about market timing? What if we're turning down opportunities that won't come again?"

The question hangs between us, heavy with implications neither of us wants to examine too closely. In the workshop, Ryn's voice drifts through the doorway as she explains our process to a new customer, her tone confident and warm. Through the front window, the late afternoon light makes our displays glow like small beacons of something precious.

What we've built is beautiful. It's ours. It's enough.

Isn't it?

EIGHT

Aria

____

THURSDAY ARRIVES FASTER THAN I WANT IT TO, BRINGING WITH IT
the kind of nervous energy that makes coffee taste like anxiety
and every conversation feel loaded with subtext. Miranda
Anderson arrives at precisely two o'clock, dressed in the kind of
understated elegance that costs more than most people's rent and
signals serious professional credibility with every thread.

She's younger than I expected—maybe early thirties—with
sharp, intelligent eyes and the confident handshake that comes
from being very good at what you do. Dad's introductions flow
with characteristic effusiveness, full of phrases like "rising star in
brand development" and "incredible track record with artisanal
scaling."

"I've been looking forward to this." Miranda's voice carries
polished professionalism as we begin the tour. "Your father
showed me some photos, but seeing the actual space... The
aesthetic is quite sophisticated."

We walk through the shop methodically, Miranda asking
questions that demonstrate she's done her homework thoroughly.
Customer demographics, average transaction size, and seasonal

fluctuations. Her attention to detail impresses and intimidates in equal measure, like being examined by a particularly thorough machine.

Ember answers the operational questions with increasing tension, her responses growing shorter as Miranda's focus shifts from admiration to analysis. By the time we reach the workshop, the atmosphere feels more like an audit than a consultation.

"This is where the magic happens." I try to lighten the mood as we enter the creative space, gesturing toward the workstations where half-finished pieces wait for completion.

Miranda examines the workstations, picking up tools and examining half-finished pieces with the careful attention of someone evaluating assets. "The craftsmanship is excellent. However, I must ask about production capacity. How many units can you realistically complete per week?"

"It depends on the complexity." Ember's response carries careful politeness. "The kintsugi pieces take significantly longer than standard pours."

"Right. Time investment versus profit margin." Miranda makes notes on her tablet, fingers moving efficiently across the screen. "Have you considered developing a simplified version of the technique? Something that captures the aesthetic appeal but reduces labor costs?"

Ember's jaw tightens almost imperceptibly, the only outward sign of her internal reaction.

"The technique is meaningful because of the time investment. Each crack, each gold line—it's intentional. Personal."

"Of course. But from a scaling perspective, you'd need to balance personal touch with production efficiency." Miranda's tone remains gentle but firm, like someone explaining mathematics to a child. "Customers who aren't familiar with the backstory might not distinguish between hand-applied details and machine precision."

The conversation continues in this vein for another hour—Miranda offering suggestions that sound reasonable in isolation but collectively add up to transforming everything we've built into something entirely different. Standardized scent profiles. Simplified production processes. Strategic wholesale partnerships that would put our candles in major retailers within six months.

"The brand equity is strong." Miranda's conclusion carries the authority of expert assessment. "The story resonates, the aesthetic is marketable, and you've proven consumer demand. With the right strategic approach, I could see this becoming a significant player in the luxury lifestyle space."

Dad nods with satisfaction, as if Miranda has confirmed something he already knew. "What kind of investment would we be looking at for that level of growth?"

"Initial capital requirements would depend on the scope, but for national rollout... Probably starting around two million for inventory, marketing, and distribution infrastructure."

The number hits like a physical blow. Two million dollars. More money than I've ever seriously contemplated spending on a business, even growing up in Dad's world of casual wealth.

"That's quite a jump from where we are now." I keep my voice carefully measured.

"Growth requires investment." Miranda's response conveys a matter-of-fact tone, as if stating a universal truth. "But the potential returns... If you capture even a small percentage of the luxury candle market, you're looking at eight-figure annual revenue within three years."

Eight figures. The number should generate excitement—proof that what we've built has real value, real potential. Instead, it feels overwhelming, like we're being asked to trade something precious for something profitable.

"I'd need to run some detailed projections..." Miranda continues, her enthusiasm building as she speaks. "But based on what I've seen today, this has all the elements of a scalable luxury brand. The question is whether you're ready to take that step."

After she leaves—with promises to send detailed proposals and projections—the shop feels unnaturally quiet. Ember disappears into the workshop while I help Ryn close out the register, both of us processing what just happened in the weighted silence.

"She seemed nice." Ryn offers the diplomatic assessment while counting bills.

"She did." I count the day's receipts automatically, my mind elsewhere. "Very professional."

"The kind of professional that turns handmade into mass-produced?"

I glance up, surprised by the insight in Ryn's question. She has become more perceptive as she's grown more confident, picking up on undercurrents that would have escaped her six months ago.

"Maybe." The admission tastes bitter. "I'm not sure."

"Ember looked like she wanted to throw something."

That assessment strikes me as probably accurate. By the time we finish closing, Ember still hasn't emerged from the workshop. I find her hunched over a half-completed kintsugi piece, her movements more aggressive than usual as she applies gold leaf to a hairline crack.

"Want to talk about it?" I settle into the chair across from her workbench, watching her hands work with familiar precision.

"Not particularly." She doesn't look up from her work, her focus intense and deliberately narrow. "But I suppose we have to."

"We don't have to do anything. It was just a consultation."

"Was it?" Now she does look up, her eyes sharp with frustration. "Because it felt like a sales pitch. Like she had already decided what we should become and was explaining the process."

I can't argue with that assessment. Miranda's enthusiasm felt predetermined, as if she'd seen dozens of small businesses like ours and knew exactly how to transform them into something bigger and more profitable.

"The numbers were impressive." The words feel weak even as I speak them.

"Were they? Two million dollars to turn our shop into a factory. Eight-figure revenue from selling mass-produced versions of something that matters because it's personal." Ember sets down her brush with more force than necessary, the small sound echoing in the quiet workshop. "At what point does success become failure in disguise?"

It's a good question, one for which I don't have a ready answer. In Dad's world, bigger is always better, growth is always positive, and maximum profit represents the ultimate goal. But sitting in this space we've created together, surrounded by the careful work of our hands and the evidence of our shared vision, those assumptions feel less certain.

"What if we're thinking about this wrong?" I lean forward in my chair. "What if it's not about choosing between small and personal versus big and profitable? What if there's a middle ground?"

"Such as?"

"Selective growth. Maintaining control over the quality and process while expanding carefully. Maybe wholesale to a few high-end boutiques instead of national retail chains. Maybe developing new product lines instead of simplifying existing ones."

Ember considers this, her expression softening slightly as she sets down her tools.

"Like Ryn's crystal work. That's become its own thing without compromising what we originally built."

"Exactly. Growth that feels like evolution instead of trans-formation."

We sit in silence for a few minutes, the tension beginning to ease like steam escaping from a pressure valve. Through the workshop window, the main shop basks in late afternoon light, empty now but holding the memory of the day's customers and conversations.

"There's something else." I lean back in my chair, knowing I need to address the elephant that's been lurking in our discussions. "Dad's involvement. How do you feel about him—taking point on this?"

Ember's laughter carries no humor. It's short and sharp in the quiet space.

"You mean how do I feel about him treating me like the talented employee while you're the real business owner?"

The directness of her response catches me off guard, even though I knew it was coming.

"He doesn't mean it that way."

"Doesn't he?" She turns to face me fully, her expression serious. "I love your dad. He has been generous and supportive, and I'm grateful for everything he has done. But he fundamentally doesn't understand what we are to each other. In his mind, you're the Holbrook who's managing the idiot artistic girl's cute little business."

The accuracy of that assessment stings because I've seen it too—the subtle ways Dad frames our partnership, the assumptions embedded in his language, the way he addresses strategic questions to me while treating Ember's input as creative consultation.

"I could talk to him." The offer emerges automatically. "Clarify how our partnership actually works."

"Could you? Because every time we have these conversations, you end up defending his perspective instead of challenging it."

That hits harder than I expect because it's at least partially true. The habit of managing Dad's expectations and smoothing over tensions runs so deep that I sometimes do it automatically, even when it undermines people I care about.

"That's not fair." The words carry little conviction.

"Isn't it? When Miranda suggested simplifying the kintsugi technique, what did you say?"

I think back to the conversation, trying to remember my exact words. The silence stretches long enough to become its own answer.

"I didn't say anything." The admission tastes like ash.

"You didn't say anything because agreeing with her would have hurt my feelings, but disagreeing with her would have contradicted your father's vision. So you stayed quiet and let me defend something that shouldn't need defending."

The workshop feels smaller suddenly, the weight of unspoken tensions making the air thick and difficult to breathe. We've navigated numerous challenges together—the initial awkwardness of our different backgrounds, the trauma that brought us together, and the delicate process of building trust and friendship. But this feels different.

More fundamental.

"I don't want to lose what we've built." My voice emerges quieter than intended.

"Which part? The business or the friendship?"

"Both. Either. I don't know." I run my hands through my hair, feeling suddenly exhausted. "Three months ago, this felt simple. We were successful, we were happy, we had a clear vision. Now everything feels complicated."

"It got complicated when your father decided our success needed management."

There's truth in that, even though it feels disloyal to acknowledge it. Dad's involvement has brought opportunities and resources, but it has also brought expectations and assumptions that don't align with what we've built.

My phone buzzes with a text, and I glance at the screen automatically. Jon asking if I want to grab dinner after he finishes at Guardian HRS. The simple message carries its own complication—our relationship that exists in secrecy, another thing I haven't figured out how to integrate with Dad's vision of my life.

"I should go." I stand and gather my things, movements feeling heavy and uncertain. "Jon and I have plans."

Ember nods, already turning back to her work. "Tell him I said hi. And, Aria… Think about what I said. About choosing sides."

"I'm not choosing sides. I've already chosen *my* side. We're partners."

"Are we? Because sometimes it feels like you're caught between your old life and your new one, and I'm not sure which side I'm on."

The question follows me out of the shop and throughout the evening, coloring every conversation with Jon and making sleep elusive when I finally get home. By the time Friday morning arrives, I still don't have answers, but I have a growing certainty that something fundamental needs to change.

I'm reviewing inventory reports when Dad calls, his voice bright with enthusiasm.

"Miranda sent over her preliminary projections." He speaks without preamble, excitement crackling through the phone line. "The numbers are extraordinary. We need to move on this opportunity."

"Good morning to you, too, Dad."

"Sorry, sweetheart. Good morning. But seriously, these projections… She's talking about achieving a national presence within eighteen months. The investment requirements are significant, but the potential returns…"

I pull up my email, finding Miranda's report waiting with the kind of detailed spreadsheets that make Dad's eyes light up.

Revenue projections, market analysis, competitive positioning—all the language of serious business that transforms our personal venture into something abstract and strategic.

"Have you had a chance to discuss this with Ember?" I scroll through pages of charts and graphs that reduce our work to numbers and percentages.

"I thought we'd review it together, then present the opportunity to her. This is the kind of decision that requires strategic thinking, not artistic input."

There it is again—the fundamental assumption that Ember's role is creative while mine is strategic, that business decisions happen between the adults while she provides artistic consultation.

"Ember is my business partner. We're equal partners. Any decisions about the company's future need to include her from the beginning."

"Of course, of course. I just meant… Well, you understand the financial implications better. You can help translate the strategic elements into terms that make sense from her perspective."

"Her perspective is as my business partner."

"Right. Your business partner who's phenomenally talented but doesn't necessarily have the background to evaluate complex financial projections."

The conversation continues in circles, Dad enthusiastic about opportunities while I struggle to articulate why his approach feels wrong without seeming ungrateful or unprofessional. By the time we hang up, I have a stack of printouts that represent someone else's vision of our future and a growing sense that I'm standing at a crossroads I never saw coming.

The shop bustles with Friday morning energy when I arrive, the crowd comprising regular customers and weekend tourists who have heard about us through social media or word of mouth. Ryn handles the newcomers while Ember works with a customer on a custom scent blend, her attention focused and genuine.

Watching her interact with customers, something Miranda's analysis missed entirely, strikes me—the personal connection that drives our success. Ember doesn't sell candles; she listens to stories, suggests scents that match memories, and creates pieces that feel meaningful to their eventual owners.

It's not a technique that can be scaled or systematized. It's the heart of everything we've built.

"Heavy thoughts?" Ember appears beside me as the morning rush slows, her voice carrying the kind of gentle concern that's become familiar between us.

"Miranda's projections." I gesture toward the printouts I've spread across our shared desk, as if they were evidence of some crime. "Dad's excited about the potential."

Ember glances at the spreadsheets, her expression carefully neutral. "What kind of potential?"

"National retail presence. Licensing deals. Revenue projections that would make us millionaires within three years."

"Millionaires making what?"

It's a simple question that cuts to the core of my growing unease. Millionaires making mass-produced candles that capture the aesthetic of our work without the meaning. Millionaires who've optimized the soul out of something that mattered because it was personal.

"I don't know." The admission emerges with startling honesty. "That's the problem."

NINE

Jon

THE SCENT OF ROASTED GARLIC MINGLES WITH THE SAUTÉING OF onions—rich, warm, and grounding. My knife slices clean through the red pepper, the steady rhythm soothing—almost.

But tonight, peace is an illusion. My focus keeps drifting.

To her.

Aria moves barefoot across my kitchen like she belongs there. Like this is her space too. Her hair's down, wild and golden, tumbling over her shoulders in soft waves instead of that polished curtain she wears like armor. She's in jeans—my T-shirt hanging loose over her curves, brushing the tops of her thighs—and I can't stop looking.

It does something to me. Primal. Possessive. She's in my home, dressed in my clothes, cooking beside me like this is what we do every night.

"Stop staring," she says, not even glancing up from the garlic she's mincing.

"Hard not to," I murmur, watching the smile tug at her lips. She doesn't deny me the pleasure of it, just keeps chopping, precise and unfazed, like she doesn't realize how easily she's unraveling me.

I lean on the counter, arms crossed, letting my gaze linger. "Where'd you learn to handle a knife like that?"

"Boarding school in Switzerland. We had a chef who taught cooking classes on weekends." She shrugs. "Dad thought it was ridiculous—his exact words were *'why learn to cook when you can pay someone to do it better.'* But I liked it."

That small rebellion against her father's expectations—it's the first of many glimpses I'll get tonight of the real Aria beneath the polished heiress exterior.

"What about you?" she asks. "You're pretty handy in the kitchen yourself."

"Mom's influence. She refused to raise sons who couldn't fend for themselves." I reach past her for the olive oil, letting my body brush against hers. "She said no partner of mine should have to do everything."

"Smart woman, your mom." Aria leans into the contact, her body warm against mine.

"The smartest." I press a kiss to her temple before stepping back to the stove. "Pour us some wine?"

"This place suits you."

My new apartment is a far cry from the one I shared with Charlie and Brett—deliberately so. After they moved on and started building their life together, I needed something that was just mine. Something without memories haunting every corner.

"Feels good to have my own space again." I stir the risotto, focusing on the smooth, creamy consistency forming.

She hands me a glass of wine, our fingers brushing. "I can see why. It's very—you."

"And what exactly is 'me'?" I ask, curious about how she sees me.

Aria takes a thoughtful sip of wine, looking around the apartment. "Practical, but not austere. Comfortable, without being showy." Her eyes meet mine over the rim of her glass. "Strong, steady, with unexpected depth."

The way she says it—like she's describing more than just my apartment—warms something in my chest.

"You've thought about this," I say.

"I've thought about a lot of things." She moves to the stove beside me, peering into the pot. "Including how good that risotto smells. What's your secret?"

"Patience." I stir slowly, methodically. "And knowing when to let things simmer."

"Is that just for cooking, or life advice?" Her eyes catch mine, a smile playing at the corners of her mouth.

"Take it however you want." I nudge her playfully with my shoulder.

We work in companionable silence for a while, the kitchen filling with the aromas of garlic, wine, and simmering rice. Outside the window, the city lights glitter against the darkening sky, a private universe of our own making.

"Tell me about growing up in Montana," she requests, settling onto one of the barstools at the kitchen island. "You mentioned your grandfather taught you to track and hunt?"

"Yeah, he was old-school. Believed a man should know how to provide, how to read the land." I smile at the memory. "He'd take me out at dawn, show me how to spot broken twigs, disturbed soil, the signs most people miss. Said it wasn't just about hunting—it was about understanding your place in the world."

"And what place was that?"

"Part of something bigger. Not separate from nature, not above it. Just another link in the chain." I add the last of the stock to the rice. "Those lessons came in handy later, in the military. The ability to observe, to really see what's in front of you—it's saved my life more than once."

"Is that why you enlisted? To use those skills?"

I consider the question, wanting to give her an honest answer. "Partly. But mostly it was about service. Grandpa fought in Vietnam, Dad in Desert Storm. Service is in our blood."

"But not forced?"

"No." I shake my head. "They would've respected whatever path I chose. But the military felt right. I wanted to protect people, to stand between them and harm."

"And that led you to the Guardians?"

"Eventually. After my second tour, I was recruited for special operations. The work was important, but—impersonal. Too much politics, too much distance between the mission and the people we were supposedly helping." I stir the risotto one final time before turning off the heat. "Guardian HRS is different. We see the direct impact of what we do. The people we help—they have faces, names, stories."

"People like me," she says softly.

"People like you." Our eyes meet across the kitchen, and I clear my throat. "Dinner's ready. Why don't you grab the salad?"

We settle at the small dining table, knees brushing underneath. I've kept the setting simple—no fancy tablecloth or candles, just good food and better company. Still, Aria looks around with appreciation.

"This is nice."

"It's just dinner."

"No, it's—real." She takes a bite of the risotto, closing her eyes briefly in appreciation. "My father's idea of dinner is a seven-course meal with the correct wine pairing for each course, served by staff who've been instructed to remain practically invisible."

"Sounds suffocating."

"It is." She takes a sip of wine. "Everything in his world has to be perfect, controlled. Including me."

"Tell me about him." I keep my tone casual, despite the surge of protectiveness I feel whenever she mentions her father. The man has always struck me as calculating, even during our brief interaction after Aria's rescue. "What was it like growing up with Marcus Holbrook as your father?"

Aria's fork pauses halfway to her mouth. She sets it down, considering. "He wasn't always—like he is now. After Mom died, something changed. He became obsessed with legacy, with control. Everything had to be perfect because she wasn't there to see it."

"How old were you when she passed?"

"Eight." Her voice softens. "Young enough to forget details, old enough to miss her. Dad sent me to boarding school the following year. Said it was for the best education, but I think he couldn't bear to see her in me every day."

The casual cruelty of it—shipping off a grieving child— makes my jaw tighten.

"That must have been hard."

"It was—lonely. But I adapted. Became exactly what was expected of me—perfect grades, perfect manners, perfect friends from perfect families." She twirls her wine glass absently. "Perfect Aria, the ideal daughter, the flawless heiress."

"Until the kidnapping."

She nods. "Until then, I'd never really questioned my path. Graduate from Stanford, take an executive position at Holbrook Pharmaceuticals, marriage to someone with the right connec- tions… It was all laid out."

"And now?"

"Now I know what it feels like to truly be taken from your life. To be erased." Her eyes meet mine, clear and determined. "I don't want to follow his blueprint anymore. I want the freedom to choose my own path. Work that matters. People who see me, not just my father's name or my trust fund."

"Where do I fit into this new vision?" I reach across the table, taking her hand in mine.

"You don't fit into my father's plan at all." A small smile curves her lips. "A security specialist with no Ivy League degree and no family connections? Dating his daughter? He'd have a coronary."

"Is that why you haven't told him about us?" I keep my tone neutral, no accusation.

"Partly." She squeezes my hand. "And partly because until recently, I wasn't entirely sure where we stood. Whether this was just... casual for you."

"Aria, there's nothing casual about how I feel about you." I can't help the laugh that escapes me.

"Good to know." The simple declaration visibly affects her, color rising in her cheeks.

"Is it?" I stroke my thumb across her knuckles. "Because it means eventually, we're going to have to deal with your father."

"I know. I need time to figure out how to make him understand that my life is my own." Uncertainty shadows her eyes.

"We'll figure it out together." I lift her hand to my lips, pressing a kiss to her palm. "No rush."

The conversation shifts to lighter topics as we finish dinner.

As I clear our plates, Aria follows me into the kitchen, hip leaning against the counter as she finishes her wine.

"What about your missions? Did you ever worry you wouldn't make it back?"

"Not really." I consider the question while loading the dishwasher. "In the moment, there's just the mission, the team. Fear comes later, when you have time to think."

"That's interesting." She swirls the last of her wine. "The things that really scare us aren't always what they should be."

"Meaning?"

"Meaning…" She sets her glass down, eyes finding mine. "Sometimes, I was more afraid of disappointing my father than I was of actual danger. How messed up is that?"

"Not messed up. Just human." I close the dishwasher and straighten, wiping my hands on a towel.

"What about you?" Her voice softens. "What scares Jon when he's not on a mission?"

The question catches me off guard—not because it's difficult, but because the answer rises so immediately I can taste it. I move closer, drawn by something I can't name.

"This," I say simply, the word hanging between us.

"Define '*this*.'" She doesn't back away.

"This thing between us. How it feels different." My eyes hold hers, the kitchen suddenly too warm, too small.

"Different how?" Her breath catches slightly.

I search for words that won't sound ridiculous coming from a man who's faced down armed hostiles without blinking. "More—consequential."

"That's a cautious word." Her lips curve in a small smile.

"I'm being careful." I toss the towel onto the counter. "Maybe too careful."

"Maybe." She steps closer, eliminating the last bit of distance between us. Her hand comes up to rest against my chest, light but deliberate. "I've never seen you hesitate before. Not in anything."

"The stakes were different before." The weight of her palm against my heartbeat anchors me.

Understanding dawns in her eyes, and something else—vulnerability mixed with desire. I lean down, resting my forehead against hers, breathing in the scent of her—floral and warm with undertones of wine.

"Your father would definitely not approve of this," I murmur.

"That just makes it better." A small laugh escapes her.

"Rebellious streak." I smile against her skin.

"You have no idea." She tilts her face up, lips a breath away from mine.

Her boldness ignites something raw in me. No more holding back, no more careful distance. We've already laid our cards on the table at the beach—her fears about not being enough, my assurances that what we have is whole and complete. Now there's nothing left but action.

I slide my hand into her hair, tilting her face up to mine. Her eyes darken, pupils dilating until only a thin ring of blue remains.

With deliberate slowness, I cup the back of her neck, my other hand settling at her waist, drawing her in until our bodies press together.

Her breath quickens as she rises on tiptoes. My restraint snaps like a wire pulled too tight.

The first touch of her lips is tentative, questioning. The second is not. I kiss her deeply, thoroughly, pouring months of restraint and longing into the contact. Her mouth opens under mine, a small sound of pleasure escaping her as my tongue sweeps inside.

I back her up against the counter, lifting her easily to sit on the edge. Her legs part, allowing me to step between them, bringing us closer still. The new position puts us eye to eye, her thighs warm against my hips. I cup her face, my thumb tracing the delicate curve of her cheekbone as I break the kiss to study her flushed cheeks, parted lips, eyes dark with desire.

"You have no idea how long I've wanted this," I murmur, my voice rough even to my own ears.

Her answer is to draw me back in, her kiss hungrier now, more demanding. Her hands slide under my shirt, exploring the planes of my back, nails dragging lightly along my spine. The sensation sends heat flooding through me.

I trail my lips along the line of her jaw, tasting the softness of her skin. Her head falls back, offering her throat to me. I accept the invitation, pressing open-mouthed kisses down the column of her neck, feeling her pulse racing beneath my lips. She tastes like salt and wine, and something uniquely her own.

Her fingers thread through my hair, guiding me, urging me on. When I find a particularly sensitive spot where her neck meets her shoulder, she gasps, her body arching against mine.

"More," she whispers, the single word both command and plea.

I smile against her skin, taking my time, learning what makes her breath catch. My hands slide beneath her borrowed T-shirt, tracing the curve of her waist and the warm softness of her back. Her skin is like silk beneath my calloused palms.

"Take this off." She tugs at my shirt, impatient.

I oblige, stepping back just long enough to pull the shirt over my head. Her eyes darken as she takes me in, her hands immediately reaching to explore newly exposed skin. The sensation of her touch—gentle yet possessive—sends electricity racing through my veins.

"Your turn," I say, fingers playing with the hem of her shirt.

She lifts her arms in answer. I peel the shirt slowly upward, revealing smooth skin inch by inch, the lace edge of her bra, the gentle swell of her breasts. The sight of her half-undressed in my kitchen, looking at me with undisguised hunger, nearly brings me to my knees.

I drop the shirt to the floor and step back between her legs, my hands spanning her waist. Her skin is warm against mine as I bend to press my lips to the hollow of her throat, then lower, tracing the edge of her collarbone with my tongue. Her hands grip my shoulders, nails digging in slightly when I brush my lips against the swell of her breast just above her bra.

A small, breathy sound escapes her. I look up—she's watching me, lips parted, cheeks flushed. God, she's beautiful like this.

Unraveled. Wanting. I capture her mouth again, the kiss deeper, hungrier, claiming every soft gasp she gives me like I've earned it.

Her legs lock around my waist, pulling me in until there's not a breath of space left between us. Heat radiates through the denim where we press—scorching, unrelenting. It short-circuits every rational thought in my head.

My hands slide down to cup her ass, dragging her tighter. I need her to feel it—that she's driving me insane. That she owns me right now, in every way that counts.

No games. No flings. This isn't about sex. It's her. All of her. And she's mine.

She breaks the kiss with a gasp, her forehead pressed to mine, both of us breathing hard, like we've run miles just to get here. Her fingers drift over my chest—circling, teasing—each touch branding me. Her eyes meet mine, wide open, dark with certainty.

"Jon." My name, wrecked and reverent, falls from her lips. "I want you."

Three words. That's all it takes. The rest of the world ceases to exist.

I lift her in one smooth motion, her thighs clinging tight to my waist, her breath catching as I hold her there, pressed against me like she belongs. She does. God, she does.

The hallway blurs as I carry her, the only light a soft spill from the kitchen behind us. My shoulder nudges the bedroom door open, and then we're inside. My sanctuary. And now it's ours.

I lower her to the bed, slow and reverent. Her hair fans across the pillow, a golden halo in the low light. And fuck, the way she looks at me—no fear, no hesitation. Just hunger. Trust.

It slams into me like a punch to the chest.

"You're beautiful." The words feel too small, too tame for what I feel. But I need her to hear them. I need her to know.

She reaches up, fingers curling into my hair, voice low and trembling with need. "Show me."

God help me. I will.

I dip my head, catching her mouth with mine. This kiss—this one is slower, deeper. Not a question. A vow. My fingers trace the warm silk of her skin. She arches into me, breath shivering from her lungs as I skim higher, memorizing the curve of her waist, the lift of her ribs, the soft catch in her breath when I brush the underside of her breast.

She's trembling. Or maybe it's me.

I want to go slow, draw this out, worship every inch of her. But the need pulsing through my veins is savage. Primal.

Still, I force myself to pause, hovering above her, breathing her in. "Last chance to stop me," I murmur, my voice raw with restraint.

Her eyes blaze. "Don't you dare."

And just like that, I'm gone.

TEN

Aria

———

MOONLIGHT SPILLS ACROSS THE HARDWOOD FLOOR LIKE SILVER ink, calm and luminous. Jon's hands don't leave me—not right away. They linger at my waist, fingers splayed, thumbs circling in a way that makes it hard to think.

Harder to breathe.

Even through the denim of my jeans, my skin burns where he touches me.

Because he touches me.

He watches me like he's memorizing every reaction, every flicker of need I'm too proud to name aloud. His eyes have gone dark in the low light, pupils dilated, irises almost swallowed whole. There's heat in them—yes—but something steadier, too. Something that makes me feel seen, not just wanted.

I shiver, and it has nothing to do with the night air.

"We can take this as slow as you want." His voice is low and rough, scraped raw at the edges. Like, restraint costs him something.

I don't want slow.

I want to drown in him.

I want to forget every version of myself that ever felt the need to be perfect, polite, or polished.

"I don't want slow." I reach for him, fingers finding the sharp line of his jaw, the faint rasp of stubble.

"Too bad." His smile flickers—wolfish, wicked—and my stomach flips in response.

The words shouldn't make me ache, but they do. They shouldn't turn me inside out, but they're a fuse in my bloodstream, lit and hissing.

Before I can argue, his mouth is on mine again—this time controlled. Purposeful. Not rushed or ravenous like before, but deliberate in a way that makes every nerve stand up and beg. His hands stay at my waist, not roaming. His thumbs keep circling those maddening, tender patterns.

It's maddening. It's everything.

I fumble at his belt, urgency clawing up my spine. I want him, now. Need the drag of skin on skin, the sharp gasp of connection, but he catches my wrists before I get anywhere.

Gently. Firmly.

My breath stutters. Not from fear, but from the way my body listens to him.

"No." Just one word. Quiet. Certain.

My pulse trips. My hands go still.

He lifts them between us, pressing a kiss to one palm. Then the other. My chest squeezes.

"My way," he murmurs. "Tonight is about you."

The words splinter something open inside me. Not just arousal—though that pulses hot and thick in my core—but something more dangerous. Something terrifying.

Trust.

"What if I want it to be about us?" I tilt my chin up.

"It will be." His calloused fingertips brush a strand of hair from my face with impossible gentleness. "But first, I want to learn you."

No one has ever spoken to me like this—like I'm a landscape to be explored, a text to be studied. The men I've been with before treated sex like a transaction, a race to completion. Quick, efficient, focused on their pleasure. Even those who made token efforts to satisfy me approached it like a task to be checked off a list.

Jon holds himself back, every motion careful, restrained, like he's walking a tightrope between control and surrender. His touch adjusts with each breath I take, as if my body's reactions are commands he's wired to obey. The air between us thickens, charged with something I don't have words for, only instinct. He's not just touching me. He's studying me.

Memorizing me.

His words settle over me like velvet and steel.

My way.

It's not a threat. He makes it a promise.

Something inside me softens—and tightens. My pulse thrums beneath my skin like a second heartbeat, desperate and unsteady. I should protest. Push for control. That's what I've always done— take the lead, set the terms, never surrender. But right now, with Jon standing before me, gaze steady, hands reverent... I don't want control.

I want to be unraveled.

I fight the instinct to cover myself, to hide the way my breath hitches, the way my nipples harden under his gaze, but Jon doesn't leer. Doesn't smirk.

He looks at me like I'm art.

"Perfect," he murmurs—not to flatter, not to seduce. Just truth. Plain and undoing.

He bends his head, lips brushing just beneath my collarbone. Every nerve in my body wires to that single point of contact. He maps me with his mouth, kissing me along my jaw, neck, and shoulder. Each kiss is slow. Intentional.

Claiming.

I arch into him, greedy for more, but his hands settle at my hips, holding me steady. Not pushing. Just anchoring.

"You're shaking." His voice, low and warm against my throat.

Of course I am. How do I explain this isn't just lust? That no one's ever touched me like this—seen me like this. I've been naked before, sure, but never stripped like this.

Never laid bare in the quiet between heartbeats.

"I'm okay," I whisper, but it's shaky. Real.

"Tell me if that changes." He kisses the corner of my mouth like a reward.

Jon moves with a patience I didn't know men like him possessed. Each kiss is a tether. Each touch peeling away another layer I've hidden behind for years. The silk-and-champagne heiress. The polished socialite. The perfect daughter.

None of that matters here.

Here, I'm just Aria.

And I'm his.

His lips brush the curve where my neck meets my shoulder, and my thoughts scatter. His mouth trails upward, finding a spot behind my ear that makes me shudder. One strong arm wraps around my waist, supporting me, while his other hand slides into my hair, angling my head to give him better access.

"I've thought about this," he murmurs against my skin. "About all the ways I want to touch you. All the sounds I want to hear you make."

Heat pools low in my belly at his words. I've never been one for talking during sex—it always felt forced, performative. But Jon's low voice sends electricity racing along my nerves.

"Show me," I whisper.

The hunger in his eyes makes my breath catch. He's waiting

for something. Waiting for me to yield, to acknowledge he's in charge of this dance.

A lifetime of rebellion makes me hesitate, if only for a moment. I've spent years fighting against control, resisting the paths laid out for me. But this is different. This isn't my father's suffocating control or society's rigid expectations. This is Jon asking me to trust him, to let go.

I sit on the edge of the bed, then lie back, my hair fanning across his sheets. A wordless surrender.

His smile is worth it—approving, appreciative, with a hint of something primal that makes my pulse quicken.

He stands over me, broad shoulders blocking out the moonlight, creating his own eclipse. The power in his stance should be intimidating, but instead, it feels like shelter. Protection.

"You are so beautiful." His eyes travel slowly down my body.

I fight the urge to cross my arms over my chest, to hide from the intensity of his gaze. I'm used to being looked at—I've been on display my entire life—but never like this. Never with such focus, such intent.

He kneels on the bed, one knee between my legs, and leans down to kiss me again. This kiss consumes me completely. His tongue explores my mouth with the same deliberate attention I imagine he'll give to the rest of my body. One large hand cups my face, tilting it for better access, while the other slides beneath me to cradle the back of my neck.

The position is subtly controlling—I can't move my head, can't escape the onslaught of sensation. Not that I want to. The way he holds me, possesses me, sends heat spiraling through my core.

When he finally breaks the kiss, we're both breathing hard. He rests his forehead against mine for a moment, eyes closed, and I realize he's fighting for control. The knowledge that I affect him this strongly is intoxicating.

"May I?" His fingers trace the edge of my bra, where lace meets skin.

"Please." The request, so formal and courteous, makes me smile despite the tension humming between us.

Rather than removing the bra immediately, he slides the straps down my shoulders slowly, maintaining eye contact as he peels the lace away.

The cool air on my exposed skin makes me shiver, or maybe it's the heat in his gaze as he looks at me. I resist the impulse to cover myself. Instead, I arch my back slightly, offering myself to his view.

A muscle ticks in his jaw—sharp, barely restrained. Heat pools low in my belly.

"Do you have any idea what you do to me?"

"Show me." My fingertip traces the taut line of his jaw, drawn to the tension coiled beneath his skin.

"Patience." His hands curve around my waist, thumbs brushing just under the swell of my breasts.

That word again. Patience. I've never had much use for it—always sprinting toward the next thing, the next high, the next win. But with him, everything slows. Every second stretches like it matters.

He lowers his mouth to the center of my chest, lips brushing the frantic rhythm beneath my skin. Then he shifts, trailing kisses to the side—closer, closer—until the heat of his mouth closes over my nipple.

The shock of it pulls a gasp from deep inside me. My spine bows off the bed before I realize I'm moving.

"Stay still." His palm presses flat to my stomach, a grounding weight that stills everything but the pounding of my pulse.

The command slices through me like lightning—clean and hot and electric. I should bristle at it. Should rebel. But instead, something in me stills. Anchors me. There's power in surrender.

In choosing it.

His mouth returns with slow, agonizing intent—lips, tongue, the occasional scrape of teeth making my skin hypersensitive, my breath stutter. His hands move with purpose, skimming every inch of me, coaxing sounds I've never made, and never thought I would make.

Not from sex.

Not from this aching tenderness that feels like worship.

I reach for him, instinct over thought, desperate to feel the muscles that make up his torso, to ground myself in him.

But he catches my wrists, easing them above my head and holding them there with a gentle, unyielding grip.

"Not yet." His breath ghosts across my breast, and I nearly come apart at the contrast. "Let me take care of you."

And God help me, I will.

ELEVEN

Aria

———

Jon's hand trails down my stomach, fingers skimming just beneath the hem of my panties before shifting to the button of my jeans. He flicks it open with maddening ease, then slowly drags the zipper down. The sound—slow, metallic—cracks through the quiet like a promise. My pulse stutters.

He doesn't blink. Just watches me as he hooks his thumbs into the waistband and starts to slide the denim down my legs, inch by torturous inch. I lift my hips without being asked, hungry for more of his hands, more of that delicious friction. The moment his grip loosens to tug the jeans free, my skin prickles with the absence of his touch.

He drops them over the edge of the bed without looking away. The air feels cooler against my bare legs, my panties suddenly the only barrier between his gaze and everything I ache to give him.

He just—looks. And God, the way he looks at me—like he's savoring every inch, every curve, every breath I take. His jeans still cling to his hips, low enough to hint at the lines that disappear beneath the waistband. I'm the one stripped down, but it doesn't feel unequal. It feels electric. Exhilarating. As if he's unwrapped me and is now deciding which part of me to taste first.

He kneels at the foot of the bed, his large hands circling my ankles. His thumbs stroke once—slow, possessive—before his mouth joins in. A kiss to the arch of my foot. Another, warmer, to my ankle. Then his tongue, hot and unhurried, slides up the length of my calf.

I grip the sheets.

When he reaches the sensitive crease behind my knee, his teeth graze gently, just enough to send a jolt straight between my legs. My thighs twitch. His hands hold me still, steady, as his mouth climbs higher. Higher.

The trail he leaves is fire. Wet heat. Teasing pressure.

By the time his breath ghosts over the inside of my thighs, I'm shaking. My hips tilt toward him instinctively, desperate, shameless.

"Jon—" It slips out, breathless. Not a command. A plea.

"Patience." He glances up, mouth hovering just inches from my center, a smile playing at the corners of his lips. His fingers ghost along the edge of my panties, just beneath the lace, warm skin brushing silk. Then he pulls back—again. The retreat is intentional, maddening. A whimper slips from my throat before I can stop it. "Tell me what you want."

His voice is silk over steel. Teasing. Commanding. He knows exactly what he's doing. My breath hitches as I meet his gaze, dark and focused like a storm ready to break.

I freeze.

No one's ever asked me that before. Not like this. Sex was always about what someone else wanted. What I was supposed to give. I learned the script early—how to arch, how to moan, how to pretend it was enough. No one ever asked what I needed.

"I want…" The words catch in my throat. God, why is this so hard? "I want you to touch me."

"I am touching you." His fingers slide along the waistband again, tracing lazy circles that do nothing to relieve the ache pounding between my thighs.

"More." My voice is barely above a whisper. "I want more."

"Be specific." He leans closer, breath warm against my cheek.

The flush crawls down my neck, but the embarrassment is no match for the hunger burning in my gut. His demand strips me bare in a way that has nothing to do with nudity. I swallow hard.

"I want your hands on me. All over me. I want your mouth. I want to feel you…" I falter, pulse thundering. "Inside me."

A muscle in his jaw flexes, hard enough that I see it even in the dim light. His control fractures, just slightly, and the crack is beautiful.

"Good." His voice roughens. "I like hearing what you want."

Then finally—finally—his fingers slip beneath the lace. The first brush against my swollen, slick flesh steals the air from my lungs. My hips jerk upward, desperate for more, for anything.

"Patience," he murmurs, the word both a promise and punishment. One hand holds me firm by the hip, anchoring me, while the other moves with excruciating slowness, exploring and learning. He touches me like it's a privilege. Like I'm the gift, not the prize.

It's torture. Exquisite, breathless torture.

I want to scream. Claw at him. Beg.

But I don't. Because every second of this torment makes the need sharper, the pleasure deeper. And when he finally gives me what I want, it's going to shatter me.

With deliberate slowness, he draws my panties down my legs. I've never felt so exposed, so vulnerable—or so desired. The way he looks at me makes me feel like the most precious thing he's ever seen.

"Perfect," he murmurs, running his hands up my now-bare legs, parting them gently.

The cool air hits my heated skin, making me shiver. I should feel self-conscious, laid bare like this, but the reverence in his eyes banishes any uncertainty.

His hands grip the insides of my thighs and ease them farther apart, but it's his mouth that undoes me. The first swipe of his tongue lands like a lightning strike—sharp, wet, devastating. A cry rips from my throat before I can stop it.

My spine bows off the mattress. His hands clamp down on my hips, anchoring me to the bed as his mouth works lower, deeper, with maddening purpose. No hesitation. No mercy.

He explores me like he's memorizing every gasp, every tremble, every stuttered breath. Tongue and lips and the faint scrape of teeth—all of it driving me higher. My fingers twist in the sheets, my legs shaking around his shoulders. I teeter there, so close I can taste it—and then he stops.

Air punches from my lungs.

"Jon—" The sound barely forms, half a plea, half a sob.

"Not yet." He rises onto his knees between my thighs, mouth slick, gaze dark and unreadable. Hunger simmers beneath the restraint, that same careful control I've come to crave and curse.

"Please." I reach for him. No shame left.

He stands. Unbuttons. Unzips. The quiet rasp of denim fills the room.

No boxers. No briefs.

My breath catches.

He's bare beneath the jeans, and his cock springs free—thick, hard, flushed dark with need. My mouth goes dry. Every inch of him is all lean muscle and raw power, but it's the way he stands there, unashamed and utterly in control, that makes my thighs press together instinctively.

He doesn't touch himself. Doesn't smirk or show off. He just watches me watching him, letting the tension coil tighter and tighter.

Then he climbs onto the bed, the mattress dipping under his weight, and I rise on trembling elbows.

He's beautiful in a way that feels dangerous—like looking straight into a fire and wanting it anyway. Scars slice across his body—pale ridges, brutal memories carved into skin. They make him real.

Raw.

Human.

My palms meet the heat of his chest—solid muscle, the rough texture of hair, the raised line of a scar that curves under his ribs.

"IED in Kandahar," he murmurs.

My fingertips glide over another, thin, silvery line, like a whisper across his shoulder.

"Training knife. Went too deep."

Every scar tells a story. Not just of pain, but of survival. Of the man he is beneath all that strength and stillness. So different from the polished, pampered men I grew up around. Men who earned their muscles at boutique gyms, not warzones.

Jon lowers himself over me, weight supported on his forearms, his body pressing into mine—hot skin against skin, chest hair rasping over my breasts, thighs bracketed by his. His cock rests heavy and hard between us, a promise and a threat.

"Last chance to back out," he murmurs, voice low, breath hot against my mouth. "First chance to surrender."

That word—*surrender*—it crackles through me like lightning, short-circuiting all thought. Not a command. An invitation. And yet it hits deeper than any demand ever could.

Not just surrendering my body. Surrendering control. Letting someone else lead… Letting him lead.

The instinct to push back flares like muscle memory—I've spent years guarding my independence like armor. But his voice, the steady weight of him above me, the reverent way he looks at me like I'm something sacred, not something to conquer—God, it frees me.

A shiver rips through me, part fear, part need. My fingers dig into his shoulders.

"I'm exactly where I want to be." My voice sounds foreign, wrecked, raw, and honest.

Something in his eyes changes. The restraint shatters. Control slips as his hunger takes over. He crashes his mouth to mine, all teeth and heat, the kiss bruising and wild and perfect. And when he finally pushes inside me—slow, deep, overwhelming—I shatter.

Eyes shut. Breath gone. Body his.

And for the first time in my life, I surrender and want everything that comes with it.

"Look at me." His hand cups my face, thumb brushing my cheekbone.

I open my eyes, meeting his gaze. The connection is almost too much, too intimate, too real. I've never looked into someone's eyes during sex before. It always seemed too vulnerable, too honest.

"Stay with me." He holds still within me. "I want to see you."

And I do. I stay present, entirely in the moment as we move together. No performance, no carefully constructed façade. Just me and him, finding our rhythm, learning each other's bodies.

He sets a pace that's deliberately slow at first, each movement deep and purposeful. One hand slides beneath me, changing the angle, making each thrust hit exactly right. The other tangles in my hair, holding me in place as he kisses me deeply.

The dual sensation—the physical pleasure building inside me and the emotional connection in his unwavering gaze—is almost too much to bear. I dig my nails into his back, urging him on.

He responds to my silent plea, increasing his pace, his movements becoming more forceful. The control he's maintained all night begins to fray at the edges, and there's something thrilling about that—about knowing I can push him to the brink of his restraint.

"Jon," I gasp, feeling myself getting close. "I need—"

"I know what you need." He shifts his weight to slide a hand between us. His fingers find exactly the right spot, applying perfect pressure in time with his thrusts.

The combination pushes me over the edge. Wave after wave of pleasure crashes through me, my body arching against his, his name a cry on my lips. Through it all, he watches me, his eyes dark with satisfaction and need.

Only when the last tremor subsides does he let himself go, his rhythm faltering as he follows me into release. The vulnerability on his face in that moment—the usually controlled Jon completely undone—is perhaps the most intimate thing I've ever witnessed.

He collapses beside me, gathering me close in the same movement so I'm draped across his chest. His heartbeat thunders beneath my ear, gradually slowing as our breathing steadies.

His fingers trace lazy patterns on my back. I feel oddly peaceful. Complete. As if I've discovered a piece of myself I didn't know was missing.

"You okay?" His voice rumbles through his chest into mine.

I nod, not trusting my voice yet. The intensity of what just happened—not just physically, but emotionally—has left me raw in ways I hadn't expected.

"Talk to me." He tilts my face up to his.

"I'm good. Better than good. Just—processing."

"Processing, what?" His eyes search mine.

I take a deep breath, seeking words for something I've never had to articulate before. "That was—different."

"Different good or different bad?" A small frown creases his brow.

"Good. Definitely good." I trace the line of his collarbone, gathering courage. "I've never… It's never been like that before."

"Like, what?" Understanding dawns in his eyes.

"So—present. So connected." I hide my face against his chest, embarrassed by my own vulnerability. "The men I've been with before—they were never really there with me. It was always just about the act itself."

"Their loss." His arm tightens around me, protective.

The simple statement warms something in my chest. I press a kiss to his skin, tasting salt and something uniquely him.

"I liked how you took control," I admit, surprising myself with the confession. "How you knew exactly what to do, what I needed."

"I pay attention." His hand strokes my hair, gentle but possessive.

"You certainly do." I prop myself up on his chest, looking into his face. "How did you know I would respond to that?"

"I didn't. Not for sure." A smile plays at the corners of his mouth. "But I notice how you react when I take the lead in other situations. How you relax when you don't have to make every decision."

His observation strikes me silent. He's right. All my life, I've had to be the perfect daughter, the flawless heiress, constantly calculating and performing. The weight of expectations—my father's, society's, my own—has been exhausting. With Jon, I can simply be. Can let someone else take the reins for a while.

"Thank you."

"For what?" He traces my jawline with his thumb.

"For seeing me. The real me, not just what I show the world." I run my fingers along the strong line of his jaw. "For making me feel like a person, not a conquest or a trophy."

Pain flashes across his features, quickly replaced by tenderness. He rolls us so I'm beneath him again, his weight a comforting pressure. He kisses me—gentle, unhurried, a contrast to the intensity of before.

"You're not a conquest. You're someone I want to know. All of you. Not just this part." His eyes hold mine, serious now. "I can't wait to show you all the things I enjoy, all the ways we can explore this. Together."

"What does that mean?" My pulse quickens at his words.

"The very way you have to ask tells me everything I need to know." He smiles, a knowing look crossing his face. His fingers trail down my side, raising goosebumps. "You're a blank canvas, and I can't wait to educate you in all things about sex…" His voice drops lower, "…especially the things I want you to do to me."

"I'd like that." Heat floods my face, but curiosity and desire follow close behind.

"Good." He brushes a strand of hair from my face. "We've got all the time in the world."

We stay like that, talking in the darkness, learning each other in new ways. He tells me about his first deployment, about the terror and the camaraderie. I tell him about the loneliness of boarding school, about finding ways to rebel within the strict confines of privilege.

As the night deepens, we come together again—slower this time, more tender but no less intense. Afterward, wrapped in his arms, I drift toward sleep with the realization that for the first time in my life, I'm not playing a role. Not the perfect daughter, not the polished socialite, not even the rebellious heiress.

With Jon, I'm just me. And somehow, that's enough.

TWELVE

Aria

———

Aria breathes like she trusts me. Slow, steady. One hand curled against my chest, her bare leg tangled with mine, her skin still carrying the heat of the night we didn't stop touching.

I haven't moved in twenty minutes. Not because I'm asleep. Because I don't want to break this moment.

Don't want to wake her.

Don't want to lose the feel of her against me.

She's different like this. Unmasked. Vulnerable in a way she never lets the world see. The sharp edges smoothed, the steel in her spine softened. She's not the cool, calculating heiress. She's mine. And fuck if that doesn't hit somewhere I didn't know was empty.

A soft strand of hair clings to her cheek, and I brush it back. She murmurs something against my chest, too soft to catch, and shifts closer. Her body fits against mine like it was always meant to be here.

Last night wasn't just sex. It was something deeper. The way she let go, gave in—gave herself—it wrecked me. The way she listened, obeyed, surrendered. I didn't expect that. But now that I've seen it... Now that I've felt it...

My hand traces the curve of her waist, over the slope of her hip, and up the length of her back. She shivers. Still mostly asleep, but her body reacts like it remembers me.

Like it wants more.

"Mmm." She makes that soft, satisfied sound, barely lifting her head. "What time is it?"

"Early." I press a kiss to the place where her neck meets her shoulder, tasting sleep and skin and something unmistakably hers. "Go back to sleep."

She stretches with that feline elegance that drives me crazy. And then her ass nestles against my cock, already half hard from just existing next to her. She pauses. Smiles. That small, knowing sound escapes her throat—a low hum of discovery—and the tension in my body coils tight.

"Doesn't feel that early to me." Her voice—rough with sleep, rich with promise—slides through me like warm whiskey.

"Smartass." I nip her shoulder, just enough pressure to make her gasp, to remind her who she gave herself to last night.

She rolls toward me, lashes fluttering open, sleepy mischief dancing in those impossibly blue eyes. "Good morning to you too."

I don't bother answering. Just catch her mouth with mine, not caring about morning breath or anything else that isn't the taste of her, the feel of her melting into me like she's already forgotten where she ends and I begin. Her hand finds its way up my chest, fingers curling at my neck like she needs the contact as much as I do.

When we pull apart, she's smiling. That soft, sleepy kind of smile that punches straight through every defense I've built.

"I could get used to waking up like this." Her lashes flutter, voice husky.

Something shifts. Sharp and unexpected. Dangerous. Like my chest can't decide if it's aching or expanding.

"Like, what?" I let my fingers drift down her side, slow enough to draw goosebumps, controlled enough to keep from losing myself in how perfect she feels under my touch. "Tired? Sore?"

"Happy." One word. Soft. Uncomplicated. But it lands with the weight of a goddamn bomb.

I kiss her again—because I need to. Because I can't look at her and not want to claim her all over again. This kiss is different. Hungrier. Deeper. Her leg hooks over my hip, grinding her slick heat against my cock, and I don't need a single word to know she wants more.

"Hands above your head." My voice is low. Measured. I watch her closely, reading every flicker of emotion on her face.

No hesitation. No nerves. Just a slow, sensual stretch as she obeys, wrists crossing above her like she was made to be restrained. Like she trusts me with the power she never gives away.

Fuck.

"Good girl." The praise slips out on instinct, and the flush that blooms across her cheeks is better than anything I've ever seen.

I wrap one hand around both wrists, pressing them into the pillow. Not rough, but firm. A reminder. A promise. My other hand trails from the base of her throat, over the rise of her breasts, down to her navel, watching every twitch, every tremble as sensation unfurls across her skin.

"Keep these here," I murmur, releasing her wrists with a final press. "Don't move them unless I say so."

She draws in a sharp breath. Eyes wide. Chest rising in anticipation.

And she nods. Slow. Certain.

Trusting me to lead.

Trusting me to own her pleasure.

I take my time.

Not to tease her, but to learn her. Every gasp. Every catch of breath. Every place my mouth grazes that makes her body arch off the mattress like she's offering herself up to me.

Her nipple tightens against my tongue, and she shudders. Hands still pinned obediently above her head, knuckles white from the effort not to move.

Her hips roll, searching for friction, heat, me.

"Jon…" A low sound. Need wrapped in surrender.

"Patience." I move lower, mouth trailing a path of open-mouthed kisses down her stomach. "We've got all morning."

She spreads her thighs without hesitation. No shame. No modesty. Just an open invitation. One I'd die before refusing.

My mouth finds her.

She cries out, body jerking. Slick heat and her taste hit me like a punch to the chest, like I've been starving for this without realizing it.

I drag my tongue through her folds, slow at first, savoring. Then I focus—learn the rhythm that makes her tremble, the pressure that makes her curse, the soft suck against her clit that makes her breath stutter.

She's falling apart. Voice going high, hips chasing every movement. She's right there.

I slide two fingers inside her, curling forward until I feel the exact spot that—

"Fuck!" She bucks violently, hands flying down, clutching at my shoulders like she needs an anchor.

I stop. Immediately.

Lift my head. Lock eyes.

"What did I say about your hands?"

Her eyes are huge. Lips parted, cheeks flushed. Still drunk on the edge of pleasure but desperate to obey.

"I'm sorry..." Her voice is barely a whisper. She lifts her arms, returning them to the pillow. Exposed again. Vulnerable. Trusting.

"Better."

I reward her with my mouth. Slower now. Drawing it out. Building her higher. Higher.

Her hips rock in time with my fingers, greedy for every stroke. She's so close. Teetering.

"Jon, please..." My name wrecked on her tongue. Guttural. Gorgeous.

"Let go," I murmur against her skin, voice low and firm. "I want to hear you fall apart."

She shatters.

Body arching. Mouth open in a scream. Inner muscles clenching so tightly around my fingers, it's as if her body never wants to let me go. Wave after wave rolls through her, and I keep going—drawing it out, giving her everything, owning her pleasure until she's trembling and wrecked.

When I finally crawl up her body, she's still panting, her hands still above her head, shaking now.

"You can touch me," I say softly.

Her arms wrap around me instantly, nails digging into my back, pulling me down like she needs me inside her more than air.

I slide in with one slow, deep thrust. Her gasp is muffled by my mouth as I swallow her cry.

She's hot. Slick. Still pulsing around me.

And fuck, I'm already so close.

But this moment—this woman—deserves more than fast and desperate. She deserves everything.

I grit my teeth and slow down, setting a rhythm that will take us both apart, piece by aching piece.

"Open your eyes," I demand softly when I notice they've fluttered closed. "I want to see you."

She complies, her gaze locking with mine, vulnerable and trusting. The intimacy of it nearly undoes me.

I slide a hand beneath her, angling her hips to take me deeper, and she moans, a sound so purely feminine it sends a jolt of pleasure down my spine. Her legs wrap around my waist, heels digging into my lower back, urging me on.

"Harder," she whispers, and I comply, driving into her with enough force to make the headboard knock against the wall.

The sounds she makes—breathy gasps and broken moans—push me closer to the edge. When I feel her begin to tighten around me again, I slip a hand between us, circling her clit with my thumb.

"Come for me again," I growl against her neck. "I want to feel you."

Her second orgasm crashes through her with even more intensity than the first, her body clenching around me so tightly that I follow her over the edge, my own release hitting me like a physical blow.

For long moments afterward, we lie tangled together, breathing hard, sweat cooling on our skin. I roll to the side to avoid crushing her, but keep her close, one arm wrapped possessively around her waist.

"Holy shit," she finally manages, her voice hoarse. "Now, that's a nice way to wake up."

"Nice?"

"Decadently wonderful."

"I'll take that as a compliment." I can't help the satisfied smile that spreads across my face.

"That was… I didn't know it could be like that." She turns to look at me, her expression a mixture of wonder and satisfaction.

The simple admission makes my chest swell with something between pride and tenderness. I press a kiss to her forehead, unable to find words for what I'm feeling.

After a while, she stretches, wincing slightly. "I think I need a shower."

"Mmm." I trace patterns on her hip. "Good idea."

"Join me?" She sits up, looking over her shoulder at me with a mischievous smile.

"You're insatiable." But I'm already following her out of bed, enjoying the view as she pads naked toward the bathroom.

The shower is barely big enough for one person, let alone two, but we manage to make it work, our bodies sliding against each other under the spray. I wash her hair, massaging her scalp until she practically purrs with contentment. She returns the favor, her soapy hands exploring my body with newfound confidence.

I'm just rinsing the last of the shampoo from my hair when I notice her expression. She's biting her lower lip, a gesture I've come to recognize as her thinking face, her eyes fixed somewhere around my chest but clearly not seeing it.

"What's going on in that head of yours?" I tilt her chin up with one finger.

"Nothing." She blushes, avoiding my eyes.

"Bullshit," I say it gently, no heat in the word. "Tell me what you're thinking about."

She takes a deep breath, as if gathering courage. "I was just —wondering about something."

"Something?"

"Something I've never done before." Her blush deepens. "With anyone."

I still. Heart slowing even as blood rushes south.

"And what might that be?"

She lifts her eyes to mine—open, searching. There's heat there, yes. But also a kind of fragile courage.

"I've never—gone down on someone before." Her voice barely carries over the sound of the water, but the words hit like a detonator. "But with you, I want to. I'm curious… Eager, even."

Christ.

It's not the sex. Not the mental image of Aria on her knees—though fuck, that alone nearly unravels me. It's the offering. The trust laced into every word. The quiet way she's giving this to me—not just her mouth, but her vulnerability. Her first time. And she wants it to be with me.

A bolt of heat sears through me, dark and possessive.

I step forward, close the space between us, and back her against the cold tile. My palm curves around her cheek, anchoring us both.

"And you want to try it? With me?"

She nods, breath quickening. "But I don't know what I'm doing." Her voice is unsteady, but her eyes are steady. "I want to make it good for you."

Jesus.

Most women I've known have performed. Polished. Practiced. But this? This is raw. Honest. She doesn't want to impress me—she wants to please me. Not because she has to. Not because she thinks she owes me something. But because she wants to.

That difference does something to me I don't have a name for.

"You couldn't be bad at it if you tried." My voice comes out rough, unfiltered. The need to protect what she's giving me runs parallel to the hunger clawing at my control.

I kiss her. Not with heat—yet—but with reverence. Letting her feel how much this moment matters.

She leans into me.

"Will you—show me? Tell me what to do?"

A groan slips out before I can stop it. I press my forehead to hers, trying to ground myself, trying not to lose it completely just from the fantasy of her asking to be taught by me.

"Are you sure that's what you want?"

No teasing. No coaxing. I need her answer to be clear.

Certain.

"Yes." No hesitation. No fear. Just quiet, blazing intent. "I want to learn what you like."

My restraint frays another inch.

She has no idea what she's doing to me.

And I'm going to make damn sure her first time doing this becomes something she never forgets.

I reach behind her to shut off the water. "Not here. Too cramped, too slippery."

My voice is hoarse with restraint. I step out of the shower, grab a towel, and wrap it around her still-shivering body. The scent of her—steamed skin, warm shampoo, sex—clings to me as I take a second towel and sling it low around my hips.

"Bedroom. Now."

THIRTEEN

Jon

Aria follows me into the bedroom, her steps small and tentative, towel clutched in front of her like armor. There's a flicker of uncertainty in her eyes again. But it only tightens the heat coiling in my gut. That vulnerability? It wrecks me.

In the bedroom, I sit on the edge of the bed and look up at her.

"Come here."

She hesitates for just a beat before stepping between my knees. Her lips part, uncertain. Anticipation shadows every line of her posture, but she holds my gaze, brave, trembling, mine.

"First rule," I murmur, forcing calm into my voice. "If at any point you want to stop, you stop. No questions, no explanations."

She nods. Some of the tension slips from her spine.

"Second rule—this isn't a performance. I don't want perfect. I want you. Curious. Unfiltered. Real."

A flush rises on her cheeks. Not embarrassment. Heat.

"Third rule—tell me what you're okay with. What you're not. That's non-negotiable. I want your voice as much as your mouth." I lift her hand and press a kiss to her palm, letting her feel the shake in my breath.

She swallows. "Okay."

The quiet confidence in her voice sends heat rushing to my cock. I want to kiss her, want to lay her down and worship every inch of her skin—but this? Watching her choose this, choose me for this first? It's its own kind of reverence. And I'll be damned if I rush it.

"Where do I start?" she asks, that blush deepening.

"Here." I guide her gently to her knees, cushioning them on the rug between my legs. I don't strip the towel from her—yet. She's still holding it like a shield. And as much as I want to see her bare, open, I want her comfortable more.

She kneels between my thighs, wide eyes flicking up to mine.

"Start with your hands," I murmur. "Get used to the weight. The texture. How I react."

Her fingers wrap around my cock—tentative, exploratory.

Fuck.

A harsh breath escapes me. "Jesus. Yeah. Just like that."

"Like this?" she whispers, watching my face.

Her grip is too soft, but the look in her eyes is anything but.

"A little firmer." I cover her hand with mine, adjusting her pressure. "That's it. Good."

Pleasure spears through me at the touch—imperfect and perfect all at once. The fact that she's learning me this way, choosing to offer this piece of herself, makes it feel bigger than just lust.

It feels like trust.

And I want to earn every fucking inch of it.

She experiments slowly at first, but she's watching me—really watching me—like she's studying the cause and effect of every breath I take. Every twitch of my fingers in her hair. Every rough exhale that escapes me when she does something just right.

And fuck, there's a lot she's doing right.

The longer she explores, the more her hesitation gives way to instinct. Her curiosity sharpens into boldness. Each stroke of her hand grows surer, more deliberate, and I can feel her confidence rising in the way her grip adjusts, the way her shoulders square. She wants this. Wants me undone beneath her.

"What about…" She glances up, lashes fanning as she leans in.

I barely hang on. That look? It could bring me to my knees.

"Start slow," I manage, fingers threading gently into her damp hair, anchoring me. "Just the tip. Use your tongue."

And then she does.

One tentative lick, one swirl—hot and wet and so fucking reverent—and my world narrows to the place where her mouth touches me.

"Holy shit." My voice is ragged, head tipping back as pleasure spikes through me. "That's… *Fuuuuck.*"

Words fail. Sanity splinters. My jaw clenches with the effort not to move, not to take over. But I won't. This is hers—her exploration, her control. And it wrecks me more than anything I've ever felt.

She pulls back, breath cool against my wet skin. I groan, hips twitching despite myself.

Then she takes me deeper. Too deep. Perfectly deep.

My hands fist in the sheets. My vision goes white at the edges, like a fuse has been lit low in my spine and it's burning fast toward detonation.

"Jesus, Aria—" Her name breaks from me like a prayer. Or a plea. Maybe both.

Every part of me is trembling, holding on by a frayed thread as she learns me with her mouth, her hands, her goddamn gorgeous eyes still locked on mine.

She wants to please me.

But I'm the one unraveling.

"Christ, you're a natural." The words scrape out of me, half prayer, half damnation, as I fist a hand in her damp hair. She moans softly around me, and the vibration punches straight through my spine, heat coiling deep in my gut.

"You sure you haven't done this before?" My voice is shot, barely holding.

She pulls back just enough to smirk, lips slick and eyes gleaming. "Maybe I just have excellent instincts."

Then she takes me again—deeper, slower, with intent that feels like worship—and I swear I nearly come right then.

The velvet slide of her tongue along the underside is pure sin, her suction so sharp and focused I groan out loud, head falling back as the edge rushes closer. My grip tightens, knuckles white, legs locked to keep from thrusting.

She finds a rhythm—perfect, practiced chaos—and flashes me a look that lands like a gut punch. Gone is the shy, uncertain heiress. In her place? A woman awakening to her power. Discovering how completely she can undo me.

"Use your hand too," I rasp, reaching down to guide her fingers to the base of my cock. "Tight, but not too tight."

She follows my lead, her touch curious, responsive. Intent.

"Twist slightly, like this…" I wrap my hand over hers, guiding her through the motion. "Yeah—fuck—that's it."

She catches on fast. Learns me faster. Every shift, every stroke perfectly synced to the sounds dragging out of me like confessions I never meant to give voice to.

"Squeeze harder at the base," I pant. "Lighter at the top. Just like that—yes."

My hand falls away, useless now, because I can't not let her take over. Because she's driving this now, and I'm barely keeping it together.

When my hips jerk forward, instinct overpowering control, I grit out, "Sorry."

She pulls off me, just enough to say, "Don't be." And fuck me, that tone—confident, commanding—is the hottest thing I've ever heard.

"Your other hand," I choke out. "Cup my balls. Gentle, firm."

She obeys instantly, and the moment she does—mouth, hand, both hands—my body loses the plot.

A broken sound tears from my throat. Raw. Animalistic. My head drops forward, eyes locked on the impossible sight of her on her knees, wrapped around me like she was made for this.

"Aria," I growl, voice shredded. "Fuck, baby, you keep going like that…"

I don't finish the warning. Can't. Because I'm too close. Too far gone.

And she knows it.

"Fucking perfect," I groan, head thudding back against the wall as the orgasm rips through me—raw, unrelenting, electric. It detonates in waves, my entire body locking tight before shuddering loose under her mouth, her hands, her unwavering focus.

And goddamn, she stays with me through it. Every twitch. Every tremble. Never looking away.

By the time I come back to myself, she's easing off me, sitting back on her heels with a flushed face, lips swollen and slick. She wipes her chin with the back of her hand, hesitating as if she's not sure if she did it right.

And all I can do is stare.

Aria Holbrook. The elegant, guarded woman who walked into my life with diamond armor and fire in her eyes—on her knees, mouth-wrecked, looking up at me with tentative pride and the barest hint of vulnerability.

The image brands itself behind my eyes. Permanent. Fucking sacred.

"Was that okay?" she asks softly, as if the answer isn't already written all over my fucked-out expression, in every shuddering breath still dragging through my lungs.

I haul her up into my arms before she can second-guess herself again, crushing my mouth to hers in a kiss that's all teeth and gratitude, messy and consuming. I don't give a damn where her mouth just was. It's mine, and I want it again and again.

When I finally pull back, I'm grinning like a lunatic. Still dazed. Still shaking.

"Holy shit. That was easily the best fucking head I've ever had." My voice comes out hoarse, reverent. "And you said you've never done that before? Christ."

She laughs, and it's that unguarded, startled kind of joy that punches straight through my chest. Pure. Beautiful.

"You, my darling," I murmur, brushing damp hair back from her face, "are a fucking natural." I keep my arm around her, holding her against my chest like I can't stand the idea of space between us. "We're definitely going to do that again. Often."

Her eyes spark at the praise, heat, and satisfaction glowing where hesitation used to live. "I had an excellent teacher."

"Damn right you did." I kiss her again—gentler this time. A promise, not a demand.

We linger in the afterglow, trading soft kisses, idle touches, both of us reluctant to move from the cocoon of warmth between us. But eventually, her stomach growls, loud enough to make her laugh again.

"Okay," I chuckle, finally dragging myself upright, still a little unsteady. "Time to feed the beast." I head for the kitchen, pausing with the fridge open, bare-assed and unapologetic. "Pancakes?"

She leans in the doorway, wrapped in a towel, hair mussed and face flushed, looking every bit like temptation incarnate.

"Only if you make them shirtless."

I arch a brow. "That a kink I should know about?"

"Only if you flip them with those sexy forearms." Her smile is smug, playful, and God help me, I want to take her right there against the counter.

"Hope you're hungry, baby. Because after breakfast, I'm returning the favor."

"Is there anything you're not good at?" She settles onto the barstool, towel still clutched like she's forgotten to let go.

I snort, cracking eggs one-handed into a bowl. "Plenty. Dancing, for one. Two left feet. Charlie tried to teach me once, an undercover op where we had to blend in. Nearly broke her toes."

Her smile falters. Just for a second. Not jealousy. Something quieter. Uncertainty, maybe. The way her fingers tighten around the edge of the stool betrays the thought behind the look.

"You miss them?" she asks, voice low. "Working with them, I mean."

"In some ways." I stir the eggs, let the silence stretch a beat longer than necessary. "We had rhythm. Trusted each other without needing to speak."

She doesn't press, but the weight of her gaze lingers.

"Things change. Teams evolve." I add milk, whisking until the mixture froths. "They've got their life now. I'm building mine, with you, I hope."

She nods. Some of the tension in her posture loosens.

"What's on your agenda today?"

"Training drill at HQ." I pour batter onto the griddle, the sizzle cutting through the quiet. "Jenny's been running us hard since Charlie and Brett stepped down. Making sure we still operate like a single mind."

"What kind of training?"

I flip the first pancake. Golden, perfect.

"Everything. Endurance, weapons, and tactical response. But the real test is in the cohesion—how fast we adapt. Read each other. Move like one unit."

"Sounds intense."

"It is." I slide a stack onto a plate and nudge it toward her. "Anyone can learn to shoot. But knowing when not to—when to wait, to cover, to trust your team—that's where it matters."

She drizzles syrup, biting in with a moan that nearly derails all my good intentions.

"These are obscene," she mumbles through a mouthful. "I might love you for these."

"My mom's recipe." I smirk. "Sunday mornings smelled like butter and vanilla and a million arguments over who got the last one."

We eat in a silence that doesn't feel empty. It feels earned. Warm. Lived-in. Her leg brushes mine under the counter, and neither of us pull away.

When I finally glance at the clock, I curse under my breath. "Shit. If I'm late, Jenny'll skin me alive. Last guy to show up ten minutes late, ran laps until he puked. Then mopped the whole gym."

Aria's eyes widen. "Jenny sounds terrifying."

"She's brilliant, brutal, and has zero tolerance for bullshit." I rinse our plates, setting them in the drying rack. "Once, she made Charlie do burpees for an hour straight because Charlie answered a text during a briefing."

"Oof. Okay, yeah. Terrifying." Aria winces in solidarity. She stands, stretching with a soft sound that draws my attention straight to the exposed line of her throat. "I should check in at the shop. Ember's been texting."

"What'd you tell her?" I dry my hands.

"That I was engaged in high-level business negotiations." Her mouth curves with mischief.

"Is that what we're calling it?"

I close the distance, one hand finding her waist, the other tilting her chin. She rises onto her toes, pressing her body against mine like it's the most natural thing in the world.

"Very important negotiations," she murmurs. "Highly satisfactory outcome for all parties involved."

"Glad to hear it." I kiss her—slow, deep, a promise tucked into every pass of my lips over hers.

We move around each other with a rhythm that feels older than it is—passing shirts, brushing shoulders, sharing the mirror. I hand her one of my shirts to replace the one we destroyed last night, and she slips it on without hesitation. It hangs loose on her frame, swallowing her in cotton and the scent of me. Something primal stirs in my gut.

At the door, I tug her close again. One last kiss. One last brush of lips against skin before the day starts pulling us apart.

"Dinner?" I ask. "My place again?"

"I'd like that." She smooths the front of my shirt, fingers lingering at the collar like she belongs there. Like she's always belonged there.

"Good luck at training." She lifts on tiptoe to kiss my cheek.

"Stay out of trouble," I warn, opening the door for her.

"Where's the fun in that?" She glances back over her shoulder with a wink that hits like a match to dry kindling.

I watch her walk to her car, the early sunlight turning her hair to gold, and stand there until she pulls away, my heart thudding, and my pulse still echoing her name.

Only when she's gone do I head to my truck, already calculating how fast I can get through the day and back to her.

FOURTEEN

Aria

———

JON's SHIRT STILL SMELLS LIKE HIM—CEDAR AND SOMETHING
spicy, distinctively masculine. I catch myself inhaling deeply as I
push open the door to The Little Matchstick Girl, the brass bell
jingles announcing my arrival. Two hours later than usual, but
who's counting?

Ember, apparently.

She looks up from her workstation, a knowing smile
spreading across her face as she takes in my disheveled appearance and borrowed clothing. Even through the haze of scented
wax and essential oils filling the shop, I feel her amusement.

"Well, well, well. Look who the cat dragged in." Her smile
turns positively feline, green eyes gleaming with mischief.

"Good morning to you too." I set my purse on the counter,
trying and failing to suppress my own smile. My body still hums
with the ghost of Jon's touch, a pleasant soreness in muscles I'd
forgotten I had.

"It's almost noon," she points out, eyebrows raised as she
gestures to the vintage clock on the wall. "And that's definitely
not your shirt."

I glance down at Jon's black shirt, several sizes too big and rolled at the sleeves to keep my hands free. The soft cotton against my skin feels like an embrace, a reminder of this morning's goodbye.

"Very observant," I reply, aiming for dry but landing somewhere closer to smug.

"So." She sets down the candle she's working on and leans forward, elbows on the worktable, wax-stained fingers tented beneath her chin. "What kept you? Or should I say who?"

Heat rises to my cheeks, but I don't mind her teasing. This easy friendship we've built still surprises me sometimes—the socialite and the street kid, now business partners and confidantes. If anyone had told me six months ago that I'd be standing in a candle shop in borrowed clothes, trading innuendos with a former street kid, I'd have called them delusional.

Yet here we are, and it feels more real than anything in my previous life.

"I was conducting important business negotiations." I primly echo the text I sent her earlier when she bombarded me with question marks and fruit and vegetable shaped emojis.

"Oh, I'll bet you were." Ember laughs, the sound bright and knowing. "With Jon, I'm guessing? Since you're wearing his shirt and all."

From the corner, Ryn glances up from where she's carefully placing crystal inclusions in her signature gemstone candles. She's still finding her footing after everything she's been through, but she's talented, with an eye for beauty that transforms Ember's practical creations into works of art.

Barely eighteen, Ryn seems both younger and older than her years—her slender frame and wide eyes giving her a deceptive fragility, while the shadows behind those eyes speak of experiences no one should have to endure.

"Fine, yes." I move behind the counter, checking the register out of habit. The familiar routine grounds me, bringing me back from memories of Jon's bedroom to the present moment. "I was with Jon."

"And?" Ember prods, not about to let me off that easily. She abandons her workstation to follow me, the scent of cinnamon and clove clinging to her clothes.

"And, what?" I busy myself with straightening a display of travel-sized candles, though it doesn't need it. The glass containers catch the morning light, sending prisms dancing across the polished wood counter.

"Oh, come on." She hip-checks me gently, her voice dropping to a conspiratorial whisper. "Details. How was it? Is he as intense in bed as he is in the field?"

The memory floods back unbidden—Jon's hands pinning mine above my head, his voice rough against my ear, commanding me to stay still. The weight of his body over mine, controlled yet barely contained. A shiver races down my spine, my skin prickling with goosebumps despite the shop's warmth.

"I don't kiss and tell," I manage, though the flush creeping up my neck probably tells its own story.

"That good, huh?" Ember grins, green eyes dancing. "I knew it. The quiet, intense ones always are."

I can't help but laugh, the sound releasing some of the giddy energy bubbling inside me.

"Alright, fine. It was…" I search for a word that won't reveal too much while still acknowledging the seismic shift I feel. "Educational."

"Educational?" She raises an eyebrow, her expression incredulous. "That's the word you're going with? Not mind-blowing? Earth-shattering? Religious experience?"

"Among others." I bite my lower lip, the memories of the morning still fresh enough to warm my blood. His hands in my hair, on my hips, guiding me with gentle insistence. "He's very—directive."

"Bossy in bed? Called it." Ember's eyes widen with delight, her smile turning triumphant. She lowers her voice further, though Ryn is the only other person in the shop, seemingly absorbed in her work across the room. "Something about these military types. They're used to giving orders, and damn if it isn't hot when they bring that energy to the bedroom."

The casual revelation makes me curious. I've wondered about Ember and Blaze, how their relationship works. They seem such opposites—her fiery independence against his steady command presence.

"So Blaze is...?" I leave the question hanging, not wanting to pry too deeply, but genuinely curious.

"Dominant as hell." Ember nods, a slight flush coloring her cheeks, making the faint scattering of freckles stand out. "First time we were together, he literally picked me up and pinned me against the wall. Didn't even make it to the bedroom."

The image is vivid and not entirely surprising. Blaze, with his imposing presence and intense hazel eyes, strikes me as a man accustomed to taking control. The thought of him and tiny, fierce Ember together creates an interesting picture.

"Jon's like that too," I admit, keeping my voice low as I arrange candles that don't need arranging. "Last night he just—took over. And this morning—" I stop, suddenly self-conscious about how much I'm revealing.

"This morning...?" Ember prompts, eyes gleaming with interest as she leans closer.

I glance around, confirming we're still alone except for Ryn, who remains focused on her work.

"He had me put my hands above my head. Told me not to move them." The memory sends another wave of heat through me, settling low in my belly. "And when I did move them, he..." I trail off, still not quite believing how much I enjoyed his reprimand.

"He, what?" Ember's practically vibrating with curiosity now, her attention laser-focused.

"He stopped. Completely." I shake my head, remembering my frustration, the desperate need to touch him. "Made me put them back. Said if I couldn't follow instructions, he'd stop altogether."

Ember lets out a low whistle. "And did you behave after that?"

"Completely." I laugh softly, surprised by my own admission. "It was… God, I never thought I'd be into that. I've spent my entire life fighting against being controlled. My father micromanages every aspect of my existence. The idea of voluntarily giving up control to someone else should be my worst nightmare."

"It's different when you choose it," Ember says, her expression suddenly serious, voice thoughtful. "When it's play, not real control. When it's someone you trust." She shrugs, fingers toying with a chunk of beeswax. "With Blaze, I know I can say stop, and he will. Immediately. No questions asked. That's what makes it okay to let go—knowing I still have the power to take it back."

Her insight strikes me like a revelation. She's right—what Jon and I share isn't about him controlling me. It's about me choosing to yield, knowing I could take back control at any moment. The difference between a cage and a sanctuary.

"Exactly." The truth settles in my bones. "That's exactly it."

A small sound from across the room draws our attention. Ryn stands frozen, a polished rose quartz crystal halfway inserted into melted wax, her face pale beneath her auburn hair. She blinks rapidly, gaze fixed on the candle in front of her.

"Ryn?" Ember's voice softens with concern, all teasing gone. "You okay?"

The girl nods jerkily, not meeting our eyes. "Fine," she says, but her hand trembles slightly, disturbing the perfect surface of the wax.

Shit. In our enthusiasm to share experiences, we completely forgot about Ryn's history. Of course, talk about dominant men and control would upset her after what she'd been through. How insensitive could we be?

I cross the room, stopping a respectful distance from her workspace. The scent of lavender and sage rises from her candles, calming and protective.

"I'm sorry, Ryn. That was thoughtless of us."

"God, I'm such an idiot." Ember joins us, her expression stricken. "We shouldn't have been talking about that stuff with you here."

"No, please." Ryn finally looks up, her expression complicated—not quite distress, but something harder to define. "You don't have to stop on my account."

"We don't want to make you uncomfortable," I say gently.

"You're not. Not really." She sets down her crystal, wiping her hands on her apron with deliberate care. "It's actually… It helps. In a weird way."

"Helps?" Ember asks, confused.

Ryn nods, a strand of auburn hair falling across her face. She tucks it behind her ear with a self-conscious gesture. "Hearing you talk like that. About—sex. Like it's normal. Fun." Her voice drops on the last word, as if testing how it feels in her mouth. "That you can still be in control…"

"It *should* be fun," Ember says softly.

"I know." Ryn takes a deep breath, her narrow shoulders rising and falling. "And I need to hear that. Especially after— everything."

The weight of unspoken history hangs between us. We know pieces of Ryn's story—snippets she's shared. Enough to understand the horror she escaped, but not the full picture.

"It's not what you think, though," she continues, her voice steadying. "What happened to me. Or what didn't happen."

"What do you mean?" I'm careful to keep my tone neutral and non-pressuring.

Ryn's fingers trace the edge of a crystal, the repetitive motion seeming to calm her. "I wasn't... They didn't..." She takes another breath, deeper this time. "They never touched me. That way."

Ember and I exchange confused glances. The trafficking ring that had taken Ryn specialized in selling young women to wealthy buyers. We naturally assumed...

"I was supposed to be auctioned." Ryn's voice turns flat, matter-of-fact, a defense mechanism I recognize all too well. "High-dollar sale. They keep the merchandise pristine for that kind of transaction."

The clinical way she refers to herself—merchandise—makes my stomach turn. I've spent my life among the ultra-wealthy, have seen the casual objectification of women in those circles, but this is something far darker.

"They told me I'd fetch a premium price because I was..." She looks down at her hands, slender fingers stained with wax and oils. "Because I've never been with anyone."

The revelation settles between us like a stone dropped in still water, ripples of understanding spreading outward. Not horror at abuse suffered, but horror at what almost happened. What would have happened if Guardian HRS hadn't found her in time.

"I'm eighteen, although they thought I was much younger," she continues, her voice stronger now. "Most of the other girls were... Younger, that is. The men who buy girls pay extra for firsts."

The casual brutality of the statement lands hard. I think of my own first time—awkward, fumbling, with a prep-school boyfriend who'd been as nervous as I was. The luxury of that normal experience, which I'd taken for granted, now seems impossibly precious.

"I'm sorry," I say again, the words hopelessly inadequate. "We shouldn't have been so flippant."

"No, really, it's okay." Ryn looks up, a small smile ghosting across her face. "It's actually—nice. Hearing you talk about choice. About trust." She picks up her crystal again, turning it in the light so it catches fire with inner colors. "Someday, maybe I'll have that too. With someone who sees me as a person, not a-a thing to be bought."

The simple statement, full of quiet hope, brings unexpected tears to my eyes. At eighteen, I'd been focused on college applications and social status. Ryn, at the same age, is rebuilding a life from shattered pieces, finding the courage to hope for something as basic as human connection.

Ember reaches out, squeezing Ryn's shoulder gently. "You will," she promises, her voice fierce with conviction. "When you're ready. On your terms."

Ryn nods, returning to her work with renewed focus, carefully placing the rose quartz in its wax bed. "So," she says, the deliberate change of subject clear, "Jon makes you keep your hands above your head?"

"Yes. He did." The unexpected question startles a laugh from me.

"And you like it?" There's genuine curiosity in Ryn's voice, no judgment.

"I do." The honesty feels like freedom. "I really did."

"Huh." She considers this, head tilted thoughtfully. "And Blaze pins you to walls?" This directed at Ember, who grins.

"Among other things."

"Good to know." Ryn nods again, absorbing this information with serious consideration.

"For future reference?" Ember asks, a teasing note returning to her voice.

"Maybe." The smile that crosses Ryn's face this time is real, if fleeting. "When I'm ready."

Ember and I retreat to give her space, moving to the small office at the back of the shop. The room smells of paper and ink, with hints of the various candles that have passed through over time. I sink into the chair behind the desk, the gravity of what Ryn shared settling on me.

"I keep forgetting how young she is," Ember murmurs once we're out of earshot, leaning against the doorframe. "Not much younger than us, but——"

"A lifetime of difference. For me, at least." At twenty-five, I feel ancient compared to Ryn's eighteen years, though the gap is small in actual time. "And how much she's been through."

"She's remarkably resilient." Ember's eyes drift back to where Ryn works, her movements precise and focused.

"Aren't we all?" I observe, thinking of Ember's own journey from living on the streets as a kid to a business owner. "Survivors adapt."

"Some are better than others." Her smile is wry as she pushes off from the doorframe. "Back to work. Those candles won't pour themselves."

The rest of the morning passes in comfortable productivity. Ember works on a new winter collection, the scents of pine and cinnamon filling the shop. Ryn meticulously crafts her crystal candles, each one unique and stunning. I handle customers, review inventory, and finally settle at the desk to tackle the paperwork I've been avoiding.

Miranda's business proposal sits at the top of the stack, my father's handwritten notes visible in the margins. The heavy cream stationery bears the Holbrook Pharmaceuticals watermark

—my father never misses an opportunity to brand himself, even in personal correspondence.

I open the folder and scan the executive summary. The strategy is aggressive—triple production, move to larger commercial space, automated manufacturing, and wider distribution within eighteen months. National presence within three years.

It's a sound business plan. The projections are realistic, the growth attainable. It would mean significant profit and notable success in the business world my father understands.

It would also mean the end of what makes The Little Matchstick Girl special.

I flip through the pages, noting my father's annotations in his precise, slanted handwriting. *"Eliminate artisanal processes—inefficient." "Outsource crystal work—too labor-intensive." "Standardize product line—reduce to 5-7 core offerings."*

Each note feels like a knife to what we've built. To what Ember created. To the purpose that has given Ryn a new start.

I close my eyes, remembering the weight of Jon's body over mine this morning, the security of his arms around me. The way he looked at me when I told him about my father's expectations.

"You deserve to make your own choices," Jon's voice was rough with conviction. *"Not his. Yours."*

I glance through the office doorway. Ember stands at her workbench, head bent in concentration as she carefully measures essential oils, testing different combinations. The tip of her tongue peeks out between her teeth, a sign of intense focus I've come to recognize. Across the room, Ryn places a final crystal in a candle, her face lighting up with quiet satisfaction at the result.

This is the heart of our business. Not efficiency, not standardization, not market share. This is passion, craftsmanship, and a human touch.

I close the folder with a decisive snap. My father's vision for The Little Matchstick Girl is not *our* vision.

Pulling out my phone, I compose a text to my father. I type, delete, retype, struggling to find the right balance between respectful and firm:

"Reviewed Miranda's proposal. Cannot proceed as outlined. Fundamental misalignment with our brand identity and values. Will develop an alternative strategy that preserves the core business while allowing sustainable growth. Can discuss further at dinner Sunday."

My finger hovers over the send button. This is more than rejecting a business plan. It's the first time I've directly opposed my father's vision for my life. The first real step toward independence, toward becoming the woman Jon sees when he looks at me, capable, strong, worthy of making her own decisions, rather than the child my father sees.

I press send.

The response is almost immediate; my phone buzzing in my hand before I can set it down:

"Unacceptable. My office. 7pm tonight."

Not a request. A summons, delivered with the expectation of unquestioning obedience.

My stomach tightens with familiar anxiety, the lifetime habit of wanting to please him, to earn his approval. For a moment, I'm eight years old again, standing in his study as he coldly lists my shortcomings.

But beneath that old fear, something new takes root. Determination. Resolve. I think of Ember's fierce independence, of Ryn's quiet courage. Of Jon's faith in me.

I set the phone down without replying. Whatever comes next, I've made my choice. For Ember, for the business we've built together. For the vision of who I'm becoming.

For myself.

FIFTEEN

Jon

———

THE COMBAT KNIFE SLICES THROUGH THE AIR INCHES FROM MY throat. I twist, letting momentum carry the blade past as I pivot into my attacker's space. One hand traps the wrist, the other drives the heel of my palm under the chin. Not enough force to cause damage.

Enough to make a point.

"Dead." I release my hold on Razor. "That's three."

"Lucky counter." Razor rubs his jaw with a grudging half-smile.

His dark eyes narrow, already calculating his next approach. In the short time we've been training together, I've come to respect his quick adaptability and focused intensity.

"Luck had nothing to do with it." I step back, resetting my stance on the training mat. "You telegraph with your shoulder. Every time."

Sweat drips down my spine, soaking the back of my shirt. We've been at this for nearly two hours, and neither of us show any sign of calling it quits. Across the training facility, Storm and

Mac run shooting drills, the rhythmic pop of suppressed rounds punctuating our sparring session.

It's only been a few weeks, but already, I see it—Storm's voice carrying across the range, the easy rhythm of his movements syncing with Mac's timing. Razor falling into step during drills without needing to be told twice.

The edges are starting to smooth out. Personalities clicking into place. The new dynamic forming its own shape.

Not a replacement of Charlie and Brett.

Just—something new that works.

Razor circles, danger radiating from his powerful frame. Former Navy SEAL, he moves with that silent, deadly control— like violence lives just under his skin, waiting for an excuse to surface. He's a man who's spent years perfecting the art of violence. Every step, every shift of muscle, honed by years of breaking bodies and walking away. His knife flips between his fingers—a nervous habit rather than showmanship.

"Again." He drops into a fighter's crouch.

I mirror his stance, watching for the tell I know is coming. Despite the exhaustion burning in my muscles, a familiar calm settles over me—the clarity that comes with combat.

This is simple. This makes sense. This I understand.

The attack comes faster this time. A feint high, then the real thrust low toward my kidney. I pivot, catching his forearm, using his momentum to throw him off balance. We grapple, a controlled chaos of blocks and counters. He's good—better than good.

But experience trumps raw talent.

I lock his arm, twist, and suddenly he's face down on the mat, my knee in his back, training knife pressed against his carotid.

"And four." I release Razor's arm and step back. He stays down a beat longer, breathing hard, then grabs my hand. I haul him up.

He winces, sweat dripping down his neck.

"Better." I grab a towel off the bench and toss it at his chest. "You almost got me with the feint."

"Almost doesn't count for shit," he mutters, toweling off.

"It does here. That's the gap between dead and not-dead. You keep closing it."

"Still feels like getting my ass kicked."

From the doorway comes slow, sarcastic applause.

Storm leans against the frame, grinning widely, water bottle tucked under one arm. "Razor, are you seriously getting folded by Delta-Three again?"

"Step in the ring, I'll fold you next." Razor flips him off.

Storm strolls in, easy swagger, shirt damp, hair still wet from his last workout.

"You'd have to land a hit first. I watched that last round. I've seen toddlers move with more unpredictability."

"Bite me," Razor says, but there's no real heat.

"Tempting, but you're not my type." Storm grins, takes a long drink, then jerks his chin toward me. "Besides, I know better than to throw hands with Jon unless I've updated my will."

"Smart choice." I grab my water, crack the cap.

The three of us breathe in the stillness—sweat cooling, adrenaline thinning, just the low hum of the ventilation system above and the distant clank of weights from the other room.

"You know, I was thinking about this earlier—something weird about our team setup." Storm wipes his mouth, still watching me.

"Just one thing?" I give him a look.

He smirks. "Blaze has his callsign. Razor's got his. Hell, even Mac's stuck with his because, let's be real, the guy's built like a damn truck."

"Dude's a walking refrigerator with arms." Razor chuckles.

"Exactly. And Jenny?" Storm asks.

"No one's dumb enough to slap a name on her. She'd rip you in half." I can't help the cheeky grin. I almost want him to *try* to see the fireworks.

"You're the only one who's just… Jon." Storm's eyes stay locked on mine. "What gives?"

"Nobody ever gave you one?" Razor turns toward me.

"Plenty tried." I twist the cap off and take a drink. Cold water, sharp in the back of my throat. "None of 'em stuck."

"You? Quiet. Unshakable. Intimidating as hell. No callsign?" Storm tilts his head. "That's just—unsettling, man."

"Don't." I point my bottle at him, voice low but clear. "Don't start."

"I'm just saying… It's a missed opportunity." Storm's grin sharpens.

"Try giving Jenny a nickname," I say. "If you survive that, we can revisit the topic."

Razor laughs.

"Hey, I like living." Storm's brows pinch together, thinking. "I'll start with something easier. Like poking a bear with a short stick." He's still smiling. Still thinking.

"I suggest you don't…" I know damn well he's not letting this go.

"Sounds like a challenge." Razor chuckles.

"It's not." I glance between them. "You try and stick me with something, I'll make you regret it."

"Alright, alright. Damn." Storm whistles low, hands raised in mock surrender.

But he's still smiling and already filing through options, as if a challenge's been issued, whether I meant it or not.

And just like that, the room feels different.

The rhythm between them—the joking, the shots thrown and caught without flinching—it's starting to land.

Not forced. Not artificial.

Just—settling.

The team is starting to click, and that should feel good. It should feel like progress, but something in me resists because it's happening too fast. Faster than I thought it would.

Storm with his constant grin and restless energy. Razor running sharp with something to prove. They're filling the space where Charlie's quiet steadiness used to be. Where Brett's dry, bone-deep loyalty used to hold the line beside me.

They stepped away. Left Guardian HRS to start their next chapter—family, peace, and an everyday life. They earned it, but I'm still here.

Still carrying the weight.

Still watching the gaps close around me as if the shape of this new team was always meant to form.

"Earth to Jon." Storm's voice breaks through, a hand waving casually in front of my face. "You in there?"

I blink, drag my thoughts back. "Yeah." I clear my throat. "Just thinking we should wrap it up. After-action review in fifteen."

"Copy that." Razor's already tugging on his shirt.

Storm lingers half a second longer, gaze steady. He doesn't ask. Doesn't push. Just nods once, then follows Razor out.

I roll my shoulders, working out the lingering tension. The facility hums around me—the sound of professionals honing their craft. The steady rhythm of gunfire from the range, the distant clack of keyboards from the tech hub where Mitzy's team works their magic.

My phone vibrates in my gym bag. A message lights up the screen, bringing an involuntary smile to my face. The sight of Aria's name triggers something warm in my chest.

"Hey." I press the phone to my ear, suddenly aware of how much I've missed her voice today.

"Jon." My name in her mouth carries a tension that instantly puts me on alert. "I need a favor, and I completely understand if you can't, but I'm kind of desperate."

"What's wrong?" I'm already moving toward the Delta team's bullpen.

"My father." The two words carry volumes of complication. "He demanded I come to his office at seven tonight for some 'urgent business discussion' that can't wait, but I managed to negotiate dinner at Mastro's instead. I—I don't want to face him alone."

I pause by my locker, weighing the implications of what she's not saying. Marcus Holbrook—billionaire, power broker, and Aria's father—remains unaware of our relationship. Aria's choice, and one I've respected, though the secrecy sits uneasily with me. Asking me to join her represents a significant shift in her approach to our relationship.

"What do you need?"

"Come with me?" A pause, then, "I know it's last-minute, and probably crossing all kinds of lines since I've been keeping you secret from him, but—"

"I'll be there." The decision comes without hesitation. "What time?"

The relief in her voice is palpable. "Seven, at Mastro's. God, thank you. You have no idea—"

"Aria." I cut through her stream of gratitude. "It's fine. I've got your back. I'm just surprised you want me there, given how careful you've been about keeping us separate from your father."

"I know. But after today…" She sighs with a heaviness I want to lighten. "I rejected his business expansion plans for the shop, and I'm done hiding parts of my life from him. It's time."

"Whatever you need, it's yours." Her words send a rush of pride through me.

"That's why I—" She stops herself. "That's why you're you."

The unspoken words hang between us, a bridge neither of us is quite ready to cross. Not yet. I smile into the phone.

"I need to clean up. I'll meet you at the shop at six?"

"Perfect. And, Jon? Brace yourself. He's… Well, he's Marcus Holbrook."

"I've faced worse." I keep my tone light, though we both know it's not entirely a joke.

SIXTEEN

Jon

———

After we disconnect, I shower quickly, my mind already shifting gears. As I'm changing into street clothes, the facility intercom crackles to life.

"Delta Team to Briefing Room One. Repeat: Delta Team to Briefing One."

The formal summons raises the hair on my neck. Briefing One is reserved for high-priority situations. Whatever this is, it's not routine.

I finish dressing in record time, then stride through the corridors of Guardian HRS's compound with growing unease.

Storm and Razor are already in the briefing room when I arrive, along with Mac, whose massive frame makes the tactical chair look like doll furniture. Jenny stands at the head of the table, deep in conversation with CJ and Blaze.

But it's the man standing by the window that raises my pulse. Forest—Guardian HRS's founder and the reason we all exist as a team. His presence at a standard briefing is unprecedented.

The room falls silent as I enter. Forest turns, his face unreadable as always. Our eyes meet, and he gives the barest nod of acknowledgment.

"Good. We're all here." His voice carries the weight of mountains.

Jenny takes her customary position at the briefing terminal. "We have a situation."

Before Jenny can continue, the door opens again.

Mitzy strides in, tablet in hand, her expression sharper than usual—calm, but with an edge.

"Sorry, I'm late." She slides into a chair, fingers moving across her screen. "Still pulling the threads together, but you need to see this."

The main display lights up with surveillance footage—an exterior camera feed from a warehouse lot, timestamped three nights ago.

"This was a chemical supply facility in Houston. Not military, but with restricted access and decent private security. On paper, nothing about it screams high-value. But three nights ago, it got hit."

She switches to interior cams—grainy black-and-white footage of armed men rushing in. Hoodies, jeans, cheap masks. Not pro. But fast. Brutal.

"Twelve dead," Mitzy says. "All security or warehouse staff. Locals ruled it gang violence. Said it was a turf thing. But look…"

She zooms in on one of the attackers dragging a body. The guy's forearm is bare—a full tattoo sleeve, crudely inked. The wolf skull in the center is unmistakable.

"That's Night Pack." A sharp scrape of metal against tile—Blaze pushes back from the table, jaw tight, fists curled at his sides. "Motherfuckers," he mutters. "That's their mark."

He doesn't look at the screen. Doesn't need to. I see it in the way his whole body's gone still, coiled—like violence is a tide rising fast beneath the surface.

"Exactly." Mitzy taps to another angle. "Two of them had that same tat. Third had a version across his neck. It's not armor or insignia—but it's branding. And it's consistent."

"Night Pack?" Storm says it like a bad taste. "I thought they went down with Wolfe."

Jenny shakes her head. "We crippled their leadership, but the network's always been decentralized—local cells with their own muscle, same playbook."

"What were they after?" Razor asks. "Why hit a supply warehouse?"

Mitzy's jaw tightens. "Records show the facility was holding a short-term shipment of sedatives and paralytics. Medical-grade. Black-market value is high, especially if you're moving product."

No one needs her to explain what kind of *product*.

Children.

A knot tightens in my gut.

We thought we ended this. Six months ago, we raided Wolfe's compound. Rescued Aria and Ember. Ryn too. Burned the place down.

"But Wolfe is dead," Razor says, uncertain. "Ember killed him?" He looks around the room. "I read the reports."

The room goes still.

Forest steps forward, placing his hands flat on the table.

"We never recovered a body," he says quietly. "We assumed. The fire. The blast. But this?" He looks at the screen. "This doesn't feel like someone picking up the pieces. This feels like orders."

"From Wolfe?" The weight of it settles like concrete.

If he's alive—if Night Pack's rebuilding—then this isn't unfinished business.

It's the beginning of something worse.

"There's more." Mitzy swipes to a new image—a photograph taken in what appears to be a high-end shopping district. "This was captured yesterday in San Francisco."

The image shows a tall man in an expensive suit, face partially obscured by sunglasses. But even with the disguise, there's something familiar in the bearing, the way he carries himself.

"Facial recognition is inconclusive," Mitzy continues. "But gait analysis gives us an 87% match."

"Damien Wolfe." The name falls from my lips like a curse.

Forest straightens, his gaze sweeping the room. "As of this moment, we operate under the assumption that Damien Wolfe is alive and rebuilding Night Pack's operations. All previous targets should be considered at potential risk."

"Aria, Ember, and Ryn…" I meet Forest's eyes directly. "Previous targets."

"They won't get near her again." Blaze is already on his feet, fists clenched against the table, tension radiating off him in waves.

He doesn't say Ember's name. He doesn't have to. It's written in the tight line of his shoulders, the muscle ticking in his jaw.

"If Wolfe's moving pieces, this isn't about leverage—it's about revenge," Blaze says. "He's sending a message. We need to answer it."

"We will." Forest meets his eyes, something unreadable flickering across his features.

Jenny continues outlining preliminary security protocols, but my mind races ahead. If Damien Wolfe is alive, if he's rebuilding Night Pack, then Aria isn't just dealing with her father's controlling nature tonight. She's potentially walking back into the crosshairs of a man who nearly destroyed her life.

The briefing concludes with assignments for increased surveillance and intelligence gathering. As the team files out,

Forest remains, his stoic presence a gravitational force in the room.

"Jon." Forest's voice pulls me back to the moment. "A word, please."

I comply, years of military discipline kicking in automatically. Forest is a legend in our world, a man who built Guardian HRS from nothing into a premier private security and hostage rescue organization globally.

"Your relationship with Aria Holbrook." He doesn't phrase it as a question. "How serious is it?"

"Excuse me?" The directness catches me off guard.

"Don't insult either of us by pretending you don't know what I'm talking about, loverboy." His tone remains neutral, but his eyes don't miss a thing.

"Wasn't pretending. Just caught off guard." I weigh my response carefully. "It's—significant."

"I see." Forest leans back, fingers steepled. "And Marcus Holbrook's awareness of this significance?"

"Limited." I meet his gaze steadily. "Aria's choice, though that's changing tonight. She asked me to join her for dinner with him."

Forest nods slowly, as if confirming something to himself. "Marcus Holbrook is not just a wealthy man. He's powerful. The kind who makes problems disappear."

"I'm aware of his reputation."

"Are you?" A rare smile touches Forest's lips, there and gone in an instant. "Marcus and I have history. Complex history. When his daughter was taken, he came to me specifically because of that history."

This is new information. Forest's connection to our clients typically remains professional and detached. The implication of personal history with someone like Marcus Holbrook raises questions I'm not sure I want answered.

"Marcus Holbrook protects what he considers his, and he very much considers his daughter his to protect. Do you understand what I'm saying?"

"You're warning me off."

"I'm providing context. I've learned warning men off from the women they protect is an exercise in futility." Forest stands, moving back to the window. "Guardian HRS operates in the shadows by necessity. We cannot afford complications with clients of Marcus's caliber."

I feel my jaw tighten. "With respect, sir, my personal life—"

"Is inextricably linked to your professional one." Forest turns, his expression softening marginally. "I'm not telling you what to do. I'm certainly not telling you who you can and can't date. None of you listen to me anyway. I'm smarter than that, but I'm telling you to proceed with your eyes open. Especially now, with Night Pack potentially back in play."

My phone vibrates again. This time, I glance at the screen. A text from Aria: *Meet me at the shop?*

"I appreciate the concern." I stand, straightening my shoulders. "But I can handle Marcus Holbrook."

"For your sake, I hope that's true." Forest's expression suggests I've just claimed I could handle a hurricane with an umbrella. "If Damien Wolfe is targeting Aria again, Marcus will pull out all stops to protect her. Including removing anyone he perceives as—complicating factors."

The warning settles like ice in my veins. Not for my safety—Marcus is many things, but not a murderer—but for what it could mean for Aria. For us.

"I should go." I check my watch. "I'm meeting her at six."

Forest nods, dismissal clear. As I reach the door, his voice stops me.

"Jon." When I turn, something almost like concern shows on

his weathered face. "You're one of my best. Don't let personal feelings cloud your judgment when it matters most."

The advice—warning, really—follows me out into the corridor. I check my phone again, typing a quick reply to Aria: *On my way. Be there soon.*

As I head to my truck, Storm falls into step beside me, his expression unusually serious.

"So. Damien Wolfe." He keeps his voice low. "Think the boss is right?"

"Forest is always right. Whether I like it or not."

"And Aria?" Storm's question carries layers of meaning.

"Could be in danger again. Along with Ember, the shop, and everything they've built. Ryn too." Although I hope that's not the case.

"Want me to run surveillance tonight? I'll get Razor to join. Although I bet Blaze beats us to the shop. "Quiet, unobtrusive. Just an extra set of eyes while you're playing bodyguard at dinner."

"That would help. We're meeting Marcus at Mastro's." The offer reminds me why I trust this man with my life.

"Fancy." Storm grins, though it doesn't reach his eyes. "Wear your good suit, pretty boy."

I shoot him a look. "Just keep an eye on the shop. Razor can back you up. I don't want Ember or Ryn alone tonight."

"Consider it done." Storm claps me on the shoulder. "Watch yourself with Holbrook. Men like that don't share their toys easily."

"Aria isn't a toy."

"No." Storm's expression turns serious again. "But I doubt Daddy Warbucks sees it that way."

The observation follows me to my truck, mixing uneasily with Forest's warning and the specter of Damien Wolfe's return. As I navigate toward The Little Matchstick Girl, I can't shake the feeling that tonight's dinner is about to become much more than just an awkward meeting with Aria's father.

The shop comes into view, its warm glow a beacon against the darkening evening. Through the front window, Aria moves about, her graceful figure haloed by soft light. Something in my chest tightens at the sight—a feeling I'm still learning to name.

I park across the street, taking a moment to survey the area. Old habits. The commercial district is winding down for the evening, and most stores are closed or closing. A few pedestrians stroll the sidewalks, headed home or to dinner. Nothing out of place, nothing suspicious.

And yet…

My gaze catches on a sedan parked half a block down. Dark, nondescript. The kind designed to blend in. The driver's silhouette sits motionless, face obscured by the gathering dusk.

It could be nothing. A rideshare driver waiting for a fare. Someone checking their phone before heading home.

Or it could be something else entirely.

I exit my truck, making a show of checking my watch while angling for a better view of the sedan. As I do, it pulls smoothly away from the curb, merging into traffic.

Coincidence? Maybe.

But in my experience, coincidences are usually anything but.

My phone buzzes with a text from Razor: *In position at north corner. Storm taking south. Locked and loaded for Operation Dinner Date.*

Despite everything, I smile. Then I cross the street toward the warm light of the shop, toward Aria, and toward whatever complications the evening holds.

SEVENTEEN

Aria

—————

MY PHONE LIES FACE DOWN ON THE COUNTER, A SMALL
rectangle of doom I can't bring myself to check again. That two-line text from my father—"*Unacceptable. My office. 7 pm tonight.*"—still burns in my mind, the digital equivalent of a summons to the principal's office. Except that the principal is Marcus Holbrook, and disappointing him has consequences far beyond detention.

I take a deep breath, focusing on the task at hand. A middle-aged woman with kind eyes and an expensive handbag examines our winter collection, lifting each candle to inhale its scent.

"This one is incredible," she says, holding up Ember's newest creation. "What's in it?"

"Pine, cinnamon, and just a hint of vanilla." I move closer, grateful for the distraction. "Ember calls it 'Hearth and Home.' It's designed to evoke memories of holiday gatherings."

"It works." The woman closes her eyes and inhales deeply. "Reminds me of my grandmother's house when I was little."

From her workstation, Ember glances up with a small smile of satisfaction. Creating emotional connections through scent is her gift, her art. She understands intuitively how fragrance bypasses the rational mind, speaking directly to memory and emotion.

"I'll take three," the customer decides. "One for me, one for my sister, and one for my daughter. Can you gift wrap them?"

"Of course." I move behind the counter, pulling out our signature packaging—recycled paper embedded with wildflower seeds, tied with jute twine, and a sprig of dried lavender. Sustainable, beautiful, and distinctively ours.

As I wrap each candle, I can't help thinking about Miranda's proposal, still sitting in the office. *Standardize product line. Eliminate artisanal processes. Outsource.*

My father's vision would turn these hand-poured creations into mass-produced commodities. The personal touch—Ember's careful blending, my custom packaging, Ryn's crystal work—all sacrificed for efficiency and scale.

"Here you are." I hand over the beautifully wrapped package. "The paper can be planted in the spring. It'll grow California wildflowers."

"How lovely." The woman's delight confirms what I already know—these touches matter. They create connection, loyalty, and meaning beyond the product itself.

After she leaves, Ember wipes her hands on her apron and approaches the counter. "You okay? You've been staring at your phone like it might bite you."

"I texted my father." The words come out more strained than intended. "About Miranda's proposal."

"And?" Ember's expression turns guarded. Her relationship with my father has always been complicated—gratitude for his investment mixed with wariness of his control.

"I told him no." My voice strengthens as I say it aloud. "I said we can't proceed with the plan as outlined. That it doesn't align with our values."

Ember's eyebrows shoot up. "You told Marcus Holbrook no?"

A slow smile spreads across her face. "Damn, Aria. I didn't think anyone could do that and live to tell the tale."

"The jury's still out on the survival part." I flip my phone over, showing her his response. "He summoned me. Like a disobedient employee."

"That's bullshit. This is your business. Our business." Ember reads the text, her smile fading.

"Exactly." I square my shoulders. "That's why I'm not backing down. The Little Matchstick Girl isn't just a business opportunity—it's your creation. Your dream. I won't let him turn it into something unrecognizable."

"*Our* dream," Ember corrects gently. "I may have started it, but it's ours now. Yours and mine. And Ryn's too."

From across the shop, Ryn glances up at the sound of her name. She's arranging a display of her newest crystal candles— amethyst and clear quartz suspended in pale purple wax; the effect is ethereal and somehow hopeful.

"What's going on?" She approaches, wiping wax from her hands.

"Aria just stood up to her father." Ember's voice carries pride I'm not sure I deserve. "Told him we're not selling out."

"What did he say?" Ryn's eyes widen slightly.

"He's not happy." I try for casual, though my stomach knots at the thought of facing him tonight. "But that's not new. I've been disappointing Marcus Holbrook since I was about six years old."

"That's his problem, not yours." Ember's matter-of-fact tone cuts through my anxiety. "You're running a successful business, making your own choices. If that disappoints him, he needs to adjust his expectations."

The bell above the door chimes, interrupting our conversation. A young couple enters, holding hands and looking around with interest. Ember moves to greet them, slipping into her role as creator and guide.

"Welcome to The Little Matchstick Girl." Her smile is genuine and welcoming. "Is this your first visit?"

"Yes." The woman looks around, taking in the warm atmosphere. "It smells amazing in here."

"That's kind of our thing." Ember's laugh is easy and confident. "Each candle tells a story through scent. Are you looking for something specific?"

As she leads them through the shop, I'm struck again by how far she's come from the wary street kid I first met. The transformation isn't just in her circumstances but in her presence—the confidence of someone who knows her worth, who has built something meaningful with her own hands.

"This one is called 'Ocean Memory.'" Ember holds up a sea-glass blue candle. "Salt, citrus, and a hint of driftwood. It captures that moment when you're sitting on the beach at sunset, when the day's heat is fading and the first cool breeze comes off the water."

The couple exchange impressed glances. The man lifts the candle, inhaling deeply.

"Wow. That's exactly what it smells like." He looks at Ember with new respect. "How do you do that?"

"It's about understanding what makes a memory powerful." Ember's passion shines through as she explains her process. "Scent is the sense most directly connected to emotion. The right combination can transport you instantly to a specific moment in time."

"What about this one?" The woman points to a deep amber candle.

"'Campfire Stories.'" Ember smiles. "Smoke, pine, and marshmallow. For when you want to feel like you're sitting around a fire with your favorite people, telling stories under the stars."

They move through the shop, entranced by Ember's descriptions and the emotional journey she creates. This is what would be lost under my father's plan—the artistry, the personal touch, the connection between creator and customer.

My phone buzzes with another text. Not my father this time, but Jon: *Picking you up at 6:30 for dinner. Dress sexy.*

The message sends a flutter through my stomach, momentarily displacing my anxiety about facing my father. Jon is coming with me. I won't be alone.

"Good news?" Ember asks, returning to the counter after the couple leaves with four candles and Ryn's business card for a custom order.

"Jon's coming to dinner with me." I show her the text.

"Smart move." She nods approvingly. "Marcus's less likely to go full dictator with witnesses present."

"You underestimate his capacity for public tyranny." I sigh, tucking my phone away. "But yes, having Jon there will help."

"Your father's never met a man he couldn't intimidate or buy off." Ember begins cleaning her workspace, methodically organizing tools and ingredients. "I'm curious to see how he handles Jon."

"Jon can't be intimidated or bought," I say with complete conviction. After last night, after this morning, I know this with absolute certainty. "He's not motivated by money or power."

"Which makes him completely incomprehensible to your father." Ember's laugh holds a hint of satisfaction. "Oh, to be a fly on that wall. It should be an interesting dinner."

The bell chimes again, but this time it's not customers.

Storm and Razor step through the door, casual enough to fool a civilian—but their gazes sweep the shop with the precision of men trained to spot threats in their sleep.

"Ladies." Storm flashes a charismatic smile, the kind that should feel easy, but doesn't. "Just in the neighborhood, thought we'd stop by."

"Since when do you guys make social calls during working hours?" Ember's brows draw together, confusion hardening into wariness.

"Can't a guy visit his favorite candle shop?" Storm's tone is light, bordering on amused, but there's an edge beneath it. "Maybe I need another candle?"

Razor says nothing as he crosses to the front window, scanning the street, cataloging exits, shadows, and movement.

"Nice display," he mutters, but it's clear he's not looking at the jars of wax.

"Hey, everything okay?" Ryn steps out from the stockroom, ponytail swinging.

The moment Razor registers her, something shifts in his posture. Almost imperceptible—but I catch it. Shoulders relax. Head tilts. Eyes soften just a notch.

"Didn't know you were here," he says, voice low, almost thoughtful.

"Inventory day." Ryn grins, unaware—or maybe not—of the way his gaze lingers a fraction too long.

"You always do the labels by hand?" He nods toward the tray of calligraphy tags she carries, then steps closer to examine one, closer than necessary.

"I like the way it looks," she says. "Cleaner. More personal."

"Yeah. Looks good." His fingers brush the edge of a tag, not touching her, but close enough to notice her scent—citrus and clove from the oils she mixes.

My brows lift. Razor doesn't do small talk. Doesn't compliment, but here he is, all subtle shifts and soft edges.

The hair on the back of my neck prickles. Something's off.

These men don't show up together unless it's tactical—and whatever Razor's doing now, the rest of his body screams alert.

"What's going on?" I ask, stepping closer. "Why are you here?"

Storm and Razor exchange a glance, a silent confirmation of what I already suspect.

"Just keeping an eye on things," Storm says with a shrug that doesn't reach his eyes. "Jon asked us to swing by."

"Why would Jon—" I stop mid-sentence. "This is about my father, isn't it?"

Storm hesitates. And that tells me everything I need to know.

"Not exactly."

"Then *what* exactly?" Ember's voice sharpens, the old edge cutting through. "Because you're scaring off customers with the whole Men in Black routine."

Razor tears his gaze away from Ryn—reluctantly—and turns back toward us.

"Sorry. We'll tone it down." He gestures toward the back table. "Mind if we hang out for a bit? Promise we'll buy something."

"Better be the expensive stuff." Ryn arches a brow.

"Only the best." His grin flickers, real this time.

But even as he takes the seat closest to her station, I clock the way he angles his body—half-alert, half-interested. I can't tell which instinct is stronger.

"Is someone in danger?" I press. "Is it the shop?"

No one answers right away.

Which is an answer all by itself.

The men exchange another glance. Finally, Storm sighs.

"Look, it's probably nothing. Just some chatter that has Jon concerned. He thought it might be good to have extra eyes around until things settle."

"What kind of chatter?" Ember asks, her voice suddenly tight.

The bell chimes once more.

This time it's Jon.

His tall frame fills the doorway like he owns it—like he owns me. His broad shoulders, stormy eyes, and lethal calm are barely reined in. His gaze locks with mine the second he steps inside, and the noise of the shop fades to static.

Everything else disappears. The shop. The people. The air.

It's just him. And me.

Something inside me loosens, unclenches, breathes. Then tightens all over again at the look he gives me—dark, searching, and a little too intense.

He crosses the room in long, purposeful strides, no wasted movement. That quiet intensity that turns my blood to wildfire. His hand comes to rest at the small of my back—hot, firm, possessive.

But it's not just the way he touches me. It's the weight of memory behind it. That mouth on my thighs, my breasts, my name rasped against my skin as he shattered me, slow and unrelenting. The way he held me open with nothing but his voice, whispering filth and worship in equal measure.

The way he took his time.

The way he didn't.

I suck in a sharp breath, my body already reacting—spine straightening, thighs clenching, heat unfurling low in my belly.

"Hey." His voice is pitched for me alone, low and rough with something he doesn't bother to name. "You okay?"

"Yeah."

He doesn't move his hand. If anything, his fingers curl a little tighter against my back, like he doesn't want to let go.

"Good." His mouth finds mine, slow and molten—nothing frantic, nothing rushed. Just a kiss that owns. That seals the promise in his words with the heat of his mouth and the sure grip of his hand.

When he pulls away, I'm flushed, breathless, my whole body humming.

"Will you be okay here?" I turn to Ember, struggling to sound normal, to remember the world beyond Jon's kiss.

"We'll be fine." She gestures to Storm and Razor. "Apparently, we have our own security detail now."

"Just until closing," Razor clarifies.

Ember rolls her eyes but doesn't argue. She's been through enough to recognize when protection is necessary, even if she chafes at the constraint.

"Call me if anything happens," I tell her, gathering my purse. "Anything at all."

"You too." She meets my eyes directly. "And, Aria? Don't let your father bulldoze you about the business. We'll figure it out our way, whatever happens."

"Our way. Not his." I nod, drawing strength from her confidence.

Jon's hand settles at the small of my back as we exit the shop, the warm weight both reassuring and thrilling.

Whatever my father has planned, I'm not the same woman who was kidnapped months ago. I've changed—found my voice, my strength, my place.

And I've made my choice. Now I have to stand by it.

EIGHTEEN

Jon

Mastro's gleams like a polished gem in the evening light, all sleek lines and understated luxury. The kind of restaurant where the menu has no prices because if you need to ask, you can't afford it. The kind of place where Marcus Holbrook is undoubtedly a regular.

"Relax," Aria murmurs, her hand light on my arm as we approach the entrance. "You look like you're walking into an ambush."

"Force of habit." I manage a smile, though the comparison isn't far off. "Professional hazard."

She stops just short of the door, turning to face me. The transformation I've watched unfold during our drive here is complete now—Aria Holbrook, socialite daughter, poised and perfect. Her simple black dress and subtle jewelry scream money in the way only true wealth can—effortlessly. Even her posture has shifted, spine straighter, chin lifted, a polished armor sliding into place.

But her eyes—those haven't changed. They still look at me

with the same warmth, the same quiet strength that first drew me in.

"Thank you for doing this." Her voice drops, meant only for me. "I know it's not exactly how you wanted to spend your evening."

"I'm with you." I brush a strand of hair from her face, a small intimacy. "That makes it exactly where I want to be."

Her smile softens something in my chest. Then she takes a deep breath, squares her shoulders, and nods to the host who has appeared silently at the door.

"Ms. Holbrook." He inclines his head. "Your father is waiting in the private dining room."

Of course he is. Nothing so pedestrian as the main floor for Marcus Holbrook.

We follow the host through the dimly lit restaurant, past tables of power brokers and celebrities pretending not to notice each other. The private dining area occupies the rear of the building—exclusive, separated from the common folk by frosted glass doors that whisper open at our approach.

Marcus Holbrook rises from his seat at the sole table, his movement as precise as everything else about him. Tall, imposing, with silver-streaked dark hair and the kind of face that's never known uncertainty. His bespoke suit is impeccable, custom-tailored to his frame.

His eyes—so similar to Aria's in color but utterly different in warmth—widen fractionally at the sight of me. The only tell in his otherwise perfect composure.

"Aria, darling." He steps forward, pressing a kiss to her cheek. Then his gaze shifts to me, assessment as tangible as a physical touch. "I wasn't aware you were bringing a guest."

The words are neutral, but the undercurrent isn't. This is a man unaccustomed to surprises.

"Dad, you remember Jon, from Guardian HRS?" Aria's voice

carries just the right amount of casual lightness. "He's part of Delta team that—well, you know."

"Of course." Marcus extends his hand. His grip is firm, calibrated to convey strength without becoming a contest. "Mr. Knutt. I wasn't expecting to see you again under such—pleasant circumstances."

"Life is full of surprises, Mr. Holbrook." I match his pressure exactly.

A flicker of something—amusement? Irritation?—crosses his features. "Indeed, it is. Please, join us."

He gestures to the table, where a third place setting has already appeared as if by magic. The server who arranged it vanishes with the same silent efficiency.

I pull out Aria's chair, a small gesture that doesn't escape Marcus's notice. His eyes narrow fractionally as he retakes his seat.

"I must say, your timing is fortuitous." Marcus signals to the sommelier hovering nearby. "I was just telling Aria about some security concerns regarding our latest venture."

Our latest venture. Not "Aria's shop" or "the candle business." Ours. The distinction speaks volumes.

"Oh?" I accept the wine list with a nod to the sommelier, then pass it directly to Marcus. His territory, his rules—for now.

"The Château Margaux 2015," he tells the sommelier without consulting the list. "And bring the Krug Grande Cuvée for my daughter. She prefers champagne."

I glance at Aria, catching the slight tightening around her eyes. A small rebellion forms before I can think better of it.

"Actually," I address the sommelier directly, "Ms. Holbrook was telling me how much she enjoyed the Caymus Special Selection last time. Perhaps that instead?"

Marcus's eyebrow rises a fraction of an inch. The sommelier freezes, caught between conflicting authorities.

"The Caymus would be perfect." Aria's eyes sparkle, and the tiniest smile curves the corners of her lips. "Thank you, Jon, for remembering."

Score a point for Aria. Marcus inclines his head in gracious defeat, though something calculative enters his gaze as he studies me with renewed interest.

"Very well," he tells the sommelier. "The Caymus for my daughter and her—friend. The Margaux for me."

The brief power play settles, leaving charged silence in its wake. Marcus breaks it smoothly, turning to business like a shark returning to familiar waters.

"As I was saying, our expansion plans for The Little Matchstick Girl present certain security considerations. The increased inventory alone will require upgraded systems."

"Expansion plans?" I keep my tone neutral, though Aria's sudden tension beside me speaks volumes.

"Dad." Aria sets her napkin down with deliberate care. "We haven't finalized anything yet. Ember and I are still discussing options."

Marcus waves a dismissive hand. "Details, darling. The direction is clear. Miranda's projections show the growth potential is too significant to ignore."

"Miranda?" I glance at Aria.

"My father's business consultant." Her voice carries a tightness I've rarely heard. "She's been running numbers."

"At my request," Marcus adds smoothly. "And her findings are quite compelling. We're looking at potential national distribution within eighteen months."

We again. Aria's fingers curl around her water glass, knuckles whitening slightly.

"That's an aggressive timeline." I glance at Aria, wondering how hard I can push. She asked me here for a reason, and I've got her back. "Especially for an artisanal product."

"That's precisely what makes it such an attractive opportunity." Marcus leans forward, his intensity palpable. "The artisanal narrative provides excellent marketing leverage. Consumers love a good story—the street girl made good, the handcrafted touch. It differentiates in a crowded market."

The street girl made good. Ember reduced to a marketing angle. I catch the flash of anger in Aria's eyes before she masks it.

"Ember isn't a narrative, Dad." Her voice remains level, controlled. "And her candles aren't mass-market products."

"Not yet." Marcus's smile doesn't reach his eyes. "But with the right scaling strategies, proper quality control protocols—"

"The hand-crafting is the quality control." Aria sets her glass down with just enough force to create a small sound. "That's the entire point."

"Darling, I understand the emotional attachment." Marcus's expression softens into something patronizing. "It's charming, really, but business is business. Sentiment makes for poor strategy."

The sommelier returns with our wines, creating a brief respite in the tension. As he pours, I study Marcus Holbrook more carefully. This isn't just a controlling father. This is a man who genuinely cannot conceive of a world where his vision isn't the correct one—the only one.

The sommelier returns, and I accept the wine he pours, taking a moment to taste it properly. Marcus watches the ritual with barely concealed impatience.

"Mr. Holbrook." I wait until the sommelier retreats. "Having seen The Little Matchstick Girl's operations firsthand, I can tell you what makes it special is precisely what makes it difficult to scale. The craftsmanship, the personal touch—these aren't just marketing angles. They're the product."

"You seem unusually informed about candle making, Mr. Knutt." Marcus's gaze shifts to me, reassessing.

"Jon has been very supportive of the business." Aria's hand finds mine under the table, a silent *thank you.* "He understands what we're trying to build."

"Does he?" Marcus's eyes drop to where our hands have disappeared, though the tablecloth hides the actual contact. His expression remains pleasant, but something sharp enters his gaze. "How—involved have you become with my daughter's venture, Mr. Knutt?"

The double meaning hangs in the air between us. Before I can respond, a server appears with our appetizers—small plates of artfully arranged seafood.

"I've always believed in supporting local businesses." I meet his gaze directly. "Especially ones with integrity and vision."

"Admirable." Marcus samples his dish with appreciation. "Though I wonder if your expertise in security translates well to retail strategy. Different skill sets entirely."

"You'd be surprised what skills transfer." I keep my tone light. "Risk assessment, identifying vulnerabilities, distinguishing between actual value and perceived value—these apply in many contexts."

Marcus's mouth curves into something not quite a smile. "Indeed. Though in my experience, security professionals tend to focus on threats rather than opportunities. A necessarily limited perspective."

"Dad." Aria's voice carries a warning note. "Jon is here as my guest…"

"Of course, darling." Marcus dabs his mouth with his napkin. "Merely making conversation. After all, I should get to know your—*friends.*"

The slight pause before "friends" carries weighted implication. The game is now fully open. He knows. Or at least, he strongly suspects.

"Speaking of friends," Marcus continues smoothly,

"Hampton Greaves was asking after you just the other day. His son Julian is back from London. Perhaps a dinner?"

The suggestion hangs in the air like an expensive trap. Aria stiffens beside me.

"Julian Greaves?" I keep my tone casually curious. "The investment banker?"

"You're familiar with the Greaves family?" Marcus's eyes flick to mine, narrowing slightly at my knowledge.

"We've crossed paths." I don't elaborate that those paths involved pulling Julian out of a compromising situation in Monaco that would have embarrassed both his family and his firm. Client confidentiality still applies, even during uncomfortable dinner table conversations.

But Marcus's mentioning of Julian is deliberately aggressive, sending a clear message as to who he considers worthy of dating his daughter.

"Julian is focused on his career." Aria's dismissal is polite but firm. "As am I."

"One should never be too focused when advantageous connections are present." Marcus signals for our main courses. "The Greaves family has considerable influence in circles that could benefit your—candle shop."

The subtle diminishment in his tone when he mentions the shop doesn't escape me. Nor does the implication that Julian Greaves represents a more suitable match for his daughter than a security specialist.

"The shop is doing quite well without those particular connections." Aria's smile carries a practiced brightness that doesn't reach her eyes. "Our customer base grows every week."

"Yes, your little boutique operation has its charm." Marcus accepts his steak from the server with a regal nod. "But we're discussing real growth now. Scale. Significance."

"It's already significant." The words escape before I can filter them. "To the people who work there, and the customers who value what they create."

Marcus studies me over the rim of his wineglass. "Significance is measured in impact, Mr. Knutt. A few hundred candles sold to local customers is—*quaint*. Millions sold nationwide is *significant*."

"Different metrics for different values." I cut into my steak, perfectly cooked but somehow less appetizing than it should be. "Not everything worth doing scales well."

"An interesting philosophy." Marcus's tone suggests it's anything but. "Is that Guardian HRS's approach as well? Deliberately remaining small and—limited?"

The jab is precise, targeting both professional and personal goals. Aria once again tenses beside me, ready to intervene, but I touch her knee gently under the table.

"Guardian HRS is selective." I meet his gaze directly. "Quality over quantity. Depth over breadth. It's served us well, as you know." I'm not letting this bastard diminish Guardian HRS, especially since he owes his daughter's life to our rescue.

"I imagine it limits your earning potential considerably." Marcus smiles, but there's no warmth behind it. The curve of his lips is all performance—his eyes stay flat. It's the kind of smile meant to disarm, not to connect. "Security work is already a modest field, financially speaking. Deliberately constraining growth seems—unnecessarily restrictive."

"Dad." Aria's voice now carries a sharp edge. "That's enough."

"It's merely an observation, darling." He turns his attention back to his meal. "I'm sure Mr. Knutt is quite comfortable with his choices."

"Quite." I maintain my composure, though something hot and defensive burns beneath it. "Some of us define success beyond balance sheets."

"A luxury many can't afford." Marcus's eyes flick up, something almost like respect flickering briefly.

"Or a priority many choose to make." Aria's quiet contribution lands with unexpected weight. "Like I have with the shop."

A silent moment stretches between father and daughter—some private communication I'm not privy to. Marcus breaks it first, setting down his cutlery with precision.

"Which brings us back to the matter at hand." His tone shifts to business mode, the personal attack apparently complete for now. "I've scheduled meetings with potential investors for next week. People who understand vision and scale."

"You did what?" Aria's fork stills midway to her mouth.

"Several key players in the luxury retail space," Marcus continues as if her shock is merely a minor detail. "Miranda has prepared a comprehensive prospectus. With the right capital infusion, we could begin production expansion by quarter's end."

"Dad." Aria sets down her fork carefully, her control visibly tenuous. "We haven't agreed to any of this. Ember and I don't want to expand beyond our current operation."

"Discussions are well and good, darling, but opportunities have windows." Marcus makes a dismissive gesture. "These particular investors won't wait indefinitely."

"Then they can invest elsewhere." Aria's voice gains strength. "This isn't your decision to make."

"I've invested considerable resources into your—project."

Aria cuts her father off before he can finish.

Sharp. Controlled. Deadly calm.

"My resources," she says. "Not yours. I used my investment. *My* money."

Marcus's expression shifts, just barely. No visible flinch, but his eyes turn cold and calculating. The man doesn't like being corrected, especially not by his daughter.

He adjusts his cuff like he's brushing off lint. "True. You

provided the capital, but I'm contributing something far more valuable—my connections, my reputation, my name." He lets it hang there like a noose. "That gives me a vested interest in seeing this venture succeed—properly."

I lean back, every instinct on edge. The way he says "properly" makes my jaw tick. Not because he's threatening her outright. He's too polished for that. It's the way he talks like she's still some ambitious little girl playing CEO, and he's humoring her. Letting her think she's in control.

Aria's hand tightens around her knife—not dramatic, not performative. Just firm. Deliberate. Her spine straightens. Shoulders squared.

"It is succeeding *properly*," she says, her voice like cut glass.

He smiles again, that thin, polished thing that doesn't reach his eyes—doesn't even try. "You always did have a rebellious streak. Just like your mother."

Fucking hell.

Low blow. Deliberate. And he watches her like he's gauging damage.

She doesn't move. Doesn't speak. But I see the flicker—just a flash—in her eyes. The kind of pain that sharpens into fury when held too long.

I shift closer, just enough for my knee to brush hers under the table. Not to soothe. Not to pull her back.

To anchor her.

To remind her she's not alone in this room with him.

She doesn't look at me. Doesn't need to. Her fingers loosen on the blade. But she doesn't let go.

Good.

Let him see that too.

The tension between them crackles, years of similar conflicts visible in the practiced way they square off. I remain silent, watching Marcus calculate his next move.

His phone buzzes discreetly. With a slight nod of apology that feels entirely perfunctory, he glances at the screen. Whatever he sees causes a momentary furrow in his brow before he masks it.

"Excuse me a moment." He rises smoothly. "A matter that requires immediate attention."

As he steps away toward the private dining room's entrance, Aria exhales heavily, shoulders dropping slightly.

"I'm sorry." Her voice drops to a whisper. "He's always like this, but tonight he's especially…"

"Testing boundaries?" I offer, covering her hand with mine. "Marking his territory?"

A small, sad smile touches her lips. "That obvious?"

"Only to someone trained to read people." I squeeze her hand gently. "You're handling him well."

"Years of practice." She glances toward where Marcus stands near the door, engaged in an intense conversation on his phone. "God, I can't believe he scheduled investor meetings without even telling me. Ember will—"

My phone vibrates in my pocket. I withdraw it discreetly, expecting a check-in from Storm or Razor.

Instead, I see CJ's name with a single message: *Surveillance footage at the shop. Check now.*

NINETEEN

Jon

A COLD SPIKE SHOOTS THROUGH MY CHEST AS I TAP OPEN THE file. Blood pounds in my ears, drowning out the ambient restaurant noise. CJ doesn't send messages like this unless it matters.

I angle the screen away from Aria, shielding it with my body while the video loads.

Surveillance footage from The Little Matchstick Girl. Timestamp: less than fifteen minutes ago.

A man steps into the frame. No rush. No hesitation. Hoodie up, posture loose, almost casual—like he owns the night. He strolls to the front door, crouches, and presses something against the glass.

My stomach tightens as he straightens, glances directly at the camera, and walks unhurriedly back to a waiting car.

Not an attack. A message.

I'm back. And I know where to find you.

"What is it?" Aria's voice cuts through my thoughts, sharper than the knife beside the salmon she barely touched.

I lock the screen, already calculating our next moves.

"We need to leave."

"Is it the shop? Is Ember okay?" Her hand finds my forearm, fingers digging in with surprising strength.

Before I can answer, Marcus returns to the table, tucking his own phone into his suit jacket.

"I apologize for the interruption." His gaze shifts between us, registering the tension. "Is everything alright?"

"No. Someone just left a package at The Little Matchstick Girl." I stand, hand automatically checking my concealed weapon. "I need to get Aria somewhere secure while my team investigates."

"Somewhere secure? My penthouse has security measures that rival the Pentagon." Marcus's eyebrow arches with affronted surprise.

"Dad, please." Aria rises, already gathering her purse. "If Jon thinks we should—"

"My security team is the best money can buy." Marcus cuts her off with the same tone he likely uses to silence boardroom dissent. "The penthouse is a fortress. You're coming home, where I can ensure your safety."

My phone vibrates with incoming messages. Delta team deploying. Razor and Storm are already on site. Blaze is five minutes out. Mac and Jenny another ten minutes.

"Ember and Ryn are at the shop right now." I keep my voice steady despite the growing urgency. "My team is moving to secure them and the scene."

Something shifts in Marcus's expression—a calculation happening behind cold eyes. "Then by all means, handle the situation at the shop. I'll take my daughter home where she'll be safe."

"I'm staying with Jon." Aria's spine straightens.

"Aria—" The muscle in Marcus's jaw jumps, the only sign that his control isn't absolute.

"Dad. I'm not going anywhere until I know Ember and Ryn are safe."

I guide them toward the exit, sending rapid texts while scanning the restaurant. Too many windows. Too many unknown faces.

Marcus's sleek town car idles at the curb, driver already holding the door open. It's the safest option. Bulletproof. GPS-tracked. Secure comms already built in.

I hate relying on his resources, but right now, this isn't about pride. I can retrieve my truck later.

As we slide into the leather interior, I send a detailed alert: *Have Aria and Marcus Holbrook.*

CJ's response comes instantly: *Storm and Razor on scene. Blaze ETA three minutes. Wolfe signature confirmed. Extraction to HQ planned. Will see you there.*

Ice floods my veins. Wolfe's signature confirmed. Not just Night Pack—Wolfe himself.

I open the secure video feed as Marcus's driver pulls into traffic. Four camera angles show The Little Matchstick Girl from different perspectives. Storm maintains his position near the main entrance while security protocols are activated around the perimeter.

Inside, Ember moves between candle displays, unaware of the danger. Ryn arranges a crystal-embedded collection near the register.

"What's happening?" Aria leans closer, breath warm against my neck as she tries to see my screen.

I tilt the phone so she can watch. "Storm and Razor are securing the area. Blaze is almost there for extraction. Jenny and Mac are inbound as well."

"Extraction?" Marcus leans forward, eyes narrowing. "You make it sound like a military operation."

"It is." My attention stays on the feed as Blaze's vehicle

appears at the edge of one camera's range. "Night Pack doesn't leave warning notes unless they're planning something bigger."

On screen, Storm enters the shop. Ember's face transforms—confusion melting into the hard focus I recognize from our previous encounters with danger. She immediately moves to Ryn, placing herself slightly ahead of the younger woman—protective instinct kicking in.

Blaze enters the frame, shoulders set, expression severe. His tall frame and confident movements make him unmistakable even on the low-res feed. Ember rushes to him, abandoning caution as he folds her into his protective embrace. The St. Michael medallion—his sister's gift—glints briefly as he presses his lips to her forehead, whispering something that makes her nod.

Ryn stands a few feet away, arms wrapped around herself, looking suddenly small and alone without Ember's sheltering presence. Then Razor enters from the back, his stride quick but controlled as he reaches her side. He doesn't touch her—respecting boundaries—but positions himself as a shield, head bent toward her as he speaks. Her shoulders lower slightly as he stays close, providing the security she needs without demanding contact she might not want.

"What was in that package?" Aria's voice has gone hollow.

I switch camera views to where Mac establishes a small perimeter around a plain brown package leaning against the door. He lifts it in gloved hands, his movements methodical—the instinct of someone who's handled explosive ordnance for decades. His gruff demeanor doesn't waver as he examines all sides before carrying it to a portable containment unit.

A quick glimpse of the box reveals what triggered CJ's alert—a stylized wolf's head stamped in black ink on one corner. Wolfe's signature. His calling card, just like before.

"Guardian HRS protocols include secure transport and technical analysis of potential threats." I keep my voice clinical, detached. "The package will be examined in a controlled environment."

"Guardian HRS has grown more efficient since I last employed them." Marcus watches the operation unfold, his assessment as much for his own benefit as mine.

The backhanded observation barely registers as Blaze escorts Ember toward an armored SUV. Razor does the same with Ryn. The shop's lights go dark as Storm activates security protocols, sealing the building.

"They're safe." Aria's shoulders drop a fraction. "Where are they taking them?"

"Guardian HQ." I meet Marcus's gaze directly. "Which is where we're heading too."

"Absolutely not. I have no intention of placing my daughter in your facility when my own security is perfectly adequate." His fingers curl into a fist on his knee.

"Dad, please. If Ember and Ryn are going there, that's where I need to be." Aria's hand finds mine in the darkness of the car.

"This isn't open for discussion." Marcus's tone cuts like a blade. "Mr. Knutt, I appreciate your organization's assistance with the shop, but my daughter will be under my protection."

The feed on my phone shows Blaze's vehicle pulling away, Ember visible in the back seat. Another SUV follows with Razor and Ryn.

"Mr. Holbrook." I keep my voice level despite the tension knotting between my shoulder blades. "Night Pack specializes in penetrating high-security locations. They've compromised government facilities, corporate headquarters, and private residences."

"Not mine." The certainty in his voice borders on arrogance.

"They've been watching your daughter for weeks." I turn my phone so he can see the newest image CJ has sent through—

three photos found in the package. Aria behind the counter. Ember making candles in what should have been a secure back room. Ryn walking to her apartment, marked with a red X.

Marcus's expression doesn't change, but something flickers in his eyes—the first genuine fear I've seen from him. Not surprising. After what Night Pack did the last time, after what his half-brother nearly accomplished…

"Guardian HQ was designed specifically to counter organizations like Night Pack." I press the advantage. "The facility changes access protocols every twelve hours and maintains active counter-surveillance measures at all times."

"I want my daughter with me." He's not standing down.

"Dad, please. I need to be with Ember and Ryn."

"These people are not your responsibility." Marcus's voice softens when he addresses his daughter, a manipulation so subtle she probably doesn't even recognize it.

"They're my friends." She sits straighter, chin lifting. "And my business partners. I won't hide in your penthouse while they're in danger because of me."

"Because of you?" Marcus's eyes narrow. "What makes you think this has anything to do with you?"

The question hangs between us, loaded with implications.

My phone vibrates with another message from CJ: *Penthouse security protocols received. Analysis indicates significant vulnerabilities. Recommends immediate transport to HQ.*

I study Marcus's face in the dim car interior, noting the slight tightening around his eyes, the calculated mask of paternal concern that doesn't quite reach those cold depths.

"You know why Wolfe is targeting Aria." The words come out harder than intended.

"You're treading on personal ground, Mr. Knutt." Marcus's face goes rigid, eyes narrowing dangerously at me.

"This turned personal when he kidnapped your daughter." I

hold his gaze without flinching. "When he built an entire criminal organization to get revenge on you."

"What are you talking about?" Aria looks between us, confusion clear on her face.

"You didn't know." It's not a question. I mentally curse myself for blurting it out. "I'm so sorry. I thought you knew." The realization that she doesn't know strikes hard. Marcus's eyes flash a warning, but it's too late to retreat.

"Damien Wolfe is your father's half-brother." The words land in the car like stones dropped into still water. "That's why he targeted you. Why he kidnapped you. It wasn't random."

"What?" Aria's gasp cuts through the tension. Her hand pulls away from mine as she stares between us. "Dad? Is this… Wolfe is your brother?" The shock in her voice makes me turn. The color has drained from her face, eyes wide with disbelief and betrayal.

Marcus's eyes close briefly, a rare moment of visible weakness. When he opens them, something shifts behind that calculated mask—resignation, perhaps. Or simply the recognition that this secret can no longer be contained.

"Half-brother." He nearly spits the word. "We share a father. Nothing else."

"How could you keep this from me?" Aria's question comes out raw, wounded.

"I assumed Ember would have told you." I reach for her hand again, but she pulls away. "She was there when Wolfe admitted it. If she was truly your friend, she would have."

"Well, she didn't, and it wasn't her place or responsibility. You should've said something." Aria's jaw clenches as she turns to her father. "Everyone knew except me? Your own daughter?"

Marcus's expression hardens. "It wasn't relevant to your recovery."

"Wasn't relevant?" Her laugh holds no humor. "The man

who kidnapped me did it to hurt you specifically, and that wasn't relevant?"

"You got the empire, the power, and the name." I echo Wolfe's words from the files we compiled after the last encounter. "And he got scraps and shadows."

Marcus's jaw tightens. "You seem well-informed."

"He told us during the last rescue operation." My fingers squeeze Aria's hand reassuringly. "Called her 'the perfect tool to dismantle everything my dear brother holds dear.'"

The car slows at a red light, city shadows playing across Marcus's face. For a moment, he looks decades older, wearied by old sins and long-buried history.

"Guardian HQ." He finally concedes, voice tight with controlled anger.

I nod once, sending confirmation to CJ. The light changes, and the driver adjusts course based on coordinates now appearing on his navigation system.

Aria's fingers remain intertwined with mine, her grip betraying the fear she's working so hard to contain.

"It'll be okay." The reassurance feels hollow even as I say it.

"Will it?" Her voice barely rises above a whisper. "He's back, Jon. After everything… He's back."

I have no answer that isn't a lie, so I simply tighten my grip on her hand.

Marcus watches this exchange, reassessing the nature of my relationship with his daughter. Whatever he sees displeases him, but he remains silent, his attention turning to the phone now vibrating in his hand.

As the car carries us toward Guardian HQ, I can't shake the feeling we're missing something crucial. Marcus knows more than he's saying. This blood feud between half-brothers runs deeper than we've uncovered. Wolfe is targeting not just Aria but

Ember and Ryn as well. Somewhere beneath it all runs a current of old hatred that makes this more than just business.

My free hand checks my weapon again, a grounding ritual learned through years of combat. Whatever's coming, whatever Wolfe has planned, one thing is certain—he won't get to Aria.

Not while I'm breathing.

TWENTY

Jon

Something's wrong with the driver.

The first hint is subtle—just a half-second hesitation at the green light two blocks back. Nothing anyone else would notice. Then comes the missed turn that would have taken us directly toward Guardian HQ.

"Taking an alternate route, sir," the driver explained when Marcus questioned it. "Traffic alert on the main thoroughfare."

Plausible. Except Marcus's driver would have notified us before deviating from the planned route. This man keeps his cap pulled low, his shoulders tense. And there's something about the way he holds the wheel. Too tight. Knuckles pale against the black leather.

I shift slightly, creating space between my hip and the door where my weapon rests. Marcus's town car is luxury-armored, meant to stop bullets from getting in.

Right now, I'm more concerned about us getting out.

The streets grow less familiar with each turn. We should be heading north toward the coast, but instead we're moving east, toward the inland hills. Reynolds makes another turn, this one sharper than necessary. His eyes flick to the rearview mirror, not checking traffic.

Checking us.

"The restaurant was lovely." Aria fills the silence that's stretched too long. "Thank you for dinner. I'm sorry we didn't get to enjoy it."

Her voice sounds normal, but her fingers tighten around mine beneath the fold of her dress. She senses the tension radiating from me, even if she doesn't understand its source.

Marcus nods, still focused on his phone. "Garrison always prepares something special when I bring guests."

I've been in enough dangerous situations to recognize the familiar calm settling over me—heart rate steady, senses sharpening, mind calculating options and outcomes. We've traveled at least six blocks in the wrong direction now.

Too far for coincidence. Too deliberate for a mistake.

The car makes another turn onto a road leading away from city lights. That's the fourth deviation from our route.

This isn't a detour. It's an abduction in progress.

My phone vibrates.

Driver not responding to dispatch calls. Everything okay? CJ's message confirms what I've already concluded.

Three options: wait and gather intelligence, attempt to overpower the driver, or exit the vehicle at the next stop. The first feels right. We don't know how many hostiles are involved or what weapons they have. Better to wait, gather intel, and choose the moment.

I type back one-handed, keeping my movements casual: *Compromised. Prepare extraction team.*

The car slows for a red light. For half a second, I consider changing plans. The three of us could exit now, but we'd be exposed on an unfamiliar street with limited cover. I glance at Aria, at the thin fabric of her dress, at Marcus's polished shoes unsuited for running. The temperature outside hovers around fifty degrees according to the car's display.

"Is everything alright, Mr. Knutt?" Marcus's gaze lifts from his phone, sharp and assessing. "You seem—distracted."

"Just planning our security protocols for when we arrive." The lie comes easily. No need to escalate until I have more information.

The light changes. The driver accelerates too quickly, then makes another turn onto a street lined with shuttered businesses. We're heading into an industrial area now. Buildings grow sparse, streetlights fewer. The expensive shops and restaurants have given way to manufacturing plants and warehouses.

"I think we're going the wrong way." Aria's voice carries the first hint of concern.

Marcus frowns, leaning forward to tap the privacy glass. "Driver, you've missed the turn for Guardian HQ."

No response.

"I'm speaking to you, son." He taps harder.

The privacy partition slides up fully instead of down, sealing us in the back compartment. The locks engage with an audible click.

"What the hell is this?" Marcus reaches for the door handle, yanking it uselessly. "Do you know who I am? I'll have your job for this."

His face reddens, more offended than frightened, like a customer receiving poor service rather than a man in danger.

"We're being taken." I drop all pretense, drawing my weapon. "Stay down and away from the windows."

Aria's eyes widen, but she immediately slides lower in her seat. Marcus stares at my gun with naked disapproval.

"Is this really necessary? It's likely just a misunderstanding with the service—"

"It's not." I cut him off, checking the magazine of my Glock even though I know exactly how many rounds it contains. "Your driver's been replaced. This was planned."

The car swerves hard right, throwing Marcus against the door. He curses, more indignant than frightened, as if this is an inconvenience rather than a life-threatening situation. We screech down an access road, emerging into an empty lot surrounded by abandoned warehouses.

Three black SUVs appear from side streets, blocking every escape route. The town car halts, trapped by the larger vehicles. The SUVs move, each vehicle positioned to prevent escape, engines still running, headlights illuminating our car from multiple angles.

"Call Guardian HRS," I tell Aria, passing her my phone. "Tell them our location."

She takes it, fingers trembling but resolute as she swipes at the screen. Her jaw tightens. "No signal."

Of course. Jammers.

"I pay half a million dollars annually for security." Marcus straightens his jacket, fury replacing shock. "Whoever's responsible will regret—"

"Get down!" I grab his shoulder, forcing him lower as the first SUV's doors open. "These aren't ordinary kidnappers."

Instead of complying, Marcus shoves my hand away.

"Don't manhandle me. I've dealt with extortion attempts before." He turns to Aria, his expression showing more annoyance than concern for his daughter's safety. "This is precisely why I didn't want you involved in that ridiculous candle shop in that neighborhood. You've attracted attention we don't need."

The callousness of his response—blaming Aria while ignoring the immediate threat to her safety—sends a spike of disgust through my chest. Not the reaction of a protective father.

"Dad, this isn't about the shop—" Aria begins, but Marcus cuts her off.

"Of course it is. You've been parading around town with those—former street people. Did you really think that wouldn't make you a target? Your association with them has compromised our security."

Even now, with armed men surrounding us, Marcus's priority is assigning blame rather than protecting his daughter. I catch Aria's expression, the hurt quickly masked behind resignation. This isn't new behavior for him.

Four men emerge from each vehicle. Black tactical gear, faces obscured by balaclavas, weapons drawn but held low. Their movement is coordinated and disciplined. This has to be Night Pack, but with a level of military precision that wasn't present in our previous encounters.

"Jon?" Aria's voice is steady despite the fear in her eyes. "What do we do?"

The bulletproof glass buys us minutes, but not salvation. I assess our position: outnumbered, outgunned, with no communication and no backup arriving in time.

"We—"

A hissing sound cuts me off. Cold mist seeps through the car's ventilation system, filling the cabin with chemical sweetness.

Gas. Fuck.

I rip off my jacket and press it against Aria's face. "Shallow breaths through this."

Her eyes meet mine, wide with understanding. She nods, pressing the fabric tighter.

Marcus coughs once, then lurches for the cloth.

"Give me that—"

I shove him back with more force than necessary.

His eyes flash with something dangerous—possessiveness, not protection—before he controls his expression. But his actions betray him. Instead of trying to protect Aria, he fumbles for his phone, fingers desperately typing what I suspect is a call to his security team.

Not a word to comfort his daughter. Not a move to shield her. Just self-preservation wrapped in expensive tailoring.

"Your phone will be blocked," I tell him, disgust barely contained. "They're using jammers."

"I have private channels," he snaps, continuing to type. "Unlike your organization, my security team has proper contingencies."

Even as the gas fills the car, Marcus's priority is clear: Marcus Holbrook. Not his daughter. Not the woman he insisted on protecting at his penthouse rather than Guardian HQ.

His own damn skin.

I want to kill him.

I try the emergency release under the seat. Nothing. They've thought of everything. The gas thickens, clouding my vision. My lungs burn despite my attempt to hold my breath. My limbs grow heavy, and my responses grow sluggish.

"Jon…" Aria's voice sounds distant despite her proximity. The jacket slips from her grasp as the sedative takes effect.

"Stay awake," I manage, even as darkness edges my vision. "Remember everything you see. Count… Count the men. Note details."

Marcus slumps against the window, unconscious. Aria fights longer, her training from our previous ordeal evident in her resistance. However, the gas is too potent and professionally formulated. Her eyelids flutter as she struggles to remain conscious.

A sharp tap on the window draws my attention. I force my head to turn, fighting the chemicals pulling me under.

Damien Wolfe stands there, immaculate in a charcoal suit that whispers new money. Not the rabid dog from our intelligence files—this man looks refined, controlled. His hair is perfectly styled, his posture relaxed. No visible weapon, yet he radiates danger more effectively than his armed men.

He smiles, satisfaction gleaming in his eyes, too similar to Marcus's.

Something about that smile stops my heart colder than the gas. This is revenge.

Something beyond the half-brothers' feud.

The door opens. Hands reach for Aria. I lunge forward on instinct, muscles betraying me as I collapse half across her lap. My gun clatters uselessly to the floor.

"Jon." Her fingers brush my cheek as they pull her away, the touch featherlight but deliberate. A goodbye, or perhaps a promise.

I fight the darkness, memorizing faces, counting men, gathering intelligence even as my consciousness slips. Marcus is dragged out next. Even sedated, his body language speaks of entitlement, chin lifted as if he's being inconvenienced rather than kidnapped. The contrast between father and daughter is stark.

Aria thinks of others in danger.

Marcus is concerned only with himself.

The last thing I see before blackness takes me is Wolfe bending to whisper something in Aria's ear, his lips close to her temple, almost tender. Her eyes widen with shock before they roll back in sedated sleep.

TWENTY-ONE

Aria

———

Cold air hits my face, and the world tilts sideways.

Hands grip my arms, too tight, dragging me from the car. My legs won't work. My head lolls against someone's shoulder. Chemical sweetness coats my tongue.

Jon. Where's Jon?

A flash of awareness breaks through the fog. Men in black tactical gear. The gleam of weapons. Jon's crumpled form, still in the car, his arm outstretched toward me.

"Jon…" My voice sounds foreign, distant.

"Shh, Aria." A man's voice. Familiar yet not. "You're safe."

My father appears in fragmented vision, limp between two masked men. His head hangs forward, unconscious. A second kidnapping. The statistical improbability of it would be almost funny if terror wasn't clawing up my throat.

Another car. Black SUV. The interior smells of leather and pine.

"Separate vehicles." The same voice, commanding. "Marcus goes with Team Two."

I try to turn my head to see who's speaking, but my muscles refuse to cooperate. My vision swims, darkness encroaching.

A face leans close. Sharp cheekbones. Eyes that are too familiar.

"It's time you learned the truth about your father," he whispers. "About your mother. About me."

The words make no sense. The gas pulls me under before I can process them.

Darkness.

Light burns through my eyelids.

I jerk awake, heart hammering against my ribs. Where am I? What happened?

The ceiling above me is coffered, cream-colored with gold inlay. Not a hospital. Not my bedroom.

My mouth feels like cotton, my throat raw. The sedative. The kidnapping. Jon.

Oh, where is Jon? If they've hurt him…

I sit up too quickly. The room spins. Nausea rises. I grip silk sheets—emerald green, high thread count—until the dizziness passes.

This isn't the warehouse from last time. No wire cage. No concrete floor.

Instead, I'm in a bedroom that belongs in an architectural magazine. King-sized bed with a mahogany frame. Artwork on the walls—originals, not prints. Fresh flowers on the nightstand beside a crystal carafe of water.

A prison disguised as a five-star hotel suite.

I swing my legs over the edge of the bed. My black dress clings, wrinkled from sleep, the fabric heavy against my skin. No shoes. Just bare feet sinking into unexpected warmth—not concrete, not linoleum. Heated marble. Smooth, polished. Luxurious.

Too luxurious for a prison.

But that's what this is.

My limbs drag, the lingering haze of sedation dulling the edges of everything, but the floor is unmistakably rich and warm, like something out of a spa or a mansion. Not a cage, like before, and that contrast makes my stomach turn.

The details jar against my memory of the last kidnapping—the cage, the filth, the terror. Ember... My light in the darkness.

Jon.

Where is he? The memory of his body sprawled across the car seat, reaching for me as they pulled me away, tightens my chest. Is he alive?

And my father... I remember his limp form being loaded into a different vehicle.

My head throbs as fragments of last night reassemble. The driver. The gas. Hands pulling me from the car. And that whisper...

"It's time you learned the truth about your father..."

Damien Wolfe. The man we believed dead after the last rescue operation. My father's half-brother. The crime lord who traffics children now wants me to know "the truth."

I push myself to standing, fighting a wave of dizziness. I need to assess my situation. Find an escape route. Locate Jon.

The room is approximately twenty by twenty feet. Double doors that presumably lead to a hallway. Another door slightly ajar, showing an en-suite bathroom. Two tall windows with a view of pine-covered mountains. Coastal mountains. We're still in California at least.

I try the main doors first. Locked, as expected. The knob doesn't even turn. I press my ear against the wood, listening for guards. Nothing.

The windows next. They stretch from floor to ceiling, filling the room with morning light. The view is spectacular—gentle hills rolling toward the distant Pacific. I'm high up, on the second or third floor of a building perched on a hillside. The windows are fixed panes. No latches, no way to open them. And the glass, when I tap it, returns a solid, heavy sound. Security glass. Unbreakable without tools.

I sweep the room for surveillance—corners, ceiling edges, recessed panels. If cameras are here, they're expertly concealed. The ceiling's too high to reach, even standing on the bed. Whoever designed this space knew exactly how far I could stretch.

The bathroom is another mindfuck. Marble gleams under recessed lighting, accented by gold fixtures so polished they reflect. The floor radiates warmth underfoot. A rainfall shower with digital controls and jets. Everything screams luxury.

But it's the details that make my stomach knot.

A row of toiletries lines the marble counter—every brand I use, down to the exact vanilla-cedar shampoo I hoard from that boutique in SoHo. The moisturizer I keep in my travel bag. Even the lip balm I reorder compulsively. My scent, my routine.

Monogrammed towels wait beside the sink. A single letter stitched in gold thread: **W**.

There's no razor. No scissors. Nothing sharp. Nothing dangerous.

Except the implication.

This isn't random. This is curated. Customized. Whoever orchestrated this didn't just want a hostage. They wanted me. Not just the woman I am now, but every version of me. The girl who still texts her housekeeper for skincare refills. The woman who used to leave her straightener on the bathroom counter.

They studied me. Prepared for me.

I splash cold water on my face, hoping to wake up from whatever carefully gilded nightmare this is. The mirror answers with the truth—pale skin, mascara smudged beneath my eyes, hair twisted into knots. I look like hell.

But beneath the wreckage, there's something new. A tightness around the mouth. A quiet defiance in my eyes.

The socialite who walked into that restaurant last night wouldn't have lasted here.

But I will.

Back in the bedroom, I notice a closet I missed during my initial sweep. Inside, a selection of clothing hangs in obsessive order. Casual wear, athletic clothes, evening dresses. All in my size. All in styles and colors I would choose for myself.

But one garment stops my breath.

A pale blue wrap dress with a delicate floral pattern. Almost identical to one my mother used to wear. I haven't seen that dress since I was eight years old, but I remember her wearing it to Sunday brunches, to gallery openings, to afternoons in the garden.

I touch the fabric, a chill racing up my spine. How would Wolfe know about this? The dress isn't vintage—it's new, tags still attached. Custom-made to duplicate a twenty-year-old memory.

I yank my hand back as if burned. This goes beyond stalking. Beyond research. This is—personal. Intimate in a way that makes my skin crawl.

"It's time you learned the truth about your father."

What truth? What could this monster possibly know about my father that I don't?

As for my mother and the blue dress, Rebecca Holbrook died when I was eight. One day, she was there, singing off-key in the kitchen, braiding my hair too tightly. The next—gone. Sudden. No explanation, I was old enough to understand, just whispered voices behind closed doors, and a funeral I barely remember.

Closed casket.

My father never spoke of her again. Her photos vanished

from the walls. Her name dropped from conversation like it carried disease. Any time I asked, he redirected. *It was a tragedy, darling, let it rest.* Eventually, I stopped asking.

I used to think it was grief.

Now… I'm not so sure.

The door lock clicks. I spin toward the sound, heart leaping into my throat. My gaze darts around the room for a weapon. The lamp is too unwieldy. The pen on the nightstand is too flimsy.

The carafe. Heavy crystal. I grab it, water sloshing over my hand as I position myself against the wall where the door will hide me when it opens.

The handle turns. The door swings inward with a soft click.

A girl enters carrying a breakfast tray—no older than seventeen, maybe eighteen at most. She's dressed in a simple black shift that's too formal for a housemaid and too polished for someone free. Dark hair pinned into a neat bun, eyes downcast in practiced submission.

When she doesn't immediately see me, her brows lift slightly.

"Miss Holbrook?"

I stay silent, still half-shadowed, still gripping the carafe like a weapon.

She turns, spots me near the corner, and freezes.

Only for a second.

Her expression shifts—not to fear. But recognition. Understanding. Like she's seen worse reactions. Like girls with wild eyes and weaponized carafes are part of her daily routine.

"I've brought your breakfast." Her voice is soft, with a hint of an accent I can't place. Maybe Southern. Maybe midwestern. Something scrubbed clean. "Mr. Wolfe thought you might be hungry when you woke."

"Where is Jon?" My voice cracks from disuse, rough as gravel.

She flinches. It's quick—barely perceptible—but it's there.

"I'm not allowed to speak about the other guests," she says. The tray lands on a small table by the window with quiet precision. "Mr. Wolfe will answer your questions when he joins you."

"I'm not hungry." Another lie. My stomach betrays me with a low, aching growl at the scent of strong coffee and buttered pastry.

She doesn't smile. Doesn't smirk. Just nods like she's heard it before. Like everyone says that in the beginning.

"As you wish." She straightens, hands folded in front of her. Up close, she's even younger than I thought. Slender wrists. A fading bruise on her forearm, half-hidden by the cuff of her sleeve. Her gaze lifts, finally meeting mine.

She doesn't blink.

Not cold. Not cruel. Just—resigned.

"The bathroom has everything you'll need. Fresh towels, toiletries. Mr. Wolfe requests you make yourself comfortable."

I take a step forward, still holding the carafe tightly. "Comfortable? I've been kidnapped. I'm a prisoner."

Her mouth parts as if to answer. Then she stops herself. Eyes flick—not toward the door. Not toward me. But toward the corner of the ceiling. Subtle. A single twitch of her gaze.

Then she looks back. Carefully blank. "Mr. Wolfe prefers the term *guest*." Her voice dips, just a little. "He'll explain everything shortly."

I watch her. The tension in her frame. The perfect stillness of someone trained not to flinch, not to resist.

"There are no cameras in the bathroom," she says, so softly it could almost be for herself. "You don't need to worry about taking a shower."

The implication chills me far more than a direct warning ever could.

Everywhere else—watched.

I study her face. "How long have you been here?"

"I'm not at liberty to say." She lowers her gaze.

"But you're not here by choice."

That makes her look up.

The stillness cracks. Not enough to draw attention from whatever surveillance monitors this room, but I see it—in the way her lips press tight, her throat swallows hard.

"Mr. Wolfe—can be a difficult master, but he's not the worst. I'm lucky to serve him."

The word *master* lodges like a shard of glass in my chest.

"Lucky?" My heart bleeds for this poor soul.

"There are men—worse than him. Others I've seen. He doesn't let them… Not here. Not with us." She shudders—barely a tremor, like her body's remembering something it wishes it could forget.

Us.

How many girls?

She lifts her chin, and for the first time, there's something fiercely defiant behind the quiet mask. A kind of brittle pride. She's survived. She's still surviving.

"What's your name?"

Another subtle glance toward the ceiling.

"I have none." A pause. Then, under her breath, "But thank you for asking."

She moves toward the door, keeping her back straight, every step rehearsed.

"Is there anything else you require, Miss Holbrook?"

"My freedom. A phone. Information about my companions."

She hesitates, hand on the knob.

"I'll let Mr. Wolfe know." Her voice softens again. "He'll be with you shortly."

The door closes with a mechanical click. The lock engages.

And I'm alone.

I set down the carafe, hands trembling—not just from adrenaline, or the last shadows of whatever Wolfe used to drug me—but from something deeper. That girl had no bruises on her face. No torn clothes. Nothing visible.

But she's a prisoner, like me.

A polished, well-trained, quietly broken girl.

And now I can't stop thinking about her.

I approach the tray she left behind with caution, examining the food without touching it. No obvious signs of tampering, but that means nothing. The coffee smells rich and tempting after the chemical taste that still lingers in my mouth.

Could it be drugged? Possibly. But if Wolfe wanted me unconscious, why bother with the pretense? The gas worked efficiently enough.

I pour a small amount of coffee and sip cautiously. The flavor explodes across my tongue—expensive, perfectly brewed. My body craves the caffeine, the normalcy of the ritual.

As I drink, I take stock of my situation.

I've been kidnapped by my father's half-brother, a man who should be dead. I'm being held in luxury rather than squalor. Jon and my father are somewhere in this building—or perhaps not. The woman's comment about "other guests" suggests they're alive, at least.

Wolfe wants me to know some "truth" about my family. Given his criminal enterprise, this is likely psychological warfare, an attempt to turn me against my father.

And yet…

I glance again at the blue dress hanging in the closet. An exact replica of my mother's favorite. How would he know that? What else might he know about her that I don't?

I've spent my life in my father's world. His rules. His expectations. His version of our family history. The candle shop was my first real act of independence, and even that came with strings attached—my money, but his conditions, his constant reminders of how it reflects on the Holbrook name.

Jon saw through my father almost immediately. I dismissed his concerns as professional paranoia, but now…

The coffee turns bitter on my tongue.

I need to escape. Find Jon. But first, I need information. And Damien Wolfe seems eager to provide it. I don't know that, but the young girl—young woman—said he wants to speak with me.

The question is whether I'm prepared for what I might learn.

I set down the cup, suddenly cold despite the room's perfect temperature. My father has always been controlling, demanding, and critical, but he's still my father. The only family I have.

"It's time you learned the truth about your father."

Wolfe's words echo in my mind, carrying a weight I can't ignore. There was something in his eyes when he looked at me. Something beyond the satisfaction of a kidnapper. Something almost like—recognition.

I shake off the thought. This is what he wants—to make me doubt, to make me vulnerable. Classic manipulation tactics. I won't fall for it.

I move to the bathroom, splash more cold water on my face. The woman was right about one thing. I need to gather my strength and clean up. Whatever game Wolfe is playing, I need to be clear-headed to counter it.

The shower controls are intuitive despite their complexity. Hot water pounds against tense muscles, washing away the lingering scent of the sedative gas. I use the provided shampoo— the same brand I use at home, another unsettling detail, and try to focus on practical matters.

The room has no obvious escape routes. The door is secured from the outside. The windows won't open and are too strong to break. I'm at least twenty feet above ground level, with no ledges or nearby trees.

I'll need to get out of this room. That means either overpowering someone when they enter or convincing them to take me elsewhere. Given the level of security I've seen, the latter seems more probable.

Which means I need to play along with whatever Wolfe has planned. At least for now.

I step out of the shower and dry off with the monogrammed towel. My black dress from last night is gone—removed while I was in the bathroom. The message is clear: *wear what's been provided or wear nothing.*

I examine the closet options again, deliberately avoiding the blue dress that so resembles my mother's. Instead, I select black pants and a simple white blouse. Casual but dignified. Clothes, I can move in if an escape opportunity presents itself.

They fit perfectly. Of course they do.

I'm brushing my hair when the door unlocks again. This time, I don't reach for a weapon. I turn slowly, brush still in hand, composing my features into the mask of calm I've perfected at a thousand society functions.

TWENTY-TWO

Aria

———

Damien Wolfe steps into the room.

He's tall, well-built, with that same confidence that seems genetic in the Holbrook line. His suit is impeccably tailored, navy blue with a subtle striped pattern. He looks more like a CEO than a crime lord, but it's his eyes that hold me frozen. The exact shade of steel-blue as my father's.

As mine.

"Good morning, Aria." His voice carries the faintest trace of an accent I can't place. "I trust you slept well, all things considered."

I say nothing, just watch him, and catalog the details. The way he stands—weight evenly distributed, ready to move in any direction. Military training or something similar. The watch on his left wrist—Patek Philippe, understated wealth. The St. Christopher medal partially visible beneath his collar—unexpected religiosity from a man who traffics children.

"Please, don't let me interrupt your meal." He gestures to the breakfast tray.

"Where is Jon?" I keep my voice level.

"Mr. Knutt is unharmed." He moves further into the room, maintaining a respectful distance. "I have no quarrel with Guardian HRS personnel. They're simply doing their job."

"And my father?"

"Marcus is another matter." Something flickers across his face —too fast to identify.

The hesitation tells me more than the words. Whatever "truth" Wolfe wants to reveal, it centers on my father.

"Why am I here?" I set down the brush, turning fully to face him. "If this is about money—"

"This has never been about money." He cuts me off, voice hardening briefly before he controls it. "Please, sit. This conversation will be easier if we're both comfortable."

I remain standing. Small defiances matter in captivity—I learned that the first time.

He sighs, then moves to sit in an armchair near the window. The morning light catches his profile, highlighting the bone structure that mirrors my father's. He's not an unattractive man. Some might call him beautiful. Handsome even.

I struggle to categorize my thoughts and feelings about this man.

"I understand your reluctance." He crosses one leg over the other, the picture of relaxed confidence. "But I'm not here to hurt you. Quite the opposite."

"Kidnapping is a strange way to show concern for another person, and this is the *second* time you've taken me."

"I prefer to think of this time as a family reunion. It's long overdue, and I apologize for the first kidnapping. My intent wasn't to cause you any harm." His lips curve in a smile that doesn't reach his eyes.

"And yet, you did."

"A necessary inconvenience, and you have my apologies, but *this* is a family matter."

"We're not family." The words come automatically, reflexively.

"Are you certain of that?" He studies me for a long moment, head tilted slightly.

"What do you want from me?" A chill runs through me despite the room's warmth.

"I want you to know the truth." He leans forward, intensity bleeding through his composed exterior. "About who you are. About who Marcus is. About what happened to your mother."

"My mother died when I was eight. It was an accident." My mouth goes dry.

I remember standing in my father's study, clutching my stuffed rabbit while he delivered the news in that clipped, clinical tone he used for boardroom briefings. *"A tragic fall,"* he said. *"Quick. Painless. Nothing anyone could have done."*

No comfort. No visible grief. Just sterile words designed to close the door before I could even step through it.

When I asked how it happened—why she'd been walking down the stairs so late, or why no one heard her fall—he cut me off. *"It's time to move forward, Aria."* That tone. The one that made further questions feel like a threat.

Her funeral was closed casket. Her photos vanished from the walls within a week. Her name dissolved into silence like it had never existed.

Even then, something felt—off. The way the house went still around him. The way I learned to stop wondering.

It was easier that way.

Safer.

"Is that what he told you?" There's genuine curiosity in his voice, as if my answer matters to him.

"That's what happened." But even to my own ears, the words sound hollow, uncertain.

"Sit, Aria." His tone gentles. "Please. This isn't a conversation to have standing."

Against my better judgment, I perch on the edge of the bed, as far from him as possible while still in conversational range. My heart pounds against my ribs, but I keep my expression neutral. Another skill learned at Marcus Holbrook's dinner table.

"Many years ago," Wolfe begins, "I loved a woman named Rebecca Price."

My mother's maiden name. A name I've rarely heard spoken aloud.

"We were going to build a life together." His gaze shifts to the window. "Until Marcus took her from me."

"That's not—" I stop myself. What do I know about my parents' courtship?

Nothing but the sanitized version my father occasionally referenced. They met at a charity function. A whirlwind romance. Society's perfect couple.

"Your father is not the man you believe him to be." Wolfe's eyes return to mine, searching. "And neither am I."

"You're a criminal." The words come out sharper than intended. "You traffic children. You kidnapped me and intended to sell me to the highest bidder. I think I know more than enough to formulate an opinion about you."

"Is that what you've been told?" Pain flashes across his features, genuine and raw.

"Told? It's what happened. It's what you are." But an unwelcome uncertainty creeps in.

"Marcus always excelled at controlling narratives." He rises slowly and moves to the closet. "Just as he's controlled you your entire life. I was never going to sell you…"

He stands, crosses the space, and removes the blue dress from the closet, holding it with unexpected reverence.

"Your mother wore a dress like this the day I told her I loved her. A picnic in Golden Gate Park. She made sandwiches with the crusts cut off because she didn't like crusts and said it made things *fancy*."

The specificity of the memory catches me off guard. This isn't information he could have researched. This is personal knowledge and intimate details.

"She hated crusts," I whisper, the words escaping before I can stop them. "She always cut them off my sandwiches too."

His smile turns genuine for the first time. "She would sing while she made them. Fleetwood Mac. Dreams."

Another detail that rings true. My earliest memories include my mother singing that song as she moved around the kitchen.

"How do you know these things?" My voice sounds small, even to me.

"Because I knew your mother." He carefully returns the dress to the closet. "Better than Marcus ever did. And she knew me."

I want to dismiss his words as manipulation, but they've found purchase in soil I didn't know was fertile—longstanding questions about my mother, about her death, about the strange emptiness that always existed in my father's carefully constructed world.

"What do you want from me?" I ask again, but the question now holds a different meaning.

"I want you to listen." He moves toward the door. "I want you to ask questions. I want you to decide for yourself what's true."

"What have you done with Jon? With my father?"

"Interesting that you ask about the Guardian over your father. He's special to you."

"Will you use that against me?"

"I will use what I need to do what must be done, but all in good time." He pauses at the threshold. "Rest today. Think about what I've said. Tonight, I'll show you evidence that will change everything you know about your family."

"I want to see Jon." I stand, finding strength in concern for someone else. "I need to know he's safe."

"Your loyalty does you credit." Wolfe studies me, something like approval warming his gaze. "He's not injured, merely—inconvenienced; but I'll consider your request."

The door opens, revealing a guard outside, professional security rather than the tattooed thugs from the previous kidnapping.

"One more thing," Wolfe says. "The blue dress. Your mother made it herself. The pattern was French lilac—her favorite flower. Marcus always told people it was roses."

The door closes before I can respond, lock engaging with an audible click.

I sink back onto the bed, mind racing with implications I'm not ready to face. My hands tremble as I reach for the coffee cup, now cold.

Wolfe is manipulating me. Using personal details to build credibility before the larger lies come. He must be.

Because none of that can be true.

But how does he know about the lilacs? About the Fleetwood Mac song? About details, I myself had forgotten until he mentioned them?

I close my eyes, trying to focus on what matters. Jon is alive. My father, too. I'm not in immediate danger. I need to stay calm, gather information, and look for opportunities to escape.

But Wolfe's parting words echo, impossible to dismiss.

My mother's favorite flowers were lilacs, not roses. I remember the scent of them in our garden, the way she would bury her face in the purple blooms each spring.

Yet every year on her birthday, my father placed roses on her grave.

TWENTY-THREE

Jon

Cold water shocks me awake.

I gasp, choking as it streams down my face and soaks the collar of my shirt. My head pounds with the aftermath of the sedative, mouth cotton dry, muscles aching from being held in one position too long.

"Good morning, Mr. Knutt." Wolfe's voice carries the faintest trace of an accent—one that wasn't in any of our intelligence files. "I apologize for the accommodations."

I blink water from my eyes, taking stock through the disorientation. Metal chair, wrists and ankles secured with proper restraints, not zip ties. Concrete room, perhaps fifteen by fifteen feet. Single door, heavy steel. No windows. One camera in each corner. Temperature cool but not uncomfortable.

And Damien Wolfe, seated across from me in a chair that doesn't belong in this prison cell—antique leather, expensively worn. The kind of chair you'd find in a private study. His suit is different from earlier. Still perfectly tailored, but now a deep navy rather than charcoal. I've been unconscious long enough for him to change clothes.

"Where is she?" My voice comes out ragged, throat raw from the gas.

What time is it?

"Ah." He smiles slightly. "No questions about your location? No demands to be released? No threats about what Guardian HRS will do when they find you? Just concern for Ms. Holbrook. How touching."

I remain silent, conserving my energy and gathering intel. Every second he talks, I gain valuable information. The room is soundproofed—the heavy door and concrete construction confirm this. No ambient noise filters through, which means we could be anywhere—a warehouse, a bunker, or an office building with a renovated interior.

"She's quite comfortable, I assure you. Unlike her father." Wolfe leans forward, elbows on his knees like we're having a casual chat instead of sitting across from a predator. "You've chosen an interesting woman to protect. Aria Holbrook isn't what she seems. Neither is Marcus."

Blood roars in my ears.

My fists clench slow and tight, my fingers curling as much as they can with the restraints. "If you've hurt her—"

"I would never harm her." He raises a hand, placating. Mocking.

"Liar."

"It's the truth." He leans back, crossing one leg over the other with that same calculated ease. His gaze sharpens, cutting into me like a scalpel, quiet and precise. "Though I wonder if the same can be said for her father."

My pulse spikes. My muscles coil, ready to snap. But I don't move. Not yet. He wants a reaction. Wants me off balance. Wants to remind me she's in his hands.

He doesn't get what he wants.

Instead, I lock eyes with him and let him see it—that if he's touched her, even once, even wrong, I'll rip this room apart brick by brick.

"Never harmed her? You kidnapped her… Twice. Drugged her. Locked her in a cage. Planned to sell her like property—"

"I was *never* going to sell her. That was for Marcus's benefit."

"Does it matter? You used her as leverage, and she suffered as a result." The metal of the restraints bite into my wrists. I don't raise my voice. Don't flinch. But every word lands like a warning shot.

"You think because you didn't lay a hand on her, that makes you innocent?" I meet his gaze, steady and cold. "You broke into her life. Ripped away her safety. Turned her into a bargaining chip in a game she never agreed to play."

His expression doesn't change—but I see it. That flicker of regret behind the eyes.

"You don't get to say you haven't *hurt* her. Or whatever the hell you're telling yourself to sleep at night."

Silence stretches, taut and thin.

I lean forward as much as the restraints allow, voice low and sharp.

"What you did leaves bruises no one can see. That's still harm. That's still violence."

The sheer audacity of it makes my jaw clench. Heat sparks low in my chest—not panic, not fear. Rage. Controlled. Contained. But rising.

I shift in the chair, just enough for Wolfe to notice. Not aggression. Not yet. Just a quiet signal: you're not safe here either.

"You keep using her as leverage," I say, voice flat. "Don't pretend that's not harm."

"You assume I want to hurt her. I don't." Wolfe's mouth curves, but there's no pleasure in it. "I want to free her. From him. From the lie she's living."

Something in his tone raises the hair on my arms. Not the

threat I expected. There's bitterness there, yes, but also what sounds like genuine concern.

"What do you want?" I test the restraints subtly. Professional grade, properly applied. No give in the metal, no weakness in the chair legs. Those who secured me knew what they were doing.

"I want the truth." Wolfe stands, straightening his suit jacket. "And for Aria to hear it."

"Truth? What the fuck does that mean?"

He moves to a small table, tucked in the corner of the room. Pours water from a crystal decanter into a glass. Returns and holds it to my lips. I hesitate, then drink. No point refusing hydration. If he wanted me dead, I'd be dead already.

The water is cold and clean, washing away some of the chemical aftertaste from the sedative.

"You believe you understand what's happening here." He sets the glass aside. "A criminal taking revenge on his half-brother. A kidnapping motivated by greed or power or simple malice."

"Enlighten me."

"Marcus stole something precious from me many years ago." Wolfe's smile is all teeth, his eyes cold and unreadable. "Before Aria was born. I'm simply reclaiming what's mine." There's a curve to his mouth, but his eyes stay flat—empty of anything human. The smile is hollow, as if his face remembers the motion even when he doesn't feel it.

"Aria isn't property."

"No."

Something flashes across his face—genuine emotion breaking through the controlled exterior. Pain, perhaps. Or grief. "She's not, but she is family. More than Marcus deserves."

He turns away, adjusting the cuffs of his shirt like the conversation hasn't cracked open something raw beneath his practiced calm. Then—like flipping a switch—the warmth drains from his voice.

Wolfe paces toward the door, hand resting briefly on the frame. He doesn't turn back.

"You know, you don't have to stay involved." He glances over his shoulder, gaze flicking over me. Calculating. Cold. "You could walk away. No chains. No threat. Just—freedom."

He lets the word hang in the air like bait.

"Leave this to Marcus and me. Let Aria decide what matters most without your influence."

I lift my head. Say nothing. Just watch him.

A slow breath cools the fire building in my chest. He wants to frame this as mercy. A noble out. Pretend he's offering peace.

But it's nothing more than manipulation. Smoke dressed as virtue.

"You're wasting your breath." My voice stays level. "I'm not leaving her."

Wolfe smiles, but it's hollow—like his face remembers the shape of the expression, even if he's forgotten how it's meant to feel.

"Didn't think so. But I had to offer. Optics. You'll be fed. Given water. Monitored. But for now…" His gaze drops to the restraints, his mouth twitching. "You stay here."

I tense—not from fear, but from instinct. The itch to move, to fight, coiling under my skin.

"If you hurt her—"

"I won't." The words cut sharply. Offended. Defensive. "But Marcus will. And she deserves to know what kind of man raised her."

He steps to the door, fingers brushing the panel beside it. A low mechanical click signals the lock disengaging. He pauses there, half-shadowed by the hall light, then looks back.

"She's lucky, you know." His voice is quieter now, almost reflective. "To have someone like you. A man who'll walk through hell to save her." His head tilts slightly, admiration laced with something darker. "But that kind of interference?" He shakes his head once, slow. "That, I can't allow. Things need to happen. She needs to see the truth."

His smile returns—thin and final.

"Get comfortable, Jon. This part of the story? It's not about you."

The door closes. The click of reinforced steel echoes like a sentence.

And I'm left alone. Restrained. Pulse steady. Jaw clenched.

Not because I'm afraid.

But because I believe Wolfe means every word he says, and that makes him far more dangerous than I ever imagined.

I immediately test the restraints, searching for weaknesses. The chair is bolted to the floor. The restraints show no sign of poor maintenance or improper application. Over the next few hours, I catalog details—the time between guard checks, the type of locks on the door, the camera angles.

But beneath the professional assessment runs a current of dread.

Not for myself.

But for Aria.

She is family. More than Marcus deserves.

Something is very wrong here. Wolfe's words weren't just the ranting of a criminal seeking revenge. They held conviction—and worse, they held pain.

I remember Marcus in the car—his instinct to save himself first, the way he blamed Aria for the kidnapping, the possessive rather than protective nature of his concern. Not the behavior of a loving father. Something cold settles in my stomach at the implications.

Whatever truth Wolfe is planning to reveal, I suspect it will shatter Aria more thoroughly than any physical threat could.

And I need to reach her before that happens.

TWENTY-FOUR

Aria

———

THE SOFT KNOCK AT THE DOOR BARELY REGISTERS. I'M STILL cataloging my surroundings: heavy damask curtains over windows that don't open, antique furniture that could fetch thousands at auction, and the unsettling knowledge that everything in this room has been selected with purpose.

"Come in," I call, expecting another guard.

Instead, a slight figure slips through the doorway. It's the girl from before. The one with no name. Her movements are careful, measured—the deliberate steps of someone trained to be invisible. Her eyes remain fixed on the floor as she sets a tray on the dresser.

"Mr. Wolfe requests your presence for dinner in one hour," she says, voice barely above a whisper. "I'm to help you prepare."

"Please, tell me your name." I stand, moving slowly so as not to startle her.

She flinches at the direct question, eyes darting up to meet mine before quickly returning to the floor. In that brief connection, I see exhaustion etched into features too young for such weariness.

"I don't have one." Her fingers twist in the fabric of her dress. "Mr. Wolfe calls me 'girl.'"

Something cold slides down my spine. "Everyone has a name."

"I had one. Before." She moves to the closet and opens it. "Mr. Wolfe says names are for people, not property."

The clinical way she says it—like reciting a fact about the weather—makes my stomach clench. I've heard about Wolfe's operation from Jon and the Guardian files. Human trafficking. But seeing this girl, hearing the empty acceptance in her voice, makes the horror visceral in a way statistics never could.

"How long have you been here?" I approach slowly, afraid of startling the girl.

Her hands pause on a hanger. "Three years, four months, two weeks." The precision of her answer speaks volumes. She's counting.

Still tracking time. Still hoping.

"I'm going to get you out of here," I say it as if it's something I can accomplish, but how am I going to free her? I need Jon. I can't do this alone. Where is he? What has Wolfe done to him?

Is he being held? Tortured? Is he already dead?

My hand flies to my chest. I'd feel it, wouldn't I? If Jon were dead?

For the first time, something flickers in her eyes—not quite hope, but the ghost of it. "That's what the last girl said too." She pulls a dress from the closet, and the sight of it punches the air from my lungs.

Azure blue silk, with a sweetheart neckline and delicate beading along the bodice. An exact replica of the dress my mother wore in the photographs on my father's desk. The dress she was wearing the night she met him, according to the story he's told countless times.

"He wants you to wear this." The girl holds it out, and I can't help but take a step back.

"No." The word comes out sharper than intended. "I won't."

"Please." Fear threads through her whisper. "He'll punish me if you refuse."

Our eyes meet, and something unspoken passes between us. She nods once, slow, but her posture doesn't change—shoulders still tucked tight, spine drawn inward like she's trying to disappear.

Her body tells the truth that Wolfe would rather hide.

Faint scars ring her wrists, pale ridges that speak of restraint—not once, but often.

A fading bruise shadows the curve of her collarbone, yellow blooming into green beneath the neckline of her dress.

It makes me sick. Not just the marks, but the quiet way she wears them. As if she believes she earned them.

"Alright," I whisper, bile thick in my throat. "I'll wear it."

Relief flickers across her face—too fleeting, too cautious to be real comfort. She moves behind me, hands trembling as she reaches for the zipper at my back.

I lift my arms to gather my hair.

She flinches.

Not a subtle twitch, not a blink. She jerks away, body recoiling like a dog bracing for the belt. Her breath stutters. Her hands fly up, defensive, before she catches herself—before shame and submission fold her back into place.

My chest tightens like it's collapsing inward.

She thought I was going to hit her.

That motion—so simple, so thoughtless—read as a threat in her world. A raised hand equals pain.

Always.

I want to scream. I want to burn Wolfe's empire to ash and drag him through the ruins.

But I stay still. I don't speak. I don't reach for her.

Because even kindness might feel like danger.

She smooths the zipper with shaking fingers. Her eyes never rise.

And I swear, whatever it takes, I'll make sure no one ever makes her flinch again.

"Has he hurt you?" The question is unnecessary; the answer is written in every careful movement she makes.

She doesn't respond, focusing instead on preparing the blue dress. As I step into it, the silk slides cool against my skin, and I fight a shudder. It fits perfectly—of course it does. The thought of Wolfe knowing my measurements makes my skin crawl.

The girl works silently, fastening closures and adjusting the fabric. When she steps back, she studies me with an odd expression.

"What is it?"

She shakes her head slightly. "You look like her. The woman in the photograph. In his study."

"My mother," I confirm softly.

She nods, then moves to the vanity, gesturing for me to sit. As she begins arranging my hair, her fingers work with surprising skill. For someone so damaged, her touch holds surprising tenderness.

"Did you know her?" I ask, watching her reflection in the mirror.

"No." She pins a section of my hair, recreating an updo I recognize from my mother's photos. "But he talks to her picture sometimes. When he drinks."

My throat tightens. "What does he say?"

"That he should have fought for her." Her eyes meet mine in the mirror, then dart away. "That he should have saved her from him."

"From who?"

"Your father." She secures the final pin. "Mr. Wolfe says your father stole her. That he destroyed her."

Before I can respond, the door swings open. Wolfe stands in the threshold, immaculate in a tailored black suit. His eyes sweep over me, satisfaction and something darker flickering in their depths.

"Perfect," he says, gaze lingering on the dress. "Rebecca would be proud."

The casual use of my mother's name in his mouth sends a surge of anger through me. I rise from the vanity, squaring my shoulders. "What do you want from me?"

His smile doesn't reach his eyes. "Just dinner, Aria. A *family* dinner. Truth and all that comes from it." He extends his arm. "Your father is waiting."

I hesitate, glancing back at the girl who stands with her head bowed, hands clasped before her.

"The girl will join us," Wolfe adds, catching my concern. "I insist."

The girl's shoulders tense, but she follows silently as Wolfe leads me through corridors lined with artwork worth more than most people's homes. The juxtaposition is jarring—such beauty in a place built on suffering.

We descend a grand staircase into a dining room pulled from some warped fairy tale.

Gleaming mahogany stretches the length of the room, set for three with polished silver and blood-red crystal. Chandeliers drip prisms of fractured light across gleaming floors, casting shimmering ghosts that dance between us. A fire snaps behind a carved stone hearth—too ornate, too controlled, like everything in this house.

At the far end of the table sits my father.

His hands are bound to the arms of a high-backed chair, thick leather straps pulled taut. A bruise blooms over his left cheekbone—angry, fresh—but his posture remains unbowed. Chin lifted. Spine ramrod straight. The same unflappable force that presides over Fortune 500 boardrooms and black-tie galas. Even now, blood drying at his temple, he radiates power.

"Aria, my darling," His voice cracks—not from weakness, but sheer relief. "Are you hurt?"

"I'm fine." I step toward him, heart hammering—but Wolfe's fingers curl around my arm, stopping me cold.

A low chuckle rumbles from him, dark and indulgent.

"Family reunions are so touching." He guides me not to my father, but to the chair opposite him, separating us by a battlefield of linen and crystal. A deliberate move. A message. "Please, sit. We have much to discuss."

The room is a study in contrast—beauty and threat, elegance and menace layered in equal measure. But the real tension isn't in the place settings or the guards stationed at the door.

It's between the men flanking me.

Blood enemies. Bound by one woman. Torn apart by the same.

My mother's ghost sits with us too, invisible but heavy in the air. Her absence sharpens the edge of every glance, every word.

I wear her. Or close enough.

The blue dress clings to my skin like memory—an exact replica of my mother's favorite. The same midnight hue, the same elegant lines, the same fragile silk that used to shimmer when she twirled beneath ballroom chandeliers. I found it hanging in the closet. Not chosen by accident.

Wolfe knew exactly what he was doing.

My father sees it. His gaze skims the neckline, catches on the familiar slope of the shoulders, then hardens. His eyes flick to the neckline, then back to my face. No flicker of recognition. No change in expression. But I feel the tension bleed into the room like smoke.

No flinch. No reaction. Not even a blink.

But I see the effort it costs him.

The tightening of his jaw. The steel in his spine.

He knows what this is and refuses to give Wolfe the satisfaction of seeing it land.

But the silence between them isn't empty. It says more than a scream ever could.

It's loaded. Cracking.

And my mother's memory sits between them like a lit fuse.

Marcus's eyes dart to me again, hungry for confirmation that I'm whole. But Wolfe withholds it—casually, cruelly—savoring the way it twists the knife.

"Let her speak to me," Marcus grits out, a growl buried beneath cultured restraint. "Let me know she's okay."

Wolfe leans back, relaxed as a king presiding over court.

"You're in no position to demand anything." He folds his napkin slowly, deliberately. "But don't worry. She's here. Breathing. For now, that's enough."

My father's jaw clenches, but he doesn't lash out. That's not his way. He bleeds power without needing to raise his voice.

But I see it—the crack in his composure. Not from fear for himself. But for me.

He doesn't know what Wolfe wants, but I'm the prize they're both fighting over.

The nameless girl materializes beside me, pulling out my chair. As I sit, she keeps her eyes downcast, particularly when near Wolfe. Her presence at the edge of the room—not quite servant, not quite guest—creates a constant undercurrent of tension.

Wolfe takes the head of the table, signaling to the girl. She moves immediately to pour wine into crystal glasses that catch the light like liquid rubies. When she reaches Wolfe, he casually rests his hand on her arm, fingers digging in possessively.

She freezes, bottle still poised, until he removes his hand with a smirk in my direction. The message is clear: everything here belongs to him.

I fight the urge to stand up for her, but drawing his attention to her would only make things worse. I've seen that dynamic play out in charity galas where wealthy men treat their trophy wives as accessories. Making a scene never helps the victim. So I swallow my disgust, filing it away with all the other reasons Wolfe deserves to rot in prison.

"To family." Wolfe raises his glass. "The one thing that can never truly be escaped."

My father's face remains impassive, but I catch the slight tightening around his eyes. "If this is another attempt to rehash ancient history, I'm not interested."

"Ancient history?" Wolfe laughs, the sound sharp and without humor. "Is that what you call stealing the love of my life?"

The girl sets a plate before me—something artfully arranged that I have no appetite for. Her hands tremble slightly, and I see the faint outline of fingerprints still visible on her wrist from Wolfe's grip. She catches me looking and quickly tucks her arm against her side, as if hiding evidence of a crime we both know occurred.

"I stole nothing," my father replies coolly. "Rebecca chose me."

"Did she?" Wolfe snaps his fingers, and the girl hurries to a sideboard, retrieving a leather portfolio. "Perhaps we should let Aria decide that for herself."

The girl places a portfolio before me, then retreats to the shadows along the wall. Her presence is a constant reminder of what Wolfe is capable of—the human cost of his empire. I want to tell her to sit, to eat with us, but I know such a gesture would only bring Wolfe's wrath down on her later.

"Open it," Wolfe instructs.

With reluctant fingers, I lift the cover. Inside are photographs —dozens of them, carefully preserved. My mother, younger than I ever knew her, laughing in the sunlight. Her head thrown back, eyes crinkled with genuine joy. Beside her, a younger Wolfe, looking at her with unmistakable adoration.

The contrast is startling. In my father's photographs, my mother always looks composed, elegant—the perfect society wife. In these, she's radiant with unguarded happiness. I've never seen her smile like this in any picture with my father.

Something flickers across Wolfe's face—surprise, perhaps, that this revelation isn't landing with the impact he expected.

"That changes nothing." I close the portfolio, refusing to be manipulated. "Whatever ancient grudge exists between you two, it doesn't justify kidnapping me."

The nameless girl moves silently around the table, refilling water glasses with trembling hands. The crystal pitcher looks heavy in her thin arms. When she passes behind Wolfe, his hand darts out, catching her wrist. She goes utterly still, like a deer in headlights. His thumb traces slow circles on her inner wrist while he continues the conversation as if this casual violation is perfectly normal.

I taste bile in the back of my throat, but force my expression to remain neutral. Any reaction would only encourage him, make things worse for her. The helplessness burns like acid.

"Did you know," Wolfe leans forward, finally releasing the girl's wrist, "that your mother and I were in love before your father ever entered the picture?"

"You mentioned something, but I don't trust you." I look up, my gaze moving between them. I want to be loyal to my father, but in the photographs, my mother looks happier with Wolfe than in any image I've ever seen of her with my father. The contrast is stark—this laughing, vibrant woman versus the composed, reserved mother I remember.

"A brief infatuation," my father dismisses with a wave of his bound hand. "Rebecca quickly realized her mistake."

"Did she?" Wolfe's voice drops dangerously. He gestures to the girl again, who brings another folder, placing it before me with trembling hands. "Or did you threaten her family's financial security? Did you tell her what would happen if she didn't comply?"

My father's jaw tightens. "Ridiculous accusations."

I open the second folder. Bank statements. Loan documents with my grandfather's signature. Foreclosure notices dated shortly after my mother began dating my father, then mysteriously withdrawn.

"Your maternal grandparents were facing financial ruin," Wolfe explains, his eyes never leaving my father's face. "Until suddenly, they weren't. Miraculous timing, wouldn't you say?"

The girl moves silently around the table, refilling water glasses… again. When she reaches Wolfe, he absently runs his hand up her arm. She goes completely still, eyes fixed on the floor, until he releases her. The casual ownership in the gesture makes my stomach turn, but I force myself to remain impassive. Drawing attention to her would only make things worse.

The touch is proprietary, lingering. The girl's face remains carefully blank, but I catch the slight tremor in the pitcher, the way her knuckles whiten around its handle. This isn't the first time. Won't be the last. Each subtle interaction between them tells a story of systematic abuse, ownership rather than employment.

"You manipulated her," I say quietly, looking at my father.

"I protected her," he counters. "Damien was already involved in criminal activities. I offered Rebecca security, legitimacy."

"You offered her a prison," Wolfe hisses. He pulls something from his jacket—a small recorder. "Perhaps you'd like to hear Rebecca's own words on the matter?"

"Don't you dare—" My father lunges forward, straining against his restraints.

The girl flinches at the sudden movement, backing against the wall. The water pitcher clutched to her chest like a shield. Her fear is palpable, a living thing in the room with us.

Wolfe presses play, and my mother's voice fills the dining room. She sounds tired, defeated.

"He watches everything. Controls everything. The money, the staff, who I speak to. He says it's for my protection, but I'm suffocating, Damien. I made a terrible mistake."

"Edited. Manipulated." My father's face has gone ashen. "This proves nothing."

"There's more," Wolfe promises, his smile cruel. "So much more, Marcus. Shall we discuss the bruises her maid documented? The 'accidents' that always seemed to happen when Rebecca spoke of leaving you?"

The recording continues, my mother's voice growing more desperate. *"If anything happens to me, promise you'll watch over Aria. Marcus will try to control her like he controls me. Don't let him break her."*

The blood drains from my face. These words—my mother's voice—shatter something fundamental in my understanding of my childhood. The expensive schools, the security details, the careful monitoring of my friends… Protection or control?

The girl's eyes lift, watching me with something like recognition. Perhaps she sees in me what my mother once was—another beautiful possession in a gilded cage.

The crystal chandeliers suddenly seem too bright, the room too small. Every luxury around us—the hand-painted china, the sterling silver cutlery, the priceless artwork on the walls—all of it built on suffering. My mother's. This girl's. How many others?

The scent of expensive perfume mingles with the aroma of food neither of us will eat. Somewhere in the house, a clock chimes nine times, the sound echoing through marble hallways.

The girl shifts her weight, a barely perceptible movement that speaks volumes about how long she's been standing.

My gaze returns to the photographs of my mother—her smile, her obvious love for the younger Wolfe. I try to reconcile that joyful woman with the reserved, anxious mother I remember. The mother who flinched at loud noises. Who checked my father's schedule obsessively. Who taught me to be perfect, quiet, unobtrusive—to avoid his moods.

"Why this elaborate setup?" I ask, forcing strength into my voice. "Why the dinner theatrics?"

"Because you deserve to know the truth," Wolfe answers, something almost human flickering across his features. "About who your father is. About what happened to your mother."

A terrible suspicion begins to form. The "accident" that took my mother—a fall down the stairs. The closed-casket funeral. The way my father controlled the narrative so completely.

I look at my father, searching for denial, for outrage at these accusations. Instead, I see calculation in his eyes—assessing how much I believe, how to spin this, how to maintain control of the situation—of me.

And for the first time, I wonder if I've been living with a monster all these years.

TWENTY-FIVE

Jon

Blood pounds in my temples. Not fear—focus.

My wrists burn where the restraints bite into my skin. The thought of Aria alone with Wolfe sends something primal clawing up my spine. I force it down. Emotion is a luxury I can't afford.

"Family reunion," Wolfe said. *Tonight.* The words twist in my gut like a knife.

I work methodically at the right restraint. Seventeen minutes of silent, controlled movements. The sedative hasn't fully cleared my system, making each twist of my wrist require double the concentration. Blood slicks the metal as I work the padding, creating just enough space.

I dislocate my thumb. There's no alternative. White-hot pain explodes up my arm. My teeth clench against it, jaw muscles bunching. One smooth pull, and my right hand slips free.

With my free hand, the remaining restraints take seconds to release. The hidden pressure points give way easily when attacked from the outside.

Standing sends the room tilting. I breathe through it, riding the vertigo until it subsides. The concrete floor is ice against my bare feet.

The crystal decanter Wolfe left. I drink, washing away the chemical taste lingering in my mouth. Water. Not drugged—he wouldn't bother. He thinks the restraints are enough.

His mistake.

The antique leather chair he brought specially catches my eye. Symbol of his arrogance. I strip off my bloodied shirt, wrap it around my fist, and strike the chair where the wooden frame is weakest. The crack seems deafening in the silent room. Three more strikes and I have what I need—a foot-long metal support rod with a jagged end.

Now the waiting. I position myself in the blind spot beneath the northwest camera and go still. Heart rate sixty-two beats per minute. Breathing shallow and silent.

The guards rotate every thirty minutes.

Minutes stretch. My muscles remain loose, ready. The lock finally disengages with a soft click.

A guard steps in, hand resting casually on his holstered weapon. His eyes track to the empty chair, the bloody restraints. Pupils dilate. Breathing accelerates. He reaches for his radio.

Too late.

I drive the metal bar into the side of his knee. Cartilage tears with a wet sound. As he drops, a strangled cry catches in his throat. My hand clamps over his mouth, driving him backward. The taser from his belt is in my hand before his back hits the floor.

"Not a sound." Metal presses against his windpipe. "Blink if you understand."

Terror widens his eyes. He blinks rapidly.

"How many guards in the compound?"

He hesitates. I increase pressure on his throat, just enough to restrict airflow without crushing the larynx.

"Eight," he chokes. "Plus Mr. Wolfe."

"Where's Aria Holbrook?"

His eyes dart away. The subtle tension in his facial muscles tells me he's preparing a lie.

I activate the taser an inch from his face. The crack and sizzle of electricity fills the small room. "Try again."

"Main house," he gasps. "But I swear I don't know which room. Security rotation keeps us down here. We don't go upstairs."

The micro-expressions match his words. He's telling the truth —or at least what he believes is true.

"The other prisoner? Marcus Holbrook."

"Cell B-2. One corridor over."

"When's the next guard check?"

"Fifteen minutes. Johnson will radio when I don't respond."

I zip tie his hands and feet with his own restraints, gag him with strips of my torn shirt. The radio at his belt crackles to life.

"Check-in, Section C."

I adjust my pitch, mimicking the cadence and inflection I heard in his voice earlier. "All clear."

Silence stretches for three heartbeats. "Repeat check-in."

They're suspicious. The timing's off, or my voice wasn't close enough. I place the guard's radio into my pocket.

I drag the unconscious guard to the camera blind spot, take his security pass, and check his weapon—9mm Glock, full magazine, round chambered.

The corridor beyond is deserted—concrete walls, industrial lighting, numbered doors. Cameras every twenty feet, positioned for maximum coverage with minimal blind spots. Professional security setup. No windows, cool dry air—we're underground.

The security station at the end of the hall shows feeds from around the compound. A sprawling estate. Main house, outbuildings, perimeter fence. One monitor displays another cell—Marcus pacing like a caged animal, disheveled and haggard.

I scan the security system, memorizing the compound layout. We're beneath the main house. Two guards assigned to detention level, four patrolling the grounds, two in the main house, plus Wolfe. Nine total.

Whatever "family reunion" Wolfe mentioned could be happening soon. I need to move.

The stairwell door requires the guard's keycard. It opens with a soft click that sounds thunderous in the quiet corridor. Three steps up, and alarms begin to wail.

"Security breach, detention level. All personnel, secure positions."

I take the stairs three at a time, emerging into a service corridor. Red emergency lights pulse along the ceiling. A voice echoes over an intercom system—controlled, professional. Not panicked. These aren't amateur security contractors. They're trained professionals.

The corridor splits ahead—left toward the main house, right toward what looks like a utility area.

I move right, staying tight to the walls where cameras are less likely to catch movement. The corridor opens into a maintenance area—tools, electrical panels, a door marked "Server Room."

It's locked. The guard's keycard doesn't work here. Different security protocol.

Footsteps echo behind me—heavy, multiple sets. I duck behind a stack of supply crates as two guards rush past, weapons drawn, heading toward the detention level.

The maintenance room across the hall is unlocked. Inside, I find tool racks, supply shelves, and—jackpot—a building systems diagram on the wall showing electrical, plumbing, and communications infrastructure.

The main house has a dedicated office on the first floor, east wing. If Wolfe runs his operation from here, that's where I'll find information.

I grab tools that might prove useful—screwdriver, wire cutters, electrical tape—and stuff them in my pockets. The radio chatter from the fallen guard's unit crackles with coordinated search patterns. They're sweeping the compound systematically, working outward from the detention level.

The service corridor continues past the maintenance area, eventually connecting to the main house through a pantry adjacent to the kitchen. According to the diagram, it's the least monitored approach.

Three minutes of careful movement brings me to the pantry door. Voices filter through—kitchen staff preparing dinner. The smell of roasting meat and expensive wine wafts under the door. My stomach tightens. The "family reunion" must be happening soon.

I wait until the voices move away, then slip through into a gleaming industrial kitchen. Steam rises from pots on professional-grade burners. A rack of knives gleams on the wall. I take one—six-inch blade, perfectly balanced. It disappears into my waistband.

The kitchen opens onto a service hallway that connects to the main house. I follow it, encountering no one. The security alerts must be contained to avoid alarming whoever's in the main house.

The hall opens into a grand foyer—marble floors, crystal chandelier, sweeping staircase. Opulent. Old money mixed with new. I press against the wall, listening. Voices drift from somewhere deeper in the house—muffled, indistinct, but one is definitely female.

Aria.

Something loosens in my chest. She's alive. The relief is physical, a wave that nearly throws my focus.

Steady. Focus. Plan.

Don't rush in. Stop and think. Process.

It's saved my ass more times than I can count. I can't rush in blind. I need backup, which means I need to communicate with my team. From the sounds in the dining room, Aria's not under immediate threat. This gives me time.

The office should be down the east corridor according to the building diagram. I move silently across the foyer, staying low, using columns and furniture for cover. My bare feet make no sound on the cold marble.

The east corridor is lined with closed doors. The third one—slightly ajar—shows a slice of what looks like an office. No voices or movement inside.

I slip in, close the door silently behind me. The room is everything you'd expect from a man like Wolfe—leather-bound books, antique desk, oil paintings. But it's the modern equipment that catches my attention—a computer, an encrypted phone system, and a document safe in the corner.

The computer is password-protected. The safe is biometric. But there's a file cabinet against the wall, old-fashioned with a simple lock. The kind of place someone might keep less sensitive but still important documents.

I should keep moving, rescue Aria, but Wolfe said he wanted her to hear "the truth" about Marcus. If there's evidence of what that might be... I'll give that time to marinate.

The lock picks easily with the screwdriver from maintenance. Inside, folders are meticulously organized by name and date. One label jumps out: "Holbrook, Marcus - 1997-Present."

I pull it, flip it open. My blood turns to ice.

Police reports. Hospital records. Surveillance photos.

Marcus standing over a woman's body, blood staining his hands. Crime scene photos of a luxury apartment, furniture overturned, signs of struggle. Autopsy report: cause of death, blunt force trauma.

Newspaper clippings. "Business Mogul's Wife Dies in Tragic Accident." "Marcus Holbrook Cleared of All Charges." "Influential Family Mourns Loss of Rebecca Holbrook."

Rebecca. Aria's mother.

My hands don't shake. Training overrides the shock. I keep turning pages. Bank statements showing massive payments to police officers, medical examiners, witnesses. Evidence of a cover-up so thorough it's breathtaking—heartbreaking.

More folders. More evidence. A pattern spanning decades— women silenced, accidents staged, investigations derailed. Marcus isn't just corrupt; he's a monster.

And Wolfe has been documenting it all. For years. Building a case piece by piece.

The question pulses behind my eyes: Why? What's his endgame?

A thicker folder catches my eye. "Project Eclipse - 1995." Inside, papers so old the edges have yellowed. Shipping manifests to countries with lax regulations. Bank statements showing millions flowing through shell corporations. Photographs of Marcus at private airfields, shaking hands with men whose faces are familiar from international watchlists.

Then more disturbing images—makeshift medical facilities in what look like abandoned warehouses. People strapped to beds. Kids. Surgical equipment. Body parts labeled and packaged.

Organ harvesting. A criminal operation Marcus apparently ran in developing countries.

The folder contains meticulous financial records. Profits funneled through offshore accounts. Bribes to officials. All with Marcus's signature or personal authorization codes. It's sickening.

The last page is a newspaper clipping, dated April 12, 1997. Three months before Aria was born. A small article about a humanitarian investigation shut down due to "lack of evidence." In the margin, a handwritten note in precise script: "He buried it all, but I kept copies."

The pieces click together with sickening clarity. Marcus ran a horrific criminal enterprise. When investigators got close, he used his wealth and influence to bury the evidence and silence witnesses, but somehow, Wolfe obtained proof of everything.

And now he wants Aria to know the truth about her father.

Footsteps echo down the hall—approaching. I stuff the most damning documents into my waistband, replace the folder, and close the cabinet.

A landline phone sits on the desk. Direct line out. I pick up the receiver, dial Guardian HRS's secure emergency number from memory, and press it to my ear. It rings once.

"Guardian HRS, code verification." The operator's voice is crisp and professional.

"Delta-Three, authorization echo-seven-niner-tango-four." My voice barely above a whisper. "Requesting immediate assistance. Hostage situation. Marcus and Aria Holbrook held by Damien Wolfe. Nine hostiles, heavily armed."

"Location?"

"Unknown estate, forested area. Tracking my implant?"

"Signal acquired. Delta team already mobilized. ETA thirty-eight minutes."

Too long. "Tell them to hurry. Wolfe's planning something tonight. Some kind of 'family reunion.' I've found evidence—"

Footsteps in the hall, approaching fast.

"On the move. Will maintain radio silence." I hang up before she can respond.

I move to the door. Voices grow louder—coming this way.

"Please, just tell me what this is about." Aria's voice, strained but steady.

"Patience, my dear. Marcus will be joining us shortly. Then all will be explained."

Wolfe. They're coming this way.

I slip out of the office, scanning for cover. A door across the hall stands partially open—a small library or sitting room. I duck inside just as Wolfe and Aria turn the corner.

Through the crack in the door, I see her—hair pulled back, wearing a pale blue dress that isn't hers, face pale but composed. No visible injuries. The tight knot in my chest loosens fractionally.

They pass the library, continuing down the hall. Wolfe's voice drifts back to me.

"Dinner is almost ready. I've instructed the staff to bring Marcus up shortly."

"Why are you doing this?" Aria's question carries the edge of someone maintaining control by sheer will.

"Because you deserve the truth, my dear. And tonight, you'll finally have it."

Their voices fade as they turn the corner. The dining room. That's where this is happening.

The documents press against my skin, burning like a brand. Evidence of the monster who raised her. The truth Wolfe wants her to hear.

But not like this. Not as a weapon in whatever vendetta he's pursuing.

I check the Glock—full magazine, round chambered. The knife at my waistband sits ready. With my implant, Guardian HRS will have my location. Delta team is already en route.

All I need is time.

But how long? An hour? More?

Too long.

From down the hall comes the sound of chairs moving,

crystal clinking. Dinner is starting. The "family reunion" Wolfe promised.

I move silently toward the dining room, every sense hyper-alert. My bare feet make no sound on the polished floors. The knife's weight is familiar against my hip. The gun sits ready in my hand.

The documents burn against my skin. Truth as a weapon. More devastating than any bullet.

Eight guards plus Wolfe. Bad odds.

I've faced worse.

TWENTY-SIX

Aria

———

THE SILENCE THAT FOLLOWS MY QUESTION HANGS IN THE AIR, thick and oppressive. Wolfe twirls his wine glass, the burgundy liquid catching the light like blood. His smile is that of a predator who knows his prey is cornered.

"Marcus has always been a master of appearances," Wolfe says finally. "The perfect son. The perfect businessman. The perfect father." He sets his glass down. "Perfection requires rigorous control, doesn't it, brother?"

My father's face betrays nothing, but his knuckles whiten where they grip the chair arms.

"Let's continue our little history lesson." Wolfe signals the nameless girl, who brings another folder to the table. Her movements are mechanical now, fatigue evident in the slight tremor of her hands. Wolfe doesn't acknowledge her beyond a casual glance. She's disposable, and that hurts more than anything so far. For a human being to be so—degraded. I'm in the company of a monster.

"Rebecca's medical records," Wolfe explains as the folder is placed before me. "From her private physician. A man who mysteriously received a position at your father's flagship hospital shortly after your mother's—'heart failure.'"

The insinuation lands like a physical blow. I can't bring myself to open the folder. My fingers hover over its edge.

"More fabrications," my father says, but there's a new tension in his voice. "Rebecca had a congenital heart condition. It was tragic, but natural."

"Open it, Aria," Wolfe urges softly. "See what your father's definition of 'natural' truly is."

The girl has retreated to her position against the wall, but I catch her watching me from beneath lowered lashes. There's something in her expression—a terrible understanding, perhaps. Or recognition. The look of someone who knows exactly what I'm about to discover.

I flip open the folder. Medical charts. Doctor's notes. Photographs.

My breath catches. My mother on an examination table. Bruises bloom across her ribs in sickening purple-yellow patterns. Another image: finger marks around her throat. Another: a healed fracture noted on an X-ray of her wrist.

"Treatment for a fall down the stairs," reads one notation. "Patient reports accident with kitchen cabinet door," says another. "Patient declined to explain injuries," a third states clinically.

A familiar pattern emerges across years of documentation. Injuries. Explanations that don't match the trauma. A physician's carefully worded concern, followed by a sudden transfer to another doctor.

"This is…" I can't find words.

"They are lies," my father says.

"They are the systematic destruction of a courageous

woman," Wolfe finishes. His voice has lost its mocking edge, replaced by something colder, harder. "Your mother was dying by inches, Aria. Long before her heart gave out."

The chandelier light suddenly seems harsh, exposing. The crystal facets scatter light like accusing eyes across the room. The ornate wallpaper, with its intricate pattern, feels suffocating—luxury disguising the rot beneath.

"These could be anyone," my father dismisses, but a muscle twitches in his jaw. "Doctored images. Forged records."

"You've never denied being controlling, Marcus," Wolfe continues as if my father hadn't spoken. "You've simply rebranded it as protection. As love. The same way you've rebranded your entire existence."

My father's eyes narrow. "Coming from a man who traffics in human beings—in children—your moral outrage is somewhat laughable."

The nameless girl flinches almost imperceptibly at this direct reference to Wolfe's business. Her gaze remains fixed on the floor, but her shoulders draw up, as if anticipating a blow.

"At least I don't pretend to be anything other than what I am," Wolfe responds. He reaches into his jacket again, producing another recorder. "Rebecca knew exactly what she married, in the end. Listen."

He presses play. My mother's voice emerges, so familiar it physically hurts to hear it after all these years. But this isn't the serene, composed woman I remember. This voice is frantic, frightened.

"I can't stay anymore, Damien. The things he's doing, the business in Thailand—those people aren't volunteers. They don't survive the procedures. He's built everything on suffering, and if I try to leave, he'll—" Her voice breaks. *"He says he'll make sure I never see Aria again. That I'll be committed. That no one will believe me."*

"Turn it off," my father says, his voice low and dangerous. "Damien, I swear to God—"

"No, no. The best part is coming." Wolfe's smile is vicious. "The part where she begs me to help her escape. Where she tells me about the bruises you hid with the designer clothes you forced her to wear. Where she wonders if Aria might not be yours after all."

My father's mask slips. Rage contorts his features into something unrecognizable—something ugly and raw and terrifying.

"You bastard," he hisses. "You've always been jealous. Always wanted what was mine."

"She was never meant to be '*yours*,'" Wolfe counters, voice rising to match my father's intensity. "She was a person, Marcus. Not a possession. Not a trophy. Not another asset for your portfolio."

The recording continues, my mother's voice growing more desperate: "*If I stay, he'll kill me. It's just a matter of time. I need to get Aria away from him before she's old enough to become another victim—another decoration for his perfect life.*"

The serving girl edges further from the table, pressing herself against the wall as if trying to disappear into it. The tension between the men feels like a living thing, expanding to fill the room, squeezing the air from my lungs.

"You manipulated her," my father snarls. "Filled her head with paranoia—"

"I loved her!" Wolfe slams his hand on the table, making the crystal jump and the girl startle violently. "I loved her, and you destroyed her because you couldn't stand that she loved me first."

Something shifts in my father's expression—a calculation, a reassessment. When he speaks again, his voice has regained some of its habitual control.

"Rebecca made her choice. She chose stability over chaos. Legitimacy over criminality. She chose me."

"Did she?" Wolfe's rage recedes, replaced by something more dangerous—a cold certainty. "Or did she choose to protect her parents from financial ruin? To protect me from whatever threats you made? Did she *'choose'* to endure your control, your violence, your ownership for over a decade?"

The chandelier light catches on the silverware, flashing like blades. The heavy draperies seem to absorb sound, creating a suffocating intimacy to this destruction of everything I thought I knew.

"This is pointless," my father says, looking at me rather than Wolfe. His expression shifts, softening into the concerned father I've always known. "Aria, darling, you can't possibly believe these fabrications. Your mother loved us. We were happy."

But I'm remembering differently now. The way my mother startled at loud noises. How she always seemed to know my father's schedule better than her own. The "spa retreats" that coincided with visible exhaustion or unexplained injuries. The way she taught me to be perfect, compliant, unobtrusive—especially around my father.

"Were we?" My voice sounds strange to my own ears.

Something flashes in my father's eyes—surprise, quickly masked. He's not used to me questioning him. Not used to me seeing beneath the perfect façade.

"Of course we were," he insists, voice gentle but firm—the tone he uses in board meetings when someone has suggested something inconvenient. "Damien has always been disturbed. Jealous. Vindictive."

"And yet," Wolfe interjects softly, "Rebecca came back to me. When she tried to escape you."

The silence that follows is absolute. Even the girl has gone completely still, barely breathing.

"What are you talking about?" I ask, though something in me already knows the answer.

Wolfe's gaze shifts to me, something almost gentle in his expression. "Twenty-four years ago, your mother contacted me. She'd finally gathered the courage to leave Marcus. She had evidence of his business dealings, his abuse—enough to ensure her freedom, or so she thought."

My father's breathing has changed, becoming shallow and rapid. His control is slipping.

"Your mother, Aria… She stayed with me for three weeks while we made arrangements," Wolfe continues. "Three weeks of planning a new life, away from him. Three weeks of—*reconnection*."

The way he says *reconnection* makes my blood go cold. The implication hangs in the air between us. The timing… I count the years, coming to a conclusion I refuse to admit.

"And then?" I prompt, my heart pounding.

"And then he found her," Wolfe's voice hardens. "Threatened her parents. Threatened me. Threatened you. Threatened to use his connections to ensure she'd never see you again." His gaze shifts to my father. "But there was a complication by then, wasn't there, Marcus?"

My father's face has gone pale beneath his tan, jaw clenched so tight I can see a muscle jumping in his cheek.

"She was pregnant," Wolfe says simply. "And neither of us could be certain who the father was."

The room spins slightly. The crystal chandelier fragments into a thousand points of light, the silk wallpaper swirls with its damask pattern. I grip the edge of the table, anchoring myself.

"You might be my daughter, Aria," Wolfe says quietly. "Rebecca believed you were. Said she could see it in your eyes from the moment you were born."

My father explodes. There's no other word for it. The careful control shatters completely, revealing something monstrous beneath. He strains against his restraints with such force that the chair creaks.

"You delusional bastard!" he roars. "You think you can steal my daughter the way you tried to steal my wife? Aria is MINE!"

The possessive pronoun lands like a blow. Not "my child" but "mine"—a thing owned, a possession.

The girl drops a glass, startled by my father's outburst. It shatters on the marble floor, the sound like a gunshot in the tension-filled room. She immediately drops to her knees, frantically gathering the shards with trembling hands.

"Leave it," Wolfe snaps at her, but there's no real heat in his voice. His attention remains fixed on my father, whose rage has transformed his familiar features into those of a stranger.

"I should have ended you years ago," my father says, voice low and vicious. "When you first started sniffing around Rebecca. Should have buried you in the same hole as your whore mother."

Wolfe doesn't rise to the bait. Instead, he smiles coldly. "And there he is. The real Marcus Holbrook, ladies and gentlemen. Not the philanthropist. Not the grieving widower. Not the doting father. Just a vicious, entitled little boy who breaks his toys rather than sharing them."

The girl has retreated to the far corner, glass forgotten. Her wide eyes dart between the men, assessing the threat level, calculating escape routes. It's the instinctive response of someone who has learned that male rage typically precedes violence.

"Enough," I say, my voice steadier than I feel. "I want to understand what happened to my mother. How she really died."

"Heart failure," my father insists, but the rage has made him careless. His eyes shift away—the tell I've seen when he's lying to business associates.

"The night your mother died," Wolfe says quietly, "she called me. She'd finally gathered enough evidence of Marcus's operations overseas. Proof that Holbrook Medical Technologies was harvesting organs from 'donors' who rarely survived the procedures."

My stomach turns. Holbrook Medical Technologies—my father's legacy. Revolutionary transplant techniques. Life-saving innovations. Built on death?

"She was going to expose everything," Wolfe continues. "She'd made copies of documents, recordings of conversations. She was ready to take you and run."

"Lies," my father spits, but his eyes are wild now, darting between Wolfe and me.

"I told her to wait. That I'd come for her the next day," Wolfe's voice catches slightly. "By morning, she was dead. Fell down the stairs. Sudden heart failure. Got dizzy and *tripped*. How convenient."

The implication sits heavy in the air between us.

"That's absurd," my father says, but the denial lacks conviction. "I was out of town when it happened. There are witnesses."

"Yes," Wolfe agrees smoothly. "Your alibi was perfect. Just like everything else you orchestrate."

He slides another folder toward me. This one is marked with the Holbrook Medical Technologies logo. I open it with numb fingers.

Financial reports. Shipping manifests. Patient records from clinics in Thailand, Nigeria, Honduras. Mortality rates hidden in footnotes. Payments to families labeled as "compensatory settlements."

"Your father's real business," Wolfe explains. "High-end medical technology built on a foundation of harvested organs from people desperate enough to sell them—except they don't survive the 'donations' as promised. The perfect captive donor pool: poor, desperate, and disposable."

The clinical language makes the horror worse somehow.

These aren't statistics—they're people. Hundreds of them, reduced to "donors" in a spreadsheet. Lives exchanged for medical advancements and profit margins.

"Thousands of lives saved," my father counters, his voice steadying as he falls back on familiar justifications. "Revolutionary techniques that wouldn't exist otherwise. The greater good requires sacrifice."

"But not your sacrifice," I find my voice. "Father, how could you? These people had no choice." I don't know that, but the pictures tell a story of poverty and choices only the desperate make.

Something flickers in my father's eyes—surprise that I'm not accepting his explanation. That I'm seeing through him, perhaps for the first time.

"You don't understand the complexity—" he begins.

"I understand perfectly," I interrupt. "You built your empire on suffering. Just like Wolfe." I turn to Wolfe. "You're both monsters. Just different kinds."

Wolfe inclines his head, accepting the assessment with unexpected grace. "The difference, Aria, is that I've never pretended to be anything else. I traffic in human beings—a crime I don't deny, but those I sell survive the transaction." His gaze hardens as he looks at my father. "I don't murder them for parts."

The casual way he acknowledges his crimes sends a chill through me. The nameless girl stands perfectly still in her corner, her expression carefully blank at this discussion of people like her —people sold and bought like commodities.

"And my mother discovered this?" I connect the pieces. "That's why she died?" I hesitate to say *killed*, although I wonder now.

"She knew too much," Wolfe confirms. "Was ready to expose everything."

"You have no proof I was involved," my father says, but his

voice has changed—harder, colder. The mask isn't just slipping now; it's been discarded entirely.

"Don't I?" Wolfe produces a final envelope. "Rebecca sent me this the day before she died. Insurance, she called it."

He removes a handwritten letter, yellowed with age, and begins to read: "*Marcus knows I've found the files. He threatened me tonight—said no one would believe 'a mentally unstable woman' over a respected businessman. Said arrangements could be made for my 'care' that would ensure I never saw Aria again. I'm afraid, Damien. If anything happens to me, it won't be an accident, no matter what he claims.*"

My father's breathing changes, becoming shallow and rapid. His eyes dart to the door, calculating escape like a cornered animal.

"You killed her," I whisper, the truth finally crystallizing. "You killed my mother."

"She was going to destroy everything," my father snarls, abandoning pretense entirely. "Take you away. Ruin the company. Thousands of lives saved, medical advancements that changed the world—and she was ready to burn it all down over some worthless donors who would have died in poverty anyway."

The confession hangs in the air, stark and terrible. The nameless girl's eyes widen, her hand flying to her mouth in shock at his admission.

"She was hysterical," he continues, voice rising. "Unstable. The medication was just supposed to calm her, make her manageable until I could arrange more permanent care. How was I to know her heart would stop, or that she would trip?"

The coldness in his voice—the complete absence of remorse —is more terrifying than rage would be. This is the real Marcus Holbrook: calculating, ruthless, seeing people only as means to his ends.

"So you didn't mean to kill her," Wolfe says softly. "Just drug her into compliance. Make her 'manageable.' Lock her away from her daughter. That's so much better, isn't it?"

The sarcasm cuts, but my father doesn't flinch.

"You could never understand what I've built," he says, chin lifting with the arrogance I've seen in a thousand business negotiations. "The lives saved. The advancements made. A few hundred worthless donors against thousands of valuable lives extended. The mathematics is simple."

"Worthless?" I repeat, the word like ash in my mouth. "You think some lives are worthless?"

His gaze shifts to me, calculating even now. "Don't be naive, Aria. Of course they are. Society has always made these calculations—we just don't speak of them in polite company. A beggar in Bangladesh or a brain surgeon in Boston? Which life matters more? I simply acted on what everyone knows but won't admit."

The girl against the wall has gone completely pale, likely recognizing that in my father's worldview, she falls firmly into the "worthless" category. Disposable. A means to an end.

"And my mother?" I ask, voice shaking. "Was she worthless too, in the end?"

Something flickers in his eyes—not remorse, but irritation. "Rebecca became a liability. She chose that path."

"By discovering what you really are," I say softly.

His expression hardens. "By betraying me. By threatening everything I built. By running back to him." He jerks his head toward Wolfe. "After everything I gave her—security, luxury, position—she was going to throw it all away. Take you away."

"To protect me from you," I realize.

My father's laugh is bitter. "To turn you against me. To poison you with her weakness, her sentimentality." His gaze sharpens. "But I raised you better than that, didn't I? You understand what it takes to build something that matters. The necessary sacrifices."

The confidence in his voice—the certainty that I share his monstrous worldview—turns my stomach. Have I been complicit all these years? Benefiting from suffering I chose not to see? I don't think so, but I've certainly benefited from his crimes.

"I understand exactly what you are now," I say, each word deliberate. "What you've done. What you've built on the bodies of people you deemed expendable."

Something dangerous flashes in his eyes. "Don't be dramatic. You've never minded the benefits of my work. The lifestyle. The security. The opportunities."

"Because I didn't know the cost," I counter.

"Didn't you?" His smile is cold, knowing. "Or did you simply choose not to ask the questions that might have uncomfortable answers?"

The accusation lands like a physical blow because there's truth in it. How many times did I notice inconsistencies in my father's explanations? Staff who disappeared after asking too many questions? The secretive facilities overseas that were always "too dangerous" for me to visit?

"That's how he works," Wolfe interjects softly. "Makes you complicit. Binds you to him with beautiful chains you don't want to examine too closely."

My father's attention snaps back to Wolfe, hatred blazing in his eyes. "As if you're any better. Shall we discuss your 'merchandise'? The children you've sold? The lives you've destroyed?"

"I've never claimed moral superiority," Wolfe acknowledges, his gaze flickering to the nameless girl still pressed against the wall. Something like regret crosses his features. "Merely honest about what I am."

The girl's eyes meet mine briefly, and in that moment, I understand that neither of these men deserves my loyalty. They're two sides of the same coin—one operating in shadows, the other behind a veil of respectability, but both building empires on suffering.

The elegant dining room suddenly feels like a stage set—all beauty and no substance, disguising the ugly reality beneath. The crystal, the silver, the priceless art on the walls—all of it paid for with blood.

"You're both monsters," I say again, my voice stronger now. "And neither of you deserves to call yourselves my father."

TWENTY-SEVEN

Jon

The documents press against my skin as I move toward the dining room, each step silent on the polished marble. The weight of what I carry—names, dates, proof—burns like a brand against my lower back. Evidence enough to dismantle Marcus Holbrook, to finally expose the puppet strings he's been yanking for decades. But that only matters if I make it to Aria.

I press forward, each movement deliberate, blending into the opulence around me. The corridor stretches like a gauntlet, chandeliers dripping with crystal casting refracted halos across glossy walls. I stay in the shadows, slipping between the pools of light like a ghost. Every creak of the floorboards, every shift of air registers like an alarm in my head. I've made it this far, but the longer I'm loose, the tighter the noose will draw.

The dining room door stands partially ajar at the end of the hall. Voices float out in low cadence, muffled by thick oak. Wolfe's drawl, theatrical and deliberate. Marcus's tone, clipped and calculating. And woven somewhere between them, Aria's silence.

My Glock is warm in my hand. Full magazine. Round chambered. Knife tucked at my waistband. Delta team is still twenty minutes out—an eternity when you're running out of time.

Ten more steps. Eight. Six.

A guard rounds the corner, sharp and sudden. His eyes lock on mine. Recognition hits a second later—the prisoner who shouldn't be free.

"Intruder!" he shouts, reaching for his weapon.

Shit.

I lift the Glock, aim instinctively, calculate the angle to avoid hitting the dining room beyond. Before I can pull the trigger, chaos erupts.

Three more appear—one from a hidden side entrance I hadn't noticed, and two from the far end of the corridor. The door bursts open, and out comes Wolfe's head of security. Big, fast, and pissed.

"Target located," he barks into his radio, weapon trained on my center mass. "East corridor, approaching dining hall."

Four against one. Bad odds just became impossible odds. I've survived worse. But not often.

I fire as I dive, aiming for the closest threat. One guard drops with a grunt, shot in the shoulder. The second round misses as the chief barrels into me, driving me down hard. My ribs scream on impact with the marble.

The Glock skitters across the floor.

Rough hands grab for me. I twist, elbow connecting with someone's jaw, but it buys me seconds, not freedom. A boot slams against my neck, pinning me down. The cold seeps into my skin, into my bones. I'm face first on the polished floor, vision swimming.

So close. Five more seconds and I would have reached her.

"Sir, we have him," the security chief growls into his radio, pressing harder. "Threat contained."

Through the buzz in my ears, I catch the sound of Wolfe responding. Garbled. Dismissive.

Hands wrench my wrists behind my back, zip ties slicing into skin. Another set digs through my waistband, retrieving the knife with a satisfied grunt. But it's the documents they want. One of the guards yanks them free, the folded pages crinkling with the sound of damning truths.

"What about these?" A gloved hand pulls the documents from where they're pressed against my lower back. Marcus's crimes, exposed.

"Give them to me." A guard behind him pulls out a radio. "Sir, we have him. What are your orders?"

"Secure him in Containment Level B," Wolfe's voice crackles through. Cold. Impatient. "I'm in the middle of something important. No interruptions."

They drag me back the way I came, away from the dining room, away from Aria. Every footstep feels like a blade. Each inch of distance is a wound.

I memorize the route reflexively. Two right turns. Down a narrow staircase that stinks of concrete and bleach. Past a biometric scanner and a steel door requiring both keycard and numeric code. I log every detail.

Containment level B. Not back to my previous cell—somewhere deeper, more secure. The kind of place designed to hold someone who's already escaped once.

The lights change from the warm glow of the upper floors to harsh fluorescents that cast everything in unforgiving clarity. The air grows colder, heavy with the scent of concrete and steel. Underground bunker, professionally constructed.

They shove me into a room that redefines the word prison. Cement walls, harsh fluorescent light, and a single steel chair bolted to the center. No windows. No distractions. Only surveillance—four cameras in each corner, red lights blinking like eyes that never blink.

The security chief oversees the process like a man taking pleasure in his craft. He straps my ankles and wrists to the chair with reinforced steel cuffs, checking each one himself.

"Mr. Wolfe will deal with you after tonight's dinner concludes," the chief says, checking each restraint personally. "He's planned this evening for years. You're merely an inconvenience, not a real threat."

I don't respond. He wants a reaction. Instead, I lock onto him with silence sharper than any blade.

His jaw ticks. He leans in, voice a low snarl. "Your team's not coming. The girl will listen to everything Wolfe has to say, and when he's done ruining her, he'll come for you."

He straightens, nodding to the guards. "Triple the patrols. I want eyes on every entrance, every exit. No one gets in or out without direct authorization from me or Mr. Wolfe."

The guards file out. The door slams shut. Electronic locks hiss into place, sealing me in. I test the restraints one by one. Industrial strength. No give. No weakness.

I'm completely alone and on my own.

The chair doesn't budge—welded directly to the floor. The cuffs show no sign of manufacturing defects or improper application. Whoever designed this cell knew exactly what they were doing.

But they missed one thing.

Sewn into the inner lining of my waistband—my backup. A lock-pick set thin as wire, invisible to the untrained eye. They found the knife. Found the documents. But not the thing that's saved my life more times than I can count.

I close my eyes. Breathe.

Pain throbs across my ribs. Left side—definitely bruised. Maybe cracked. Vision blurred slightly on the right. Cut above the eyebrow—bleeding has stopped. Thumb dislocation immi-nent. It'll hurt like hell. I'll deal.

Above me, Aria sits at a table surrounded by monsters.

Wolfe wants to use the truth like a weapon. Wants to unravel everything she knows. The reunion he promised will be nothing but a calculated psychological ambush. If he succeeds in turning her against herself, against me, we lose everything.

And I can't let that happen.

Even if I have to break myself apart to stop him.

TWENTY-EIGHT

Aria

———

"You don't mean that." My father's eyes narrow, the calculation in them shifting to something darker. "You're upset, confused by Damien's manipulations."

"I'm seeing clearly for the first time," I counter. The crystal chandelier light suddenly seems harsh, exposing every line in my father's face, every flicker of his expression. The mask is gone now, revealing something cold and alien beneath the familiar features.

Wolfe watches our exchange, like a chess player observing an unexpected move. The nameless girl edges closer to the door, sensing the dangerous shift in the room's atmosphere.

"After everything I've given you," my father says, voice low and dangerous. "After all I've done to protect you, to provide for you—this is how you repay me?"

"Protect me?" I laugh, the sound brittle in the opulent room. "Like you protected my mother?"

His face contorts. "Your mother was weak. Sentimental. She would have destroyed everything I built—everything that would have been your legacy."

"My legacy?" I repeat, revulsion rising like bile. "Built on suffering? On exploitation? On murder?"

"Built on vision," he snaps. "On understanding that progress requires sacrifice. That greatness demands difficult choices." He leans forward against his restraints. "Do you think the world's advancements come without cost? That medical breakthroughs appear by magic? Someone always pays the price. I simply ensured it wasn't us."

The clinical coldness in his voice sends a chill down my spine. This is my father stripped of pretense—the ruthless calculator who sees human lives as entries on a balance sheet.

"So you admit it," I say quietly. "Everything Wolfe said about your business. About what happened to my mother."

Something shifts in his expression—a recognition that he's said too much, revealed too much—but instead of retreating behind his mask, something darker emerges. If he can't reclaim control through manipulation, perhaps force will serve.

"What I admit," he says, voice dropping to a dangerous register, "is that I've built something extraordinary. Something that has saved thousands of lives that matter." His emphasis on the last word is deliberate, cutting. "And I won't apologize for the methods required."

"And my mother?" I press. "Did she deserve to die for threatening your precious company?"

His jaw tightens. "Rebecca made her choice when she betrayed me. When she ran to him." His eyes shoot daggers at Wolfe. "When she threatened to destroy everything with her misguided morality."

"So you killed her." The words hang in the air between us.

For a moment, I think he'll deny it. Instead, his expression hardens with a terrible resolve.

"I did what was necessary," he says coldly.

No remorse colors his voice, only irritation at an unforeseen complication. "An unfortunate escalation, but the result was the same. The company was protected. You were protected."

The casual admission steals my breath. The dining room seems to contract around us, the ornate wallpaper closing in, the crystal chandelier light harsh and accusing. My father—the man who raised me, who I spent my life trying to please—just admitted to killing my mother as if discussing a business merger that had unexpected complications.

"Protected? Is that what you call it? Keeping me ignorant? Controlling every aspect of my life? Ensuring I became exactly what you wanted?"

"I gave you everything," he says, genuine bewilderment in his tone that I'm not grateful. "The best education. Every advantage. A legacy that will endure for generations."

"A legacy built on blood," I counter.

"Don't be melodramatic." His face darkens. "It's unbecoming."

"Unbecoming," I repeat, a hysterical laugh threatening. "My father admits to killing my mother, to building his empire on the deaths of countless 'worthless' people, and I'm being 'unbecoming' by opening my eyes and seeing you for who you really are?"

Something dangerous flashes in his eyes. The restraints on his chair creak as he strains against them.

"You've been corrupted." His voice rises. "First by Rebecca's weakness, now by Damien's manipulations. I won't allow it."

"You won't allow it?" I echo, finding strength in my growing rage. "You don't get to 'allow' anything anymore. Not with me."

His expression transforms into something I've never seen before—a raw, primal fury that erases all traces of the controlled businessman I've known my entire life.

"You are *my* daughter," he snarls. "*Mine!* Not his. Never his. Everything you are, everything you have, comes from *me*."

The possessiveness in his voice is terrifying. Not love—ownership. I realize with sudden clarity that I've never been his child. I've been his possession. His creation. His legacy.

"Maybe biologically," I acknowledge, my voice steadier than I feel. "But in every way that matters, I am not your daughter. Not anymore. You're dead to me."

Something snaps in him. With a roar, he throws his weight sideways, toppling the heavy chair. The restraints loosen as the chair arm cracks against the marble floor. Before anyone can react, he frees one hand, then the other.

The nameless girl shrinks back against the wall, terror etched across her face. Wolfe rises swiftly, but he's too slow. My father lunges across the table, crystal and silver scattering in his wake.

"You ungrateful little bitch," he snarls, lunging for me with hands outstretched. "After everything I've done for you—"

I stumble backward, my chair toppling as I scramble away from his rage. The chandelier light fractures across shattered crystal on the floor, each shard reflecting his contorted features as he advances.

Wolfe intercepts him, catching him mid-lunge. Despite their age, both men are powerful, driven by decades of hatred. They crash into the sideboard, expensive china shattering around them.

My father breaks free of Wolfe's grip, shoving him hard against the wall. I hear the sickening crack as Wolfe's head connects with the ornate molding. Blood streaks the cream-colored paint as Wolfe slides to the floor, momentarily stunned.

My father seizes the advantage, grabbing a heavy crystal decanter from the sideboard. He brings it down against Wolfe's skull. More blood spatters across the expensive carpet as Wolfe crumples further.

"I should have ended you years ago." My father raises the decanter for another blow.

The scene freezes my blood. My father stands over Wolfe,

who lies crumpled on an antique Persian rug, blood staining the intricate patterns.

"Always the same story, isn't it, Damien?" my father says conversationally, as if they're discussing business over brandy. "You want what's mine. First Rebecca. Now Aria. You never did understand your place."

Wolfe struggles to push himself upright, blood streaming from a gash on his temple. "Rebecca was never yours," he manages, voice thick with pain. "Neither is Aria."

The nameless girl has frozen by the wall, her eyes wide with terror. She's seen this violence before—lived it. For her, this isn't shocking; it's confirmation of the world she already knows.

I need to do something. The girl won't move—can't move. She knows what happens to slaves who run. My gaze darts around the room, searching for a weapon, an escape route, anything.

"Goodbye, brother," my father says. "This time, I'll ensure the job is finished properly."

My father strikes Wolfe again, the decanter coming down with brutal force. Wolfe's body goes limp, blood pooling beneath his head. Whether he's unconscious or dead, I can't tell.

"Now for you," my father says, turning toward me. Blood—Wolfe's blood—spatters his expensive suit, flecks his face. The civilized mask is gone completely, revealing the predator beneath.

I back away, my legs hitting a serving cart. Without thinking, I grab a carving knife from its surface.

"Stay back," I warn, holding the blade before me.

My father's laugh is cold, dismissive. "Really? You think you can use that? On me?" He advances, confident in his control over me—the control he's cultivated my entire life. "Put it down before you embarrass yourself. This unpleasantness has gone on long enough."

My hand trembles, but I don't lower the knife. My entire life has been about pleasing this man, earning his approval, obeying his commands. Breaking that pattern takes everything I have.

"I said stay back," I repeat.

"This rebellious phase is tedious." He shakes his head, disappointed. "We're leaving now. Once we're home, we'll discuss your future—away from these—influences."

He reaches for me, utterly confident I won't strike. That's his mistake. As his hand extends, I slash outward with the knife. The blade catches his palm, opening a shallow cut. He jerks back, genuine shock registering on his face.

"You little—" he snarls, looking at the blood welling on his hand. "You'll regret that."

His eyes darken with something I've never seen directed at me before—the same cold calculation I've glimpsed when he discusses business rivals who've crossed him. Opponents who later disappeared or were destroyed financially, personally, completely.

I'm no longer his precious daughter. I'm an obstacle. A problem to eliminate.

He lunges again, faster than I expect. The knife clatters from my grip as he seizes my wrist, twisting until pain forces me to my knees.

"I've given you everything." Spittle flies from his lips. His face inches from mine. "And this is how you repay me? With betrayal? With violence?"

His grip tightens, grinding the bones in my wrist. I bite back a cry, refusing to give him the satisfaction. Behind him, the nameless girl edges toward the fallen knife.

"You're coming home," my father says, his voice flat with certainty. "We'll undo whatever poison Damien has fed you. Whatever weakness he's cultivated."

"I'd rather die," I tell him, meaning it.

Something flickers in his eyes—consideration. "That can be

arranged, if necessary." The casual threat chills me to the bone. "But I prefer rehabilitation. You're a valuable asset."

Not a daughter. An asset. The mask has fallen completely now.

The nameless girl moves suddenly, darting forward to grab the knife. My father whirls, sensing movement behind him. The distraction is enough—I wrench free of his grip and scramble away.

"Run!" the girl shouts, brandishing the knife.

My father's laugh is dismissive. "Put that down, you stupid little whore, before I show you what real pain feels like."

She doesn't waver, doesn't flinch at his words. Something in her has snapped—the fear replaced by desperate resolve. She's trapped in this house with two monsters, one unconscious, one raging. She has nothing left to lose.

"Go," she tells me again, her eyes never leaving my father.

My father lunges for the girl, clearly expecting her to crumble in fear. Instead, she slashes outward. The blade catches his forearm, slicing through expensive wool and skin beneath. He roars in pain and rage.

I can't leave her—won't leave her to his rage. Not after everything I've witnessed. Not after understanding what men like my father do to people they consider disposable.

I grab a silver serving tray from the sideboard and swing it with all my strength. It connects with the back of my father's head. He staggers, turning toward me with shock and fury contorting his features.

"You dare—" he begins, but the girl uses his distraction. She slashes forward with the knife, catching him across the shoulder.

He roars in pain, spinning back toward her. Blood blooms across his expensive shirt, spreading like ink on silk.

"Come on." I grab the girl's arm, pulling her toward the

service door. My father stumbles after us, rage overriding the pain of his injuries.

We burst through the door into the service corridor. The service corridor is dimly lit and narrow, clearly meant for staff to move unseen through the house. I have no idea where it leads, but away from my father is the only direction that matters.

"We need to find Jon," I tell her, still gripping her arm. "Do you know where they're keeping him?"

"Basement cells," she finally says. "Through the kitchen, past the laundry." Terror and uncertainty war in her eyes. Helping me is already more rebellion than she's dared in years.

Behind us, the service door crashes open. My father stands there, blood streaming from his shoulder, fury transforming his familiar features into something monstrous.

"Run!" I pull the girl forward, down the dimly lit corridor. We race around a corner, my father's footsteps pounding behind us.

"This way," the girl gasps, tugging me toward a narrow staircase. We descend rapidly, the steps creaking beneath our weight.

My father's voice echoes from above, shouting threats and promises of what he'll do when he catches us. The sound drives us faster, deeper into the house.

We reach the bottom of the stairs, emerging into another corridor. The lighting is harsher here, fluorescent tubes casting everything in cold, unforgiving light. Utilitarian. Functional. The hidden machinery of Wolfe's operation.

"The cells are through there," the girl points ahead, where the corridor branches. "But there will be guards."

I move quickly, following the corridor as it turns left, then right. Ahead, light spills from an open doorway. Voices carry— male, gruff. Guards. I slow my pace, easing toward the light.

"—check the east wing again," someone says. "Wolfe wants the boyfriend found before midnight."

The boyfriend. Jon. He's alive, and they're looking for him. Which means he's escaped his cell.

A surge of hope rises in me. If Jon is free, moving through the house, there's a chance. A real chance we might get out of here.

"We need a distraction." My gaze falls on a fire alarm mounted on the wall. Without hesitation, I pull it.

Sirens wail immediately, the sound deafening in the confined space. Emergency lights begin flashing, bathing everything in pulses of red.

"This way," I shout over the alarm, pulling her toward where she indicated the cells would be.

A narrow staircase leads down toward storage areas. Away from the voices, at least.

I descend silently, one hand trailing along the wall for guidance. At the bottom, another corridor stretches into darkness. A service area, most likely—the unseen veins of the house where staff move like ghosts, attending to the needs of those above.

Perfect for someone who doesn't want to be seen.

I move forward cautiously, ears straining for any sound. In the distance, I hear the faint hum of machinery. I follow the sound, hoping it leads to a utility area. Somewhere with an exit.

We round a corner and nearly collide with two guards rushing toward the stairs. They halt, recognizing me instantly.

The girl moves with surprising speed, darting forward to slam her knife into the guard's thigh. He goes down with a cry of pain as his partner lunges for her.

I grab a fire extinguisher from the wall and swing it at the second guard's head. He staggers but doesn't fall. His hand closes around my throat, lifting me off my feet and slamming me against the wall.

Black spots dance before my eyes as oxygen dwindles. Behind

the guard, the girl hesitates, knife dripping with blood, clearly torn between running and helping.

TWENTY-NINE

Jon

———

The restraints are professional grade. Industrial, military, top-tier. Cold stainless steel embedded with reinforced lock housings and pressure-force pivots. There's no give. No loosened loop or warped hinge. Engineered with intent: to hold someone dangerous. Someone like me.

They've done their homework.

But they missed something.

No restraint is flawless. Not forever. There's always a weakness—we're just trained not to see them. A seam in the weld. A pressure point in the design. Something waiting. Something hidden. It just takes someone desperate enough—someone broken in all the right ways.

I let my body be still.

Breathe shallow.

My heartbeat thuds in my temples, strained and echoing like sonar. The metal wraps too tight around my wrist, tight enough to sing with each pulse. The edge has already peeled back the skin to raw meat. Blood warms the inner curve of my arm. Doesn't matter. I catalog pain now like an ally, not a warning.

I tense my hand. Flex. Rotate.

Skin peels more. My wrist slides just far enough that I can turn my thumb inward.

The next movement has to be fast. One motion, absolute. There's no halfway.

I grit my teeth and snap it.

The sound is liquid and brutal—like violent bubble wrap. The knuckle pops right out of the socket, sinew and tendon yanking free. Pain doesn't just bloom—it explodes. A white-hot fracture down my arm that punches through my lungs.

Motherfucker.

My throat locks. Vision fuzzes, the world narrowing to a white tunnel with a grenade siren screaming inside it. Can't think. Can't breathe. Everything collapses for a searing moment.

Then I come swimming back.

I sag forward and suck in air through clenched teeth. The burn lingers, but it's background now. Manageable.

Functional pain. Necessary pain. The kind that buys escape.

That buys time.

I wrench against the cuffs. The change in joint angle creates just enough slack—microscopic—and I force my hand backward through the ring. Bone grinds. Skin splits wider. The taste of copper hits the back of my throat—I've bitten my tongue. Fingertips stretch, shaking and numb, reaching for one thing.

The waistband seam.

Custom-stitched. Double-knit. Reinforced. I find the edge beneath the layered fabric and twist two fingers into it. I pull.

It holds.

More pressure. Pull harder.

Then—a single strand snaps like a tendon. And everything starts to unravel.

The thread parts, then the fabric. A tiny notch opens, revealing a silver sliver tucked deep in the fold.

My pick set.

I crush it in my palm like a relic, dizzy with relief. A breath escapes me—sharp, short—and vanishes into the shadows. I'm not out yet. But I'm close.

I wedge the first tool into the inner lip of the cuff. My other wrist is still trapped behind my back, so I'm working blind, fingertips numb and trembling. I rotate the tension wrench gently —too much pressure and the pin shears.

Sweat curls down my back in threads. My nose stings with the stench of blood and iron, along with something moldy in the walls. I tune it all out.

Focus.

Click.

Too soft to be sure—was that real?

I adjust the angle and try again.

Another click. This one is cleaner.

Then the cuff slips off with a faint, metallic chime.

My hand falls forward, swelling already setting in. I stifle the groan, press my fist to the floor, panting.

Not yet. One last step.

I grab my dislocated thumb, anchor hard against my thigh, and shove.

The joint crunches back into place with a sickening slap.

Black spots flutter across my vision. My stomach convulses. But I stay upright.

Everything tastes like rust.

I flex my fingers. They shake. The nerves are on fire.

But they move.

I stand, slow and low, legs aching from blood pooling at awkward angles. My equilibrium teeters, but I steady myself against the wall.

Next: the door.

It's unmarked. No obvious handle. Seamless flush paneling.

Tri-lock system. Clean. Surgical. But that kind of control? Means electronics. Electronics mean wiring.

Wiring means options.

Guardian HRS embedded it in us as instinct: Every system has an override. Fire codes demand it. Natural disasters. System crashes. Even the most secure facilities have panic contingencies wired beneath the surface.

I run my fingertips around the frame, every millimeter painstakingly cataloged. Then—there. A vertical seam just left of center. Less than a fingernail thick. Matte texture interrupts the smooth lacquered surface.

I slot my pick into the edge. Drag slowly. It catches. I let it ride the groove down until the panel wiggles free with a breath of friction and pops slightly outward.

Behind it—nestled in foam insulation—is a tangled, color-coded mess of wires.

Someone cobbled this together fast. No labels. No redundancy. It wasn't supposed to be found.

That means it might kill me.

I mutter under my breath, half memory, half prayer. "Red to black. Yellow bypass. Blue disconnect. Ground the circuit."

My fingers twitch over each decision. Mistakes here mean alarms. Gas. Fail-safes.

I isolate the wires, using the tip of the pick to strip connections. One wire sparks. I flinch, heart leaping—but the circuit holds.

I ground it to a stripped anchor bolt embedded in the floor.

A soft trio of clicks. Quiet. Final. Like coffin lids, one by one.

The lock disengages.

I don't savor the moment. No fist-pump. No breath of victory.

I'm moving.

The hallway beyond is near-dark. A sickly yellow light faintly fluoresces from the broken bulbs overhead. The air is heavy. Dust thick enough to taste. Mold creeps up corners. Every shadow could be a camera.

Could be a gun.

Far off, voices echo. Cuts of radio chatter. Words clipped and panicked: "Sector two breach… no visual confirmation… he's gone dark."

Damn right I have.

Noise swells ahead—boots. Close. Fast.

I duck back and press into a crumbling alcove just before two guards barrel past. Tactical armor. High alert.

Their guns are hot. Their strides purposeful. They're not performing a sweep. They're hunting and carrying the scent of urgency. They know I'm out.

I wait. Five seconds. Ten. Until the hallway quiets and the sound of their boots fades into nothing.

Then I move.

I sink into every shadow. My pulse leads me now—thunderous, but focused. Each movement is practiced and deliberate. I scan corners, wait for the telltale rotations of camera eyes. Up ahead—a vent, bricked shut. New. Not in Wolfe's blueprints.

He's changed the maze. Tightened the net.

Cameras dot the main thoroughfares now. Laser tripwires glow when you catch them at the right angles. If I hadn't trained for this, I'd already be dust and blood on the floor.

I slide into a maintenance corridor—too narrow to turn around in fully. Smells like burned dust and bleach. Pipes sweat condensation overhead. The air pressure shifts, like I've dipped below sea level. The architecture mutates.

This wasn't planned by architects.

This was carved by Wolfe's paranoia. Buried beneath everything official.

I hit a junction. Left is the luxury wing—wine cellars and imported Italian marble displays. Symbolic power. Public-facing.

Right angles downward. Archives. Old storage. Noise hums through the corridor—generators? Pumps? Something mechanical and private.

Something hidden.

I head left.

The walls shift to rough brick. Conduits hum to my left. Somewhere water trickles. The smell's different here—wet insulation, mixed with ozone and faint masks of ammonia. Chemicals meant to sterilize, to hide rot. It makes my stomach curl.

I round a bend—and freeze.

Two guards. Talking in low voices. One nods toward the stairwell I just came from.

I slide back into the shadows, pulse slowing. My breath catches in my chest, tucked behind cracked plaster and exposed wires. One boot scrapes nearby—then hope.

They walk past.

They don't see me.

I wait.

Slow count to ten.

Then I'm moving again.

Ahead—something new. A door with a keypad and reinforced paneling. Fresh wiring runs along the molding.

Beside it—blood.

A thin palm smear. Downward drag. Not enough to kill. Enough to warn.

My stomach lurches.

Too small to be Aria.

But someone was here.

I don't risk time with the keypad. Brute-forcing it in the dark might trigger a failsafe and bolt the place permanently.

I look. Behind the crates—barely visible—a recessed panel. Cleaner air slips through its seams.

An emergency hatch.

Slide latch. Manual.

I try it.

The creaking metal feels loud enough to wake the dead.

I slip inside.

And I know instantly—

Too quiet.

Then it hits—the sound. Sharp, sudden.

Crash! A piece of furniture screeching across tile.

Voices yelling. Frantic.

A scream. Female. Young.

My blood turns to ice and starts to boil.

Aria.

No conscious thought—just adrenaline. Motion. Velocity. I don't track where I'm going—I charge.

Past tumbled debris. Broken screens. A corridor spattered with aging blood.

Then—a corner.

I see her.

Choked. Lifted off the floor. A brute of a guard presses her against the concrete wall, arm flexed. Her legs kick weakly. Her hands claw at his wrist.

Near them, a body lies still. Another guard. A teenage girl crouched by him. Bloodied. Blade shaking in her grip.

Time stops. Something inside me snaps.

I'm on him before thinking. I snatch a length of rusted rebar from ruined shelving mid-charge. My first swing connects with the guard's head—solid and brutal. He grunts, stumbles.

Drops Aria.

She crumples.

I swing again. Catch him in the temple, full force.

His knees give out. He crashes to the floor.

I swing once more for certainty.

Then I'm beside Aria.

Catching her, holding her close as her body shakes and gasps for air. Tears stream down her dust-covered cheeks. Blood from a temple cut threads into her hairline.

My voice comes apart.

"Aria—" My hands desperately check for injuries. Jaw. Sides. Arms. Shoulders. "God, you're bleeding—"

She clutches my wrist like it's the only real thing left on earth.

"Jon…" she croaks.

THIRTY

Aria

Am I? I touch my cheek, feeling wetness. Not my blood—
Wolfe's, or my father's, or the nameless girl's. The thought makes
me shudder.

"Not mine," I tell him. "My father—he's free. He attacked
Wolfe. I think he might have killed him."

Jon's expression darkens as he takes in my disheveled appearance, the blood staining my clothes—not mine, but evidence of
violence nonetheless. His gaze shifts to the nameless girl, who
stands frozen, knife still clutched in her hand.

"Who's this?" he asks, though I suspect he already knows.

"She helped me," I explain quickly. "She's been Wolfe's prisoner. We're taking her with us."

"We need to move," he says, already assessing our options.
"The alarm will bring every guard in the building."

As if confirming his words, shouts echo from multiple directions. The house is mobilizing around us.

"This way." Jon leads us down a utility corridor I hadn't
noticed. "I've mapped most of the east wing while looking for
you."

The girl follows hesitantly, staying close to me, clearly uncertain about this new variable in her escape attempt.

"He'll help us," I assure her. "Jon rescues people. It's what he does."

We follow Jon through a maze of service corridors, the wailing alarm masking our movements. He pauses at intersections to check for guards before waving us forward.

"How did you escape?" I ask as we duck into what appears to be a laundry room.

"They underestimated my training." He doesn't elaborate, and I don't need him to. The unconscious guard we left behind in the cell tells enough of the story.

"My implant's transmitting." He taps behind his ear where Guardian operatives have tracking devices embedded. "Delta team is already en route. They should be—"

The building shudders suddenly, the concrete floor vibrating beneath our feet. In the distance, I hear what sounds like an explosion.

"That would be them." Jon's grim expression breaks into a slight smile.

"Your team has perfect timing." Relief washes through me.

"Delta team is clearing the building," Jon explains, checking the fallen guards' weapons and pocketing extra ammunition. "We need to head for the main entrance. They'll secure an extraction path."

We move toward the sound, Jon now more confident in our path. The alarm continues its relentless wail, but beneath it, there's gunfire. Controlled bursts, professional. Delta team making their entrance.

We move quickly through the corridors, Jon taking point, the girl and I following close behind. The sound of fighting grows louder—professional, coordinated assaults meeting desperate resistance.

"Almost there," Jon encourages as we reach a service stairwell. "Up two flights, then across the main foyer."

We ascend rapidly, the girl struggling to keep pace after years of malnutrition and abuse. Without a word, Jon slows, offering her his arm for support. She hesitates, then accepts, her wary eyes showing surprise at this simple act of human decency.

At the top of the stairs, Jon pauses, listening. "Delta is in the building," he says with certainty. "I recognize Jenny's breach pattern."

He eases the door open, peering into what appears to be a grand entrance hall. The opulence of the upper floors is a stark contrast to the utilitarian spaces below—crystal chandeliers, marble floors, and priceless artwork lining the walls. All of it built on suffering.

"Clear," Jon whispers, waving us forward.

We move swiftly across the open space, heading for the massive front doors that stand partially open. Freedom is meters away.

"Aria!" My father's voice cuts through the chaos. He stands at the top of the grand staircase, a gun in his hand—the same one he took from Wolfe's dining room. Blood soaks his left side, but his aim is steady.

"You're not leaving," he says, his voice eerily calm despite the madness in his eyes. "You belong to me."

Jon pushes me behind him, weapon raised. "It's over, Marcus. Delta team is here. You've lost."

My father's laugh is hollow, unhinged. "Lost? I never lose, Mr. Knutt. I simply adjust the parameters of acceptable outcomes." The gun shifts, aiming not at Jon or me, but at the nameless girl. "Drop your weapon, or I put a bullet between her eyes. One worthless life to secure what's mine."

The girl freezes, terror rendering her immobile. After everything—the knife, the escape, the hope of freedom—to be reduced once again to a bargaining chip. A disposable object.

"I don't belong to anyone." I find my voice. "Especially not a murderer."

Confusion and then rage flicker across my father's face. He's not used to direct defiance from me.

"Don't be foolish, Aria. Get over here now, and I'll let them live." Rage flashes across his features. "Everything I've done has been for you. For your future."

"You're a monster and a liar," I tell him, my voice steady despite the fear churning inside me. "You've always been a liar. You lied about my mother. You lied about your business. You've lied to me my entire life."

"I protected you from uncomfortable truths. There's a difference." His expression hardens.

"No, there isn't," I counter. "Truth is truth. And the truth is, you're a monster. You kill people you deem worthless. You killed my mother when she threatened your precious company. And you'd kill me too, if you thought you couldn't control me."

"Don't be dramatic," he dismisses, but the gun wavers slightly. "Everything I've done has been for you. For your future."

"For yourself," I correct. "Always for yourself."

"I'm a visionary," he corrects, his tone shifting to something almost reasonable. "You'll understand someday. After we're away from these—influences." His gaze shifts to the nameless girl cowering behind me. "Leave the trash behind. She's nothing."

The casual cruelty—the absolute certainty of his superiority —ignites something in me. Years of careful obedience burn away, replaced by a rage as pure as it is righteous.

"She has more worth in her little finger than you have in your entire being," I tell him, stepping forward despite Jon's attempt to keep me behind him. "She survived. She helped me. She's brave and human and decent—everything you pretend to be but aren't."

Confusion crosses my father's features, as if he can't comprehend my defiance. "You've been brainwashed. By him." He gestures at Jon with the gun. "By Damien. When we're home—"

"I'm never going home with you," I interrupt. "Never."

His expression hardens, calculation replacing confusion. "Then perhaps we need to remove the distractions." The gun shifts, aiming at Jon. "One bullet solves many problems."

"You'll have to shoot me first." I step fully in front of Jon, arms spread.

My father's eyes widen, genuine shock registering. In all his calculations, all his manipulations, he never anticipated this—his prized possession choosing to protect others rather than being protected. Choosing to stand against him rather than with him.

"Move, Aria," he orders, voice tight with barely controlled fury. "Now."

"No."

The gun wavers slightly. For the first time in my life, I see uncertainty in my father's eyes. Real uncertainty, not the calculated kind he sometimes displays in business negotiations.

"You would choose them? These—nobodies? Over your father?" Incomprehension colors his voice.

"I choose humanity," I tell him simply. "I choose truth. I choose freedom."

"Aria, please," he tries again, desperation creeping into his voice. "Everything I've built—it's all for you. Your legacy."

"I don't want it," I say. "Not a single blood-soaked penny of it."

His face contorts with rage. "Then you'll die with the rest of these worthless—"

The main doors burst open behind us. Delta team pours in,

weapons trained on my father. Jenny's at the lead, her focus absolute, her aim unwavering.

"Marcus Holbrook," she calls, her voice carrying across the marble expanse. "Put down your weapon. You're surrounded."

My father's eyes dart around, assessing the situation. Five Delta team operatives, all with weapons trained on him. Jon beside me, equally armed. No escape.

For a moment, I think he'll surrender. Then his expression shifts to something terrible—a cold, calculated resolve that chills me to the bone.

"If I can't have her," he says quietly, "no one will."

The gun swings toward me. Jon moves instantly, shoving me aside as he fires. My father's shot goes wide, shattering a chandelier. Crystal rains down as multiple Delta team weapons discharge.

My father staggers backward, blood blooming across his chest in several places. His expression holds something I've never seen before—genuine surprise. As if he genuinely believed himself untouchable, immortal.

He crumples to his knees, the gun slipping from his fingers. His eyes find mine one last time, confusion and betrayal evident in their depths. Then he pitches forward, sprawling across the marble floor.

Silence falls, broken only by the tinkling of fallen crystal and the distant wail of the alarm.

I stare at his fallen form, emotion warring within me. Relief. Horror. Grief. Not for the man he was, but for the father he could have been.

Jon's arms encircle me, turning me away from the sight. "Don't look," he murmurs against my hair. "It's over."

But it isn't over. Not really. The revelations, the truth about my mother, about my father's empire—those will remain. The knowledge that everything I thought I knew was built on lies and blood.

Jenny approaches, holstering her weapon. "Jon. Aria." Her gaze shifts to the nameless girl who stands frozen beside us. "And who's this?"

"She helped me escape," I explain, finding my voice. "She was Wolfe's prisoner. She needs protection."

Jenny nods, not questioning further. "Storm, get up here," she calls over her shoulder.

"Let's take a look at you," he says to the girl, who shrinks back, pressing closer to me. Storm's manner turns gentle despite his imposing presence.

"It's okay," I assure her. "They're the good guys. The real ones."

She allows Storm to check her for injuries, though her eyes never leave me, as if afraid I'll disappear.

"Wolfe?" Jenny asks Jon quietly.

"Marcus got to him first," Jon explains. "Unknown status, but significant head trauma. Dining room, east wing."

"Mac, Blaze, check it out." Jenny dispatches the men with a gesture. "The rest of the house is being secured. We found three more girls locked in rooms upstairs." Her gaze shifts to the nameless girl being treated by Storm. "We'll get them all proper care."

"Thank you," I say, meaning it with every fiber of my being. These people swooped in to save not just me, but everyone they could. No calculations about who was "worthless" or expendable. Just rescue, pure and simple.

Her radio crackles. "Wolfe is alive, barely. Medevac is on the way."

"And the guards?" Jenny asks.

"Those who surrendered are secured. The rest…"

Jenny turns back to us. "Extraction in five. We need to move before local authorities respond to the alarm."

Jon keeps his arm around me as we follow Jenny toward the exit. Outside, the night air feels impossibly fresh after the blood and violence of the house. Tactical vehicles wait in the circular drive, engines running.

"What happens now?" I ask Jon as he helps me into one of the vehicles.

"Now," he says, his voice gentle, "we get you somewhere safe. The rest—the truth about your father's operations, about what happened to your mother—that will take time. But Guardian HRS has resources. We'll find all of it, expose all of it."

The nameless girl is guided into our vehicle, Storm still tending to her. She sits close to me, as if I represent her only constant in this chaos.

"What's your name?" I ask her softly as the vehicle begins to move. "Your real name, not what they called you."

She hesitates, as if the question is dangerous. Perhaps it has been, until now. "Hope," she finally whispers. "My name is Hope."

"Hope," I repeat, taking her hand in mine. "You're free now. Really free."

As we drive away from Wolfe's estate, leaving behind the blood, secrets, and lies, I realize something profound. For the first time in my life, I too am truly free. Free of my father's control, of the legacy he tried to force upon me, of the gilded cage he built around me.

Jon

"Walk me through it again." CJ's voice carries no judgment, just the detail-oriented mind of a professional piecing together fragments of an operation to form a complete picture.

I lean back in the uncomfortable metal chair. Guardian's debriefing room hasn't changed since my first mission eight years ago—same gray walls, same surveillance cameras in each corner, same table designed to make you shift your weight every ninety seconds.

"Marcus had Aria at gunpoint." My voice remains steady despite the images flashing behind my eyes. "He already discovered the documents I found in Wolfe's office—proof of his involvement in organ trafficking, his role in Rebecca's death. Evidence that would destroy him."

Jenny nods, fingers tapping notes into her tablet. Across from her, Forest remains still, weathered face revealing nothing.

"He was aiming at Aria when the team breached the main entrance." The scene replays in perfect clarity. "Multiple shots fired. Marcus took at least three to the chest. Dead before he hit the ground."

What I don't mention: the relief that flooded through me when Aria emerged unharmed. The savage satisfaction when Marcus's eyes went blank. The way my hands didn't shake, not even once, as I held Aria while her father's blood spread across imported marble.

"And Wolfe?" Forest asks, the first words he's spoken in twenty minutes.

"Marcus bludgeoned him in the dining room."

CJ's eyes narrow slightly, catching something in my tone, perhaps. He's trained operatives to compartmentalize and report facts without emotion, but this mission crossed every line between professional and personal.

"The girl?" Jenny prompts.

"Hope," I correct automatically. "Not 'the girl.' Not 'the asset.' Hope. A prisoner. She helped Aria escape and came with us during extraction."

"Current location?"

"Staying with Aria at her apartment above the candle shop."

Jenny's eyebrow lifts fractionally. "Risk assessment?"

"Minimal." I meet her gaze directly. "She's traumatized but not dangerous. Storm's been monitoring the situation."

"Storm has been monitoring the situation," CJ repeats my words, the slight emphasis suggesting he knows exactly what that means.

"He's thorough." I don't elaborate further. If Storm's growing interest in Hope mirrors my own complicated feelings for Aria, that's his business.

"Ten casualties total." Jenny scrolls through her report. "Marcus, Wolfe, and his men. No civilian losses beyond Marcus Holbrook."

Ten men. Not a record for a Delta operation, but significant. I remember each face from the compound—security professionals, not street thugs. Men doing a job. Wrong side, wrong employer, wrong time.

"The evidence recovered from Wolfe's office?" Forest asks.

"Secured in the vault." I nod toward the floor, where three levels down, steel boxes hold enough information to destroy a dozen reputations in international banking. "Financial records, medical files, surveillance photos. Marcus Holbrook was running a sophisticated organ harvesting operation in developing countries for nearly two decades."

"And his connection to Wolfe?"

"Half-brothers." The revelation still feels surreal, too convenient for fiction. "Same father, different mothers. Marcus recognized as the legitimate heir, while Wolfe was abandoned and disowned. Otherwise, no connection. Their businesses were independent of each other."

"Wolfe's motive?"

"Revenge, primarily." I lean forward, elbows on the table. "Wolfe spent years documenting Marcus's crimes. The second kidnapping wasn't about hurting Marcus—it was about revealing the truth to Aria. Making her see who her father really was."

"And did she?" CJ's gaze sharpens.

Images flash—Aria facing down Marcus in those final moments, spine straight despite the gun aimed at her chest. Her voice unwavering as she rejected his demands, his threats, his manipulations.

"Yes. She saw everything clearly. Too clearly."

CJ nods, understanding what I'm not saying. The trauma of those revelations won't fade easily. The psychological impact of learning her father murdered her mother, trafficked in human organs, and built her entire life on blood money isn't something that heals overnight.

"The official story?" Jenny asks, pragmatic as always.

"Already in motion." CJ stands, signaling the end of the

debriefing. "Marcus Holbrook died protecting his daughter from his estranged half-brother, a known criminal. Tragic family drama. Nothing about organ trafficking, nothing about Rebecca's murder. The public record remains sanitized."

"With respect…" Something in me rebels at the thought of Marcus's legacy surviving intact.

"The files remain sealed." CJ's tone allows no argument. "For now. Ms. Holbrook has enough to process without the added weight of public scrutiny. What she chooses to do with that information later is her decision."

He's right, of course. Aria needs time to grieve, to process, to rebuild before facing the inevitable media circus that would follow such revelations. The truth hasn't disappeared—it's just been contained.

"Understood." I stand, muscles protesting after hours of debriefing.

"She's going to need more than protection." His voice drops. "She's going to need someone who sees her clearly. Not as Marcus Holbrook's daughter. Not as a client. As herself."

The insight catches me off guard. CJ doesn't do personal advice or emotional counseling. He trains operatives to complete missions, not to navigate relationships.

Before I can respond, he's gone, the door closing behind him with quiet finality.

"You're compromised." Jenny waits until his footsteps fade down the corridor before speaking. There's no accusation in her tone, just a statement of fact. Jenny doesn't judge. She assesses.

"Yes." No point denying what we both know.

"How are you handling it?"

I consider the question. *Am* I handling it? The protective instincts that flare whenever Aria's out of sight. The way my heartbeat synchronizes with hers when she's near. The constant awareness of threats, exits, angles of fire—not because it's protocol but because I can't bear the thought of failing her again.

"I'm functional."

"That's more self-awareness than I expected." Jenny almost smiles.

"I'm evolving."

"Clearly." She stands, gathering her tablet.

After the debrief, I head to the evidence room. It hums with climate control systems keeping paper and digital archives at optimal preservation temperature. I sit surrounded by boxes labeled with Wolfe's precise handwriting, each containing pieces of Marcus Holbrook's carefully constructed façade.

Photos spread across the metal table. Marcus at private airstrips, shaking hands with men whose faces appear on international watch lists. Medical facilities in abandoned warehouses. Financial records show millions flowing through shell corporations. Witness statements from those who survived his enterprises, their testimonies damning even in clinical translation.

And Rebecca. Aria's mother.

Her autopsy report lies open before me, the medical examiner's findings precise and cold. Blunt force trauma to the head. Defensive wounds on forearms. Time of death estimated between 11 PM and 2 AM.

Police reports document a tragic accident. A fall down the stairs. A grieving husband, too distraught to be questioned extensively. Case closed.

Bank records show payments to the lead detective, the medical examiner, and two key witnesses. Marcus's signature on each transaction, not even bothering to hide his tracks. The arrogance of a man who believed himself untouchable.

I trace the timeline meticulously. Rebecca had been planning to leave Marcus. She discovered something about his business dealings—possibly the organ trafficking operation—and reached out to Wolfe, her former lover, for help.

Marcus found out. Eliminated the threat. Covered it up with money and influence. He then raised their daughter—or possibly Wolfe's daughter—in a home built on that foundation.

"Heavy reading."

I look up to find Jenny in the doorway, two coffee cups in hand. She crosses to the table, setting one beside me.

"Anything new?" she asks, leaning against the edge of the table.

"Nothing we didn't already know." I close the autopsy report, unable to look at it any longer. "Marcus was a monster wearing a three-piece suit."

"And Wolfe was a monster trying to avenge a monster." Jenny sips her coffee. "Leaving Aria caught between them."

The simple summation captures the grotesque symmetry of the situation. Two damaged men destroying everything in their path, including the woman they both claimed to love.

"How much does she know?" Jenny asks, her gaze falling on Rebecca's autopsy photos.

It's a legitimate question.

Standard protocol involves information management for civilians, protecting them from details that might cause additional psychological trauma without tactical benefit.

But Aria isn't any civilian.

"Everything." I gather the documents into a folder, decisions crystallizing. "Wolfe exposed the truth."

Jenny doesn't argue further. Instead, she asks, "What will you tell her about Guardian HRS sealing the records?"

This gives me pause. Guardian HRS operates in shadows by necessity. Our methods, our reach, our influence—all carefully obscured from public view. The standard protocol would be to maintain that separation, limiting civilian awareness of our capabilities.

But again, Aria isn't just any civilian.

"She deserves to make informed choices about what happens next." I stand, tucking the folder under my arm. "Just because Marcus is dead doesn't mean his operation shut down. If it becomes a media circus, all his contacts will go to ground. If we keep things quiet, it allows us to take them down ourselves."

"My thoughts exactly." Jenny nods, apparently satisfied with my answer. "Sam has authorized limited disclosure at your discretion. If Aria wants to make this public, it will limit our ability to erase the entire operation."

"Agreed, but Aria will understand. She knows what's at stake." I check my watch—nearly seven. Aria will be waiting, questions burning behind those clear blue eyes. "I should go."

Aria deserves nothing less than complete honesty, but I believe she'll understand the need to keep her father's operation out of the public eye. Although, after everything Marcus took from her, I won't take that from her. She needs to decide what happens next.

Aria's apartment, above The Little Matchstick Girl, smells of vanilla and amber, warm notes that contrast with the cool evening air. I knock lightly, and the door opens immediately—she's been waiting. Hope stands behind her, watchful but no longer flinching at sudden movements. Progress, small but significant.

"Jon." My name on her lips still does something to my pulse rate, tactical training notwithstanding. "You're late."

"Debriefing ran long." I step inside as she moves back, cataloging details automatically. Two mugs are on the coffee table. A half-empty bottle of wine. Shoes kicked off by the couch. Signs of life continuing despite everything.

Hope retreats to the guest room with a small nod in my direction, giving us privacy. Another sign of progress—trust is developing where fear once ruled.

When the door closes behind her, Aria steps into my space, arms wrapping around my waist, face pressing into my chest. I hold her, one hand cradling the back of her head, the other splayed across her back. Her heartbeat against mine, steady despite everything.

For a long moment, we breathe together. No words, no questions, no demands. Just connection, grounding, and presence.

"How did it go?" she finally asks, voice muffled against my shirt.

"Standard procedure after an operation of this magnitude."

"What will the official story be?" She pulls back slightly, eyes searching mine.

Smart, perceptive Aria—already anticipating the sanitized version that will protect reputations and limit scandal.

"That is up to you. Guardian HRS's version will be Marcus Holbrook died protecting his daughter from his estranged half-brother, a known criminal." I repeat CJ's approved narrative. "Family tragedy. Nothing about organ trafficking or your mother's death."

"They're protecting his reputation?" Her expression tightens, blue eyes sharpening.

"For now." I touch her cheek gently. "The evidence is secured, not destroyed. What happens with it is your decision, when you're ready."

She absorbs this, processing implications with the quick intelligence that continues to impress me. "And Guardian HRS? What's their interest in keeping his secrets?"

"Public investigations bring scrutiny. That scrutiny will drive those who worked for him underground…"

"And prevent Guardian HRS from taking out the entire operation?"

"Correct." I squeeze her hand gently. "A media circus is the last thing you need right now, but if you think otherwise…"

"I know what's at stake, and if it saves one person, it's enough."

She doesn't argue, which tells me more about her mental state than any words could. Normally, Aria would challenge any decision made on her behalf, any attempt to manage what she can and cannot do. That she accepts this explanation suggests her exhaustion is deeper than physical.

She nods, decision made. She leans against me, head resting on my shoulder.

"Tonight, I just want to exist without being Marcus's daughter or Wolfe's target or even Aria Holbrook."

"Whatever you need." I wrap my arm around her shoulders, drawing her closer.

"I need you." The simple word carries layers of meaning, of trust, of something deeper than operational parameters or protective protocols. "Just you."

"You have me." Three words, inadequate but honest. "However, you need me."

Her eyes close briefly, some of the tension leaving her expression. When she looks at me again, determination replaces her exhaustion.

Her bedroom is familiar territory now—the cloud-soft comforter, the candles on every surface, the photos of friends and happier times lining the dresser. I've held her here before, after nightmares and revelations and moments when the weight of everything threatened to crush her.

Tonight feels different. Not frantic with adrenaline or desperate with fear. Just quiet need for connection, for proof that we've both survived. That something remains worth saving.

She turns in my arms, face tilting up to mine. "I keep thinking I'll wake up and none of this will have happened. That

Marcus will still be alive, still be my father, still be the man I thought I knew."

"I know." I brush her hair from her face, tucking it behind her ear. "The mind tries to protect itself from trauma."

"But then I look at you." Her fingers trace my jaw, my cheekbone, the scar above my eyebrow. "And I know it's real. All of it. The kidnapping, the revelations, Marcus's death."

The admission settles in my chest, heavy with responsibility and something warmer, deeper. To be someone's anchor requires strength, stability, and presence. All things my training provides, but for different reasons, in different contexts.

"I'm here." I turn my face to press a kiss into her palm. "As long as you want me."

"What if that's forever?" The question emerges barely above a whisper, vulnerability she shows to no one else.

The word—*forever*—should trigger warning bells. Instead, it settles like certainty. Like permission to want something I've denied myself since joining Guardian HRS.

"Then I'm yours forever." The promise comes easily, truth replacing tactical assessment.

Her smile blooms slowly, warming places inside me that have long gone cold. She rises on tiptoes, lips finding mine with familiar heat. I gather her closer, one hand at the small of her back, the other cradling her head.

The kiss deepens, muscle memory guiding us toward the bed. No urgency drives us tonight—just connection, affirmation, presence. Her fingers work at buttons, mine at zippers, layers falling away until nothing separates us.

I've memorized her body through nights like this—the curve of her waist, the sensitive spot at the base of her throat, the way her breath catches when I trace patterns along her spine. Tonight, I relearn every detail, committing it to memory as something I'm ready to name.

She arches beneath me, golden in the low light, eyes holding mine with complete trust. Her hands map my scars—souvenirs from missions across continents, each one a story of survival. She knows them all now, having traced them with fingers and lips, whispering questions in the dark.

When we join, there's no awkwardness or uncertainty—just the perfect alignment of two people who have found home in each other.

Afterward, she curls against my side, her breathing slowing toward sleep, my fingers trace idle patterns along her shoulder, memorizing this moment of peace amid chaos.

"Jon?" Her voice drifts up, already blurring with approaching dreams.

"Hmm?"

"I love you." Three words, simple and devastating. "I didn't want to say it during a crisis or because of adrenaline or trauma bonding or whatever psychological term applies. But I do. I love you."

The admission stops my breath, my heart, my world. Not because it's unexpected—we've been moving toward this since the first kidnapping, perhaps since the moment I saw her, the fire reflecting in her blue eyes.

Not in crisis. Not in fear. In peace, in certainty, in choice.

"I love you too." The words come easily, truth replacing tactical language. "More than I thought possible."

She smiles against my skin, the curve of her lips felt rather than seen. Her breathing deepens, slow and steady, her body growing heavier with sleep.

I hold her throughout the night.

Outside her window, the city hums—traffic lights blinking through exhaust haze, strangers going about their lives unaware of what played out in marble foyers and bloodstained stairwells.

But in here? Everything stills.

Time bends around the woman in my arms. Around the truth we spoke. Around the possibility I spent a lifetime avoiding.

For the first time in years, I allow myself to imagine a future beyond the next mission. A life that isn't measured in op reports or threat levels. A life with her in it.

And with that vision comes clarity.

This is what Charlie and Brett wanted for me. What they whispered about when they thought I wasn't listening. Not just survival. Not just duty.

Love.

The kind that doesn't fade in the dark or fracture under pressure. The kind that roots itself deep and stays.

We never had that, the three of us. We shared fire and purpose. Pain and loyalty. But not this.

Not peace.

I breathe Aria in—lavender and warmth—and something inside me settles. Something that's been restless since Charlie and Brett left.

They were right.

This is worth everything.

And for once, the future doesn't feel like a liability.

It feels like coming home.

THIRTY-TWO

Aria

BLACK DOESN'T SUIT ME. I KNOW THIS WITH THE CERTAINTY OF someone raised to analyze every fabric, cut, and color against skin tone and social context. My father made sure I understood the importance of appearance from a young age.

Image is reality, he would say. *The world sees what you show them.*

Now, I stand before the mirror in funeral black, the dark fabric washing out my complexion, making me look as hollow as I feel. The dress is a designer piece, perfectly tailored, exactly what Marcus would have chosen for this occasion.

Perhaps that's why I hate it so much.

"You don't have to go." Jon leans against the doorframe of my bedroom, watch already on his wrist, suit pressed to perfection.

"Yes, I do." I smooth nonexistent wrinkles from the skirt. "The world is watching. Image is reality."

The words taste bitter, echoes of Marcus's endless lessons in the management of *perception is reality*. But he wasn't wrong about everything. The media is circling, waiting for the grieving daughter to make an appearance—or conspicuously avoid one. Either way, they'll craft a narrative I can't control.

At least this way, I maintain the illusion of choice.

"Whatever you decide, I'm with you." Jon steps behind me, his reflection appearing in the mirror beside mine. His hand settles at the small of my back, warm through the fabric of my dress.

The simple certainty in his voice steadies me. Jon doesn't deal in manipulation or calculation. What you see is exactly what you get—a man of his word, solid as bedrock.

The opposite of the father I will bury.

"Thank you." I lean slightly into his touch, drawing strength from the connection. "I need to see this through. For me, not for him."

Jon nods, understanding what I mean without further explanation. Closure requires a witness. Without seeing the casket lowered into the ground, some part of me might always wonder if Marcus is truly gone.

If the monster wearing my father's face is really dead.

"The car's waiting downstairs." Jon's hand slides around to my waist, turning me gently to face him. "Ready?"

No. Not even close. But I nod anyway, reaching for the folder that hasn't left my sight in three days. The one containing the truth about Marcus, about my mother, about the family legacy built on blood and lies.

"Leave it here." Jon's hand covers mine, stopping me from taking it.

"But—"

"Today is about burial and closure." His eyes hold mine, steady and certain. "The past will still be here when you get back."

He's right, of course. Carrying physical evidence of Marcus's crimes to his funeral would be both unnecessary and unwise. The media would notice, questions would follow, and the carefully crafted narrative would unravel before I'm ready to deal with the fallout.

"Let's go." I release the folder, squaring my shoulders.

The cemetery gleams with old money and careful landscaping. Marble angels and granite monuments stretch across manicured lawns, and the elite of generations are laid to rest with appropriate grandeur. The Holbrook family plot occupies prime real estate near the center, naturally. Even in death, Marcus secured the best position, the most prestigious address.

I stand beside the polished casket, Jon a silent presence at my shoulder. Around us gather the expected crowd—business associates, political connections, social elite.

Not friends.

Marcus Holbrook didn't have friends, only assets and liabilities.

Who standing here is a part of his crimes? Part of the dirty underbelly of my father's work?

The minister speaks of a man I thought I knew—devoted father, community leader, philanthropist. Each platitude scrapes against the raw truth I now carry. The Marcus being eulogized never existed. He was a carefully constructed fiction, a mask worn over the face of a monster.

I keep my expression neutral; years of social training have served me well. Inside, questions circle like vultures. Did any of them know? The board members, the politicians, the socialites? Did they glimpse behind the mask, or were they as deceived as I was?

"And now, Marcus's daughter would like to say a few words."

The minister's voice penetrates my thoughts, calling me forward. This part wasn't in the program. I didn't prepare remarks. Didn't plan to speak.

But Jon's hand presses gently against my back, reassuring. I move to the podium on autopilot, social training once again carrying me through.

The crowd blurs before me, faces indistinct behind designer sunglasses and carefully managed expressions of grief. What do I say about a father who wasn't who I thought he was? About a man whose love came wrapped in control, whose protection was just another form of possession?

"My father…" I begin, voice carrying clearly across the gathering. "My father believed in legacies."

The words come from some place beyond conscious thought, truth shaping itself into language that won't shatter the delicate social contract of this moment.

"He taught me that what we leave behind matters more than what we take with us. That the world remembers how we shaped it, for better or worse."

Heads nod. The sentiment is appropriately vague, suitable for engraving on expensive stone.

"I stand here today not just as Marcus Holbrook's daughter, but as someone shaped by his vision, his determination, his unflinching pursuit of what he believed was right."

No lies, just carefully selected truths. Marcus did shape me. Did pursue what he believed was right. That his vision was corrupted, his determination monstrous, his pursuit stained with blood—these are details I keep to myself.

"The legacy he leaves is complex." My gaze sweeps across the crowd, noting which eyes slide away from mine. "As all legacies are. As all lives are."

A murmur ripples through the gathering. This deviates from the expected platitudes. Good. Let them wonder. Let them question what I know, what I might say next.

"I will carry forward what serves life, what builds rather than destroys, what illuminates rather than obscures." My voice strengthens with each word, conviction replacing performance. "That is how I choose to honor not just his memory, but my path forward."

I step back from the podium, the brief eulogy complete. Not what they expected, perhaps, but nothing they can quote as scandalous in tomorrow's papers. A eulogy worthy of Marcus's daughter—poised, controlled, revealing exactly what I choose to reveal and nothing more.

The service continues. Prayers are said. The casket begins its mechanical descent into the ground. I take the white rose offered by the funeral director, its petals perfect and unblemished.

Another illusion of purity.

As the casket disappears from view, I drop the rose, watching it land with quiet finality. Whatever Marcus was to me—father, monster, teacher, jailer—that chapter ends today. What I carry forward will be my choice, not his legacy.

Jon's hand finds mine, fingers interlacing with quiet strength. We stand together as the crowd begins to disperse, mourners moving toward waiting cars with a solemnity befitting the occasion.

"Ms. Holbrook." A man approaches, hand extended. I recognize him vaguely—one of Marcus's board members. "Beautiful words. Your father would have been proud."

The platitude scrapes against raw nerves. Marcus would have been proud of the performance, the control, and the careful management of public perception. He would have been proud that I learned his lessons well enough to hide the ugliest truths even as I acknowledge them.

"Thank you." I accept his hand briefly, posture perfect, smile measured. The politician's daughter, the banker's heir, the role I've played my entire life.

More people approach. More condolences are offered.

Connections are reaffirmed. Business cards are discreetly exchanged. Even at a funeral, networking never stops. Marcus taught me that too.

Only, I have the might of Guardian HRS behind me. We're cataloging everything. Tracing everything. No stone unturned. We will bring down what my father created.

The evil. The lies. The suffering. The victims. I intend to raze it to the ground, one smile, one handshake at a time.

Throughout it all, Jon remains beside me, a physical anchor in the sea of social performance. His hand at the small of my back, occasional whispers asking if I need a break, water, or escape.

I need it all, but now isn't the time to rest.

When the last mourner finally departs, leaving us alone beside the grave, I allow my shoulders to drop. The performance ends, the mask slips, exhaustion floods in.

"You did well." Jon's voice carries quiet pride.

"I did what was expected." I stare at the hole in the ground that now contains Marcus Holbrook. "The perfect daughter, even at the end."

"No." Jon turns me to face him, hands gentle on my shoulders. "You did what was necessary. There's a difference."

The distinction matters, though I'm too tired to fully process why. Jon sees beyond the performance to the purpose beneath. Understands that today wasn't about honoring Marcus but about witnessing an ending.

"Take me home." My voice cracks slightly, the first sign of the emotions I've held at bay throughout the service. "Not to his penthouse. To the shop."

Jon nods, understanding immediately. The penthouse was Marcus's domain, filled with his presence, his taste, his control. The shop is mine—the life I built for myself, the space where I exist as simply Aria, not Marcus Holbrook's daughter.

As we walk toward the waiting car, I don't look back at the grave. There's nothing there for me now. Nothing but earth covering a stranger I thought I knew.

THIRTY-THREE

Aria

———

The Little Matchstick Girl welcomes me with scents of amber and vanilla, familiar and grounding. Ember looks up from behind the counter, concern evident in her expression as we enter.

"You're back earlier than expected." She sets aside the inventory clipboard, moving around the counter to meet us. "How was it?"

"Appropriate." The word contains multitudes of meanings—the perfect funeral for an imperfect man, social obligations fulfilled, appearances maintained. "Everything Marcus would have wanted."

Ember's mouth quirks slightly, understanding the layers beneath my response. She's learned to read between the lines, to hear what isn't said aloud. One of the many reasons our friendship works.

"The shop's been quiet," she reports, shifting to practical matters with characteristic sensitivity. "Just the usual Tuesday regulars. Hope helped a few customers find signature scents."

"She did?" This catches my attention, drawing me from the funeral fog toward something brighter. "On her own?"

"Completely." Pride warms Ember's voice. "Mrs. Larson was particularly impressed. Said Hope had an 'intuitive understanding of fragrance profiles.'"

A small victory, but significant. Two weeks ago, Hope could barely make eye contact with customers. Now, she's helping them find personal scents, engaging directly, and building confidence with each interaction.

"Where is she now?" I glance around, not seeing her in the main shop area.

"Back room, working on a new crystal suspension technique." Ember gestures toward the workshop. "Ryn's been teaching her. They're really bonding, and she's been experimenting all morning."

The normalcy of this—inventory counts, customer interactions, creative experimentation—settles something inside me. Life continues. The shop thrives. People heal, grow, and create, even in the shadow of death and revelation.

"That's amazing. I'm glad to hear it." The funeral dress suddenly feels suffocating; Marcus's influence wrapped around me. "I'm going to change, and I want to see what Hope's working on."

Jon touches my arm lightly. "I'll check perimeter security while you do that."

Still the protective operative, even here in this safe space. I don't argue. His routines comfort him the same way mine comfort me. We each process trauma in our own way.

Upstairs in my apartment, I shed the black dress like a snake shedding skin, hanging it in the back of my closet where I won't have to look at it. In its place, I choose soft jeans and a worn sweater—clothes Marcus would have dismissed as "casual to the point of carelessness."

Good. Let my choices be my own, not echoes of his expectations.

The folder Jon brought from Guardian HRS still sits on my coffee table, waiting. I've read through it twice now—police reports, financial records, medical files. The evidence of Marcus's crimes is laid out in meticulous detail. The truth about my mother's death. About Wolfe's connection to our family.

About who I am.

DNA tests will confirm paternity eventually. The timeline makes it possible—even likely—that Damien Wolfe, not Marcus Holbrook, was my biological father. That the half-brothers' feud extended to me, to my very existence.

The knowledge should shatter me. Should rewrite my entire sense of self, but strangely, it doesn't. Whether Marcus's blood runs in my veins or Wolfe's makes little difference to who I've chosen to become. Nature may provide the raw material, but nurture—and more importantly, choice—shapes the final form.

I close the folder, leaving it on the table. The past doesn't disappear by ignoring it, but neither does it dictate the future. What matters now is what I build from these fragments of truth, what legacy I choose to create from the ashes of illusion.

Downstairs, the workshop hums with creative energy. Hope looks up as I enter, her face brightening with genuine welcome. The change in her over these past few weeks continues to amaze me—from the terrified girl who helped me escape Wolfe's compound to this focused young woman developing her artistic voice.

"Aria." She sets down her tools carefully. "You're back."

"I am." I move closer, examining her work. A clear glass container holds suspended crystals arranged in what appears to be a constellation pattern, waiting for wax to be poured around them. "This is beautiful."

"Ursa Major." Her fingers trace the pattern in the air above the glass. "The Great Bear. I found a book about stars in your library and…" She trails off, suddenly uncertain. "Is it okay that I borrowed it?"

"Of course." I touch her shoulder gently, careful not to startle. "Everything in the apartment is available to you. Books, especially."

Relief softens her features. Even after weeks of freedom, she still expects punishment for the smallest transgressions. Wolfe's conditioning runs deep, as does the trauma of years spent as, essentially, his prisoner.

"I thought—" she hesitates, then continues with growing confidence, "I thought we could do a whole collection. Constellations in crystal. Ursa Major, Orion, Cassiopeia."

"That's brilliant." The idea sparks immediate creative possibilities. "We could market them as 'Celestial Series' for the winter collection."

Hope's smile blooms fully now, pride in her idea visible in the way her shoulders straighten. "I've already started sketching designs for the labels. If that's okay?"

She passes me a notebook filled with careful drawings—star patterns rendered in gold ink against midnight blue backgrounds. The artistic skill surprises me, another hidden talent emerging now that she has the freedom to explore.

"These are perfect." I flip through the pages, genuine admiration warming my voice. "You have a real eye for design."

Color rises in her cheeks at the praise. "Storm helped with some of the astronomy details. Making sure the star positions were accurate."

Ah. Storm.

Delta-Six, demolitions expert, tactical specialist—and apparently, amateur astronomer.

His visits to the shop have become regular occurrences, ostensibly for "security checks" but increasingly focused on the quiet young woman who works with crystals and starlight.

"That was thoughtful of him." I keep my tone neutral, not wanting to embarrass her with obvious observations about Storm's interest. "When did he stop by?"

"This morning." Her fingers trace the edge of the notebook. "While you were at the… While you were out."

The funeral remains difficult for her to mention directly. I don't push for more acknowledgment than she can comfortably give.

"Well, I'm glad Storm could help." I hand the notebook back, shifting focus from personal to professional. "How many designs do you think we could have ready for the winter collection launch?"

Hope responds eagerly to the change in topic, walking me through her ideas for production techniques, pricing structures, and display options. The business side of creativity interests her as much as the artistic elements—another way she's finding her place in this new world.

As we talk, something inside me settles. The funeral recedes, Marcus's shadow diminishes, and what remains is this: creation, connection, purpose. The shop, with its warm light and endless possibilities. Hope, with her emerging confidence and surprising talents. Ember, with her fierce loyalty and grounding presence. Ryn with her quiet magic—somehow making the broken pieces more beautiful than they ever were whole. Not despite the fractures, but because of them.

The family I've chosen, not the one thrust upon me by birth or circumstance.

Jon appears in the workshop doorway, security check complete. His expression softens as he takes in the scene—Hope animatedly explaining her constellation concept, my full engagement with her ideas. Normalcy amid chaos. Healing through creation.

"Everything secure?" I ask, though his relaxed posture already answers the question.

"All clear." He moves into the space, examining Hope's work with genuine interest. "Star patterns?"

"Constellations." Hope's voice carries more confidence when discussing her work than in any other context. "For the winter collection."

Jon studies the crystal arrangement, recognition lighting his features. "Ursa Major. The Great Bear. You've got the positioning exactly right."

Hope practically glows at the validation. "Storm helped with the astronomical accuracy."

Jon's eyebrow lifts slightly at this information, a look passing between us that contains volumes. We'll discuss Storm's increasingly frequent visits later, in private. For now, the focus remains on Hope's creative development.

"It's excellent work." Jon's praise, always measured and genuine, clearly means as much to Hope as it does to me. "Distinctive product concept with strong market potential."

The security operative and the business strategist blend seamlessly in him, an analytical mind appreciating both the artistic and commercial elements of Hope's design. Another reason we work well together is that his practical assessment balances my creative impulses.

"We were just discussing production timeline for the winter launch," I explain, including him naturally in the conversation. "Hope thinks we could have five constellation designs ready by November."

The three of us fall into an easy discussion of logistics, supplies, and marketing approaches. The rhythm of normal business operations wraps around us like a protective blanket, creating space where healing can happen quietly, alongside everyday tasks.

This is how we move forward—not through dramatic declarations or radical transformations, but through simple moments of creation and connection. Through finding purpose in work that matters, in relationships that sustain.

Later, after Hope returns to her experiments and Jon steps outside to take a call from Guardian HRS, Ember joins me behind the register. We work in comfortable silence for several minutes, restocking display items and updating inventory logs. The familiar routines ground me, remind me who I am beyond Marcus's daughter or Wolfe's potential biological child.

"You seem better than I expected." Ember's observation comes without preamble, direct as always. "After the funeral, I mean."

I consider this assessment, measuring my internal state against the morning's events. "I am. Better than I expected."

"Why do you think that is?"

The question deserves honest reflection. I pause in labeling a row of amber votives, searching for the right words.

"Because I realized something today, while standing by that grave." The understanding crystallizes as I speak it aloud. "Marcus Holbrook wasn't my father. Not really. He was my jailer, my controller, my owner. The man I grieved—the father I thought I had—never existed."

Ember nods, understanding without judgment. "So there's nothing left to mourn."

"Exactly." Relief floods through me at being so completely understood. "I already grieved the father I thought I had when Wolfe revealed the truth. Today was—witnessing an ending. Confirmation."

"And Wolfe?" Her question comes gently, aware of the complicated emotions surrounding my potential biological father.

"A monster of a different kind." I set down the pricing gun, meeting her gaze directly. "Biology doesn't make someone family. Neither of them was truly my father. Not in any way that matters."

"Family is who loves you." Ember's voice carries the weight of someone who learned this truth through experience. "It's who chooses you. Who helps you become your best self rather than controlling who you are."

"Yes." The simple affirmation contains multitudes. "And by that definition, I have more family now than I ever did living in Marcus's penthouse."

Ember's smile warms, understanding precisely what I mean —that she counts among that chosen family, along with Ryn and Hope and Jon and the Delta team, who've become fixtures in our lives.

The shop bell chimes, interrupting our moment of connection. A customer enters—a middle-aged woman, stylish yet not ostentatious, with a wedding ring that suggests a disposable income. She epitomizes the target demographic for our premium lines.

"Welcome to The Little Matchstick Girl." I slip easily into professional mode, moving from behind the counter to greet her. "First visit with us?"

As I guide the customer through our signature collections, describing scent profiles and burn times, something settles inside me. This is who I am—not defined by Marcus's crimes or Wolfe's biology or even the trauma of what I've survived.

I'm defined instead by what I choose to create. By who I choose to become. By the light I bring to darkness rather than the shadows that created me.

THIRTY-FOUR

Aria

———

Evening transforms the shop into something magical. Display candles glow from strategic locations, casting amber shadows against white walls. The day's transactions are complete, the floors are swept, and tomorrow's production schedule is finalized.

I move through our closing routine—checking door locks, adjusting the thermostat, and counting the register. The familiar checklist anchors me to life continuing despite everything that's happened.

A soft knock at the front door draws my attention. Through the glass, Storm's broad shoulders are unmistakable. I check my watch—8:15 PM, well past our posted business hours. Not a casual visit then.

I open the door; the security code temporarily disabled. "Storm. Everything okay?"

"Routine check." His response comes automatically, professional mask in place. Then, slightly less formal, "Jon asked me to verify perimeter security while he's at HQ."

The explanation makes sense, but doesn't fully account for the slight tension in his posture.

"Hope's upstairs." I step aside, allowing him entry. "Working on those constellation designs."

Something flickers across his impassive features—interest quickly masked by professional detachment. "I should complete the security sweep first."

"Of course." I hide a smile as he moves through the shop, checking windows, locks, and alarm systems. The performance of duty before personal interest.

When the security check concludes, he hesitates near the stairs, clearly wanting to go up but unwilling to ask directly.

"She was hoping to show you the Orion design." I offer the excuse he needs. "Said something about star alignment questions."

Relief crosses his face, followed immediately by an attempt to appear merely professionally interested. "I should verify her astronomical references. For accuracy."

"Naturally." I keep my expression neutral despite the amusement bubbling beneath. "Incorrect star patterns could be severe."

His eyes narrow slightly, catching my gentle teasing, but instead of retreating into professional distance, a small smile touches his lips.

"Very severe." He moves toward the stairs with newfound purpose. "I'd better address it immediately."

I watch him ascend, this mountain of a man who disarms bombs and breaches secure facilities for a living, now moving toward a young woman who arranges crystals into star patterns. The unexpected tenderness of it catches in my chest.

Life finds a way, even in the most damaged soil.

The shop phone rings, breaking my contemplation. I answer automatically, expecting a customer with a last-minute order question.

"Little Matchstick Girl, this is Aria."

"Ms. Holbrook." A woman's crisp, professional voice responds. "This is Veronica Chambers from the Wall Street Journal. I was hoping to speak with you regarding your father's estate and the allegations surrounding his international business dealings."

Ice floods my veins. The carefully constructed narrative is already fraying at the edges. Questions emerging. Investigations beginning.

"Today was my father's funeral. I'm sure you understand my need for privacy." My voice remains steady despite the internal alarm bells. "I have no comment at this time."

"Of course." The reporter's tone suggests anything but understanding. "However, our sources indicate significant irregularities in offshore accounts connected to Holbrook International. As his primary heir, you must have some knowledge of—"

"As I said, no comment." I cut her off with polite firmness. "Any questions regarding Holbrook International should be directed to the corporate communications office. Goodbye."

I hang up before she can respond, heart racing despite the outward calm I maintained. It begins. The questions. The investigations. The unraveling of Marcus's empire.

My phone buzzes with a text notification.

Jon: *On my way back. Guardian HRS intercepted press inquiries. We need to talk strategy.*

Of course, Guardian HRS would be monitoring media interest. Their operational security depends on controlling the narrative around Marcus's death and the events at Wolfe's compound.

I text back: *WSJ already called the shop. More will follow.*

His response comes quickly: *We'll handle it. Together.*

The simple reassurance steadies me. I'm not alone in this. I'm not facing Marcus's legacy without support. Jon will be here soon, with Guardian HQ resources and his unwavering presence.

Until then, I have work to do. A new candle to formulate—something I've been contemplating since reading through Wolfe's files. A scent that captures the journey from darkness to light, from illusion to truth, from imprisonment to freedom.

In the workshop, I gather ingredients. Amber for warmth and grounding. Sandalwood for strength and wisdom. Black pepper for protection against negative energy. Vanilla for comfort and healing.

Each element is selected not just for its aromatic properties but for its symbolic resonance. A candle created not for commercial appeal but for personal meaning.

For transformation.

The wax softens under steady heat, shifting from solid to liquid in slow surrender. Like truth easing free from behind carefully built walls. Like resilience forged in the quiet aftermath of being broken.

I'll call it "Truth." A personal talisman against future deception. A reminder that light reveals what darkness conceals.

As I work, the events of recent weeks take on a new perspective. Marcus's death. Wolfe's revelations. The destruction of everything I thought I knew about my family, my history, my identity.

Painful, yes. Devastating in many ways. But also liberating. The lies that shaped my life have burned away, leaving only truth in their wake—a painful truth, but mine to face, accept, and build upon.

The wax reaches the perfect temperature. I add fragrance oils in precise measurements, stirring with intention. Ember would be so proud. The scent rises—complex, multifaceted, initially sharp but warming to something rich and grounding.

Like truth itself.

Footsteps announce Jon's arrival. I don't look up from my work, knowing he'll understand this moment of creation isn't to be interrupted. He moves quietly into the workshop, taking a seat at the preparation table, watching without intruding.

When the wax and fragrance have properly bonded, I pour it into waiting vessels—clear glass that will allow the light to shine through unfiltered. No decoration, no embellishment. Just pure illumination.

Only when the last container is filled do I turn to Jon, finding his eyes already on me, patient and present.

"Truth," I say simply, gesturing to the cooling candles.

"It suits you." He nods, understanding without further explanation.

Three words that contain multitudes. That acknowledges the journey I've undertaken, the strength I've discovered, the light I've found amid darkness.

"The Journal called." I move to wash my hands, practical matters reasserting themselves. "Others will follow."

"Guardian HRS is preparing a strategy." Jon's voice carries the steady certainty I've come to rely on. "Legal is reviewing options. Forest wants to meet tomorrow to discuss the approach. You are not alone in this. We're here to support you through it."

The operational language comforts rather than alienates. Concrete steps. Clear parameters. A path forward through complicated terrain.

"Whatever happens with Marcus's legacy," I say, drying my hands on a workshop towel, "I want the truth protected. Not hidden."

"I need you to hear this." Jon studies me, gauging my certainty. Then he exhales slowly and measuredly. "If we expose everything now, we handcuff Guardian HRS. Tip our hand. We lose access, leverage, and the ability to track who else was involved."

"You're saying we lie." My spine straightens.

"I'm saying we play the long game." He closes the distance

between us, voice low but firm. "If you want to disrupt the operation—if you want Guardian HRS to take down the entire network—you may have to live with some half-truths a little longer. Not forever. Just until it's safe to burn it all down."

I search his eyes. No manipulation there. Just hard-earned reality. Strategy, not avoidance.

"I know." I meet his gaze steadily. "But I'm done living with lies. Done protecting reputations at the expense of truth."

"You need to tell us what you want. We can tell the truth, or we can save lives—on our terms. With preparation. And no compromise where it counts."

He doesn't say the rest. That going public now would set off alarms. Drive Marcus's associates into hiding. Shatter Guardian HRS's chances of exposing the whole network. It's a white lie for a greater good, and I get it even if it tastes like ash.

I'm not alone in this. Not facing Marcus's twisted legacy or Wolfe's murky truths without backup. Jon is beside me. Guardian HRS at my back. My chosen family holds the line so I don't have to carry it alone.

"I'm not afraid." The words come out before I fully realize them. But they're true. "Not of what people will say. Not of Marcus's legacy burning. Not of who I'll be without the Holbrook name and fortune."

I pause, breath tight with the weight of what I do fear.

"But I need it to stop. The suffering. The silence. The damage that keeps spreading."

Jon watches me, steady and unflinching.

"Whatever Guardian HRS needs to make that happen, I'm in. Even if it means sitting with half-truths a little longer. As long as we take the whole thing down in the end."

"We will." His hand brushes mine—solid, grounding. "And for what it's worth, you're so much more than any name or fortune could encompass."

His hands frame my face, rough palms warm against my skin, steadying more than just my breath. His eyes hold mine—not calculating, not scanning for threats—but wide open and full of everything he's never said aloud until now.

No tactical assessment. No mission protocol. Just Jon. Seeing me. Knowing me and choosing me.

"I love you," he says, like it's the most obvious thing in the world. Like it's never been in question.

"And I love you. More than I thought possible." The words don't tremble. They don't catch. They come strong, sure. "Not because you saved me or protected me, but because you see me. The real me, beneath all the expectations."

His gaze dips to my mouth. No heat this time. No urgency. Just reverence.

The kiss that follows isn't a rush of adrenaline or a storm of need—it's the kind of kiss that settles into your bones. The kind that tells the truth in a thousand quiet ways. His lips press to mine, slow and unhurried, a whisper of devotion and choice. A kiss that says you're safe now. A kiss that says we made it.

He deepens it just slightly, one hand at the nape of my neck, fingers splayed like he needs to feel every inch of me breathing. My hands slip under his shirt, palms flat against the rigid muscles of his back. Not pulling him closer. Just—holding. Being held.

There's no place else we need to be. No one watching. No fear of what comes next. Only this.

When we finally part, it's not with reluctance, but with peace. I stay pressed to him, forehead resting against his chest. His heartbeat is a metronome beneath my ear—calm, constant. My safe place.

Outside, the world keeps turning. But here, in his arms, I'm still.

Around us, the workshop hums softly. Cooling candles.

Melted wax. Scattered tools waiting to be used. It smells like lavender and old wood, the scent of things mending.

And for the first time, love doesn't feel like something fragile.

It feels like a foundation.

Like home.

Outside, the world continues—media inquiries will multiply, investigations will begin. Marcus's empire will unravel, thread by thread. But here, now, time holds still. Suspended in the warmth of this truth. This love. This clarity forged in fire.

I am Aria.

Not Marcus's heir. Not Wolfe's pawn.

Not a survivor of someone else's war.

I am the architect of my own legacy.

And I choose light.

Even if I had to walk through hell to claim it.

THIRTY-FIVE

Aria

"Perfect timing." Ember's voice cuts through the bustle of pre-opening preparations. "The Truth candles just arrived from the manufacturer."

I set down my clipboard and move toward the delivery boxes stacked near the register. After weeks of testing, refining, and scaling up production, seeing the finished product finally arrive brings a satisfaction deeper than any business achievement under Marcus's watchful eye ever did.

This is ours. Created from our experience, produced under our direction, marketed according to our vision.

Truth, bottled in glass and wax.

"They look amazing." Hope appears beside me, carefully lifting one from its protective packaging. The clear glass container allows the amber-gold wax to shine through, unobstructed and luminous. No decorative elements, no embellishment—just pure light waiting to be kindled.

"Your constellation series complements them perfectly." I gesture toward the display we've set up for tonight's event—Hope's crystal-embedded candles arranged in astronomical patterns, each labeled with gold-flecked star charts and poetic descriptions.

The contrast works exactly as I'd envisioned—my stark, unadorned Truth candles surrounding Hope's intricate celestial creations. Simplicity and complexity. Revelation and mystery. Different expressions of the same fundamental pursuit—illumination.

"Five minutes to doors open." Jon's voice carries from the entrance, where he's completing final security checks. Not because we expect trouble, but because habits formed in crisis don't simply disappear when danger passes.

The shop hums with pre-launch energy. Our biggest event since reopening after everything that happened at Wolfe's compound. The official introduction of both new collections—Truth and Celestial—to our most loyal customers and select media representatives.

Three months ago, I could barely imagine this moment. Three months ago, I stood in Wolfe's dining room learning that everything I thought I knew about my family was a lie. That Marcus, the father I'd both loved and feared, was a monster wearing a businessman's mask. That Wolfe, the man who kidnapped me, might be my biological father.

Three months of rebuilding. Of healing. Of choosing what to carry forward and what to leave buried alongside Marcus in that pristine cemetery plot.

"Nervous?" Ember appears at my elbow, voice pitched for my ears alone.

"Strangely, no." I adjust a Truth candle's position slightly, aligning it perfectly with its neighbors. "This feels right. Complete, somehow."

She nods, understanding without further explanation. Ember knows about journeys of transformation, about emerging stronger from darkness. Her own path from survivor to successful business owner parallels mine in many ways.

"Delta team is all accounted for." Ember gestures subtly toward the Guardian operatives positioned throughout the shop. Jenny by the register, Mac near the eastern window, Blaze examining candle displays with what might almost pass for interest. "Storm's watching the back entrance."

"With Hope, no doubt." I don't bother hiding my smile. The connection between the quiet, stargazing girl and the stoic demolitions expert has grown stronger each week. An unlikely pairing that somehow works perfectly.

"Naturally." Ember's grin mirrors mine. "Discussing 'security protocols' that somehow always involve constellation patterns."

But even as we share the moment, two faces are missing.

"No Razor?" I ask.

Ember's eyes gleam. "He and Ryn volunteered for *perimeter sweep*."

"Is that what we're calling it?" I raise a brow.

A knowing shrug. "Longer sweeps lately. Lot of 'detours.'"

Something in my chest warms. These Guardian men—trained to be detached, deadly, unshakable—seem to fall the hardest when they finally let themselves feel. Storm with Hope. Razor with Ryn. Men of steel discovering what it means to be tethered.

Anchored.

Our shared amusement fades as Jon approaches, expression professionally neutral but eyes carrying a warmth reserved for me alone.

"Everything secure?" I ask, though I already know the answer. Jon wouldn't be here, focused on me rather than perimeters, if any concerns remained.

"All clear." He steps closer, voice dropping. "You ready for this?"

The question carries layers of meaning beyond tonight's event. Ready for public attention. Ready for the questions that continue to follow Marcus's death and the gradual revelations about his business dealings. Ready to stand as myself, not as Marcus Holbrook's daughter.

"More than ready." I meet his gaze steadily, letting him see the certainty I feel. "It's time."

He nods, understanding without further explanation. That's become our pattern—communication that needs fewer words as our connection deepens. A look, a touch, a shared breath often says more than elaborate explanations.

"Then let's open the doors." His fingers graze mine—brief, but enough to ground me, steady me. Electric in the quiet way only he can be. "Your public awaits."

The first wave trickles in. Then more. Curious customers, local press, even a few bloggers with oversized cameras and ring lights they pretend not to notice. The air hums with energy—voices overlapping, the soft clink of candle lids being lifted and replaced, murmurs of approval as scents are sampled.

I slip into motion, answering questions, guiding people through the displays, and explaining the story behind each collection. Not reciting—sharing. This isn't about sales or performance. It's about connection.

The woman who lingers over the lavender and moss blend reminds me of my mother. The teenager who gravitates toward the citrus-basil scent looks like she just left a ballet class.

Every interaction roots me deeper in the moment.

Jon stays close without hovering, his presence a steady reassurance. Ember's laugh rings out from the back corner, Hope's voice soft and certain as she explains wick types to a reporter. This isn't just a store—it's the beginning of something new.

Something real.

No one asks directly about Marcus or Wolfe or the events that played out three months ago. They don't need to—the subtext hangs in the air, acknowledged but not confronted. The Truth collection speaks for itself, its very existence a statement about my journey from darkness into light.

"Ms. Holbrook." A woman approaches, press credentials hanging around her neck. Lifestyle section, not investigative reporting. Safe territory. "Would you tell me about your inspiration for the Truth collection? It's quite a departure from your previous luxury lines."

I consider my response carefully. The prepared marketing language sits ready on my tongue—something about authenticity in challenging times, about stripping away unnecessary embellishment to reveal essential beauty.

Instead, truth emerges.

"Sometimes life strips away illusions we didn't know we were maintaining." I lift one of the candles, allowing light to pass through its clear glass and golden contents. "This collection honors that process—painful but ultimately illuminating. When everything familiar is taken away, what remains is truth. Unadorned, unfiltered, powerful in its simplicity."

She studies me with new interest, sensing the personal nature of my response. "And the scent profile? It's quite complex for something meant to represent simplicity."

"Truth is rarely simple." I smile slightly. "It has layers, dimensions, and aspects that reveal themselves gradually. The initial sharpness mellows into something grounding and enduring. Like understanding itself."

The reporter nods, jotting notes with genuine engagement. "And the Celestial collection? The contrast between the two is striking."

I glance toward Hope, who stands with a small group of customers near her constellation display. Her posture has changed subtly over these months—spine straighter, shoulders no longer hunched protectively, hands gesturing with growing confidence as she describes her creative process.

"That's Hope's creation. I think she should tell you about it herself." I catch Hope's eye, gesturing for her to come over. The momentary flash of alarm in her expression is quickly replaced by determination. Another small victory in her ongoing journey.

As Hope explains her inspiration to the increasingly fascinated reporter, I step back, allowing her the spotlight she's earned. Storm materializes nearby, ostensibly checking the back exit, but positions himself perfectly to offer support if Hope needs it.

The careful choreography of it warms something inside me—this protective circle we've formed around each other. Not the suffocating control Marcus called "protection," but genuine support that strengthens rather than diminishes.

"You've built something remarkable here." Jon's voice comes quietly beside me, his presence a comfort I've grown to rely on. "Not just the business. The family."

Family. The word catches in my chest, weighted with new meaning. Not defined by blood, legal documents, or social expectations. Defined instead by choice, by trust, by showing up when it matters most.

"We built it," I correct gently, finding his hand with mine. "All of us together."

His fingers interlace with mine, warm and solid and real. Not the Delta operative in this moment, but simply Jon—the man who stood beside me through darkness and remains beside me in light.

The evening continues around us—sales transactions, media interviews, casual conversations. I participate as needed, my upbringing guiding me through the expected social interactions, but a part of me remains anchored to an uncomfortable realization.

I've lost family—the father I thought I knew, the history I believed was mine, but gained something infinitely more valuable. Something chosen rather than inherited. Something real rather than constructed.

As the event draws to a close, with the last customers drifting out carrying signature bags and press packets, our inner circle remains. Delta team members drop their professional pretense, rolling up their sleeves, stacking boxes, and helping with cleanup despite my half-hearted protests.

Ember and Blaze move through the closing procedures, their private smiles and subtle touches speaking volumes about what's growing between them. Hope and Storm restock the Celestial candle display for tomorrow's business hours, their conversation flowing more easily now, quiet laughter punctuating the soft clinks of glass and metal.

She glows in his presence. He softens in hers.

Razor and Ryn work near the back counter, unboxing supplies that mysteriously didn't get unpacked earlier. They don't say much, but the air between them feels charged, close, and attentive. Ryn hands him a box cutter, their fingers brushing. Razor doesn't look away. Neither does she.

Whatever's beginning there, it's not casual.

And Jon—he remains beside me, a quiet fortress at my side. His hand brushes the small of my back as I lean into him. This is a moment of completion. A circle drawn and closed. A new beginning shaped by something real.

"Success by any metric." Jenny approaches with a smile. "Media coverage positive, sales exceeded projections, security maintained without incident."

"High praise coming from you." I smile, familiar enough with Jenny's standards to recognize the compliment for what it is.

"Truth deserves recognition." Her gaze shifts meaningfully to the candle display. "In all its forms."

The acknowledgment catches me by surprise. Jenny isn't given to metaphorical speech or emotional validation. That she recognizes the deeper significance of tonight's event suggests understanding I hadn't realized she possessed.

"Thank you," I say simply.

She nods once, mission accomplished, and moves to assist Mac with final security checks. The team will depart soon, returning to Guardian HQ and whatever missions await them next.

"Home?" Jon asks quietly, once the final display is secured and the last light dimmed—except for the Truth candle still flickering on the counter. Its steady flame casts a soft glow across the space, scent curling through the air like a benediction.

That word—home—doesn't sting anymore.

It's not the penthouse, all cold marble and curated perfection, haunted by Marcus's shadow no matter how many times I rearranged the furniture. It's not even the apartment above the shop, where I found refuge in the middle of chaos, where grief and survival once lived side by side.

That apartment now belongs to someone else.

Ryn moved in first—quietly, without fuss—after Ember and I offered it. A place to land after so much turbulence. Hope followed soon after, her new possessions carried up the stairs with the help of Storm and his steady hands. They make it feel lived-in now, warm and real. There's laughter through the floorboards some nights, soft music, and the low hum of life returning to two women who deserve peace.

Jon and I found somewhere else. Somewhere new.

A renovated loft perched on the edge of the cliffs overlooking the ocean, with floor-to-ceiling windows that flood the space with light. Exposed brick, wide-plank floors, and open rooms that breathe instead of closing in. No ghosts. No legacies. No past pressing in from the corners. Just light and air, and the quiet presence of the man who stood beside me when the world split open.

We picked out the candle shelves together. He insisted on a giant couch I wasn't sure about until I fell asleep in his arms on it the first night.

"Yeah," I say softly, turning to him. "Let's go home."

He threads his fingers through mine as we step into the cooling night. Behind us, the Truth candle burns steadily. Ahead of us, something new waits—ours to build, room by room, breath by breath.

"Home," I confirm, extinguishing the display candle carefully with a unique candle snuffer.

Outside, spring air carries the promise of renewal. It has been three months since Marcus's death. Three months of rebuilding, of reclaiming, of choosing a path forward. The media's interest faded as newer scandals captured the public's attention. Guardian HRS's investigation continues, but quietly in the background.

Marcus's empire will be dismantled piece by piece. His legitimate businesses will be restructured under new leadership, while the criminal enterprises will be exposed and shuttered. Blood money transformed into foundation funding for organizations supporting trafficking victims and orphaned children.

Not redemption—some sins can't be redeemed—but redirection. Using what Marcus built for purposes that would infuriate him. Finding purpose in the wreckage of illusion.

Jon drives us home, his hand warm over mine on the console. We don't speak much—don't need to. The silence between us isn't empty. It's full of everything we've already said, everything we've come to understand without words.

At home, the night settles around us like a blanket. Familiar motions unfold without thinking—shoes off by the door, lights dimmed low, the soft beep of the security system arming. The scent of bergamot and cedar lingers in the air, a quiet reminder of the life we've built here. His toothbrush rests beside mine. His jacket hangs beside mine. Two lives slowly stitched into one.

We move around each other peacefully, no sharp edges, just the rhythm we've found. The hum of the kettle. The whisper of cotton against skin. A soft laugh when we both reach for the same towel.

"I have something for you," Jon says, breaking the stillness with that low, steady voice I'll never stop leaning into. He crosses the room and pulls a small package from his nightstand drawer—wrapped in plain brown paper, folded with care.

His eyes meet mine, and there's something tender in them. Hopeful. Steady.

"You've carried enough," he says. "This… It's just something to remind you what you deserve to carry."

"What's this?" I accept it, weighing the solid object in my palm.

"Open it."

Inside the paper lies a lighter. Not ornate or expensive, but clearly chosen with care. Silver metal engraved with a simple flame pattern. Practical. Functional. Beautiful in its purpose rather than decoration.

"For Truth," he explains, watching my reaction carefully. "For when you need light."

The gift's significance settles deep inside me. Not flowers or jewelry or conventional tokens. Something that creates flame, that transforms darkness to light, that kindles truth when shadows threaten.

Something perfectly, uniquely suited to who I am now.

"Thank you." I trace the engraved pattern with my fingertip, emotion thickening my voice. "It's perfect."

He smiles, the expression reaching his eyes in a way that still makes my heart flutter and skip beats. He's not the professional operative in this moment, but simply Jon—the man who sees me clearly, who chooses me daily, who loves me without condition or expectation.

Later, curled against him in the darkness, I think about the journey that brought us here. The first kidnapping that introduced us. The second that revealed uncomfortable truths.

"What are you thinking about?" Jon's voice comes quietly in the darkness, his fingers tracing gentle patterns along my spine.

"Everything," I admit. "How different things were just a few months ago. How much has changed."

"Regrets?" The question holds no judgment.

I consider it, honestly examining the complex tangle of emotions that remain. Grief for illusions lost. Pain for truths revealed. Fear for paths unknown.

But beneath it all, something stronger emerges. Something steady and enduring and real.

"No," I answer truthfully. "Not regrets. Just—recognition of the journey."

His arms tighten slightly around me, anchoring me in the present moment. "We keep moving forward. Together."

The simple certainty in his voice settles something inside me. Whatever comes next—the continuing investigations, the rebuilding of businesses, the memories that sometimes still wake me gasping in the night—we face it as a unit. Not handler and client. Not operative and assignment. Just Jon and Aria, connected by choice rather than circumstance.

"Together," I agree, the word carrying the weight of promise.

I am Aria—not defined by Marcus's crimes or Wolfe's biology or even the trauma of what I've survived. Defined instead by the choices I made, by the truths I've embraced, and by light created from darkness.

Tomorrow I'll return to the shop. Hope will continue developing her Celestial collection. Jon will balance Guardian responsibilities with our shared life. The journey continues, path unfolding with each step forward.

But tonight, in this moment of quiet connection, I recognize the most important truth revealed through everything we've survived: Family isn't inherited. It's chosen, day by day, moment by moment. Built through presence, truth, and unwavering support when darkness threatens to consume everything.

And like the candles that have become my signature, the brightest flames emerge from the deepest shadows. Not despite the darkness, but because of it. Transformed by it. Made more valuable through contrast.

Truth, illuminating whatever comes next.

RIGHT NOW, YOU'VE GOT **THREE WAYS TO KEEP THE ADRENALINE pumping and the heat burning**:

1. DIVE INTO THE GUARDIANS FROM THE VERY BEGINNING.

If you're new here, start with **Alpha Team**—then tear through Bravo and Delta teams. Fierce, protective, unapologetically alpha men. The women who bring them to their knees. Every mission is more dangerous, every romance is more unforgettable.

2. GO BACK TO WHERE IT ALL BEGAN.

Before the missions. Before the rescues. Before Guardian HRS existed.

It began with **Heart's Insanity**—Book One in the *Angel Fire* rock star romance series. Meet Skye as she falls in love with Ash,

Angel Fire's lead singer. In Heart's Insanity, you will also meet Skye's foster brother, Forest.

See the raw, emotional love story that built the foundation for everything the Guardians have become. Once you know Forest's past, you'll never see him the same way again.

3. STEP INTO THE NEXT EXPLOSIVE CHAPTER.

Already caught up on *Angel Fire and the Guardians*? Then it's time for **Cerberus Personal Security**—the brand-new spinoff series that takes the danger beyond the Guardians.

New men. New missions. Same heart-pounding mix of passion and peril. Book One will drag you in and won't let you go.

THE HEAT ONLY GETS HOTTER.
The danger only gets deadlier.
The mission isn't over—it's just getting started.

YOUR NEXT MISSION? **CHOOSE WHERE TO GO NEXT.**
Angel Fire Rock Romance
Guardian HRS: Alpha Team
Cerberus Personal Security

WHEREVER YOU START, ONE THING'S CERTAIN—
You won't want to stop.

Ellie Masters Romantic Suspense and Steamy Contemporary Romance by series.

Angel Fire Rock Romance
Guardian HRS: Alpha Team
Guardian HRS: Bravo Team
Guardian HRS: Charlie Team
Guardian HRS: Delta Team
Cerberus Personal Security
The LaRouge Triplets
The One I Want Series
Angel's Peak Series
Billionaire Boy's Club
The Lovers
Changing Roles

THIRTY-SIX

Aria

———

RIGHT NOW, YOU'VE GOT **THREE WAYS TO KEEP THE ADRENALINE pumping and the heat burning**:

1. DIVE INTO THE GUARDIANS FROM THE VERY BEGINNING.

If you're new here, start with **Alpha Team**—then tear through Bravo and Delta teams. Fierce, protective, unapologetically alpha men. The women who bring them to their knees. Every mission is more dangerous, every romance is more unforgettable.

2. GO BACK TO WHERE IT ALL BEGAN.

Before the missions. Before the rescues. Before Guardian HRS existed.

It began with **Heart's Insanity**—Book One in the *Angel Fire* rock star romance series. Meet Skye as she falls in love with Ash,

Angel Fire's lead singer. In *Heart's Insanity*, you will also meet Skye's foster brother, Forest.

See the raw, emotional love story that built the foundation for everything the Guardians have become. Once you know Forest's past, you'll never see him the same way again.

3. STEP INTO THE NEXT EXPLOSIVE CHAPTER.

Already caught up on *Angel Fire and the Guardians*? Then it's time for **Cerberus Personal Security**—the brand-new spinoff series that takes the danger beyond the Guardians.

New men. New missions. Same heart-pounding mix of passion and peril. Book One will drag you in and won't let you go.

THE HEAT ONLY GETS HOTTER.
The danger only gets deadlier.
The mission isn't over—it's just getting started.

YOUR NEXT MISSION? **CHOOSE WHERE TO GO NEXT.**
Angel Fire Rock Romance
Guardian HRS: Alpha Team
Cerberus Personal Security

WHEREVER YOU START, ONE THING'S CERTAIN—
You won't want to stop.

Ellie Masters Romantic Suspense and Steamy Contemporary Romance by series.

Angel Fire Rock Romance
Guardian HRS: Alpha Team
Guardian HRS: Bravo Team
Guardian HRS: Charlie Team
Guardian HRS: Delta Team
Cerberus Personal Security
The LaRouge Triplets
The One I Want Series
Angel's Peak Series
Billionaire Boy's Club
The Lovers
Changing Roles

Please consider leaving a review

I HOPE YOU ENJOYED THIS BOOK AS MUCH AS I ENJOYED WRITING it. If you like this book, please leave a review. I love reviews. I love reading your reviews, and they help other readers decide if this book is worth their time and money. I hope you think it is and decide to share this story with others. A sentence is all it takes. Thank you in advance!

ELLZ BELLZ

ELLIE'S FACEBOOK READER GROUP

If you are interested in joining the **ELLZ BELLZ**, Ellie's Facebook reader group, we'd love to have you.

Join Ellie's **ELLZ BELLZ**.
The **ELLZ BELLZ** Facebook Reader Group

Sign up for Ellie's Newsletter.
Elliemasters.com/newslettersignup

Also by Ellie Masters

The LIGHTER SIDE

Ellie Masters is the lighter side of the Jet & Ellie Masters writing duo! You will find Contemporary Romance, Military Romance, Romantic Suspense, Billionaire Romance, and Rock Star Romance in Ellie's Works.

YOU CAN FIND ELLIE'S BOOKS HERE:

ELLIEMASTERS.COM/BOOKS

Shop Ellie Masters Romantic Suspense and Steamy Contemporary Romance by series.

Angel Fire Rock Romance

Guardian HRS: Alpha Team

Guardian HRS: Bravo Team

Guardian HRS: Charlie Team

Guardian HRS: Delta Team

Cerberus Personal Security

The LaRouge Triplets

The One I Want Series

Angel's Peak Series

Billionaire Boy's Club

The Lovers

Changing Roles

SUGGESTED READING ORDER

START HERE

Rockstar Romance

The Angel Fire Rock Romance Series

EACH BOOK IN THIS SERIES CAN BE READ AS A STANDALONE AND IS ABOUT A DIFFERENT COUPLE WITH AN HEA.

IT IS RECOMMENDED THEY ARE READ IN ORDER.

Heart's Insanity

Ashes to New

Heart's Desire

Heart's Collide

Hearts Divided

Hearts Entwined

Forest's FALL

Hearts The Last Beat

CONTINUE HERE...

Military Romance

Guardian Hostage Rescue Specialists

Rescuing Melissa

(Get a FREE copy of Rescuing Melissa

when you join Ellie's Newsletter)

Alpha Team

Rescuing Zoe

Rescuing Moira

Rescuing Eve

Rescuing Lily

Rescuing Jinx

Rescuing Maria

Bravo Team

Rescuing Angie

Rescuing Isabelle

Rescuing Carmen

Rescuing Rosalie

Rescuing Kaye

Cara's Protector

Rescuing Barbi

Charlie Team

Rescuing Rebel

Rescuing Stitch

Rescuing Mia

Jenna's Protector

Rescuing Sophia

Rescuing Malia

Rescuing Ally (Part 1)

Rescuing Ally (Part 2)

Delta Team

Rescuing Ember

Rescuing Aria

STANDALONES IN THE GUARDIAN HOSTAGE RESCUE

By Jet & Ellie Masters

Saving Abby

Saving Ariel

Saving Brie

Saving Cate

Saving Dani

Saving Jen

The LaRouge Triplets

Asher

Brody

Cage

Billionaire Romance

Billionaire Boys Club

Hawke

Richard

Contemporary Romance

Cocky Captain

Romantic Suspense

The Starling

The Swan

~AND~

Science Fiction

Ellie Masters writing as L.A. Warren

Vendel Rising: a Science Fiction Serialized Novel

If you enjoyed this book by Ellie Masters, the LIGHTER SIDE of the Jet & Ellie writing duo, and aren't afraid of edgier writing, you might enjoy reading BDSM themed books written by Jet, the DARKER SIDE of the Masters' Writing Team.

The DARKER SIDE

Jet Masters is the darker side of the Jet & Ellie writing duo!

Romantic Suspense

Changing Roles Series:

THIS SERIES MUST BE READ IN ORDER.

Command Me

Control Me

Collar Me

Embracing FATE

Seizing FATE

Accepting FATE

HOT READS

A STANDALONE NOVEL.

Down the Rabbit Hole

Light BDSM Romance

The Ties that Bind

EACH BOOK IN THIS SERIES CAN BE READ AS A STANDALONE AND IS ABOUT A DIFFERENT COUPLE WITH AN HEA.

Alexa

Penny

Michelle

Ivy

HOT READS

Becoming His Series

THIS SERIES MUST BE READ IN ORDER.

The Ballet

Learning to Breathe

Becoming His

Dark Captive Romance

A STANDALONE NOVEL.

She's MINE

About the Author

Ellie Masters is a USA Today Bestselling author and Amazon Top 15 Author who writes Angsty, Steamy, Heart-Stopping, Pulse-Pounding, Can't-Stop-Reading Romantic Suspense. In addition, she's a wife, military mom, doctor, and retired Colonel. She writes romantic suspense filled with all your sexy, swoon-worthy alpha men. Her writing will tug at your heartstrings and leave your heart racing.

Born in the South, raised under the Hawaiian sun, Ellie has traveled the globe while in service to her country. The love of her life, her amazing husband, is her number one fan and biggest supporter. And yes! He's read every word she's written.

She has lived all over the United States—east, west, north, south and central—but grew up under the Hawaiian sun. She's also been privileged to have lived overseas, experiencing other cultures and making lifelong friends. Now, Ellie is proud to call herself a Southern transplant, learning to say y'all and "bless her heart" with the best of them.

Ellie's favorite way to spend an evening is curled up on a couch, laptop in place, watching a fire, drinking a good wine, and bringing forth all the characters from her mind to the page and hopefully into the hearts of her readers.

FOR MORE INFORMATION
elliemasters.com

facebook.com/elliemastersromance

x.com/Ellie__Masters

instagram.com/ellie_masters

bookbub.com/authors/ellie-masters

goodreads.com/Ellie_Masters

Connect with Ellie Masters

Website:
elliemasters.com
Purchase Direct:
elliemasters.com/shopify
Amazon Author Page:
elliemasters.com/amazon
Facebook:
elliemasters.com/Facebook
Goodreads:
elliemasters.com/Goodreads
Bookbub:
elliemasters.com/Bookbub
Instagram:
elliemasters.com/Instagram

Final Thoughts

I hope you enjoyed this book as much as I enjoyed writing it. If you enjoyed reading this story, please consider leaving a review on Amazon and Goodreads, and please let other people know. A sentence is all it takes. Friend recommendations are the strongest catalyst for readers' purchase decisions! And I'd love to be able to continue bringing the characters and stories from My-Mind-to-the-Page.

Second, call or e-mail a friend and tell them about this book. If you really want them to read it, gift it to them. If you prefer digital friends, please use the "Recommend" feature of Goodreads to spread the word.

Or visit my blog https://elliemasters.com, where you can find out more about my writing process and personal life.

Come visit The EDGE: Dark Discussions where we'll have a chance to talk about my works, their creation, and maybe what the future has in store for my writing.

Facebook Reader Group: Ellz Bellz

Thank you so much for your support!

Love,
Ellie

Dedication

This book is dedicated to you, my reader. Thank you for spending a few hours of your time with me. I wouldn't be able to write without you to cheer me on. Your wonderful words, your support, and your willingness to join me on this journey is a gift beyond measure.

Whether this is the first book of mine you've read, or if you've been with me since the very beginning, thank you for believing in me as I bring these characters 'from my mind to the page and into your hearts.'

Love,
Ellie

THE END